The Lady in the Spitfire

THE LADY IN THE SPITFIRE

Helena P. Schrader

iUniverse, Inc.
New York Lincoln Shanghai

The Lady in the Spitfire

iUniverse books may be ordered through booksellers or by contacting:

iUniverse
2021 Pine Lake Road, Suite 100
Lincoln, NE 68512
www.iuniverse.com
1-800-Authors (1-800-288-4677)

ISBN-13: 978-0-595-40151-2 (pbk)
ISBN-13: 978-0-595-84531-6 (ebk)
ISBN-10: 0-595-40151-1 (pbk)
ISBN-10: 0-595-84531-2 (ebk)

Printed in the United States of America

Acknowledgements

Many people contributed to this book–first and foremost the pilots of the ATA, USAAF and RAF, whose story inspired it. It is impossible to name them all or the many historians, photographers and archivists, who have made their story accessible. However, I wish to say special and public thanks to Christy Dickensen, my editor, whose patient and positive attitude toward the project made it happen. Without her constructive criticism combined with active encouragement to proceed, this book would never have been published. In addition special thanks is owed to Commander Lance Grunge, USN Retired, who as a pilot provided invaluable advice on details of flying and to Kythera Ann of Crystal Cloud Graphics (http://graphics.elysiumgates.com), who created the supporting website and contributed to the cover graphic.

CHAPTER 1

▼

White Waltham, England
March 1943

It was a gloomy, blustery day, with low cloud and a cross-wind. Many of the training aircraft landing and taking off in quick succession bounced about rather uncertainly. White Waltham was the central flying school for the Air Transport Auxiliary, the ATA, and many of the pilots at the controls were just learning to fly the types of aircraft they were trying to handle under adverse conditions.

As the gloom increased with the passing of the short day, the training flights came to a close and the training aircraft were rolled back into their hangars. The activity on the field diminished with the light, and then just before dark, a last Anson sank down out of the clouds and started its approach.

The ATA Adjutant, a man in his mid-fifties with thinning hair and thick glasses, came into the mess. He crossed to where an RAF Squadron Leader was gazing blindly out at the near-empty airfield, and announced softly, "That's the taxi Anson with Mrs. Priestman aboard now, sir."

"Thank you." The Squadron Leader stood, replaced his cap on his head and took his greatcoat off the back of the chair. He pulled it on as he made his way out onto the airfield to meet the twin-engine Anson that was now taxiing to its parking place outside the main hangar. The Squadron Leader stopped about twenty feet away and watched as no less than eight ATA pilots clambered out of the taxi-aircraft, stiff and tired after a long day's duty and a cold ride home. He did not try to attract attention to himself, just waited to be seen.

The only woman pilot aboard the Anson was an attractive, slender woman, with dark brown hair that she wore neatly bound at the back of her head. She was no glamour queen, but her features were pleasant and her hazel-green eyes—as the Squadron Leader knew from closer acquaintance—were lively and intelligent. Up to now, he had seen her mostly on social occasions, when she wore tasteful evening attire or her dress uniform with its smart dark-blue skirt and tunic, white shirt, black tie, and golden wings. At the moment, however, she was in the service uniform with trousers, and she had stuffed these into warm sheepskin flying boots. She had pulled an Irvine flying jacket over the tunic as well, and turned the fleece collar up against the biting wind. She looked weary as she hitched the strap of her parachute pack over her right shoulder and started for the mess.

At the sight of the waiting RAF officer, her face broke into a lovely smile. "Battie! What brings you—" And then she knew. She read it off his face, and she froze. She was so numbed that the smile melted only gradually.

Squadron Leader 'Battie' Bateman crossed the short distance between them. "I'm so sorry."

"What happened?" The question came out without a trace of emotion. She was absolutely numb. You could tell that from looking at her.

"We were supposedly looking for 'targets of opportunity,' but I think your husband was looking for something in particular. He had us down unusually low—under a thousand feet—and he kept rolling slightly as he looked left and right. Then, without any warning, over a semi-rural area where you don't expect it, there was flak. It had to be camouflaged mobile 8,8s. He was hit immediately and had no opportunity to jump."

"You saw it?"

"Yes."

"And you saw him crash?"

"Yes." There was an awkward pause, but Emily was gazing at Battie expectantly, so he continued. "From what I could see, most of his starboard wing was shot away. The Spit started to smoke, roll and lose altitude instantly. He radioed, 'I'm hit. They're yours, Battie,' and then the Spit went into a flat spin and crashed within seconds."

As a pilot, Emily had seen several crashes, particularly during the intensive air battles over England in the summer of 1940. "Did he blow up on impact?"

"No," Battie admitted, "the Spit first hit a raised rail causeway and the tail and remaining wing broke off immediately, the latter bursting into flame at once. The fuselage meanwhile rolled over several times and came to rest at the foot of the causeway." Again the Squadron Leader paused.

"Did it catch fire?" Emily asked professionally, her face unreadable.

"No, but we circled for several minutes and there was absolutely no movement in the cockpit."

"I see. Then you think there is no hope he survived the crash?"

The Squadron Leader swallowed, but then he shook his head slowly. "I think it would be a miracle if he survived that crash. Furthermore, given the risk of fire and the smoke all around him, if he had had any life in him at all, he would at least have made an attempt to get out."

"Thank you for being honest with me, Battie. And thank you for coming."

"Emily, if there's anything I can do..."

"I don't know yet. I think—I think I need to be alone." The shock was disorienting. Extraneous things loomed large. The important things were blotted out. Emily heard herself say, "You need to get back to the Station. Have you been waiting for me long?"

"A couple of hours. It doesn't matter." Another awkward pause, then Bateman tried again, "I can't tell you how sorry we *all* are. He was more than respected, you know, he was—I don't have to tell you this."

"Please do." Her voice broke as she spoke the words. The numbness was starting to wear off.

"We thought the world of him, Emily. He exuded quiet confidence without overdoing it. There was never any bunk. You felt safe with him, but at the same time he made you believe in yourself. That's the best kind of CO a man can have. Our new WingCo, whoever he will be, is going to have one hell of a hard time living up to the standards your husband set in just two months."

She nodded. "Thank you. Please keep in touch." She held out her hand, but it was weak and lifeless.

Battie bent and brushed his cheek against hers. "Please call if there is any way I can help," he urged again.

She nodded in answer, afraid to open her mouth.

The Squadron Leader turned away quickly, so he wouldn't witness anything she didn't want him to see. He straightened his shoulders and walked briskly back across the now silent aerodrome, the wind catching at his greatcoat and making it flap wildly.

Emily stood rooted to the spot where her life had ended and found herself saying over and over again: "Oh, God," meaninglessly. She didn't believe in God.

The darkness was more and more oppressive, and it was bitterly cold, but she didn't feel it for a long time. Then the cold from her hands penetrated to her brain. She stuffed them, stiff and icy, into the pockets of the flight jacket. She couldn't stay out here forever. She had to do something, go somewhere. She had to report back, turn in her chits. She had to tell the Adjutant what had happened. She had to ask for a few days compassionate leave. Then she had to drive home—to an empty house that would never be home to her ever again.

Maybe it would be better to go to a hotel?

"Emily?" It was the soft, solicitous voice of the Adjutant. "Come in and have a cup of tea to warm you up." He had hold of her elbow already, and he was leading her back to the mess.

Emily didn't protest. She knew he was right, and she was grateful to him. He obviously knew what had happened. That was good. He would tell the others. She wouldn't have to explain.

The Adjutant led her to his own little cubby-hole overflowing with sagging filing cabinets and un-filed files. He made a place for her on a rickety wooden chair beside his desk, disappeared and returned with a heavy mug full of steaming tea. It was too hot to hold in her frozen hands, so she set it on his desk and clasped her hands around it for as long as she could bear, then let go, then clasped again. She was completely absorbed in thawing out her hands, and refused to think about anything.

"Is there anyone I could call for you? Someone who could spend the night with you? Your mother, perhaps?"

Emily looked up startled. "My parents were killed in a raid on Portsmouth over two years ago."

"I'm sorry, I didn't know," the Adjutant mumbled miserably.

Poor man, Emily thought, he just wants to help and thinks he's made things worse. She tried to smile for him. "No matter. We were never close."

"A sister or friend, perhaps?" The Adjutant tried again. "There must be someone I can call. I don't think you should be alone."

Emily knew he was right. The last thing she wanted to do was be alone in Robin's house tonight. But who could she possibly call? Robin and she were both only children, and she'd never been close to his mother. His Aunt Hattie was just the person she needed, but Hattie lived up in Scotland. Emily's best friend from College was a WREN stationed in Liverpool. Robin's grandfather lived on the Isle of Wight. It had to be someone who could get to Windsor tonight. Emily couldn't think of anyone, and shook her head.

"Excuse me a minute." The Adjutant disappeared.

Emily had no idea how long she just sat there in the dark, clinging ever more firmly to the cooling mug of tea. Eventually a figure emerged in the doorway and

Emily looked up. It was Pauline Gower, the Director of Women Pilots. "I think I'd better drive you home," she announced in her simple, understated way.

Emily nodded. She knew it would be dangerous for her to drive herself, because she couldn't seem to concentrate on anything. Nor was she very alert to her surroundings. In fact, she blindly followed Commander Gower out into the dark and cold again, completely forgetting her parachute, which she left on the floor of the Adjutant's office. They were halfway to Windsor before she remembered the parachute and realised how rude she had been not to thank the Adjutant. Distressed, she mentioned this to Miss Gower.

"Don't worry about the parachute. Harry will know who it belongs to, and I'll be happy to convey your thanks, but I'm sure he understands. I want you to take as long as you need before you come back to work. A week, a fortnight. Whatever you need."

"I think I need to keep busy."

"If that's *really* what you want, you can report after the funeral. But wait and see how you feel." Gower paused and then added softly, "I'd like to attend the funeral. Please let me know when and where it is planned."

"There won't be one. He was over France."

"There'll be a Memorial Service, then."

Emily nodded and concentrated on directing her commander to the house on the outskirts of Windsor that Robin and she rented.

At the sight of it, the tears welled up so plentifully that she was all but blinded. She had been so delighted to find it. It was their first really nice house, and she had put as much effort (as work and wartime shortages allowed) into fixing it up. The prospect of living here with Robin had made her feel optimistic about the future. She should have known this was going to happen!

"I'll come in with you for a minute or two," Miss Gower decided, pulling on the hand brake and getting out of the car.

Emily found her key and let them in. The black-out blinds were still closed from this morning, so Miss Gower flipped the light switch and Emily went over to start the gas fire. It was icy cold inside. She worked entirely by rote, not really aware of what she was doing. She was vaguely aware that Miss Gower had found the kitchen and put the kettle on.

Her eye fell on her leather-bound *Collected Works of Shakespeare*, which lay carelessly on the sofa. It had been a graduation gift to her from her friend Grace, but Robin had been re-reading *Henry V* just last night before they went to bed. The day before, he had been abruptly called up to Stanmore in the morning and returned preoccupied. He had evidently been given highly classified intelligence and asked to carry out a sweep against a specific target. They would never know. In any case, he had insisted on turning in early, and left the book on the sofa.

Emily picked up the heavy volume and opened it to the bookmark. Henry V, Act III, Scene One. *Once more unto the breach, dear friends, once more—or close the wall up with our English dead.* Emily snapped the book shut.

Miss Gower was watching her from the doorway. She took Emily by the arm and gently pushed her onto the sofa. She sat down beside her and laid a hand on her arm.

Emily finally broke down and started sobbing.

At some point she remembered and gasped out, "I've got to call his mother, aunt and grandfather."

Miss Gower told her it could wait 'till the morning.

After letting her cry a while longer, Miss Gower led Emily upstairs, helped her to undress and put her to bed. Leaving Emily to cry herself to sleep, she discreetly withdrew.

Emily did not hear her leave. Instead she heard her parents scolding her, reminding her they had always said Robin would leave her crying.

Emily woke in the morning feeling very stiff, swollen and dirty. She could tell that her eyes were swollen and her make-up was smeared about. She hadn't brushed her teeth the night before either, much less had a bath. She got up and went into the cold bathroom to fix herself up.

Here she let the water splatter into the tub up to the 8-inch mark, and then stepped into it and sat there splashing water over herself to get wet enough to wash. She wasn't thinking about anything, although she reminded herself she would have to call Robin's mother, aunt and grandfather today. She dreaded talking to his mother. She would be hysterical. Robin was her only child of a brief marriage in the last war. She had always doted on Robin in a smothering, selfish way. Fortunately for Robin's character development, he had been sent to public school from the age of 7 and had spent most of his holidays with his paternal grandparents. His paternal grandfather was a retired Admiral, a formidable and sharp-witted man, who had done much to make Robin what he was. Emily liked and admired the Admiral—even if she was still rather afraid of him. She dreaded calling him, too!

It was cold in the bathroom, so Emily didn't linger. She returned to the bedroom and started to get dressed. It wasn't easy. Robin's uniforms still hung in the closet. His slippers had been kicked into the corner. Small change, a candy wrapper and a Swiss Army knife, which he must have emptied from his trouser pocket the night before, were still piled in a heap on the bed-side table. At her own dressing table was the perfume he'd given her this past Christmas, the gold bracelet from their first wedding anniversary and the garnet pendant he'd given her on the second. Somehow she found a black skirt, a white blouse and black cardigan and put them on.

She went down to the kitchen and forced herself to eat. She did it because she knew she had to. She knew she had to go on living, even if she didn't particularly want to or understand why. She reminded herself that women all over the country had to do this day after day—and had had to do it in the last war and in all the wars that had gone before all the way back to the fall of Troy. At least she didn't face being raped and carried off into slavery. Somehow the thought did not comfort her in the least.

Instead she thought grimly: This is the first day of the rest of my life. I'm a widow at 26 with no children, no close relatives and a job that, rather than distracting me, will remind me of my husband every minute of every working day. Part of her did not want to face it at all, but she kept chewing, although she couldn't taste what she was eating.

CHAPTER 2

▼

Ypsilanti, Michigan
March 1943

The sight of a taxicab in the trailer park was so unusual that the curtains in all the windows fluttered as the housewives peered out curiously. When the cab stopped in front of the Baronowsky trailer-house, one could almost hear the collective gasp of admiration as a young man in the uniform of an Army First Lieutenant got out and paid the driver.

J.B. could feel the admiring eyes on his back as he reached back into the taxi for his canvas duffel bag, and he was proud. As he straightened up, he looked around, taking in the neat rows of aluminium-sided trailers on their cinder blocks, the latter half-hidden by the piles of dirty snow from the last snowstorm. After training at air bases in Texas, Alabama, Idaho and Colorado, J.B. had seen quite a bit of the country. He'd been to New York and New Orleans on passes. After seeing so much, he was aware for the first time of just how small and how run-down the houses here were. Of course, he'd seen worse places in Texas and especially Alabama; there was real poverty down there, the kind of poverty that made you uncomfortable. This wasn't like that, but it sure wasn't Manhattan either!

The front door of the trailer opened, and a dog came bounding down the narrow walkway, wagging its whole backside from excitement. "Hi yah, boy!" J.B.

put his duffel bag down to greet the ecstatic dog that was now leaping up and try-ing to lick his face. "Watch it, fellah!" J.B. tried to calm the frenzied pet. "You're getting pretty close to assaulting an officer."

"Sadie! Get back here!" J.B.'s younger brother, Stan, called the dog from the door. Stan's voice hadn't broken yet, J.B. noted, and still had that high-pitched, slightly hysterical tone of a child trying to sound grown up. The dog ignored Stan and just continued to bound around J.B., panting with excitement, as the latter took up his duffel bag again and went up the walk to the trailer-house.

Stan was 14, all skin and bones and acne. "How ya doing, buddy?" J.B. greeted him with a playful punch to his shoulder. Any other kind of greeting would have confused and annoyed the teenager.

Before Stan could answer, however, J.B. was clasped in a bear-hug by his grandmother. She was babbling at him in Polish, as she always did when she was overcome by emotion. Although she'd lived in America almost 40 years now, she had never really mastered English. Unlike her husband, who had to go out and work, she'd remained in the home, raising her large family and speaking Polish. As long as they lived in Detroit, they naturally lived in a Polish neighbourhood and belonged to the Polish church. All her neighbours and friends had spoken Polish, too. It wasn't until her children refused to speak Polish with her and her grandchildren *couldn't* speak it that she had picked up enough English to com-municate with them. Since moving to Ypsilanti, living with a daughter-in-law who didn't speak Polish, her English had improved noticeably.

J.B.'s grandmother only came up to the middle of his chest, but she made up for her short stature with breadth. She had been petite and pretty in her youth, as her wedding picture proved, but she had worked very hard in the kitchens of a large estate right up until she and her husband emigrated to America. By that time, she had six children and was already stocky. The recent good years, when she no longer had to work, had added soft layers on top.

She held her grandson at arm's length and declared: "Beautiful! You very beautiful!"

J.B. laughed, knowing his grandmother meant well, while Stan made a crack about, "Now that's *just* the word for him! Just like a beauty *queen*!"

J.B. had caught sight of his mother drying her hands on a dish-towel in the door to the kitchen, so he gently released himself from his grandmother's grasp and went over to give his mother a hug and kiss. She was less ebullient than his grandmother had been, but she held him tightly for a moment. J.B. knew that for her, the joy of seeing him was overshadowed by the knowledge that he would be gone soon. Anxious to dispel the thoughts of gloom, he urged, "Hey, come on, Mom, give us a smile!"

She tried, but quickly looked away, nodding to Stan, "Take your brother's stuff to your room, Stan."

"Why can't he take it himself?" Stan asked rhetorically, while he dutifully did what he was told. He bumped into his grandfather coming the other way in the narrow hallway.

The old man grabbed J.B.'s hand and started pumping it vigorously, while his eyes took in the splendour of this grandson. His eyes watered with tears of pride. "You officer!" He said over and over. The Baronowskys hadn't been able to afford travelling down to see Jay's graduation from Flight School, and so this was the first time they'd seen him in a lieutenant's uniform. "Never in our family did we got officer before!" his grandfather reminded him. "That's what America is all about! Even poor son of peasant can be officer!"

"We're not so poor anymore, Granddad," J.B. pointed out, embarrassed by the old man's open display of emotion.

"My father," the old man pointed to himself, "he sleep in pig-sty. He near starve to death—"

"Yeah, Granddad, we *know* all that," Stan tried to stop the flood of stories about the 'old country' that they had all heard far too often.

His grandfather turned on the younger boy, shaking his finger at him, "You don't know how good you got it! You spoiled rotten!" This said, he turned back to J.B. and still in an angry tone admonished, "You go smash Hitler! You smash him dead! You drive him out of Poland!"

"Well, that's what we plan do to, Granddad," J.B. assured him. "When we finally get enough planes and crews over there to really start an offensive, I figure we'll smash him pretty good and fast. You've got to see a formation of B-17s to believe it. They're the most—" J.B. stopped himself from swearing just in time— "Gosh-Almighty beautiful sight there is!"

"Is it definite then?" his mother asked anxiously. "Do you have your orders?"

"Yeah, Mom," J.B. looked directly at her, wishing she wouldn't carry on so. He'd said all along that he wanted to go to Europe and help the war against Hitler. He'd requested the 8th Air Force, and they sure the hell weren't turning down volunteers.

"The Carter boy got assigned to Air Transport Command," his mother told him. "He flies planes from factories all over the country to someplace in Canada where other pilots fly them across the North Atlantic. Couldn't you do something like that?"

"I could, but I don't want to, Mom. I'm a fully trained B-17 pilot and I've got a gosh-darned good crew, and we want to make a difference to this war."

His grandfather clapped him heartily on the back in approval, while his mother just shook her head and turned away, retreating into the kitchen. Then, in a gesture of reconciliation, she called, "I've got some fresh-baked cookies in here, Jay." J.B. followed her into the kitchen.

"Where are the girls?" J.B. asked, referring to his sisters, as he settled himself at the kitchen table.

"Sally's got a job now, you know," his mother answered, setting a pottery cookie-jar in front of him on the kitchen table. "Can I get you some milk?"

"Sure," J.B. agreed, thinking how bizarre it was that he was falling back into the patterns of his childhood. He'd spent the last three months learning how to fly bombing runs to blow Hitler off the map, and here he was eating cookies with milk at the kitchen table as if he'd just come home from grade school. "Where is Sally working?" Sally was younger than he by a couple of years and had just turned 21. She'd gone to a business school, learning typing and shorthand and book-keeping.

"Mary's husband got her a job out at Willow Run," his mother explained. "She works in the accounting office there, and she's really happy about it." Mary was J.B.'s elder sister, now 25. She'd married a couple of years ago and had just had a baby. "Barb" (this was the third and youngest of J.B.'s sisters) "wants to quit her job over at Jacobsens and go work on the assembly line at Willow Run. She says they pay a lot better, but your father won't hear of it."

"I should hope not!" J.B. agreed. "Doesn't she know what it's like on those assembly lines? Work till you drop isn't the worst of it! Jeez, Mom, I've heard the worst stories—you know, if a girl is so hot on being down there with a bunch of guys, then they figure there's only one thing she wants!"

"Well, you talk to Barb about it. She says she knows lots of girls who've quit their 'five-and-dime' jobs to earn 'real' money, and she says they're all nice girls."

"Well, that may be what they were when they quit work at Jacobsens or wherever, but it sure as blazes ain't what they are after they've been working in some aircraft factory for a few months!"

"Well, you talk to Barb about it. Mary will be over with the baby later, by the way. Bobbie's just the cutest little thing you ever saw."

J.B. grunted acknowledgement, not really interested in babies at all. The sound of a car in the drive distracted them all, and a moment later J.B.'s father crashed in the kitchen door. As tall as Jay, his father was broader and a good fifty pounds heavier these days. He'd worked his way up to foreman at River Rouge, the large Ford plant nearby.

J.B. stood up and saluted his father, but it was a joke. The senior Baronowsky clapped him hard on the shoulder, grinning delightedly. "Good to see ya, son! Good to see ya! You look great! Just great! Let me see those wings! Yeah, nice! Real nice!" He clapped his son on the shoulder again, and then sat down to pull off his boots. "Don't we got any beer around here?" he asked his wife, with a contemptuous glance at the empty glass of milk in front of J.B.

"For me, too, Mom," J.B. hastened to add. His father winked at him and tossed the boots toward the back door, where a towel was spread out to absorb the melting snow. Then he stood, removed his heavy woollen hunting jacket, and hung it on a hook on the back of the door before re-seating himself opposite his son. "You really do look great, son. Put on weight."

"Muscle, Dad, pure muscle!" J.B. held up his left arm and squeezed his biceps with his right hand. "It takes one hell of a lot of muscle to fling one of them B-17s around."

"Yeah? Well, so long as you stay fit, that's what I say. Got your orders?"

"Eighth—just like I asked for."

His father nodded solemnly. He understood, but he wasn't really happy about it, you could tell that. J.B. asked his father about things at the plant, and his father willingly chatted about his world—the company, the co-workers, the Union. About an hour later, another car drew up in the drive. "That'll be the girls!" J.B.'s Mom exclaimed. "Sally always swings by and picks Barb up from work on her way home."

Sure enough, the door opened a minute later to let in the two girls. Both were bundled up in woollen hats and scarves and mittens against the damp cold. No sooner were they through the door than Sally started to ask, "Did Jay make it—" Barb had already seen him, however, and with a squeal of delight she threw herself at him. J.B. caught her in his arms and picked her up off the ground in a hug. Then Sally was clamouring for his attention, and soon they were competing with each other in telling him how good he looked. He had to turn around for them, and Sally made him put his cap on. "Oh, we've got to take a picture!" she insisted, and rushed to get her camera.

At this point, J.B.'s Mom shooed the rest of the family out of the kitchen. "How am I ever gonna get dinner made with you all standing in my way!" So the rest of them poured into the little living room, rejoining the grandparents and Stan who were collected around the radio. "Any news?" J.B. asked seeing them there.

His grandfather frowned and shook his head. "Hitler lost whole Army at Stalingrad, but Stalin—he no better than Hitler. He stomped Poland, too. Hitler and Stalin—they just two peas out of same pod—one Brown and one Red!"

The news had been replaced by music, and J.B. turned on Barb. "What's this I hear about you wanting to work on some assembly line?"

"Not just any old assembly line!" Barb shot back. "I want to build B-24s at Willow Run!"

"No daughter of mine is ever gonna work on an assembly line!" J.B.'s Dad said sternly, but his children ignored him.

Jay was telling his sister, "Look, if I thought some girl was building my B-17s, I'd be scarred sh—out of my mind!"

"Well, just get scared then, brother, because I'll bet you two-to-one that girls *are* building your precious B-17s—"

"Barb! Don't you start that gambling stuff!" Sally admonished primly. She had always been the dutiful daughter.

Barb just stuck her tongue out at her, and turned back on her brother, "You know, we girls can do just about anything you guys can do!"

Barb had always been the tomboy of the family. She'd been the best of them at baseball, and could change the oil, spark plugs or a tire on the car. J.B. knew better than to take up this challenge, so he evaded it. "I'm not saying you *can't* do it, Barb. Heck, anyone can screw bolts! I just don't see why you *want* to. Jacobsens is a nice store and you meet nice people there."

"I don't meet anyone there but fat old ladies! And who wants to work in a nice store? I want to do my part, too! The whole country is standing on its head trying to win this war, and I'm supposed to sell rich old ladies hats? I think it stinks!"

"Barb!" Sally admonished again.

"Well, your job is *useful!*" Barb turned on Sally. "You're helping get those B-24s finished by being sure that the money is paid out to all the workers and all that. What's so wrong with me wanting to help build the bombers that will win the war?"

"There are lots of other ways you can help the war effort without working with a bunch of horny guys who will pinch your bottom every time you lean over to do something!" J.B. told her in no uncertain terms.

"A bunch of guys are going get bloody noses if they do that!"

J.B. had to laugh. He liked Barb's spirit, but he was dead set against her working in some factory—any factory. He decided on a different tack. "You know, little sister, you're one heck of an attractive broad, and I think it would be a crying shame if you hid yourself in baggy old dungarees. How is a guy supposed to keep his spirits up, if the picture of his girl that he takes with him when he goes off to war looks like a filthy auto mechanic?"

Barb was caught off guard, because she didn't think of herself as particularly attractive. She was nearly as tall as her brothers, and had their solid bone structure as well. That made her rather too tall and too solid to suit feminine ideals. Unlike her elder sisters, she was also rather flat-chested. She spluttered for a moment, and then decided, "You're just saying that, Jay! You don't mean a word—and anyway, I'm not the photo *you're* gonna carry around."

Sally at once picked up the lead. "Are you really gonna ask Kathy to marry you?" she asked eagerly. Kathy was the girl Jay had been dating ever since he'd been a junior in college. She'd been a freshman then and stayed on in school when he dropped out to join the Army Air Forces. They'd corresponded the whole time he was in training.

Jay grinned. "Wait a minute," he urged, and left the living room. A minute later he was back with a little box. His sisters squealed with delight and crowded around, while his mother came in from the kitchen to see what was going on. Jay opened the box, revealing a large diamond ring, and now his sisters shrieked in excitement. "It's huge!" "It's beautiful!" "What did it cost?" "Where did you get it?" "Let me wear it!" His sisters all but fought over the ring, each trying it on their own hands and sighing with envy as they saw it flashing there.

"Can you really afford that?" his mother asked with a slight frown. Jay knew that his mother wasn't all that enthusiastic about Kathy, so he went over to her and laid his arm around her shoulders. "I can afford it, Mom. With flight pay, I earn nearly $300 a month."

"No wonder the government's got to keep issuing those war bonds!" J.B.'s father grunted as if disgusted; but J.B. knew his father would be bragging about it tomorrow in the plant.

"And are you so sure Kathy's gonna say 'yes'?" his mother pressed him. "I thought she said she wasn't ever going to marry a boy without a college degree?" Kathy had made quite a scene when Jay dropped out of school to join the USAAF.

"Well, Mom, for one thing, I intend to finish my engineering degree as soon as the war is over, and for another, Kathy changed her mind about priorities the day the Japs hit Pearl Harbour. Now she's pleased that I'm doing my part."

His mother snorted. "She only likes being seen with an Army Lieutenant with wings on his chest, that's all!"

"Don't start that again, Mom. Kathy is the girl I'm gonna marry. She's gonna be the mother of your grandchildren. It would be better if you got along with her."

His mother bit her tongue and turned away, while Jay carefully put the ring back in its box. Winning Kathy was almost as important to him as having gotten his wings. She was the classiest girl he'd ever met.

CHAPTER 3

▼

Windsor, England
April 1943

Emily's birthday fell on one of her days off. It was the worst possible scenario. If she had been working, her colleagues might have given her a little surprise party or done something special. But a day off in the middle of the week in the middle of a war was not a formula for happiness under the circumstances. The nearer it got, the more Emily dreaded it. In fact, she was so afraid of spending the day alone, she had started to make plans to go down to London and go to a museum or the cinema—anything but be by herself.

And then Aunt Hattie called. Typical Hattie, she didn't give Emily any options: just announced that she'd be arriving on the 10:52 train from Oxford.

Hattie was Robin's aunt and she was the catalyst who had brought them together, even if it was without the slightest intent or knowledge on her part. Just after Dunkirk Emily had been doing volunteer work at the Salvation Army Seaman's Mission in Portsmouth, which Hattie ran, when Robin dropped by to see his aunt.

Then after a lifetime of being the ugly older sister and the maiden aunt of Robin's little family, Hattie had astonished them all by falling in love and getting married at aged 45. Robin's mother had been scandalized and unkind about it all—not least because Hattie had "married beneath herself," to an RAF Flight Sergeant, to be precise. But Emily had been delighted from the first day when Hattie had shyly admitted that she had been asked out on a date.

The only bad thing about Hattie's late marriage, as far as Emily was concerned, was that it meant that Emily saw less of her. Because Hattie now followed her husband wherever he was stationed, Hattie had moved to Scotland more than a year ago and Emily had not seen her since.

But there was no mistaking her when she got off the train. Even without her Salvation Army uniform, Hattie was a woman who seemed "in charge" of things. She was not the least bit fat, but she was solidly built, and she had a way of moving that was forthright and determined. Not that she was pushy or masculine. In fact, she was dressed in a neat, double-breasted blue coat with white gloves and a blue hat with netting that came part way down her face—very trim, very chic— but she was totting her own suitcase without any difficulty, and even graciously turned down an offer of help from a young soldier.

When she caught sight of Emily from a distance, she smiled and waved to her at once. On reaching her, she put the suitcase down and pulled the younger woman into her arms. "You poor dear! I can see I should have come earlier! How silly of me to wait until your birthday!"

The trigger of sympathy was more than Emily was prepared to withstand, and she burst into tears.

Hattie left an arm around her shoulders, picked up her suitcase with the other hand and started out of the station saying, "That's good. You go ahead and cry, and I'll make us tea. I've brought shortbread and scones and some of my own strawberry preserves. You haven't been feeding yourself at all, have you? Here, give me the keys. I'll drive."

And so fifteen minutes later, they were back at the house and Hattie was admiring it while Emily pulled herself together. "I'll never forget how you turned that gloomy old cottage in Bosham into such a cosy little home," Hattie insisted. Emily's first home with Robin had been in an ancient stone cottage with naked stone walls and an open fireplace. As a historian, Emily had loved it, but this Victorian house with its bow windows and striped wallpaper was much more to Hattie's taste. Emily showed her to one of the three extra bedrooms, and Hattie took all the "charity packages" brought from rural Scotland out of her luggage: honey, strawberry preserves, real butter, and homemade scones and shortbread. Then they went back down to the kitchen to make tea.

Hattie opened up the cupboards and found what she needed to set the table by herself, and then settled in to a chair before demanding, "Just how much weight have you lost?"

"I don't know, actually. I haven't weighed myself."

"Well, that skirt is about to fall off. You look like you've lost ten pounds at least. This isn't going to do you any good, my dear. Robin doesn't want to fight his way across France one step ahead of the Gestapo and drag himself through the Pyrenees and talk his way out of Spanish internment to come home and find his wife starved herself to death from grief."

"Do you really think he might still be alive?" Emily asked intently, wanting to smile and hope and not really daring.

"Of course! Why else would he still be posted 'missing'? It's been more than five weeks now. If the Germans had found him, dead or alive, you would have heard from them. Besides, you know that cheating the devil is most like him. Surely *you* haven't given up all hope?" Hattie added, astonished, with a hint of reproach.

Emily sank into the chair opposite Hattie and set the teapot between them. "Oh, Hattie, if you only knew! Colin is the only one who thinks there's any hope at all—and you know what Colin is like!" (Colin was an RAF chaplain whose faith in the benevolence of God was unshakeable.) Emily continued, "Everyone else says the only reason why I've had no confirmation of death is that the Germans are excessively bureaucratic. Apparently they don't report individual casualties to the Red Cross at all; they wait until they have completed an entire form with 20 or 50 or 100 names on it or whatever, and then they forward the form along to the German Red Cross, which passes the information to the Swiss Red Cross, who in turn will pass it on to us. But everyone I've talked to claims that it often takes 6 or 8 weeks for identified casualties to get reported. Apparently, it takes less time with prisoners."

"The Germans will have nothing to report if he was found by the French Resistance," Hattie countered firmly. "I've heard the most remarkable stories about our airmen evading capture or even escaping after capture. That's just the kind of thing Robin would do!"

Emily drew a deep breath and didn't meet Hattie's eyes. Her own were watering again and her lips trembled slightly. "That's what I wanted to believe, too, but I've talked to several people and the consensus is that if Robin survived that crash at all, he would have been badly injured. The very worst thing that could have happened to him, they say, would have been to be picked up by the French. You remember Jane Leigh? The WAAF at Tangmere, who married Bridges?" Hattie nodded. "Well, she's quite senior in Intel now and she says the French resistance would be in no position to provide a downed pilot with proper medical attention. She says that if Robin fell into French hands, he would be dependent on makeshift medical care, probably in cellars or other dubious places with no proper hygiene, medical instruments or pain-killers. If he had a broken back or other serious injury…"

"But why should we assume he was that badly injured?" Hattie wanted to know, clearly a little shaken by this thought herself.

"The wing broke off and the cockpit rolled over three times at high speed. There was no movement in the cockpit afterwards. Strapped in as he was, they tell me, he probably broke his neck."

The silence was very long. Emily glanced up sharply and saw horror on Hattie's face. She realised that Hattie really had been telling herself that Robin was alive, and this was the first time *she* admitted that he might indeed be dead. "I'm sorry," Emily whispered.

Hattie pulled herself together. "Nonsense, my dear. I want to know the truth as much as you do. It makes no sense to feed oneself false hopes. And what does Colin say?"

"Oh, just a lot of rubbish about how I would know in my heart if he were dead, that souls communicate across great distances by non-verbal means and all that kind of nonsense." Emily dismissed the notions irritably.

Hattie understood. Emily had been raised atheist by her fanatically Communist parents, but Hattie *did* believe in the immortal soul and telepathy, and particularly in intuitive understanding between souls that shared affection for one another. She too believed that if Robin were dead she would *know* it in her heart. He would have come to her in some way—in dreams or just subconsciously—and she would have understood and grieved. But she hadn't had any such experience, and she could not get herself to believe Robin was dead—no matter what the experts said. But she also knew better than to try to convince Emily of these beliefs. So she settled for a much milder, "Well, I don't think we should give up hope that he is a POW either—at least not yet. After all, if Robin *was* badly injured, the Germans would give him proper medical treatment. No matter what else one thinks of the Germans, one has to give them that. Think of the gallant offer they made about Bader's legs and all? So that might delay communication, too. It is just too soon to give up hope and frankly, my dear, whether Robin is dead or not, you must take care of yourself. Robin wouldn't want you to waste away on his account. You know that."

"Honestly, Hattie, I don't know anything at all. I'm so confused and lost and—well—hopeless. Life just doesn't seem to have any meaning anymore. Certainly if he's dead it is meaningless—"

"Nonsense! You are young and pretty and talented. You have a degree, for God's sake, and you can fly more types of aeroplanes than most of the RAF. You are making a very vital contribution to the war effort, and I know that you have much, much more to give this country and us all!"

Emily reached across the table and touched Hattie's hand. "Don't worry. I'm not feeling suicidal—just exhausted and disinterested in life. Depressed, I guess. At first I thought work would be the worst, but it's not. It takes too much concentration, really. But the minute I get back here…"

Hattie looked around herself. "Well, this is rather a large house for you alone. I'm surprised the authorities haven't started billeting people with you already. Have you thought of taking in lodgers?"

"Colin asked me that, too. Apparently the Waafery at Bomber Command HQ is completely overflowing. He said a new Flight Officer was looking for a billet off station, but if Robin *is* dead then I don't want to stay here at all. I'll give notice and find someplace smaller."

"There is no harm in talking to this WAAF, is there?" Hattie countered as she picked up the teapot and poured for both of them. "If she is special to Colin, then you will see more of him, too, and that would be good for you."

"Oh, it's nothing like that. Colin said she was 'way out of his league,' poor dear. I wish he *would* find someone. But it appears that this WAAF is just an acquaintance."

"Colin is too shy for his own good," Hattie concluded, and then taking a deep breath she continued, "Emily, I truly don't think you should give up hope of Robin being alive, but it sounds as if he is more likely to be a POW than to be in hiding with the Resistance. In which case, he is not going to be back here until after the war is over. And that could be several more years."

Emily nodded. There was no sign of the war ever ending.

"So, it seems to me that it would make much more sense for you to take in one or more lodgers," Hattie continued, practical as ever, "before you get people billeted with you who you can't stand. Don't many of the other women pilots live together? At least a WAAF would also understand about flying. You need to have someone you can talk to when you come home. I wish we lived nearer. Roy at once offered to have you come live with us, you know? If you want to put in for a transfer up to the Ferry Pool in Scotland, you could have our spare bedroom. You know we'd both love to have you." Hattie almost looked hopeful as she made the offer, as if she sincerely wished Emily would move to Scotland and come live with her.

Emily smiled at that and reached out to take Hattie's hand. "Thank you. I wish you lived nearer, too, but they don't have any women up in Scotland now.

It's a pretty rough Pool, I gather, and the weather's terrible. I think I'd better stay here. But I will take your advice and talk to Colin's lady friend."

Within minutes, Emily had the feeling Philippa Wycliffe was outside of her league, too. She was the kind of woman who looked stunning even in uniform. She was beautiful, sophisticated, educated, wealthy and she had a dazzling smile, a ready wit, and a perfectly natural manner. Emily found it quite amazing that the charming young woman was still single. She must have many admirers, Emily thought; maybe she couldn't choose between them all.

"Mrs. Priestman, I'm so anxious to get away from the Waafery that I'd be quite content with a camp bed in the wine cellar. Not that I'd trust *me* in a wine cellar, if I were *you*. I only meant I'm not at all fussy about rooms, and, of course, I'll do my share of any chores."

Emily assured her that she need not worry about either cellar or chores. The house had been rented with the entertaining needs of a Wing Commander in mind. Upstairs there were four bedrooms and two baths. Emily showed her the two rooms off the second bath, either of which she was welcome to have.

Emily was fairly certain that Philippa had been raised in houses far grander than this, but the WAAF officer nevertheless expressed her delight at the accommodations with every indication of sincerity, especially the view of Windsor Park from the second bedroom. "Good heavens! If you advertised with an estate agent, you could make a *fortune* letting these rooms. You're quite sure you want to be charitable to WAAFs instead?"

"Quite. Shall we have tea?"

"Splendid idea. I'm so grateful to you, Mrs. Priestman. I hope this doesn't sound snobby or whatever, but I'm quite fed up with the collective life imposed on one at a Waafery. One feels as if one is never off duty."

Emily could sympathise with that and nodded. "Are you in Admin, then?"

"Good heavens, no! No one in his right mind would let me drill anyone. I never could tell my right foot from my left. And, frankly, I'm not a neat person by nature. I rather like a bit of chaos around me. You know, just enough to feel comfy and at home. My nanny was such a fanatic about neatness that everything had to be lined up in rows and starched and all. My first weeks in the WAAF, I felt myself transported back to the nursery! Which, of course, only made me rebellious—just like a naughty six-year-old. I was quite hopeless, I'm afraid. I probably would have ended up getting myself thrown out of the WAAF altogether, if dear old Watson-Watt hadn't come recruiting."

"The Watson-Watt who invented RDF?"

"Yes, have you ever met him? He's a darling man. He's ever so amusing, and he can explain things wonderfully well. Besides, he absolutely insisted that women would be better with his little machines than most men, and from the very start set out to select suitable women for training. I was whisked away from all that infantile nonsense about falling-in in twos and fours and whatnot, and introduced to the mysteries of cathode rays."

"You were one of the first RDF operators? Sorry, I suppose that's terribly hush-hush."

"Infantile, all this secrecy, isn't it? Yes, I was one of the first, so naturally—through no fault of my own—I was soon promoted. It was quite funny, actually. Some RAF psychologist had worked out that the people most suited to filter, plot and control our fighters would be brokers from the Stock Exchange—men used to handling loads of information coming at them very fast, men used to making split-second decisions."

"Sounds reasonable," Emily admitted.

"Oh, it is—but can you imagine all those pin-striped broker types used to City salaries being put into airmen's uniforms and expected to square-bash? Not on, is it? So the RAF thought they'd just give them all nice little commissions and let them come in and supervise *us*. That was when Stuffy said: 'The day those chaps come in here, my WAAF sergeants get rings.' The next thing I knew, I was an Assistant Section Leader, and the brokers didn't last very long. I don't know why, actually. Some of them were quite charming, and they had nerves of steel. Never saw *them* in a flap. But the best part was when the Air Ministry found out about us—the WAAFs that Stuffy had given commissions to. Their Airships dryly told him we couldn't exist, because there *were* no WAAF officers in any trade except Admin at the time. Stuffy had quite a laugh about that one." Philippa laughed just remembering.

"He doesn't sound stuffy at all."

"Oh, he wasn't—once you got to know him. He was a lovely man—a perfect gentleman at all times, with an icy dry wit, but very, very caring. Of course he was very precise, could be acidly sarcastic and he always insisted on the best for 'his boys.' His son was flying with Fighter Command then, you know? But he looked on all the pilots as his own. He really cared about each and every one of them. I'll never forgive their Airships for what they did to him—chucking him out like that after he'd won the Battle of Britain for them. If it hadn't been for Dowding, we wouldn't have *had* any RDF, or a Fighter Control system, and what's more, the PM would have given away all our Hurricanes to the French, too."

Emily nodded, remembering that Robin had been equally loyal to Dowding, and not a little miffed that he had been unceremoniously dismissed before the smoke of battle had even cleared. If this woman shared Robin's opinions, she reasoned, then they were sure to get along.

Philippa was continuing: "When they chucked him out like that, I didn't want to stay at Bently Priory anymore, so I transferred out—to one of our forward Stations. But, of course, that soon got boring, so I'm back at Headquarters, albeit Bomber Command."

Emily knew better than to ask for more details. Philippa might call secrecy 'infantile,' but she would not hold the rank she did if she was really indiscreet. Emily confined herself to asking, "And you like it there?"

"I'm not entirely sure," Philippa admitted without elaborating.

"Well, you are very welcome here." Emily declared. "In fact, I hope you'll move in sooner rather than later."

"That's very kind. In fact, I'd like to move in immediately, only..." She paused and considered Emily, apparently trying to estimate her mood. "There is one slight problem."

"What?" Emily couldn't imagine what could stand in the way, since they seemed to get on so well and the accommodations were suitable.

"Well, I'm not sure I mentioned my dog..."

"Your dog?"

"She's a very affectionate bulldog. She's hasn't any bad habits—not serious ones, anyway—but she's wasting away from grief. She was my brother's, you see, and he was a navigator in Coastal Command. His Sunderland was lost 4 months ago, so I adopted her. No one at my old Station minded at all, but here the WAAF-Commanding made a terrible fuss. Poor Penny now feels she's been abandoned a second time. She's hardly eating a thing. You wouldn't mind having a dog here, would you?"

Emily was taken aback. She'd never had pets. Her parents' flat in Portsmouth had been too small, and her mother hated them. Didn't they make messes and leave hair all over the furniture? And dogs barked at all hours of the day and night, too. Emily was sure she'd never be able to get a good night's sleep with a dog in the house.

Philippa could see her dismay and begged, "Please, at least come and meet her. She's waiting out in the car."

Emily didn't feel she could say no to this, but went along with mounting resistance to the idea of having an animal in the house. It was rented, after all, as were the bulk of the furnishings. What if the dog ruined something? And a bulldog, of all things! It might bite the neighbour children or attack the postman.

Philippa led her out to her run-down Austin parked in front. As they approached the car, a small, cream-coloured bulldog leapt up and stood with her front paws on the car-window ledge. She pressed her squashed, dark face against the glass, and her large dark eyes devoured Philippa. Philippa opened the door, the dog jumped down, and Philippa swept the dog up into her arms. Then she turned to Emily with an appealing look on her face. "She's wasting away before my eyes, all skin and bones. And she hasn't said 'wuf' once since Barry died."

The dog gazed solemnly at Emily, breathing heavily, as if she knew her fate depended on Emily's decision. The look went straight to Emily's heart; they were both grieving.

Emily tentatively reached out her hand and let the dog sniff it. The sniffing became more intense, and the dog looked up with a strange hopeful light in her eyes.

"Oh, she likes you!" Philippa exclaimed delighted. "She's wagging her tail, and she hasn't done that for *anyone* since Barry died!" At this point, very hesitantly, the bulldog gave Emily's hand a quick tentative lick, then gazed at Emily again hopefully.

Emily melted. "Poor thing. She can probably smell aircraft on my hands, and it reminds her of her master. What did you say her name was?"

"Well, I'm not *sure*. Barry gave her some very clever name, I know, but his skipper complained that she was like an 'Irish Pennant'—always trailing around after them—and so they started calling her 'the Pennant,' which soon got shortened to 'Penny.' So that's what she answers to."

Emily risked patting the dog's head and Philippa smiled encouragement. "And she likes being scratched behind the ears. Like this."

Emily did as Philippa demonstrated, astonished by how soft the short hair was and feeling, too, the frail bones through the folds of skin around Penny's neck. "Poor thing. You're sure she'll be alright when we're both gone all day?"

Philippa beamed with relief as she realised Emily had capitulated. "I'm sure she will, if we give her lots of attention when we're home."

Emily smiled back, thinking she must call Colin and thank him. It was going to be very good having Philippa—and Penny—in the house with her.

CHAPTER 4

▼

Halifax, Nova Scotia
April 1943

Typical Army—after breaking Kathy's heart because he had to report in Halifax on March 10 (and not a minute later!), J.B. was then kept cooling his heels in the icy port while a convoy and escort assembled. There were quite a few of them in the same boat. Along with the rest of his crew, which met up with him in Halifax, there were at least a dozen other replacement crews, well over 100 AAF airmen, sailing in the same convoy. They were all put up in the same hotel and had to report twice daily for orders. Otherwise they were free to do whatever they liked.

Not that there was much to do in a town like Halifax in the fourth year of war (from Canada's point of view) at the end of winter. The snow had melted, but the water and wind were still bitterly cold and all trees were still bare, so one had to pretty much keep inside. There were only a handful of movie theatres, and half of them were showing the same flick. There was a music hall with terrible local musicians trying to play Dixie and Ragtime music. There was the Public Library and the Salvation Army Mission. And there were the sleazy bars down by the port.

The first couple of nights it had been exciting checking out the bars and being accosted by hookers. It made J.B. feel like a bit of a stud, the way the girls kept making eyes at him or even leaned against him provocatively, trying to attract his attention and custom. The bolder ones even rubbed their breasts up against him when they reached across him at the bar for their drinks. Others poured their hot breath into his ear, calling him 'Lieutenant,' when they whispered indecent suggestions to him. It was definitely arousing, though not the least bit tempting—not with thoughts of Kathy so fresh in his mind.

He'd proposed to Kathy the second day of his four-day leave and she'd accepted. He'd taken her out for dinner at a fancy restaurant and "popped the question" just before dessert. She had really acted surprised—but she didn't hesitate for a second. She'd jumped up to kiss him right there in front of everyone. People at the other tables had clapped. Kathy loved that, because she was a drama major. She wanted to be a stage actress. And she'd looked stunning that night in an off-the-shoulder gown with a tight waist, just like something straight out of *Gone with the Wind.* In fact, Jay thought she looked a lot like Vivien Leigh.

The next day he'd been introduced to her folks. That had been pretty stressful, because they were a lot richer than his parents and lived in a big house in Grosse Pointe. As a result, he'd spent the whole day on his best behaviour: church, brunch, a walk, tea, and a "serious" talk with her Dad in his study in which the old man (a successful lawyer) lectured Jay on finishing college. He promised Jay a job in his own firm if he went to law school (if his grades were good enough), but he stressed that he didn't want his daughter married to some "sky jockey." Jay had assured him that he had every intention of returning to college and left the field of study open. Jay was an engineering major and he liked it. He thought being an automotive engineer would be more interesting that being a patent lawyer like Kathy's dad, but he knew better than to say so.

The best day of his leave had been the following Monday, however, when Kathy and he spent the day together alone. They'd gone to lunch in Ann Arbor; then Kathy had introduced him to some of her friends (but only briefly) and they took a long walk around the campus. The only problem had been when Kathy found out he had to leave for Halifax the next day. She had assumed he'd have a whole week and had planned for him to come see the play she was performing in. She had been really upset, but making up had been nice and she'd let him cuddle with her longer than ever before. Nothing improper, of course; she wasn't that kind of girl. But they'd kissed and he'd held her in his arms. She was so soft and she always smelled beautiful. Even thinking about holding her made his blood rush.

But instead of being with Kathy, he was stuck in Halifax, NS, waiting for the war to catch up with them. He spent the whole time with the other three officers of his crew: Tony Costino, his co-pilot; Dan Vernon, his navigator; and little

Buzz Zillner, the bombardier. In the evenings they'd hit the bars. If they happened into a bar where the enlisted members of their crew (also doing the sights of Halifax as a group) were collected, then the latter quickly disappeared. The enlisted men from other crews ignored them, but would avoid contact with their own officers. That was the unwritten code that they all lived by.

Buzz was the unquestioned, self-appointed leader of their little group on these nightly forays. He was a New Yorker, and considered himself infinitely more experienced and sophisticated than his 'provincial' crew-mates. He was only 5'2" tall, but he claimed to have the biggest dick of them all—well, he would claim that, of course, and none of the rest of them was inclined to argue the point. In addition to being short and slight, he was not particularly handsome, so he had to make up for it by bragging about all the lays he'd had. He also quickly determined that Halifax was a 'pee-hole.' He couldn't get over just how bad the place was. He kept saying, 'They call this a bar?' or 'They call this a beer?' or 'They call that a whore?' Then he'd continue with 'Back in the Bronx...'

Tony, son of an Italian immigrant, had been born and raised just across the river in Hoboken. There was a natural rivalry between Buzz and Tony in social things, just as there was between Tony and J.B. in flying. Tony didn't really think he was any less of a pilot than J.B., and figured he had as much right to the left-hand seat as J.B. did.

Dan was a very quiet, thoughtful Virginian, and he kept his opinions about just about everything to himself. J.B. knew that Dan's father had an important job in Washington at the State Department and came from an 'old' family. Dan had impeccable manners, a deep faith and a highly developed sense of duty and honour. J.B. was very glad to have Dan in his crew, and felt instinctively that he could rely on Dan more than the rest of them.

So it was in Halifax, too. While Buzz and Tony made quite a show of comparing the attributes of the bars, the drinks and most especially the whores, Dan and J.B. just watched and listened. Buzz and Tony got smashed every night, and Dan and J.B. brought them back to the hotel. As for the girls, Buzz kept making hints and suggestions about finally accepting one or the other proposition (claiming only the low quality of the girls held him back). Tony kept egging him on until one night Buzz actually got up and started to drunkenly approach one of the hookers. That was when J.B. put an end to it, ordering Buzz to sit down again. "The last thing I need is for my bombardier to get a case of VD before we even get over to England!"

Buzz grumbled, but J.B. thought he was probably secretly relieved. J.B. didn't believe he'd ever had anything to do with whores any more than the rest of them had.

After almost a week of this, however, even the hookers weren't interesting anymore. They'd seen the same girls in the same bars night after night. They'd heard the same music played in the same bars over and over. They'd seen all three flicks. They were so bored and fractious that they literally cheered out loud when they finally got their orders to report aboard the *SS Waterloo* at 19.00.

"What a shit name for a ship!" Buzz complained as they packed up their duffel bags. "Who'd be so goddamned crazy as to name a fucking ship for the most famous defeat in fucking history!"

"It was a British victory," Dan pointed out dryly.

And sure enough, it was a British ship. That surprised them. Somehow they'd assumed they'd travel across the Atlantic in an American ship. The unfamiliar red ensign on her stern and the homeport of Liverpool made them feel a little lost—even before they were met by a ship's officer speaking in a crisp English accent like they'd previously heard only in the movies or over the radio.

Somewhat intimidated, they went to their cabin in the after part of the ship in a silent little group. The *SS Waterloo* was not a proper passenger ship, but a cargo ship with limited passenger capacity. The Air Army Force officers from four crews had been booked into the two First Class cabins of the ship, while their enlisted crews occupied the Second Class cabins, a deck below. Before the war, the First Class cabins had each consisted of a sitting room, bedroom and bath; now two bunks had been built into both the sitting and the bedroom of each, so that eight men shared what had been a suite for two.

"Yeah, well, what do you expect of the AAF?" Tony commented as they threw their duffel bags down, and noted they could hardly turn around between the bunks. They were going to be tripping all over each other the whole time.

The cabin was also very dark, because the porthole had been painted over from the outside with blue-black paint and sealed shut. Discovering this fact, Buzz hit his fist against it, exclaiming angrily, "What the fuck is this? Aren't we even allowed fresh air in here?"

"It's on account of the black-out, stupid," Tony retorted.

J.B. understood, but for once he agreed with Buzz. The thought of being cooped up in this tiny cabin without any fresh air was not pleasant. In the event, it was much worse than even he had imagined.

They sailed just before midnight. Excited by the prospect of setting off at last, all of them went on deck to watch as the ship cast off and nudged her way out of the harbour. They could just barely make out the lights blinking from various buoys marking a channel; and even less distinct and very shadowy, they could sense more than see other ships from other quays that slipped their moorings one after another. Soon there were more than a score of ships slowly oozing forward in the darkness.

To their amazement, while still in sight of land, another score of ships emerged on the horizon. One of the ship's officers, hearing their surprise, stopped long enough to inform them that these ships had come up from Boston. The ships from Halifax were joining them to form a mammoth convoy of over 40 merchantmen. "It saves on escorts that way," he explained, and then clattered down to the main deck on some errand.

Scanning the horizon and straining their eyes a bit, they at last found the naval escorts. These showed up slightly lighter against the black of night, and could be seen more by their bow-waves than anything else as they dashed about like shepherds collecting the slow-moving merchantmen into a long formation. Now and then an Aldis lamp flashed, but although they'd all been trained in Morse code, the RN signallers flashed out their messages so rapidly that the airmen found they couldn't make sense of it.

"Wish we had Hank here with us," Tony admitted. Hank was their radio operator and correspondingly better with Morse.

After a couple of hours, however, the cold exceeded the excitement. All the ships seemed to be in their assigned positions by that time, and even the escorts had settled down to their stations on the flanks, so the airmen turned in for the night.

J.B. was woken sometime later. It was pitch dark in the cabin, of course, and Dan in the bunk opposite was snoring softly. J.B. was alarmed, however, by the sound of something banging overhead. It banged metallically in rhythm with the alarming corkscrewing motion of the ship. There must be a terrible sea running, J.B. thought in mounting terror, as he became aware of just how violently the ship was rolling. After that, he hardly got any sleep at all.

They were woken by a steward, who announced breakfast in the 'first class saloon' in half an hour. J.B. struggled out of bed and tried to get dressed. It was impossible to stand without holding on to something, and his stomach was feeling very, very uneasy. He forced himself to go into the sombre 'saloon' for the breakfast, but something smelled horrible. "What's that?" Buzz asked in alarm right behind him.

"Kippers for breakfast, sir," the steward announced cheerfully, and set down a plate of tinned mackerel with the eyes still on them.

J.B.'s stomach turned itself inside out, and he shoved Buzz roughly aside and banged his shins on the bulwark as he rushed to the so-called 'head.'

He spent the next 24 hours staring down into that infernal contraption. The only time the others could pry him away from it was when they had to use it themselves or there was lifeboat drill. The Captain, a very dignified and icily distant man with a grey beard, insisted on lifeboat drill once a day—and he timed how long it took to "close up lifeboat stations." Anything over 5 minutes and they all had to do it again. The others bitched about it, but J.B. was far too miserable to care.

As his third day at sea dawned, J.B. found himself being pulled away from the head by one of the ship's officers. The latter was a surprisingly young man at close scrutiny (as was inevitable when a man pulls you away from a toilet basin), hardly older than J.B. himself. He pulled J.B.'s arm over his shoulder and carried/ dragged him into the saloon, where he handed him a big square saltine cracker and ordered: "Eat that!"

J.B. shook his head.

"Eat it!"

"Just let me die," J.B. countered.

"Not on my watch!"

J.B. forced himself to bite into the dry cracker and forced himself to chew and to swallow. He was then force-fed tea with milk and sugar in the same manner. It helped. Twenty-four hours later, J.B. made his first appearance at a regular meal—to the mocking cheers of the other passengers, particularly his own crew.

After that, he started to take an interest in his surroundings, limited as they were. His fellow officers (except Dan, who was reading a heavy tome by some German titled *On War*) spent the bulk of their time playing cards in the saloon. J.B. wasn't much of a reader and he found playing cards boring at the best of times, but here particularly he found it very confining. He preferred to be up on deck. The fresh air cleared his head, and his stomach felt happier with a horizon in sight. Not that there was much 'deck,' really. They had only a small, cluttered area behind the bridge where two life-boats hung from davits, and the ensign fluttered from a short flagpole over the stern. Ladders led from here up to the bridge and down to the main deck, where J.B. occasionally caught glimpses of one or the other member of his crew stretching their legs.

By spending a lot of time on deck, J.B. became familiar with the changing of the watch every four hours. He also got a feel for the zig-zagging of the convoy— a very complicated manoeuvre with so many ships, particularly in the dark. He came to recognise the various escorts and their various duties as well. There was one corvette that was always sent to round up stragglers, for example, and a destroyer that seemed to investigate suspicious objects farther afield, while the leader of the escort group sometimes dashed about flashing signals in all directions like an indignant busy-body.

J.B. noticed at once when suddenly the watch on deck increased dramatically. Something was up. He stopped the young officer (he knew now it was the Third Mate) who had helped him conquer his seasickness, as he made his way up to the bridge.

"Excuse me. Is something up?"

"Up?"

"I mean—all the extra look-outs." He gestured vaguely toward the bows.

"Oh, that's just a precaution. We're now out of range of your long-range recce aircraft and not yet in range of our own. If the Irish would let us base aircraft in Ireland, we could virtually close the gap, but as it is—" he shrugged—"we've a couple of days here when we're blind." With that he turned his broad back, clothed in a heavy duffel coat, and clomped briskly up to the bridge in his sea boots.

How reassuring, J.B. thought, looking around at the grey horizon. Dark grey sea met light grey sky; and the ships at the end of the convoy seemed small, and those at the head were almost impossible to see. (The station of the *Waterloo* was more or less three-quarters back toward the end of convoy.) If huge freighters could seem so small and insignificant, how the hell was anyone ever going to see the tiny conning tower of a U-boat?—assuming it was on the surface, which of course it wouldn't be if it was about to attack. So why bother with look-outs?

When he got cold, J.B. went below deck again, but a lingering tension remained with him. Maybe he was imagining things, but the whole crew seemed nervous in a way they hadn't been before. Not that they said anything. No, they were as polite and cheerful as ever, but when he served the evening meal the steward was wearing his life-jacket.

"Don't mind Saines," the Second Officer dismissed it; "he's just got the wind up because he got wet on his last trip."

"That's right—middle of dinner it was, too, and I didn't have my vest with me. Had to take one off a mate."

"You *stole* another man's life vest right off him!?" Tony asked in horror.

"He didn't mind, sir, he didn't have a head either. More spuds, sir?"

J.B. didn't sleep well that night, but he seemed to have just finally drifted off when a deep boom tore him from his nightmare into a reality that was worse.

Overhead alarms were going off and feet were clattering about on the metal decks. Dan was sitting bolt upright in the bed opposite, and Tony's legs dangled down in his face as the other pilot flung them over the edge of the top bunk. "What the hell was that?" Buzz called out in obvious alarm from the fourth bunk.

For a second nobody answered. J.B. just held his breath trying to decide if they had been hit or not and, if so, how bad it was.

Dan spoke first. "I think it must have been another vessel."

Now they too swung their feet over their bunks, while Tony jumped down and Buzz (grumbling to himself) followed. They struggled in the confined space and the dark on the heavily rolling deck to get their trousers on over their pyjamas and their feet into flying boots (without socks). They grabbed their flight jackets swaying from hooks over their bunks, and clattered out of the cabin. From the adjoining cabin came the alarmed voices of other AAF officers. One of them stuck his head out of their cabin. "What's happened?"

"Don't know yet."

J.B. and the others ran up on deck. Ahead of them, the sky was an unnatural colour. Once they made the afterdeck, they realised that the night sky was lit up by fire off their starboard quarter. It was bright enough to silhouette the crewmen on the bridge, their binoculars trained on the fire. An escort swept by very close and a signal lamp flashed at them. "What's he saying?" Tony asked nervously.

"Maintain convoy course and speed," Dan answered.

The others stared at him, unsure if he could really read it or was just guessing. They certainly did just that while the airmen waited helplessly and tensely for the next blow. It didn't come. Instead it got light. The crew was rung down from their 'alarm' stations. The airmen went into breakfast unshaved, tired and rattled.

The steward was silent. No jokes this morning.

"Do we know what happened last night," J.B. asked for everyone when a very weary Third Officer made his appearance later that morning.

"The *Eliza Jane* was struck amidships and went down very rapidly. I believe 12 of her crew were picked up; 28 or so are still missing. The aft escort thought she had a contact and appears to have frightened the U-boat off, but could not report a kill."

Silence.

"They'll be back tonight at the latest, probably in force, which is why we've made a radical change in course—but that rarely fools them for long. They have greater speed on the surface and if there's a pack working together, they can cover most of the area where we have any chance to be—regardless of which way we turn. There is even the risk of turning straight into another pack on the way to join the fun."

J.B. did not like the sound of this at all.

"I shouldn't think they'll attack until dark, however. They usually don't."

J.B. decided to try to get some sleep during daylight, and retired to his cabin. He managed to doze a bit. Dan woke him for dinner. The steward was still wearing his life vest. At least the nights were getting shorter, J.B. thought to himself, as he watched the light gradually fade from the sky.

The attack was launched, as predicted, after dark. It came from the southeast. A ship well forward and on the starboard side of the convoy went up in a roar of flame. Aboard the *Waterloo*, the bells clanged, and the crew clattered up the gangways to their stations. Most of the airmen also went on deck. J.B., Dan, Tony and Buzz were all bundled in their flight gear, including scarves, and wearing their life vests. They clustered by unspoken accord near their lifeboat station.

The next explosion came from what seemed to be dead ahead. It was not accompanied by so much flame, but signal flares lit up a freighter already listing very hard to port and down by the stern. The ship directly ahead of them veered sharply to avoid a collision.

And then the next explosion racked them as a ship off their port stern was lifted into the air with a loud bang before it disintegrated into thousands of burning pieces. The debris—planking, railings, shattered lifeboats and fragments of humans—splashed down all around it, sending up spumes of water or smaller flashes into the lurid night.

The airmen stared open-mouthed at the flotsam undulating on the swells off to port, lit by the flames from the first victim. Beyond it the bow-wave of one of the escorts abruptly leapt up; an Aldis lamp winked at them. It was answered by the signalman on their own bridge. As the escort receded into the darkness, it flashed at them once again very briefly. J.B. thought he read: "Agreed."

Immediately, a bell rang on the bridge, and J.B., clinging to the railing, felt the vibrations ease. They were slowing down.

"What the hell are we doing?" Tony asked in alarm.

They turned to stare at the bridge, but there was nothing to see from their vantage point—except that the Captain had gone out onto the wing and had his binoculars focused ahead of him. They saw him turn and give an order, and the next thing they knew the First Mate was clattering down the ladder from the bridge and making straight toward them. Out of the darkness other figures emerged.

The First Mate signalled the airman out of the way. "We have to launch this lifeboat," he announced.

"Why? We haven't been hit." Buzz's voice was high with alarm.

"No, we're lowering it to collect survivors from the *Thermopylae*. They were unable to get any of their boats away."

"But you can't do that! There's at least one U-Boat out there! Maybe more!"

"I know. Please stand aside."

"But if we stop, we're a sitting duck!" Buzz protested.

The First Mate did not even bother to answer. The sailors set to work swinging the davits out and preparing to launch the lifeboat.

"This is madness!" Buzz shouted, his voice breaking in his distress. "The escorts are supposed to worry about survivors!"

"They're chasing U-boats at the moment. We're only pausing to launch a lifeboat and then will resume steaming. We'll return for the lifeboat after daybreak."

Six sailors scrambled into the lifeboat, while the remaining four prepared to lower it. The *Waterloo* had slowed to a crawl, and it rolled more noticeably in the heavy swells. Meanwhile, they had come within a couple hundred yards of the now completely capsized wreck of the *Thermopylae*. You could see men bobbing up and down in the swells around the wreck. The lights from their life vests were tiny pin-pricks of light, easily obscured by the shifting surface of the water. Voices could be heard, too, now that the reassuring throb of the engines had sunk to a low, idling rumble.

The First Mate put his hand on the gunwale of the lifeboat preparatory to climbing aboard, and at the same second a fourth explosion came from behind them. Buzz screamed and grabbed the Mate's arm. "You can't do this!" he screamed. "We're highly trained airmen. We're desperately needed for your goddamned war! You can't risk losing four full bomber crews out here in the middle of the goddamned Atlantic—"

"Are you trying to tell me airmen are more important than merchant seamen?"

"Shut up, Buzz!" J.B. ordered before anything more came out of Buzz's open mouth. "I'm sorry, sir," he added to the Chief Mate, as he pulled Buzz away.

"Lower away!" the Mate ordered without even acknowledging J.B., and the lifeboat started to squeak and squeal its way down toward the uneasy blackness below.

"Jesus God!" Buzz turned in fury on J.B. "We're all going to die out here!"

Flares were going off from the fourth ship that had been hit.

"Well, then for God's sake do it with the same dignity as these sailors!" Dan hissed at him.

"Come on, Buzz, cool it," J.B. urged.

A dull splash announced the arrival of the lifeboat on the surface of the water below. At once one of the sailors on the davits raised his voice and shouted to the bridge. "Boat's away, sir!"

They heard the bell as the Captain rang for power again, and at once the vibrations increased as if the ship was trying to shake herself to pieces. Slowly, ever so slowly, they pulled away from the little white boat bobbing on the swells in their wake as they veered around the capsized wreck. J.B. felt something like shame to be abandoning it there, even while he was intensely relieved not to be such a perfect target anymore.

He stood riveted to the rail, watching the lifeboat grow smaller. He was quite overcome with awe for the courage of the men manning that lifeboat. Not one of them had hesitated for a second, he noted. They had climbed aboard that flimsy little toy boat and were being tossed about in an ugly, bitter-cold sea amidst the debris of two shattered ships. Maybe they were too insignificant to attract the attention of the U-Boat, but J.B. knew he'd be scared to death to be out there in this vast, wintry ocean in an open boat. Who was to say anyone would be able to come back for them? How could they? They'd be miles and miles away by dawn, and would surely never find this little square of ocean again. They couldn't leave the convoy to come back, anyway.

Fascinated, Jay watched as—like little black balls floating on the surface—the survivors of the capsized vessel converged on the lifeboat. Jay strained his eyes, hoping to see the men being hauled aboard the lifeboat, but the darkness closed around them too soon.

From somewhere far away came dull thuds, almost like a heavy but rapid drum-beat. Depth charges? Then there was silence. The convoy continued doggedly through the night.

CHAPTER 5

▼

White Waltham
May 1943

Emily reported as usual to Operations and got her 'chits' for the day's flying. She was being taken by one of the taxi Ansons over to Brooklands to pick up a Wellington bound for Little Rissington. There she was to collect a Spitfire for Llandow. From there she would have to find ground transportation to St. Athan, four miles away, to collect a Mosquito bound for Henlow. There she would be collected by the taxi Anson and returned to White Waltham. If all went well, she'd be home for dinner, but then there were lots of things that could go wrong with three aircraft deliveries. They might not be ready for her when she arrived, or she might have difficulty getting ground transportation to St. Athan—one was entirely dependent upon the good will of the RAF. And the weather was always unpredictable.

She collected her parachute, went over to the Met office for the latest weather, and then read a newspaper in the Mess until she was called to a waiting taxi Anson over the loud-speaker along with the other pilots travelling together this morning. There were five of them in this Anson, all with their parachute packs and flying kit. Douglas Fairweather was flying. He was in his fifties and his wife, Margie, also flew for the ATA. He invited Emily to sit in the right-hand seat, and she gladly accepted. She knew that the other pilots would be reading their newspapers in the back (just like any other group of commuters on their way to work), but she never read while flying.

"Whatever have you done to the sleeves of your flying jacket?" Douglas asked as she settled in beside him.

Emily blushed in embarrassment; she hadn't thought anyone would notice. "Oh, nothing," she dismissed the comment nervously, holding her elbows to cover the scorched lower arms of the over-sized jacket. "I grabbed Robin's old Irvin by mistake, that's all. In too much of a rush this morning."

Douglas' eyes lingered on her for a moment, and though Emily looked doggedly straight ahead through the windshield, she was certain he guessed the truth. She'd made no mistake; she'd consciously wrapped herself in Robin's old Irvin this morning in a moment of intense loneliness.

"Still no word from Jerry, then?" Douglas asked as he re-directed his attention to flying.

"None," Emily told him simply. Nothing at all. Just impenetrable silence that left them both, Robin and herself, in suspended animation. She was unable to hope or grieve, but she unconsciously stroked the opposite elbows of his old flying jacket as she sat there. The sleeves had been ruined when Robin dragged a wounded pilot out of his burning cockpit just before it exploded. The other pilot had been horribly burned; Robin had gotten away with burns to his hands that left scars but no impairment of movement. The RAF had given him a new flying jacket, of course, the one he'd been wearing over France, but the one Emily was wearing was almost like a talisman. But that was superstitious, of course, and so she tried to dismiss the thought and concentrate on the present.

The faithful Anson took off smoothly into the morning sky. There seemed to be quite a lot of haze around, Emily noted. You could see clearly enough looking straight down, but at an angle things rapidly turned murky, rather like looking through frosted glass. But maybe it would burn off. The sun was still ascending, after all.

Emily watched carefully as Douglas made his approach into Brooklands. Although she had been flying with the ATA for 15 months and had more than 600 flying hours, she was acutely aware that she still had much to learn. In fact, she was a little nervous about the Wellington she was supposed to fly this morning. She'd converted to Class IV, twin-engine, operational aircraft just this past winter, passing out on them only days before Robin went missing. They had planned to celebrate that weekend, but Robin was shot down…This was her first ferrying assignment with a Wellington.

Moments later she scrambled with considerable difficulty into the large machine, dragging her 40-lb parachute pack behind her. Once inside, Emily felt singularly lonely in a machine designed for a crew of six. She settled down into the left-hand seat, and took her time adjusting it and the straps, making herself as comfortable as possible. Then she took out her maps and the Ferry Pilot's Notes—a ring-binder with one page (double-sided) of vital statistics about every single aircraft in service with the RAF.

When flying a more familiar aircraft, Emily usually just checked take-off data before taking off, then looked at the cruising data while in the air, and reviewed landing data as she entered the circuit, but today she was feeling nervous about the Wellington. So she read through the whole thing on the Wellington again. When there was no excuse for procrastinating any longer, she signalled the patiently waiting ground crew that she was going to start up. Soon both Hercules engines were rumbling contentedly. Everything seemed to be reading normally, so Emily waved the chocks away and eased the medium bomber onto the apron and taxied carefully out to the end of the runway.

The wind was coming from the right, Emily noted, as she got the green light from the Control Tower and started to roll forward. The heavy aircraft needed considerable starboard rudder to keep it straight on the runway, and it swung rather hard on take-off, too. After that it settled down, however, and Emily could concentrate on the route she had set herself, avoiding the barrage balloons. With the larger aircraft, she felt less comfortable close to the deck than in smaller, lighter aircraft, so she was quite happy that there was no cloud—just the heavy haze—and she eased up to nearly 3,000 feet before trimming for cruising.

At this height, however, the earth below appeared through a milky sheet, obscuring all but the most obvious landmarks. Emily found herself doing dead-reckoning in her head based on the compass and airspeed, and checking her position against landmarks on the ground at every opportunity. Fortunately, the Wellington was behaving like a gentleman, sedate and reliable.

Little Rissington was a busy Maintenance Unit and there were several other aircraft on the circuit when she arrived, but she landed without incident and gladly turned the Wellington over to the crew chief, who signed her chit for her. She reported next to the Duty Pilot and was told where to find the Spitfire she was to deliver to Llandow.

Flying Spitfires still gave Emily a thrill quite unlike any other aircraft. When she'd started seeing Robin, he'd been an instructor on Spitfires at an Operational Training Unit. It was the first aircraft she'd seen him fly, and of course it was legendary in its own right. This particular aircraft was no longer young. It had clearly been at Little Rissington for some major repairs, and both its destination, Llandow, and its orange-brown desert camouflage suggested it was destined for overseas.

The cockpit drill in a Spit was familiar, and Emily found herself relaxing and starting to enjoy the day as she taxied to the top of the runway. What a contrast to the Welllington, she thought with elation, as the little fighter seemed to lift into the air of its own accord. After the seemingly cumbersome and sedate bomber, the Spitfire was so light on the controls that Emily was tempted to roll or loop or stall-turn it—any of those lovely manoeuvres she had watched Robin and his friends perform so effortlessly.

For a moment she let herself reminisce. The first time she had seen a Spitfire put through its paces had been when Robin asked her to come up to the station, where he was an instructor. It was the first time in her entire life that she had spent a weekend with a young man, not to mention her first time in an RAF officers mess. In fact, her parents had made quite a scene about the whole thing. Her mother had ordered her not to go, and her father had sadly told her she was making an utter fool of herself and would regret it the rest of her life. Both seemed convinced she would be seduced, if not gang-raped. In the event, Robin had put her up at an eminently respectable bed-and-breakfast run by a kindly Welsh woman, and Emily had fallen head-over-heels in love with not only Robin but flying as well. There had been a dance Saturday evening and then a little, unofficial air show by the instructors the following day. That was when Emily learned that Robin had been a skilled aerobatics pilot who had competed at international competitions.

Of course, ATA pilots weren't supposed to do any aerobatics. Their job was to move the aircraft entrusted to them efficiently and safely from A to B. They were not even *taught* about aerobatics—only cross-country navigation and forced landings after engine failure. When she was learning to fly, of course, her instructor had made her do spins to teach her how to recover from them, and he had rolled the Magister with her in it, but she had never done a roll herself.

Today it was very tempting, however. There was no cloud pinning her down to a dangerously low level. True, if she went up to five or six thousand feet, she would lose all landmarks in the murk of the haze, but she need only return to her cruising altitude and everything would be visible again. There was no wind to speak of. And there were—if she kept to her route—no barrage balloons, or mountains either.

Emily knew what she had to do in theory. Her instructor, David, had explained it to her and demonstrated it—but she had been afraid to risk it back then. If something had gone wrong it would have ruined both Robin and David's careers because she had no right to be in an RAF cockpit at the time. Today, the worst that could happen was that she would crash herself and this rather elderly, already out-dated, and clearly no longer front-line Spitfire. The loss of the aircraft would not greatly impair the country's capacity to wage war, Emily reasoned, and as for her own life, she didn't see that it made that much difference to anyone in particular—unless Robin really was still alive somewhere.

Not that she was suicidal. Quite the contrary, on such a lovely, warm day with spring so obviously greening the countryside and all the hedgerows in bloom, she was feeling very happy to be alive for the first time since Robin had crashed in France. And the Spitfire invigorated her, too, giving her a feeling of even greater exuberance, even youthfulness and playfulness.

It was surely time to risk just one tiny bit of aerobatics, wasn't it? Robin, although very careful to point out that aerobatics were not terribly useful in combat, always stressed that they helped build confidence in one's mastery of the aircraft. He had told Emily very forcefully that she should *not* do them before she was ready. He told her that if she frightened herself, they would destroy rather than build confidence. But he urged her to try them *when she was ready*. So the question was: was she ready now?

Emily looked about at the pale blue sky stretching in all directions around her, and then down at the greyish-green of the earth beneath in its soft, intangible blanket of haze. The sun was now quite high and blinding—though still shaded by a thick, white haze. It didn't look like it was going to burn off today, Emily decided. She squinted towards the part of the sky where the sun burned, and decided, yes, she was ready. But just to be safe, she pleaded silently: "Robin, if you're with me as Colin claims, then help me now!"

Then, before she could change her mind, she lifted the off wing of the Spitfire until it was standing on the near wing-tip and then forced herself not to ease up, but to keep going, right over, until she was standing on her head—or rather hanging in her straps. She didn't like this feeling at all, and so rather more insistently kept right on rolling until—with some relief—she found herself upright in the cockpit again.

Good! She'd done it! That was a wonderful feeling. She'd done it without any difficulty or adverse effects. The Spitfire was still purring happily. All the instruments were reading normally. She was still more-or-less on course. She'd lost a little altitude, but it was time to return to ATA 'contact' flying anyway.

By the time Emily got back down to fifteen hundred feet, she was feeling very proud of herself. "Alright," she found herself saying to Robin, "so it wasn't anything fancy. But it was a start. And I did it very smoothly, actually, don't you think? One of the other women pilots admitted to trying one and getting stuck upside down for several minutes," she told her invisible husband proudly. And then she felt ashamed of herself for talking to him at all. All a lot of rubbish, this notion of telepathy! Her grief was clearly making her daft!

When the Bristol Channel gleamed silver through the haze, dotted with shipping, Emily started to take more care with her navigation. There were some trigger-happy Ack-Ack batteries reported along this coast. More than one ATA pilot had been shot at, although fortunately no one had been lost—yet. But today the Ack-Ack was silent. Emily found Llandow and somewhat reluctantly surrendered the Spitfire.

It was now well past mid-day, and she was quite hungry. She was tempted to go over to the Officer's Mess for lunch, knowing that this was a Station that made no fuss about women pilots entering the Mess and furthermore, that the food was quite good. Unfortunately, a lorry was just leaving for St. Athan's, and Emily didn't dare miss catching a ride with them. She lifted her parachute pack to the airmen in the back and climbed in beside the driver.

By now it was very hot here on the ground, and Emily pulled off Robin's Irvin jacket and clutched it in her lap—careful to keep the burned sleeves out of sight.

The corporal driver chatted cheerfully with her as they bounced along through the puddles in the country road. Beside them the hedgerow was blooming, and beyond, a row of apple trees were also in flower. The ploughed earth of the fields beyond the hedge, however, had been recently strewn with manure, somewhat detracting from the idyllic atmosphere.

By the time they reached St. Athan it was too late for lunch, so Emily took tea and sandwiches in the maintenance hangar with the crews, and then settled herself aboard her last aircraft of the day. The Mosquito could only be entered by way of a flimsy, telescopic ladder into the floor of the cockpit. The cockpit itself was designed for two pilots, but was too narrow for them to sit abreast of one another, so they were staggered, with the Second Pilot somewhat behind and to the right of the First Pilot. This meant that all the First Pilot's controls were crammed onto the dashboard and left-hand side. In consequence, the throttle was difficult to reach.

The take-off was a bit tricky after the Spitfire, but once in the air the Mosquito, powered by two of the familiar Merlin engines, was lovely. It flew very well on just one engine too, which made it particularly beloved by her operational crews.

Flying eastward with the sun behind her, Emily retraced her route around the barrage balloons at Cardiff and Gloucester/Cheltenham, and started across the Cotswolds. She had passed Oxford, enjoying the sight of the cluster of spires to the south, when abruptly and without any warning, she was in heavy cloud.

It came upon her so suddenly that she was completely bewildered. The Met had made no mention of a front. She had seen no front coming towards her. Yes, she'd been enjoying the view off to the south, rather than staring straight ahead, but it couldn't have been more than 30 seconds since she had last looked forward. And suddenly she was in cloud so dense that it condensed on her windshield and billowed past the side windows in eddies.

ATA pilots were not trained on instruments. Either they knew how to fly blind from earlier training and experience, or they did not. Their instructions were to fly 'contact'—always in sight of land. If the weather got too 'thick' they were to land at the nearest airfield that they could find. If they could not safely land, they were to climb to a 'safe' height and bail out. Emily had no blind-flying experience, and she had never bailed out in her life. She was suddenly very, very frightened.

"Oh, Robin, help me," she whispered without thinking as she tried to master the panic she felt rising in her. At least David had taught her the basics of instrument flying, she remembered, forcing herself to look at the bank-and-turn indicator. To her horror, she realised she was not level, and having been warned that this was dangerous in fog, she carefully righted the aircraft. Robin had always advised her to turn right around if she got caught in fog. "Go back to where you came from—you know there was no fog there. If you continue flying, you're likely to get deeper and deeper into the muck."

That made sense. She checked her course, noted the reciprocal, and started a shallow, steady turn onto it.

Altitude! The word flashed through her head like a warning. How high were the nearest hills? She wanted to check the map, but was afraid to take her eyes off her instruments. Surely she would break out of this cloud shortly. She had only just flown into it! But although she kept flying and flying, it just seemed to get thicker and thicker. Maybe she should try sinking below it? But that made more sense if she turned around again so that she would be heading east, toward the flatter, lower country of the Fens, instead of back toward the Cotswolds and mountains of Wales.

Emily was sweating now, but she refused to give in to fear. She very carefully banked around again onto her initial course and started to gently slide down toward the earth. It was a bit unsettling that the Mosquito had a relatively high stall-speed, roughly 120 mph. A Hurricane didn't stall until almost half that. Don't think about that now, she warned herself. The first thing to do was try to find a break in this cloying, blinding cloud.

She continued to ease the Mosquito toward the earth, but at 800 feet the cloud was as thick as ever. What if it went right down to the deck? What airfields were around here, anyway? Luton ought to be just a few miles ahead; it was surely an option. Emily decided she would set course for Luton. It was closer than Henlow. What had happened to that beautiful morning that had inspired her to her first roll?

Robin, don't abandon me now.

If only she'd been in a Spitfire. Well, at least it wasn't the Wellington.

Thinking she must be near to where Luton ought to be, Emily eased down, watching her instruments very carefully, no longer conscious of how badly she was sweating or how stiff she was from stretching for the throttle, trying to keep it just right. She certainly couldn't risk stalling in this muck at a couple hundred feet. But at 500 feet she still couldn't see anything.

The sensible thing to do would be to go up to 5000 feet and jump out. That was what the ATA standing orders said. But Emily resisted the thought bitterly. It meant abandoning a perfectly serviceable aircraft. Nobody was going to be happy about that, no matter what they said. And it didn't help that Robin had bashed his leg up when jumping over France back in '40. Mostly, however, the very idea of bailing out into this muck was no less terrifying than flying in it. At least if she crashed, the end would be mercifully quick—especially at 170 mph or more.

What was that?

Emily thought she saw something through the murk below her—a darker green and then something light. Yes, definitely. She was beginning to see things on the ground. She checked her altimeter: 300 feet. But that was very *definitely* a train moving steadily north. Emily altered course instantly, following the train and thereby the railway tracks while she fumbled with her map to try to see where she might be—without stalling or losing sight of the train. There were now buildings off to the right and a factory with smokestacks belching coal smoke into the clouds. Bedford? Had she already overshot Luton by that much?

Not good.

If only she could be *sure* it was Bedford.

Suddenly something loomed up on Emily's left, and she jerked the Mosquito to the right, her heart pounding in alarm. A four-engine Lancaster, painted a matt black for night operations, emerged out of the cloud not two hundred yards away! She might well have collided with it! It was now crossing her bows, and she could see the crew looking over at her in obvious astonishment and alarm. She could hardly blame them. But what were they doing flying around at this altitude? They had radios and could presumably easily fly above the cloud. Only then did Emily notice that their wheels were down and they were evidently making a landing approach.

What a stroke of luck! All she had to do was follow them down! Rather excited by this unexpected deliverance, Emily banked steeply after the Lancaster and tagged along behind it. Once she located the airfield it was making for, she broke away and circled the field, dutifully awaiting a green from the tower and checking her Handling Notes again. She certainly did not want to muck up her landing at a strange, operational airfield!

Since this was a rather large bomber station, she had plenty of runway, and could afford to come in very low at the prescribed speed and then gradually ease back on the throttle. Still, it was only after she had safely come to a complete halt that she started to breathe again. She turned off the runway and taxied toward a hangar. She cut the engines, and two airmen darted out of the hangar to put chocks around her wheels. A drizzling rain fell on the windshield.

Emily collected her maps and parachute—very grateful that she had not been forced to use it—and opened the hatch in the floor of the cockpit. As she unfolded the flimsy little ladder, she realised her hands were shaking. How embarrassing! Not wanting to make a hysterical impression before strange RAF personnel, she paused, drew a deep breath to try to get a grip on herself, and only then started down the ladder—but she was still shaking.

As she hit the tarmac under the nose of the Mosquito, an RAF medical orderly ducked under it. "Are you alright, sir?"

"I'm fine," Emily assured him, more embarrassed than ever. They must have thought she had some kind of emergency. "The weather just closed in rather unexpectedly and we aren't trained to fly blind. This was the first airfield I could find." She talked rapidly, nervously, as she concentrated on stowing the ladder properly, avoiding eye contact. Only when she was finished did she turn to face the man opposite her.

He was staring at her in obvious shock, and Emily found herself a little annoyed. It really wasn't *that* unusual for a woman to fly, was it?

Just then the first airman was joined by a second, a fitter, who asked more cheerily and with no apparent shock at seeing a woman, "Everything alright, Miss?"

"Yes, I just needed to get down in a hurry before I got lost in this cloud. It seemed to come up very suddenly. Certainly the Met made no mention of it when I left St. Athan a little over an hour ago," Emily found herself explaining defensively. She was beginning to wonder if she had misunderstood or missed something. Now that the immediate danger was over, she was starting to feel guilty for getting caught out and landing at a field she did not even recognise.

"I'll say, Miss! We've had three kites from other stations put down here in the last ten minutes—they all got caught in it. And one of our own is still up there!" He pointed toward the heavy overcast, which was unloading more and more water on them. "Best get in out of the rain," he suggested sensibly, and led the way at a dash toward the nearest hangar.

The clouds had really opened up now, and the sound of it pounding on the roof of the great hangar was almost deafening. They had to shout to be heard above it. Emily asked where she was, and the fitter told her she was at Gravely—a Pathfinder station. The fitter also gave her directions to the Officers' Mess. As she was not supposed to go into the Mess in trousers, however, she asked if there was somewhere she might change into a skirt first. The fitter obligingly took her towards the back of the hangar, to the airwoman's loo. "Have a dozen girls doing spark plugs and parachute packing here now," he told her chattily. "They say they're training WAAF flight mechanics, too, but I don't want to see Chiefy's face when *they* walk through that door." He gestured with his thumb toward the hangar entrance.

Emily removed her skirt from her parachute pack, thinking again how lucky she had been not to have to use the latter. She removed her flying boots and trousers and changed into skirt, stockings and pumps. She packed the boots, trousers and Robin's flight jacket into the parachute bag (frowned upon but practical), slung the parachute pack over her shoulder and re-emerged.

She was astonished to find that the medical orderly who had first greeted her was now standing outside the loo. "Emily Pryce?" he asked.

That took her back. He knew her. "Priestman now," she corrected automatically, trying to place his vaguely familiar face. Then it hit her: it was Michael Woolsy of the Cambridge Peace Society. "Michael!" Emily burst out, amazed and embarrassed. How could she *not* have recognised him sooner? He had been one of her closest friends when she had been up at University. They had canvassed for Labour together. They had collected signatures on petitions condemning re-armament and military expansion together. Michael and the others had locked arms and marched through the streets chanting "Hell, no, we won't go!" And Emily had watched them with enraptured and admiring eyes as they—in their light flannel trousers, dark blazers and straw boaters—proclaimed eloquently and emphatically the absolute absurdity of thinking that war ever solved anything.

But that had been more than a lifetime ago. Some of those youthful pacifists had gone off to fight for the Loyalists in Spain; some failed to come home. Certainly most of them wore military uniform now. But Michael had been one of the most ardent and consistent pacifists, coming from a Quaker family. His father had gone to gaol rather than serve in the last war. And here he was in the uniform of an RAF LAC—albeit a medical orderly. "Michael! What are you doing here! Good heavens! I can't believe it!"

"Nor can I," he admitted. "When did you learn to *fly*?"

"Oh, that's a long story! When do you get off duty? I must call in to my CO, but I'm bound to be stuck out here 'till the weather clears. Could we do dinner or something?"

"Yes, I'd like that. I'm off at 6." It was now 4.30. They agreed to meet at the main gate just after 6, and Emily continued on to the Mess to call into White Waltham.

"I'm very sorry—" she started her apologies to the Pool Commander at White Waltham.

"Did you break anything?"

"No, but I had to put down at Gravely. It's a—"

"Well, stay there!" Emily was taken aback by the tone of voice, but then the CO added in a gentler tone. "I'm sorry, Mrs. Priestman, but we've been hit by what the Met calls an 'inversion'—the air all over southern England turned into cloud just like that, and I'm afraid we're still missing 4 aircraft. We have definitely lost at least one pilot."

"I'm terribly sorry."

"Yes, and that after the two pilots killed last week up in Scotland. Damned English weather!" Then, as if getting hold of himself, he added in a gentler tone. "Get a good night's sleep, and let's hope the weather clears. Call in tomorrow."

"Yes, sir," Emily promised with a shiver at the reminder of what a close thing it had been after all—and how dangerous her job was. No time to think about that now, however. She had to call Philippa to let her know she wouldn't be coming home tonight. Calling from a bomber station to Bomber Command was much easier than from White Waltham, and Philippa's voice sounded surprisingly near.

"Oh, what a pity." Philippa responded to Emily's news. "I wanted to introduce you to a friend of mine. In fact, we were planning to take you out to dinner. You're sure you're too far away to come home by other means?"

Philippa was always bringing 'friends' home and most of them were old enough to be her father. Furthermore, they usually had either enough braid on their sleeves to sink a battleship or were MPs or senior Foreign Office officials or some such thing. Most of them were also married men. Emily did not mind missing dinner with such personages.

"I have to fly the aircraft on tomorrow. Besides, I met an old friend from University here and we're doing dinner."

"Oh, well, in that case. I'll tell you all about Teddy when you get back. He's very special, but no doubt you'll have another chance to meet him. Penny will be inconsolable, however."

Emily was assigned a bed in the WAAF Officer's Mess and left her parachute pack there, along with her small cosmetics case and change of underwear that she always carried with her for exactly this eventuality. Then she met Michael at the front gate. Fortunately, it was now only drizzling, since they had just over a mile walk to the nearest pub. Neither of them noticed the distance.

If there had been anything they'd been good at during their joint years at University, it had been talking, Emily reflected. It had always been like that with Michael and the others. Debate had been their drug—far more than tobacco and beer, although some in their circle had consumed more than enough of the latter as well. But Michael and Emily were among the most abstinent in that respect. Furthermore, there had always been a special bond between them on account of being different from the others.

The others were the sons of the 'privileged' classes, well-to-do youths from public schools with parents in 'comfortable' positions—Civil Service, Colonial Service, the City, the Professions. Emily was one of only two women and the only Scholar in their little clique. Michael had been the only Quaker and the only one whose parents had been 'in trade.' There had been a time—Emily had almost forgotten it—when she had had quite a crush on Michael, but her roommate had gently pointed out that 'all that crowd' were rather more fond of men than of women. It had come as a bit of a shock to someone raised in a prudish, lower-middle-class home as Emily had been.

"Did you say your married name was Priestman?" Michael asked almost at once. "That's a Friends family, isn't it? I'm sure the Priestmans of Newcastle are Friends."

Now that Michael mentioned it, Emily remembered Robin telling her that many of his relatives on his father's side were indeed Quakers. In fact, his grandfather had left the Society of Friends and joined the Church of England because it was the only way he could be accepted by his future wife's very High Church family. But Robin had gone to school with many of his second and third cousins who were still Friends. "I'm sure you're right," she said to Michael. "My husband went to a school in Northumberland with many of his cousins who were still

Friends, but he was C of E." No sooner were the words out that she realised with horror that she had just spoken of Robin in the past tense. Surely it was just a stupid slip of the tongue? Surely, it didn't mean anything?

Michael meanwhile delightedly jumped on her words. "Thorton? Did he go to Thorton? Then we might have known each other at school! Of course, Peter Priestman! He was three years ahead of me, but he was a wizard long-distance runner and a first-rate debater. He went to Oxford, and I know he was active in the Peace Movement. You're married to Peter Priestman?"

"No, his younger cousin, Robin." The name Peter triggered a memory, however. Emily distinctly remembered Robin telling her about an incident at school where he had been badly beaten up by an older boy while his cousin Peter looked on, pleading with the older boy to stop but refusing to interfere. As Robin explained with a shrug: "That rather put me off pacifism at an early age. I'd still rather fight the Luftwaffe than to beg them to be so kind as to stop bombing us." To Michael, Emily simply added, "Robin's father died before he was born, and he was raised by his very conventional C of E mother."

"But he went to Thorton, you said." Michael persisted.

"I was told Thorton was a non-denominational school—not just Friends but Jews and Atheists and Baptists, etc. Robin was one of the Anglican minority."

"I see." Michael was clearly disappointed, but he nodded and changed the subject. "And when did you learn to fly? I didn't know you had any interest in it at all."

"When we knew each other, just driving in a motor car was a thrill. How could I dream of flying? It was only after I was married to a pilot that I dared dream about it—and Robin made my dream come true. Enough about me. What induced you to join the RAF? I thought you had Conscientious Objector status?"

"I did or I do. I mean, I have been mustered only for non-combatant duties and I have rather a lot of medical training now."

"Doesn't it upset your parents to see you in military uniform? I always thought you'd go into the Fire Department or would drive Ambulances."

"I do. I drive the Station Blood Wagon." He nodded in the direction of the airfield behind them. "As for my parents," he shrugged, "this war is different from the last. They understand." But he didn't meet her eye as he answered, and Emily wondered if they were as understanding as he pretended.

They had reached the pub and pushed their way in through the black-out curtains. Already the pub was quite crowded and smoky. They managed to find a small table, and Michael went to place orders for them at the bar. "There's not much choice, I'm afraid: Kidney Pie, Shepherd's Pie, or a Ploughman's."

"I'll take Shepherd's Pie and white wine."

Michael went to the bar, and Emily settled back against the wood panelling. It was so odd running into Michael after all these years, and it stirred up memories she had filed away ages ago. He belonged to such a different world—the enchanted world of her University years.

Until she met Robin, her brief years at University had been the most beautiful time of her life. Emily had gone to University on a scholarship, and it was the first time in her life that she had lived away from home. She had been born and raised in the grim dockyards of Portsmouth, the daughter of two Communist teachers devoted to bringing education to the working class—and educating them about their interest in World Revolution and the destruction of the British class system. At Cambridge she encountered at first hand the "class enemy"—and discovered that they were young people who looked on life as a great opportunity and the world as their oyster. After the rigid dogma of her parental home and the grim surroundings of a docklands mired in an abysmal depression and massive unemployment, Cambridge had been like a fairyland.

Cambridge had also been an intoxicating introduction to intellectual freedom, personal independence, political plurality, and liberal morés—not to mention Emily's first taste of comradeship. For the first time in her life Emily heard ideas honestly discussed instead being told the absolute "truth" as defined by Marx, Lenin and The Party. For the first time in her life she could come and go and dress as she pleased, nor did she have to excuse herself for being late or not making up her bed or having a different opinion from her parents. For the first time she met—and found she actually liked many—Conservatives. And she also discovered that a night in a pub could be a pleasant, amusing pastime rather than the first step to alcohol addiction and domestic violence, as her parents claimed. Best of all, she had had a circle of friends her own age who accepted her and included her in all their various activities.

Emily had loved every minute of her short years at Cambridge. But they had been over too soon, and she had returned to her parental home. She took work as a clerk with an insurance company in Portsmouth, turning the bulk of her earnings over to her parents. She had found herself living again in the coal-caked, terraced cottage behind the dockyards, taking the bus to the offices of the insurers on Albert Road, and working 8 ½ hours a day filing claims and typing letters. Not even the war had changed anything—until Robin walked into her life…

There was a commotion at the pub door, and a half-dozen young men in flight jackets and flying boots clomped in noisily. The man at the front had his battered and now misshapen peaked cap pulled low over his eyes, but Emily recognised him nevertheless as one of the many men who had brought Philippa home once. As his eyes swept the room critically, he too caught sight of Emily sitting (apparently alone) in the corner. He made straight for her. "Haven't we met somewhere?" he asked at once.

His flight jacket flapped open enough to reveal the DFC on his tunic.

"Philippa Wycliffe is my lodger," Emily answered rather primly, seeing Michael's look of horror behind the Wing Commander's shoulder as the rest of his crew crowded around the bar.

"Oh, of course! You're the widowed ATA pilot."

"I'm *not* widowed *yet*," Emily retorted tartly.

"Sorry. I think I'd better go back outside and make that entrance again."

"Don't bother. I'm here with an old friend from University."

"Just what the Dickens did Philippa say about me?" he countered with a curious look.

"Nothing."

"You *know* that is the most *insulting* answer you could possibly give, don't you?" He was smiling at her far too intimately for comfort.

"No. It just happens to be the truth."

Well, not really. Emily *had* asked Philippa about the man who'd brought her home in a noisy sports car and been dismissed very abruptly before they'd hardly been introduced. Philippa had replied, "Oh, just some Wing Commander from Main Force. Terrible bore. You know what they're like. More than 60 ops and they think they're demigods."

The Wing Commander laughed. "I don't believe you. Philippa has an opinion on *everyone*." He was looking straight at her in a very disconcerting manner.

"Well, she didn't reveal it to me. Excuse me, may I introduce a dear old friend from Cambridge, Michael Woolsey?"

"Sir." Michael had his beer in one hand and Emily's wine in the other, so he couldn't salute, but he nodded his head respectfully.

The Wing Commander looked from one to the other, and then laughed again, winked at Emily, and withdrew.

"How do you know *him*?" Michael asked in obvious shock as he set their drinks down and slipped into the seat opposite.

"I don't even know who it is," Emily protested. "He brought my lodger, a WAAF officer, home one night in his sports car. That's all I know."

"He's a very famous, highly decorated and terribly popular CO of a Squadron from Main Force over at Westcott, Yves 'Steeplechase' Gorrel. Got fogged in like you did. Very famous, glamorous chap," Michael repeated, looking at her with evident confusion.

"Well, I don't know him, Michael. My lodger, Philippa Wycliffe, moves in those circles, that's all."

Michael looked down at his beer thoughtfully for a minute, but then he looked up at her with a penetrating, questioning gaze. "So do you, don't you? I mean, it didn't even make you sit up straighter—his being a Wing Commander, DFC and all."

"Good heavens, Michael. My *husband* is a Wing Commander, DFC." Only after it was out did she realise how astonishing the statement must be to Michael. At Cambridge Emily had been so much the mascot of the group, the Scholar, the naïve daughter of under-privilege, that the others had patiently—but often with considerable amusement—patronised. They had been well-meaning and good to her. She had benefited from their kindly education, but she was the last person they would have expected to make something of herself.

To be fair, Michael had been the one who had argued most ardently against her going back to Portsmouth after graduation. "Don't let your parents harness you to their out-dated ambitions, Emily. You have a right to your own life!" Michael had urged. But her parents insisted she reject a post-graduate scholarship so that she could come home and "finally start contributing to the family income and do something productive."

"I don't understand," Michael admitted now. "How did you ever meet a RAF Wing Commander?"

"Well, he was only a Flight Lieutenant when we met," Emily pointed out. "And he's certainly not like that!" She gestured with her head toward Philippa's friend. But no sooner was it out that she had to stop herself and wonder—or was he? Robin was the best-looking man she'd ever met—better looking by far than the Wing Commander from Bomber Command chatting up the barmaid with his crew around him. There were newspaper clippings of Robin from various air shows showing him with a variety of titled socialites and millionairesses—and the Duke of Windsor. Michael had every right to wonder how she had ever won the attention—much less the affection—of such a man. She didn't honestly understand herself.

"He's a pilot, isn't he?" Michael was asking.

"Yes, Fighter Command, but honestly, Michael, I didn't know that when I met him. You see, I was working as a volunteer at the Salvation Army Seaman's

Mission in Pompii, and one day this young man walked in—in civilian clothes and on crutches. I was trying to serve an interminable line of sailors come in out of the rain for a hot meal. When this civilian limped over to me and offered to help serve, I honestly thought he was a Conscientious Objector sent to give us a hand. It never, *ever* occurred to me that he might be a fighter pilot. Why should it? And then, to put him at ease—thinking how hard it must be to be a Conscientious Objector shortly after Dunkirk—I chattered away, saying all the silly things we used to say up at Cambridge. You know, about the Germans having been forced into the arms of Hitler by Versailles and the post-war policies of France, and how if only we'd been more co-operative with the Weimar Republic it would never have come to this, and, oh, you know it all. Well, after I'd talked so much nonsense, Robin revealed to me he was a fighter pilot who'd been shot down over France and broken his ankle bailing out and come out by foot with the Army at Dunkirk. It was terribly embarrassing."

"So you think all the things we worked and lived for while at Cambridge are silly nonsense?" Michael summarised.

"No, maybe not nonsense. Of course, a different foreign policy in the twenties might have stopped Hitler coming to power in the thirties, but what I mean is that war *was* necessary by 1939 and it is *certainly* necessary now. Chamberlain *tried* everything short of war. It was right to try appeasement, but it didn't work. We had no choice. War was the only option in 1939—and, thank God there were men like Robin who had trained for it while you and I and all the other intellectuals were collecting petitions against re-armament. Oh, Michael, do you realise that part of the RAF expansion we actively opposed was for the establishment of our Early Warning Stations? For the purchase of Hurricanes and Spitfires? For the training of fighter pilots? If we'd been successful then, we would have *lost* the Battle of Britain! We'd all be living in a Nazi England now!"

Michael nodded wearily. It was not easy losing all one's convictions. But Emily suddenly realised that she did have something to live for after all: fighting this very necessary war in Robin's place for him.

CHAPTER 6

▼

Beauchamp Rodding, England
May 1943

J.B. could not have said what he was expecting, but certainly not what he found. Later, when he tried to analyse it, he supposed that all the horror stories about the Battle of Britain and the Blitz, the statistics about casualties and the solemn government statements about the need to help an ally with its 'back to the wall' had made him expect a ravaged, war-torn country on the brink of collapse. American soldiers on their way to Britain had been sternly warned about rationing and shortages; admonished not to be wasteful; and told never, *never* to take advantage of their hosts. The USAAF told their officers and enlisted men that they were better fed, better clothed and *a lot* better paid than their hosts, and it was their job to be generous and neighbourly—not grasping and greedy. They were told that the British lacked gasoline, coal, cloth, leather, cigarettes, chocolate, alcohol, milk, butter and meat. Children were undernourished, housing was overcrowded, everyone wore hand-me-downs...

So why did England look so beautiful?

Well, it didn't hurt that they went alongside the quay on a glorious early May morning. Nor that they were quickly loaded onto Army busses that set off, after only a short drive through some grim, monotonous but not really appalling slums, onto a road that cut through the greenest countryside J.B. had ever seen in his life. Michigan's grass soon turned brown in summer, and Texas was dust, dirt and cow shit. J.B. didn't think he'd seen anything to compare to this rich, green grass dotted with fat sheep and sleek cattle. There were various blooming bushes and trees dotting the countryside, and the gardens of the houses were a riot of colour—not to mention the window-boxes that bedecked the windows of even the cramped houses in the towns.

The children, who waved joyously to them whenever they slowed down, seemed to be in uniforms for the most part. The boys all wore shorts, which surprised J.B. given that temperatures were still on the chilly side, but you couldn't say they looked hungry or shabby—not like the kids down in rural Alabama, say. They were certainly clean and neat, not like the slum kids of Detroit, either.

At one point they drove past this real castle—just like in a fairy tale—with ramparts and towers and turrets. Lots of the towns they passed through (lurching, rattling and crawling as they wound their way along narrow, cobbled streets) had Tudor houses that looked like they were still being lived in. And in both towns and villages there were these great stone churches with spires or square towers. It was like a story book.

Of course, every story comes to an end eventually. Just when they were getting hungry enough for some of the guys to start complaining, they turned through a gate-house and found themselves on an airfield. It wasn't as bad as Texas—there was still green grass between the buildings and the runways—but the Army had definitely left its mark. In place of the charming, natural towns they had passed through was regimentation and uniformity, Nissan huts and monotonous barracks all newly built according to Air Force guidelines. All the buildings were a dull brown or grey in colour.

Bachelor's Officers Quarters were located in huts, each of which had been divided into 'bays' or cubicles for four men apiece. Naturally, crews stuck together, so Buzz, Dan and Tony were in with J.B. again. J.B. was a little annoyed that there was some other guy's stuff hanging in his locker. Apparently the guy who'd been moved out to make room for them had left half his stuff here. A private arrived shortly afterwards, however, and threw all the stuff into a canvas bag carelessly.

"I'd be more careful with that stuff, if I were you," J.B. warned. "I wouldn't want my best duds crumpled up like that."

"Yeah, well, he's got no way of complaining about it, has he, sir?"

"How's that?"

The private drew his finger across his throat. "Hamburg."

"What?" J.B. asked, still not fully believing it.

"MIA, sir. Should have been back by 13.30 this afternoon latest. No fuel after that."

"That was only three hours ago!" J.B. protested, with a glance at the large wall clock in astonishment and disbelief.

"Well, sir, do you want this locker or not? I don't give a shit."

With the newcomers stunned into silence, the private finished stuffing the missing man's things unceremoniously into the canvas bag and disappeared. Somewhat awkwardly the four new arrivals then set about moving in, no one speaking about the little incident.

The Mess Hall was located in a huge, echoing Nissan hut, and they lined up behind seemingly hundreds of other guys—but that was no different than at all the other bases they'd ever served on. When they took their trays over to a table, however, they were told to 'buzz off' by the men already there. "Rookies eat down the other end!" they were told unceremoniously, with thumbs jerked toward the tables nearer the door. So they ended up sitting with two other new crews who had come in on the same bus but a different ship. They exchanged 'convoy' stories until someone shouted "Mail!" and everyone stampeded in the direction of the mail-room, the rookies just following the crowd.

Mail for active members of the 8th Air Force was flown over in the bombers ferried to England. While their crews had languished in Halifax and crossed the Atlantic by slow boat, the mail had piled up for them. J.B. had two letters from his Mom, one from Sally, and no less than three from Kathy. Delighted, Jay went back to his quarters, stripped down to his underwear and then stretched out on his cot to read the letters, saving Kathy's for last.

His Mom wrote in a straightforward, simple way, cataloguing the events of the week: Bobby had taken his first step, Mary's husband got a $2 a week raise in pay, there'd been an accident at the plant and one of the workers had to be taken to hospital. The second letter was equally matter-of-fact, but focused on one subject only: Barb had joined the WAAC. Since her father absolutely refused to let her work in a factory, she had gone to the WAAC recruiting station, lied about her age, and signed up. There had been a terrible scene, but in the end J.B.'s father had been ashamed to tell the recruiting sergeant that he was *against* his daughter serving her country. So Barb had 'got away with it.'

Sally's letter went into the whole incident in more detail and was heavy with disapproval and criticism. Sally didn't think Barb's actions had anything to do with patriotism 'whatsoever.' "Barb is just being her usual rebellious self. All she cares about is getting away from her responsibilities to the family and having fun." J.B. was dubious about how much *fun* any girl could have in the WAAC. From what he'd seen, the girls were drilled and chased around by bullying sergeants just like the enlisted men. J.B. hated that part of the army and only put up with all the discipline-crap because it allowed him to fly and do something for his country. But the girls only got to do the shit-jobs like washing dishes or—at best—typing. J.B. couldn't imagine Barb putting up with all the discipline; she'd always been one to talk back. She'd be racking up demerits so fast, she'd never see a day's leave—if they didn't discharge her outright for some act of grave insubordination. He'd write home and reassure his folks that Barb would *never* make it in the Army. Eagerly he turned to Kathy's letters.

Kathy wrote on pink, scented writing paper with her name and address printed in cursive in the upper left-hand corner—real class. Her handwriting was perfect and neat, too. Jay remembered that Kathy had taken penmanship classes because she claimed that "a pretty, legible handwriting is the mark of a lady." Still, Jay suspected she must have written the whole letter on scratch paper first and then copied it over, because there wasn't one mistake. The content of her letters was far less controlled, however. In fact, she gushed, pouring out her impressions and thoughts with great enthusiasm, and frequently underlined words or added multiple exclamation points. Jay could almost hear the inflection of her voice behind the written word.

The first letter was all about everyone's reaction to her engagement. Although he'd spent that day with her immediate family and met her roommates at U of M, most of her extended Irish-American family and her wider circle of friends had not been informed until after he left. Her second letter was an exuberant description of the opening of the play she had so wanted him to attend: Hamlet. Apparently it had been a terrific success and she had taken three bows and been given a dozen roses. She'd also received four letters from admirers asking to meet with her—'but, of course, I turned them all down! I'm an engaged woman!' J.B. was glad things had gone so well, but he didn't really like this bit about other men paying court to her. The longer he was away, the more tempting it would be to go out with them for some 'innocent' fun…Her third letter was reassuring again, because it was a blow-by-blow description of her wedding plans. She had decided to 'list' at Jacobsens, and wanted his approval for the china and silverware she had selected. (She enclosed glossy pictures from a catalogue.) She also had some questions about invitation styles, the exact spelling of his mother's maiden name and things like that. None of it mattered to him in the least, but he was glad she was focusing on the wedding—it would keep her from thinking about those other guys who wanted to go out with her.

By now it was getting late, and everyone but Dan had already put out their light and turned in. J.B. got up, brushed his teeth, changed into his pyjamas and went to bed. He slept very well, glad to be back on solid ground.

In the morning they were briefed. New B-17s, flown across the Atlantic by the Ferrying Division, Air Transport Command, were waiting for them. They were to take these up for test and familiarisation flights today. They would be expected to complete two cross-country flights, one to a training site for a practice bomb run and the other for air gunnery practice, and only after that would they be cleared for their first mission.

Sounded easy.

They went out to their new ship. She was beautiful. Not like the half-wrecked old crates they got in Training. She glistened. She was un-scratched, and un-dented. She even smelt new! The gunners were really excited about their clean turrets, and J.B. could hear them shouting to one another as they swung their guns and made fake machine-gun sounds. The radio operator, Sgt. Hank Roach, gave J.B. a thumbs up after fiddling with his equipment a bit.

J.B. clasped his hands around the control column and ran his hand over the throttle handles with possessive pride.

"What we gonna christen her?" Tony asked.

"We better discuss that with the whole gang. Let 'em all make suggestions and take a vote," J.B. decided.

After looking over the cockpit to his satisfaction, J.B. dropped back down onto the hardstand and found the crew chief. They shook hands. The Sergeant was a dark, small man by the name of Fuentes. He looked about 30, and J.B. figured he was peace-time army and presumed he was Puerto Rican. "You new over here, Fuentes?"

"No, sir, I been over here six months."

"Your last crew finish their tour?"

"No, sir, MIA after eleven missions."

"They didn't make it back?"

"No, sir, flamed out over Le Havre. Two 'chutes. Rest went in."

"Jeez. I didn't realise things were that bad," J.B. admitted.

"They ain't good, sir." Fuentes answered. He was chewing gum and his jaw kept working.

"Right. Well, let's start her up and give her a test flight like the Major ordered."

"Yes, sir."

The sound and feel of the massive bomber trembling under his fingers gave J.B. the same thrill it always did. But this ship was particularly magical. It was the first ship that was *his*—his own command, not a ship loaned to him from Training Command for a particular flight. They went through the pre-flight check, Tony reading off the list to him, then they started her up—one engine springing to life after the other without a single hitch. As the dials settled down, the needles all hovered just where they should. With all engines warming up, Jay tested the intercom. Everyone reported in loud and clear and eager.

They waved the chocks away and gently eased out onto the taxiway. This ship was smooth as glass. She rolled out from her parking position with the sedate grace of a big old Cadillac (not that J.B. had ever driven a Cadillac, but it was the way he imagined one would handle). They were second for take-off on the runway. Jay turned onto the runway and watched for the green from the tower. When it came, he revved up the engines against the brakes, then he eased back on the throttles, eased back on the brakes, and let the great bird with her 100-foot wing-span start down the runway. She rolled forward only sedately at first, but—without a bomb load and only half tanked up—she gathered speed rapidly. You could feel the lightness gradually overtaking her whole frame. The tail wheel started to bounce and then she came unstuck from the earth and they were flying—flying over that beautiful green and yellow patchwork of English countryside. From the air you could see the way the hedgerows wriggled their way up and around the contours of the hills. You could pick out the winding lanes, the stone walls, the rich pastures and neat fields. Everything was even prettier from up here than what they'd been able to see driving on the roads. From here you could see just how tiny and irregular the fields were—not like the big expanses of identical land chopped up into regular squares by roads like in the Midwest. Here the crops seemed to change from one field to the next, and the woods wound about in irregular shapes like the shadows of cloud. And there were clusters of houses around stone churches and criss-crossing roads and railway tracks everywhere. No way you could navigate along roads in this country, J.B. registered. They bent and curved, split and converged, and in a minute you no longer knew what road you'd been following in the first place. J.B. started concentrating harder on his compass.

They climbed upwards, leaving the countryside behind them in an increasingly milky haze. At 10,000 feet they went on oxygen. J.B. banked the great ship slowly around toward the west, putting the sun behind them, and still climbing. He took her right up to 30,000 feet and still she flew just like the lady she was. J.B. was sure it was a good sign. They had a real great ship. She'd see them through anything. She had class. The boys could decide to call her anything they liked; to J.B. she'd be Lady Kathleen, in honour of Kathy.

Their second cross-country three days later turned into a bit of an embarrassment. They'd found the bomb site alright and dropped their load more-or-less on target. Well, they were off by a little more than half-a-mile, actually, and J.B. had told Buzz off for it, saying they had to do better than that or it would take them forever to win the war. Secretly, however, he figured that after the two-month break since training, it wasn't all that bad.

On the trip home, however, they encountered cloud that obscured the earth below. Dan plotted a course and when they should have been approaching their base they eased down through the cloud, coming out at 5,000 feet. Nothing looked familiar.

Finally they caught sight of an airfield off to their left and gratefully steered for it. J.B. carefully flew over the 'T' and then swept around to get in the circuit. He called into the tower for clearance to land.

A surprised voice answered. "Where are you?"

"I'm on the circuit," J.B. answered irritably. How could the idiot in the tower not see 37,000 tons of B-17 on the landing circuit?

"I can't see you," the tower replied nevertheless.

"Uh, Jay, those planes down there look kind of funny." This helpful comment came from Buzz.

Tony, too, was looking out the side window. "All painted black, too."

"What?"

J.B. had a green from the tower now, so he straightened up, eased back and set the B-17 down on the runway. As they rolled down past the tower, however, he knew they were at the wrong base. Lining the runway were black ships with twin tails. Well, alright, better find out where they were. They turned off the runway, and somewhat abashed turned onto the taxiway. By now an ambulance was racing up, and as J.B. stopped, they could see RAF pouring out of the nearest hangar to stare at them. This was getting more embarrassing by the minute.

"Dan, I don't know where the hell we are," J.B. told him over the intercom, "but it sure as hell ain't our home base. You are going to owe me one hell of a big beer for this!" J.B. left the engines idling, unstrapped himself, and squeezed out of his seat to drop out onto the tarmac. An RAF sergeant was waiting for him. The RAF saluted and then asked, "What is the nature of your emergency, sir?"

Jay returned the salute and then admitted, "Well, I gotta be honest with you, Sarge. I'm just plum lost. Thought I was coming down at Beauchamp Rodding and since that's obviously not what I did, I sure as hell hope you can tell me where I *am* and how to get back where I belong."

The RAF Sergeant smiled, "Not a problem, sir. You're at High Wych. Beecham Rodding is just 6 miles to the southeast. Just pop over that orchard there," he pointed to an orchard on a slight rise beyond the far end of the runway, "and you'll see your station beyond the village."

J.B. wasn't sure. "Beecham Rodding?—is that the same place? I'm with the 110th Bomber Group at a place called Beauchamp Rodding."

"Yes, sir, that's how we say it."

"B-e-a-u-c-h-a-m-p?"

"Yes, sir."

"OK, it's your country," J.B. conceded, then with a grin he added, "Thanks. I'll do just as you say—over that hill, right?"

"Yes, sir."

J.B. started to climb back into the B-17, then paused and called out to the RAF sergeant, who had already turned away, "Ah, Sarge, I'm not the first B-17 to do this, am I?"

The RAF grinned again. "No, sir, you're about the 110th. Second one today."

Somehow that made it seem better. J.B. swung himself back up into the nose of bomber and squeezed his way forward to Dan's navigation table. "I'm sorry, Jay," Dan started instantly; "according to my calculations we should be right here." He pointed to the map just short of Beachamp Rodding.

"Yeah, well, you're just about three miles off. We're here!" Working backwards from Beauchamp Rodding, J.B. had found High Wych—it wasn't even marked as an airfield. Great. Dan frowned, staring at the innocent village with no airfield. "Don't sweat it, Dan. The Brits say it happens all the time." J.B. slid back into his seat and strapped himself in. "Everything OK?" he asked Tony.

"Fine. Where are we?"

"Wrong side of that orchard over there."

They taxied back to the head of the runway, got a green from the tower, and took off. J.B. climbed to just a couple of hundred feet, skimmed over the orchard and beyond, just as promised, they saw the village of Beauchamp Rodding and beyond that their own airfield. J.B. called in to the tower again and this time got clearance. "We've been waiting for you." They added with a chuckle, "Drop in at High Wych, by any chance?"

"Wonder which other crew got lost today," J.B. muttered as they taxied over to their hardstand and started to cut the engines one after the other. "Bet you anything it was one of the others on the training mission with us."

By dinnertime the whole base knew that two of the rookie crews had got lost coming back from their training mission and landed at High Wych. The Squadron Commander, Major Harkins, was pretty pissed off about it. He called the pilots and navigators of the two ships that made the mistake into his office and gave them a blasting. "You goddamned bastards have disgraced the blessed US of A *and* the Army Air Forces! The RAF is so goddamned cock-sure they know how to do everything better than us, and then you bird-brains land right in front of their fucking noses to prove you don't know your eyes from your asshole! You ever screw up like this again, and I'm gonna dock you a month's pay. Now get out of my sight before I puke!"

The four junior officers filed out solemnly. In the anteroom they exchanged one look and burst out laughing. "The RAF sergeant said we were about the 110th B-17 to land there."

"Well, it would help if they put the goddamned base on the map."

"Military secret, I guess—just like they don't have any place names in the train stations and no road signs either."

"Hi, by the way, I'm J.B. and this is Dan."

The other crew introduced themselves, Alan Pearson, and Patrick Brown, his navigator. They decided to go out and celebrate their 'adventure' at the local pub. None of them had ever been to a pub before, but they'd heard it was the thing to do around here—besides it would help them 'familiarise themselves with the local countryside.'

As they had no transport, however, they had to walk, which limited their options, and so they ended up at the *Unicorn*, which was the first pub on the very outskirts of the nearest tiny village that stretched along the country lane. The *Unicorn* was housed in a quaint redbrick building with timber framing on the upper story and a tiled roof. The four American officers entered brazenly, disguising their own sense of awkwardness with counterfeit self-assurance. Tripping over the step down, they plunged into the dingy room and were instantly more bewildered than ever.

J.B. had the feeling he'd never been inside any place so old in all his life. The ceiling was very low and made lower by huge, rough-hewn beams, blackened with age. The floor was flagstone, covered with thread-worn rugs. The windows had little diamond-shaped panes set in lead fittings. The glass wasn't even clear, but thick and yellowed. The walls were papered over with some floral print paper and the wall-lamps had shades on them. The tables were dark wood, gleaming with varnish, like the bar that looped around in the middle of the room.

An old man, serving at the bar, glanced up at them, and the men sitting at the bar turned around to see who had entered. J.B. noted that there were no other Americans here at the moment. There was a big mission planned for tomorrow and only the rookie crews, who weren't flying with it, could even get off the base. Beyond the bar a step led up into another room, and from this direction came the sound of voices and laughter. J.B. caught a glimpse of RAF blue in there. The men in front of them appeared to be local farmers, all in muddy rubber boots, open-necked shirts and tweed hats. They eyed the Americans rather suspiciously.

The Americans went up to the bar. Alan, who had taken over the leadership of the little escapade, opened with a friendly, "How y'all doing? My pals and I'd like a beer."

"Yes, sir." The bartender reached over his head and removed four glass mugs and started filling them. "That'll be 8 pence, sir."

"Eight pence?" Alan pulled a fistful of change out of his trouser pocket, looked at it for a moment and then just slapped it down on the top of the counter. "Have I got enough there?"

The bartender glanced over, finishing off one beer and starting the next. "More than enough, sir." He took a six-pence and t'pence coin and then nodded for Alan to keep the rest.

When they all had their beers, they went over to a table and sat down. "Here's to High Wych!" Alan lifted his beer and took a deep pull on it. He choked on it and gasped out. "God damn! It's warm!" Then turning toward the bartender he called over. "Hey! This beer is warm!"

"Of course, sir. That's the way we drink it over here."

"Warm beer?!" The others were tentatively sipping at their drink with expressions varying from disbelief to distaste.

"You got anything else in this joint?"

"What spirit would you like, sir?"

They ended up ordering a round of rum-and-cokes. The coke, too, was warm, but Dan muttered something about 'when in Rome do as the Romans do,' and they left it at that.

It turned out Alan was from Iowa and Patrick from Ohio; both had attended college, though Alan had quit right after Pearl Harbor. Patrick had been at Ohio State, and like J.B. had played football. At once they started talking about games, won and lost, in the age-old rivalry between the Buckeyes and the Wolverines. The friendly-familiar rivalry made both Americans feel more at home in this strange place. With part of his brain J.B. was talking football and with another part he was watching himself, thinking: "This is really me. I'm sitting in an

English pub and chatting with my buddies and we're all men of the Mighty Eighth Army Air Force on active duty." It seemed quite incredible to him.

They were on about their third round when a low pulsing rumble started to shake the little pub. A couple of empty glasses that were too close together vibrated into contact and started tinkling. Then the glasses over the bar set up a choir of clinking, and the mounting hum of engines grew steadily louder until it was a deafening roar that seemed to come straight at them. The first aircraft seemed to scream right overhead and then it was rumbling away, followed by one after another, passing just off to the right or the left.

"619 Squadron," the bartender commented as the roar slowly subsided and the rattling of the windows and glasses gradually petered out. "Like to use the pub as a landmark on take-off."

CHAPTER 7

▼

Windsor, England
May 1943

The big black car in the driveway warned Emily at once that Philippa had 'friends' over again. This car was so big and so solid and so well-polished it positively reeked of wealth and power. Emily sighed. She was feeling very tired and rather dirty after a long day. She was still in her uniform with trousers for flying, Robin's flight jacket on one arm, and she knew that her hair was in desperate need of a wash after two days in flying helmets in a row. She didn't exactly regret having Philippa as a lodger, but at times like this she sometimes wished she were a little less 'social.'

As she put the key in the lock, she could hear the scratching and puffing of Penny on the other side of the door. Penny invariably stood on the arm of the sofa in the living room with her front paws on the window-sill, keeping a vigil for Philippa and Emily until they both arrived. She never failed to be at the door.

Emily opened the door carefully, her eyes directed to the floor where she knew the bulldog would be dancing about, wagging herself energetically. Penny half-reared up, her front paws reaching for Emily's legs. Emily bent down and swept her up into her arms. Holding the soft, warm dog in her arms, she laid her cheek on the dog's head and murmured endearments. Penny was the only creature she could hold and cuddle, and Emily sometimes felt like she'd go mad if she didn't have this one physical comfort.

Penny seemed to sense her need. She had quite 'shamelessly' abandoned Philippa to sleep on the foot of Emily's bed at night. The feel of her weight and warmth in the night made it easier to go to sleep somehow. And when Emily woke up in the middle of night, terrified, hopeless and embittered at the cold, empty bed, Penny helped to calm her again. Penny responded to Emily's restlessness at night by cuddling close and demanding attention. She let Emily hold her tightly in her arms until the warmth and loud breathing of the little dog soothed her nerves enough for her to fall asleep again.

From the drawing room facing the garden came the sound of the gramophone playing big-band melodies. Emily glanced in the direction of the drawing room, but it seemed dark. Light, however, came from under the kitchen door, so Emily set Penny down again and opened the door. She surprised a plump girl in ATS uniform slumped over the table with a cup of tea beside her and a novel in front of her. "Oh!" She sat up straighter.

The girl was evidently the driver of Philippa's guest's car. As she took in Emily's uniform, she jumped to her feet, evidently over-awed by the sight of a woman with golden rings on her sleeves and wings on her breast. She even saluted in her embarrassment. "I'm sorry, Ma'am, I was told—"

"Good heavens, sit down. Do you want another cup of tea? I was just about to make one for myself."

"Ah, yes, Ma'am," the girl answered uncertainly. Still not sure what to make of Emily.

"I'm the landlady," Emily explained, as she put the kettle on and lit the gas. "I'm a pilot with the Air Transport Auxiliary. May I ask the identity of the man you are presumably driving about in that large motor-car parked in my driveway?"

"Parliamentary Under Secretary Sir Howard Edward Downs, Ma'am."

"Ah ha," Emily answered, turning her attention to the tea caddy. Whoever that was. "Well, I hope he doesn't keep you up until all hours of the night *every* night," Emily commented. She did not approve of men in positions of power exploiting their privileges at the expense of their employees. Her communist upbringing wasn't entirely lost on her, after all.

As she went to set tea-things before her own place at the table, Emily froze. A letter had been carefully laid out for her. It was from the Red Cross.

Emily's knees gave way. The uncertainty was over. Inside that letter was the news of Robin's fate. Either that he was a prisoner of war or he was dead. Suddenly Emily realised *how* much she still hoped he was alive. Knowing he was dead would NOT be better than the uncertainty. She really didn't want to *know* he was dead. She wanted to go on hoping…

The kettle screamed. Emily leaped up, took it off the stove, poured the boiling water slowly over the tea-leaves in the bottom of the pot, and then brought the tea-pot over to the table. "Help yourself," she said to the ATS girl, and forced herself to pick up the letter from the Red Cross and tear it open.

She skimmed rapidly down the letter looking for the vital information. Wing Commander R. Priestman was…? It wasn't there. It was a form letter asking for donations to help their important work 'keeping open the lines of communication to our brave boys in captivity,' etc., etc. Emily felt utterly let down. She folded the letter back together and threw it into the rubbish. Maybe certainty would have been better than this after all…

After she had fortified herself with a cup of tea and brushed her hair, Emily decided it was time to make her presence known to her lodger and her guest. Shadowed by the faithful bulldog, she left the cosy kitchen and headed for the drawing room. It was a mistake.

The drawing room was empty. The gramophone was apparently playing for no one, but the French doors opening out onto the flagstone terrace facing the garden were wide open. So that was why they hadn't turned on a light, Emily thought, and started through the gently billowing lace curtains onto the terrace.

The sound of her first footfall on the flag-stone brought a gasp and two shadows sprang apart—but not before Emily had time to register that they had been in a rather passionate embrace. "Pardon me," Emily intoned and turned on heel.

"Oh, Emily! I didn't hear you get in." Philippa exclaimed. She sounded slightly surprised, but not really discomfited. "*Do* join us out here. The moon is lovely and it's a positively *balmy* night. Teddy brought along some simply *divine* cognac as well."

The man, Sir Howard Edward Downs or 'Teddy,' cleared his throat and moved toward the wrought-iron terrace table. "Yes, indeed. Can I pour you some, Mrs. Priestman?"

Emily hesitated uncertainly, decided it would be not only rude but also petty and prudish to decline, and agreed, "Thank you, Sir. I will join you for a glass."

"Teddy, for heaven's sake! Philippa? Another?"

"Yes, please."

As they congregated around the table, 'Teddy' pouring from a bottle into cut crystal glasses, Emily's eyes adjusted more and more to the semi-darkness of the moonlit night. Emily guessed that 'Teddy' was in his fifties. He had greying hair, a moustache, and deep lines on his once-handsome face. Yes, Emily decided, he was attractive in the way a mature man definitely can be—particularly if dressed as this man was, in a flawlessly tailored three-piece pin-striped suit and clothed in an aura of power. He also wore a wedding ring.

Emily stiffened, and to hide her own disapproval bent down and stroked Penny vigorously. "Not for you, darling. Should I fetch Penny some beer?"

Philippa's brother and his friends had introduced the bulldog to beer, and Penny was quite addicted to the stuff. Emily was sure it wasn't good for her, but Philippa had demonstrated more than once how happy it made the otherwise morose dog. So they had agreed that Penny would be allowed to have beer 'on special occasions.'

"Good idea! She's been so patient waiting for you, you know."

Emily went back into the house and into the kitchen, glad to get away from the awkward situation and collect her composure. How could Philippa do this? Up to now she had never seemed to take her 'friends' very seriously. Certainly, Emily had never seen her in a man's arms before. Quite the reverse. Philippa had seemed singularly adroit at keeping her (often openly ardent) admirers at arm's length. She'd certainly known how to put a decorated and famous Wing Commander like 'Steeplechase' in his place! What could she possibly see in a married man twice her age?

Maybe it was prudish and 'petty bourgeois,' Emily admitted, but she just could not approve of a woman having an affair with a married man. There was simply no excuse. Certainly not for a woman like Philippa with so many bachelor admirers! What on earth was she thinking of?

As she approached the terrace with a beer and bowl for Penny, Emily could hear Philippa and 'Teddy' talking in low voices. They were standing very close together as she emerged again, and Emily thought she saw the important man drop Philippa's hand as he took a step back. Much as she disapproved of Philippa, Emily positively hated any man who would cheat on his wife and exploit his wealth and power to seduce younger women.

"I must say, Mrs. Priestman," he started in a low, melodious voice, "you've done a marvellous job decorating this house."

Don't patronise me! Emily thought furiously, as she took up her glass of cognac and answered pointedly. "It's all rented, I'm afraid. Robin and I haven't had the time or money to buy our own things."

"I quite understand. Philippa has told me how hard you work and what long, irregular hours you have. I must say, I find it very admirable indeed—just as I admire our WAAF and WRENs." He said this with a smile to Philippa before turning back to Emily. "But flying is quite unusual, really—and, of course, very dangerous, flying unarmed as you do. I understand a number of your pilots have been lost."

"Yes, mostly to weather, I must add, although in the early years when the Luftwaffe came over in force there were a number of incidents when we were shot at. But we've had more casualties from enemy action on the ground than in the air, actually. Several of our airfields were badly bombed in '40 and '41."

"Did you have a pilot's licence from before the war?"

"No." Emily admitted and then, because this answer alone raised more questions than it answered, since all commercial and private flying had been stopped since the start of the war, she added, "My husband gave me my first lessons. He was a Station Commander in 10 Group at the time and there were a couple of training aircraft assigned to the station for liaison work and the like. He didn't really have time to teach me properly, however, so when another pilot arrived who needed training time he asked him to give me lessons."

"Not exactly according to the King's regulations that, was it?" Teddy remarked with a wink, evidently highly amused.

"'Might as well be hung for a sheep as a lamb,' Robin used to say."

"Your husband is missing, Philippa tells me. I'm very sorry to hear that."

Well, don't let it give you any ideas! "I was very lucky to know Robin—even for the short time we had together. He was much too good for me, really."

"Now, now, I'm sure that isn't true! An attractive woman like you. I'm sure your husband felt very lucky to have such a lovely wife." As if looks were the only thing that mattered! "Were you married long?"

"Two and a half years. And you?" Emily was too tired and upset to be tactful. She was determined to dislike an adulterous man who was shamelessly seducing her lodger, and she resented this man being here when she was weary and emotionally wrung out by that letter from the Red Cross.

Philippa started visibly and caught her breath. Teddy patted her arm consolingly and answered Emily steadily. "I have been married for 29 years and separated for the last 8—ever since my youngest boy left home."

"Separated? Why not divorced?" Emily pressed him, despite Philippa's outraged look.

"It would have been political suicide to divorce my wife. Besides, she's Catholic. Would you like another, Mrs. Priestman?" He held up the bottle. She shook her head, aware vaguely that she had had too much already.

"Then I suggest we call it a night, Philippa. Mustn't keep my poor driver waiting too long, you know." Turning to Emily he added, holding out his hand, "It was a pleasure meeting you, Mrs. Priestman. I've been looking forward to it ever since Philippa told me about your kindness in taking her and her poor dog in. I do hope we'll have a chance for a nice chat another time—when you're less tired, perhaps? It would be my pleasure to take you out to dinner one of these days. You will accept, won't you?"

He'd succeeded masterfully in shaming her for her pettiness, and she had no choice but to back down. "Thank you, that's very kind. I'm sorry I've been such a poor hostess—"

"Not at all. You've had a long, hard day of it, and it is quite late. Good night." He clasped her hand one last time and then followed Philippa back into the house. Emily sank down on the nearest chair, feeling wretched.

She listened to the retreating footsteps. The ATS driver was roused from the kitchen. The front door fell shut. Philippa returned. She went straight over to the table and poured herself a large cognac.

"I'm sorry," Emily opened, admitting, "I wasn't very tactful."

"About as tactful as Herman Goering!" Philippa snapped back. She turned around and faced Emily. "Look, I'm your lodger. You can throw me out if you disapprove of my morals, but I don't think it is at all fair to be rude to my guests."

"You took me by surprise. I didn't think you were that kind."

"What's that supposed to mean?"

"He's a married man, Philippa!"

"He's a very kind, considerate, *lonely* man!"

"Then perhaps he should seek a reconciliation with his wife."

"Oh honestly! Don't be so naïve! Have you never seen a marriage that is a wasteland? I certainly have! More than one, in fact." She turned her back to Emily to pour herself another drink.

Emily didn't have an answer. Her parent's marriage had been just that: a wasteland. Even now she could close her eyes and see the indifference on their faces when they spoke to or about one another. It had always been 'your father thinks' or 'your mother says'—never first names, much less terms of endearment. And the predominant sound in a house with paper-thin walls had been the ticking of the clock or the turning of her father's newspaper. *Pravda* was read religiously every night. With adult eyes, Emily supposed it had been a relationship based entirely upon utility and shared devotion to the Party. Her parents had never quarrelled, but they had never been affectionate to one another either. Yes, of course there were bad marriages, marriages that had to be ended, but that was not an excuse for just carrying on while still married.

Philippa was saying, "Teddy's wife is positively beastly to him. She's a religious fanatic and spends half her time in church or the confessional. A Jesuit priest practically lives with her in her house. They may have been separated for 8 years, but Teddy's been banished from her bed for more like 18!"

Emily bit her tongue. She did not want to be catty.

"No, I haven't! But that isn't to say I won't!" Philippa told her, eyes blazing. "Life is too bloody short, you know, and God only knows how long this bloody war is going to go on! The way things are going, I'm going to be *100* before it stops! We were all so happy when the Americans finally got in to it. Now we'll turn the tables, we thought. Ha! Instead of learning from our mistakes and building on our experience, they think they know it all better already. They send their bombers off into enemy airspace in broad daylight without any fighter escort and just let them get slaughtered. It's bad enough the way the RAF is haemorrhaging young men, but the Americans have such inexhaustible manpower reserves that a few hundred airmen mean nothing to them. So what if their damned strategic bombing campaign costs 30, 40, 50 aircraft every week? What are a couple thousand airmen each month? Plenty more where they came from!"

Emily listened to Philippa rage and felt increasingly depressed. It wasn't just what she was saying, it was the realisation that Philippa—who always seemed so cheerful and well adjusted—was really as worn-down and hopeless as the rest of them.

"…the only sensible thing to do is grab any happiness you can while you can. That's what *they* do, and no one blames *them* for it. Why should the rules be different for you and me or Teddy, just because we're women and he's too old for this one? He went through the last one, after all—sogging it out there in the mud. Is it his fault he survived?"

The question was obviously rhetorical, and Emily replied by saying, "Did I tell you I ran into 'Steeplechase' the other day?"

"No. Drinking in a pub, I presume."

"Yes. We both had to land due to weather."

"I doubt the weather has any particular influence on his presence in a pub. He's either flying, drinking or trying to seduce someone."

"He's still single," Emily observed neutrally.

"Only because he's too bloody greedy to settle for one girl. If he ever talks some poor fool into having him, he'll cheat on her on the honeymoon—if he gets the chance."

Emily didn't particularly care one way or the other, but part of her thought that Philippa was being unfair nevertheless. She rather doubted if Philippa knew

'Steeplechase' well enough to be so certain he was completely devoid of morals or a sense of loyalty. Emily remembered how her parents had beseeched her fervently not to marry Robin because they had been sincerely convinced he would never be faithful to her. Look at him, they had argued, pointing to the pictures of him with this or the other socialite. He'll never be content with a 'plain' girl like you, they told her. When she asked Robin about the girls in the news clippings, he hadn't even bothered to deny it. "There were lots," he told her with a shrug; "does it matter?"

He had been right. What had gone before, didn't matter. What mattered was what happened after they were married. Contrary to her parents' predictions and her own fears, Robin had never given her any reason to doubt his faithfulness. Obviously, she told herself, she was the kind of naïve wife who might be easy to deceive, but *if* Robin had ever cheated on her, then it was in ways so discreet it never hurt her. And surely that was the most important fact? That he had made her feel loved, desired, cherished and irreplaceable?

Emily realised her thoughts had wandered, and she concentrated again on what Philippa was saying. Philippa had clearly had more than one drink too many by now, and she was letting off steam in a stream of words that she undoubtedly would have kept to herself under other circumstances.

"...sauce for the goose is sauce for the gander. I'm fed up with being told women should be able to do a man's job so that they can go off and get themselves killed, and *then* told that because I'm *not* risking my life, I have to behave like a 'good girl.' The fact is, they don't really want us to behave like 'good girls'—except when their backs are turned. We're supposed to be so blinded by the shine of their heroism, that we quite forget our own interests. Well, I'm not buying." She clunked her heavy glass down on the table definitively. "I'm not wasting my time and youth on someone who doesn't have much chance—and maybe no desire—to be there when *I* need him—much less when our children are growing up!"

Emily nodded wearily. "I do hope you won't regret it later."

"Don't we always?" Philippa flung back at her. "No matter what we do, we're bound to regret it sooner or later. I only hope that *if* this war ever ends, *no one* will remember all the stupid things I've done in it!"

Emily nodded again and got to her feet. "And I only hope that Robin and I will be together again with nothing to be ashamed of—not even in secret." She nodded to Philippa, and went indoors to bed.

CHAPTER 8

▼

Beauchamp Rodding, England
Late May 1943

They were woken early. 4.30 am. "Good morning, Lieutenant. You're flying today." The same words again and again, as the enlisted man shook the shoulder of each officer in the hut.

Jay hadn't slept very well. All night long trucks and tankers had been shuttling back and forth between the warehouses and the planes: ammunition, fuel and bombs. Other nights they hadn't bothered him so much, but this time they'd kept him awake. Now his throat was dry, and his mouth tasted bad. He got up to brush his teeth and shave. Then he dressed warm for the mission: long johns, Mom's socks, a pair of wool gloves to wear inside his flying gloves slipped into his trouser pockets. They wouldn't get into their flying clothes until later, but J.B. wasn't sure he'd have a chance to come back for his gloves.

The tension was almost unbearable—especially because you couldn't show it. Everyone, from the base staff to the other crews, knew it was their first mission, and of course they all looked intently at them to see how they were standing up. Had to play it cool. Hadn't they trained for this for the last 18 months? They were ready. More than that: they were eager.

Mission Breakfast: orange juice, corn flakes, huge rashers of crispy bacon, scrambled eggs, hash-browns, sausages, pancakes and maple syrup, doughnuts.

Only thing missing was the blueberry muffins. The crew fell over the food, but J.B. reminded them to go easy on the coffee. Although they didn't know the target yet, they were likely to be flying a long time and the pee-hole was not terribly accessible—not to mention that at 30,000 feet you'd freeze your—off using it.

Then the Briefing. Rows of wooden chairs faced a raised platform and a curtain, like in a movie theatre. The hut gradually filled up with the crews. Most of the men wore leather jackets, and crews sat pretty much together and talked mostly among themselves. Sometimes one or another would lean forward to talk to the man in the row in front or turn around to talk to someone behind, but the tone was subdued—not like the horseplay and joking that typified such meetings back in training. The man on his right was crushing his cap between his big-boned hands like he was willfully trying to destroy it; the whole time he was staring at the blank curtain.

Finally someone shouted out 'tenSHUN!' and they all sprang to their feet. With a loud, purposeful stomping, the Group CO, Colonel Bochanek, came down the centre aisle followed by a bevy of staff officers, Group Intelligence Officer, Group Meteorological Officer and the like. The staff officers all clattered up onto the low stage and turned to face the audience. The Colonel stood at the fore. He was a big, broad-shouldered man with his grey hair cut in a 'butch.' His face was square, his eyes hard, his jaw set. J.B. was reminded of the base CO at Napier. He'd been a real fanatic about military protocol and not much else. J.B. hadn't liked him one bit.

"At ease. Sit down."

They sat down.

"Intelligence has evaluated the results of the last raid, and there's only one way of describing it: Lousy. It looks like half the load landed miles wide of the mark. The Daimler factory you were sent to obliterate was operating again within 48 hours. We're not going to win the war that way!

"Furthermore, if you can't do better than that, we might as well bomb at night like the Brits do. When their Pathfinders are on target, they generally pile the stuff on. What you guys are doing is dropping the stuff all over the countryside like it was Christmas presents.

"I want a tight formation and a tight bomb pattern!"

He nodded to an aide, and the curtains swung back, revealing a large map of southeastern England, the North Sea and the northwest of continental Europe. A bright red ribbon stretched out from a well-perforated point surrounded by white—where sweaty fingers had worn away the name of Beauchamp Rodding. It reached northeast across the North Sea, turning east over the top of Holland, and then continued across the southern tip of Denmark at the narrowest point of the peninsula, before dropping down in an arrow aimed straight at Berlin.

That sent a surge of adrenaline to Jay's heart. Berlin itself—the heart of the monster. J.B. knew his grandfather would applaud. Jay was proud he'd be able to write home about this. (After the fact, they generally announced the targets, so he didn't see why they'd censor it.) He'd be proud to say he'd been to Berlin and back, and it would sure impress the folks at home.

But it was one hell of a long flight—almost maximum range on a normal load. And, of course, the Krauts were bound to defend their capital particularly well. A glance at the experienced crews confirmed that they looked less than thrilled. Not that any of them said anything, but their faces were so stiff you got the feeling that it was taking considerable effort to keep 'em so 'blank.' The man on his right who was crushing his cap was leaving dark sweat stains on it now.

On the podium, the Colonel was cracking his pointer against the target, saying that their targets in Berlin were certain factories located at certain co-ordinates that the navigators would be given at a separate briefing. J.B. glanced at Dan, who nodded once. The crack of the pointer against the map could be heard to the back of the room as the Colonel swung it hard again and again, pointing to concentrations of 'flak,' German fighter bases along the route, and alternative targets for crews that 'absolutely could not make the target.' The Colonel made it clear that anyone who dropped their load on these alternatives had better return with at least half a wing missing or more than 2 engines dead. Less damage than that, and they'd be in 'hot shit.' These alternatives were not 'discretionary,' but strictly for ships aborting due to acute emergencies. J.B. thought that he caught an exchanged grimace between two of the men in front of him at this remark, a rolling of the eyes, but he wasn't sure.

The weather was clear over England, but apparently there was some light cloud over the North Sea. Berlin might be in cloud or it might be clear.

When they left the briefing hut, trucks were waiting for them. They collected their flying kit from their lockers: the fleece-lined overalls, flight jackets, and flying boots, leather mittens and helmets, head-sets, oxygen masks and parachutes. Weighted down with all this gear, they crowded around the waiting transport. Suddenly, someone who was already on the truck announced that he had to take a pee. Everyone groaned. He clambered over the others to get to the back and scrambled over the tailgate, making for the latrines. Several others followed him. J.B. was tempted, but in the end was too ashamed to actually go. The truck waited, trembling slightly, until they came back. Then they set off at last. One of the guys hanging over the back of the tailgate looked up at the clear summer sky that was bright as the sun shone low over the eastern horizon and remarked, "I thought it was supposed to piss rain over here all the time. Why the fuck have we got such great weather?"

"What the fuck do you want? Fog? So we can smear ourselves all over the countryside to feed the crows when we come home?"

J.B. was just as happy to drop down onto the hardstand beside *Halifax Hooker*. That was what they'd named her. The inevitable buxom blonde wearing only skimpy panties was painted on the nose. The Hooker was primping her hair with one hand and with the other, rubbing her thumb and forefinger together in the age-old gesture of demanding payment. The bomber was also now in camouflage paint; she looked grimmer and more business-like that way.

The enlisted men were already aboard. The guns were being swung as the gunners tested them. Tony went straight up through the nose hatch to start the cockpit checks, while J.B. and Fuentes did the walk-around of the ship. J.B. went through the routine, but he was doing it by rote, without thinking about it or seeing anything. Finally he asked, "Everything OK, Ricardo?"

"Yes, sir."

"We're counting on you." He shook Fuentes' hand.

"Good luck, sir."

"Thanks."

A jeep drew up and Dan and Buzz tumbled out, their separate briefings over. J.B. nodded to them and then hauled himself up through the fore hatch, battened it down properly and continued up to the flight deck. J.B. sank into the left-hand seat and strapped himself in, squirming a bit to get as comfortable as possible. He was starting to sweat in the fleece-lined 'monkey suit,' and pushed the side windows open to let in some fresh air until they were well off the ground.

Around the field a total of four squadrons were preparing to take off; they amounted to 33 aircraft, as a couple of the squadrons couldn't put up a full complement of 9 aircraft. The Group CO, Colonel Bochanek, would be leading the formation from the lower box. Major Harkins was leading the middle box. J.B. was flying No. 5 behind him.

Jay checked his watch. 30 seconds to "start engines." Then, all at once, the buzzing and humming of the engines of the other 32 aircraft coming to life one by one came through the open windows of the cockpit. J.B. put his headphone on over his cap, and the noise from outside was dimmed. He tested the intercom, calling each man by name, and they all checked in. Good. He checked his watch. No more time to waste. "Number One engine!" It started up without any trouble. One after another the others did, too. The morning air around them was filled with a thin haze of oily smoke that drifted away as the engines settled down.

One by one, other ships were edging forward, off their hardstands onto the taxiways. They were heavy, loaded to the gills with fuel, bombs and ammo. As the chocks came away and J.B. throttled forward, he could feel how heavy *Halifax Hooker* was, too. She seemed to waddle more than roll; every tiny unevenness in the pavement magnified itself and made her sway.

Ahead of them on the taxiway was a battered old veteran with a patched horizontal stabiliser. Must have lost almost the whole thing at some point. It was a wonder it could still fly in that condition.

They stopped. At the head of the line, the first ship turned onto the runway, paused, and then—decipherable even over the steady rumble of all the other engines—came the distinctive bellow of four Wright Cyclones being whipped up to full power. The lead ship started to roll slowly forward down the runway. She gained speed gradually. The tail bounced, then the wings flexed as the whole ship started to bounce a bit. Because she was rapidly moving away, J.B. couldn't see the exact moment of take-off. The great bird just suddenly separated from the earth and climbed skywards. J.B. rolled forward one aircraft length and waited again.

Finally it was their turn. J.B. turned onto the runway with starboard engines and port rudder. Lock tail wheel. A last scan of the instruments. A green from the tower. "This is it, Gang!" he told them over the intercom and pushed the throttles forward.

She was really heavy. They were halfway down the runway before the tail lightened. J.B. was sweating hard in his monkey suit. The far perimeter fence and copse of trees beyond were getting closer and closer, and the damn bird was still on the ground. At least she was getting lighter. You could feel her start to lift at last. The air gradually, very gradually, started to carry her. At last her wheels kissed the runway goodbye and then they were airborne. The engines were screaming and the ship shuddering with apparent strain, but she was flying. She climbed, not too steeply. Jay kept it gentle, banking only slightly, spiralling her up nice and easy. Plenty of time. With a gesture of his hand, J.B. ordered Tony to raise the landing gear. Tony obeyed at once.

J.B. glanced out his side window; below, the whole base was spread out neatly. He could see one B-17 rolling forward along the runway, and the other 8 still in line on the taxi-way.

Gradually, they all circled upwards to 10,000 feet, where they formed up and flew to the rendezvous point (RP) with the other Groups taking part in this raid.

J.B. had never seen anything like that RP. There seemed to be hundreds of aircraft all swarming about in the morning sun. Slowly but steadily, the various Bomber Groups were merged into a single massive formation. Above the bombers, visible only as tiny little dots not really identifiable as aircraft, there were fighters.

The whole massive formation turned out over the North Sea, which stretched out infinite and grey beneath them. The B-17s flew forward in a massive swarm, steadily climbing again, up to a cruising altitude of 28 to 32 thousand feet, depending on where they were in the formation. J.B.'s middle box was slotted to fly at exactly 30,000. The individual ships floated gently upwards or downwards on the drafts, but held formation magnificently. J.B. found it exhilarating to be part of such an armada.

The others evidently felt the same way. From the back of the ship came the chatter of the gunners. "Get a load of that!" "How many do you reckon we are?" "Hey! Look at that broad painted on *Peek a Boo!*" "That's indecent!" "Wonder what squadron that is?" They were moving around, too, apparently trying to look out different windows; J.B. had to keep adjusting the trim of the ship to compensate. He was tempted to order them to sit down and stay put, but then decided it wasn't really a big deal. Eventually they calmed down and became still and silent on their own.

J.B. thought the aircraft were like a swarm of locusts, soon to bring destruction to the Nazi heartland. Well, they'd started this damn war. They'd bombed London. (J.B. hoped to get down to London and see some of the damage one of these days.) But he couldn't let his mind wander too much. Flying in close formation took concentration. If you slipped even a little out of position, you got bumped and shaken by the slipstream of the planes in front of you—not to mention the risk of wing-tips touching. And still they were climbing, passing through 22,000 feet now.

At cruising altitude, J.B. turned it over to Tony. His muscles were cramped from the strain of concentrating so hard on keeping station. He moved his shoulders in circles to try to loosen the muscles in his neck, then did another intercom check.

After a bit Tony nudged him. "Isn't that land down there?" He pointed down and out his window.

"Bombardier to pilot!"

"Yes, go ahead, Buzz."

"There are a bunch of islands down there."

"Navigator to Pilot, it's the Dutch island of Texel."

"OK. Thanks, Dan."

Holland. That didn't sound so bad, J.B. thought; now I've been to England and Holland—sort of. Weren't there German fighter bases somewhere about? No matter. They had an escort to take care of any trouble. It was only after the escort turned back that enemy fighters would be dangerous, J.B. told himself.

The islands kept coming up on schedule below their starboard wing. Dan had names for all of them. Then they turned onto a new course, due east. Over the airwaves came a crackle. "Good luck!" The fighters were turning for home.

"Close up!"

Christ, how much closer could they get? J.B. felt as if the B-17 next to him was already trying to stick its wing right through the window of the cockpit. They were at 30,000 feet at last and the air was so cold it hurt. How did the poem go: *if our eyes we'd close, than our lashes froze, to our face so we couldn't see...*J.B. hated the way his oxygen mask collected condensed water from his breath that oozed out on his chin. He wiped it away irritably with the back of his gloved hand. The mask was already starting to chap his face. He wiggled his toes in his flying boots to try to keep the circulation in them.

"Is that flak?"

"What?"

"Look at that!"

"Stop chattering back there!"

"Bombardier to pilot! Anti-Aircraft fire coming up."

"How far below us?"

"Oh, down there among the low formation."

"Jeeze! A Fort's been hit! Half the wing's gone. He's falling out of formation. He's going into a flat spin!"

J.B. couldn't see it. He had to concentrate on keeping in formation. The plane to his left seemed to be jinking around dangerously close. The pilot was probably trying to see what was happening below them. "Watch it, Bud!" J.B. called helplessly at the B-17 that was trying to jab its wing through his window. He leaned forward and shook his fist at the waist-gunner of the other ship. The gunner waved and pressed his intercom button. The other ship eased away again. J.B. flexed his hands inside his gloves.

"Pilot to Navigator. Are we over Denmark now?"

"No, we just crossed into German airspace."

Denmark was already behind them; that made two more countries for the tour.

A thin layer of cloud had spread across the face of the earth below them. At first you could still see through the thinner patches, but as they flew on it steadily grew thicker and soon obscured everything. Not much sight-seeing, J.B. observed, and tried to wriggle some feeling back into his shoulders. He was so stiff that he felt a tingling at the base of his neck and along his right arm. "Can you take her for a bit?" he asked Tony without using the intercom, dropping his mask for a second. Tony nodded.

J.B. unhooked from the main oxygen supply and clipped on a portable oxygen bottle. He clambered over the back of his seat and wriggled his way down into the nose to check on Buzz and Dan.

"Where do you figure we are?" He asked Dan.

Dan jabbed at the chart with his gloved hand. He had sheepskin-lined leather mittens to wear when he wasn't working, but to do any plotting he needed fingers, and so he wore silk gloves inside woollen gloves. They were over a place called Wittstock, according to Dan. That was getting pretty close to Berlin. J.B. climbed back up to the flight deck, settled into his seat and re-connected to the main oxygen supply, but he left the controls with Tony for a bit longer. Tony signalled with his hand that they were in a descent, and J.B. glanced at the altimeter. It was unwinding alright. The bombing run was to be made at 18,000 feet. They were coming down for it now. Not more than 15 minutes to go.

J.B. tried to swallow, but his mouth was dry. He wriggled a bit in his seat. Flexed his hands again. Looked out the side window to the lower formation. The lower bombers were sinking into the cloud. One after another they just disappeared into the white fluff and were obliterated. It was quite astonishing—seeing so many aircraft gently disappear. Then they were into the cloud themselves.

Jesus! Don't let anyone lose position now, J.B. prayed, and looked sharply over at Tony. Tony held grimly to the controls, his jaw muscles working with concentration. J.B. stared out the window, half expecting a wing-tip to poke his eye out any minute. And just when he was about to let out his breath from relief, he heard a faint popping sound, and Buzz shouted. "Flak! It's opening up all over the place down there!"

They were out of the cloud and into the shit.

With a nod, J.B. took the controls back from Tony. In the distance ahead of them, spread out on a vast flat plain, was a large city. It had to be Berlin. What a thought! He was flying over Berlin and Adolf Hitler himself was down there somewhere. The dictator must hear the deep-throated rumble of twelve hundred engines. The air-raid sirens must be going off and people running to the shelters.

Hitler would have a big, safe bunker, of course. No chance of killing him. Still it was good to think of sending him scurrying to safety underground like a rabbit.

A burst of flak found their altitude and exploded just ahead to the left. It shook the whole ship as if a giant had taken hold of it and left a filthy smudge in the sky. J.B. was sweating again, his hands cramped on the control column. Somehow he'd never imagined flak could be *that* powerful!

And it was getting thicker all the time. "Flak-suits and helmets, everybody!" J.B. ordered the others, but he didn't dare take his own hands off the controls long enough to pull on his own helmet, much less his flak-vest. They were being shaken about the sky as if they were in the midst of a terrible thunderstorm. First up, then dropping like a stone, then left or right. Around them the other ships were being flung about in the same way. The risk of collision was multiplied a thousand fold.

Flak blossomed right in front of a ship in the upper box on the right. It seemed to fly serenely into it and then, quite abruptly, it was veering off to the right in a steep dive. J.B. didn't understand, but he didn't have time to work it out either.

Abruptly the flak stopped. Which seemed OK until Jay's tail gunner started shouting: "Holy Shit! Fighters! Fighters! Coming in! Six-o'clock low. Brier, can you see it?"

"Yeah, I've got it!" An instant later J.B. heard and felt the ball-turret gun go off. The whole aircraft shuddered.

"Jesus! There's another one! 8 o'clock!" the left waist gunner called out. "Turning in now!" The guns started chattering again, the waist gunner screamed. "Guns jammed! Can you see him, Logan? Brier? Have one of you guys got him?"

"What?! I can't see fucking shit!"

"Jesus!"

J.B. ducked instinctively as something dark seemed to flash right overhead. A second later he saw with appalling clarity the grey belly of a small aircraft. He could see the outline of the wheels tucked up into the wings, and the stark black crosses outlined in white, and then the tail wheel was right in front of his nose.

To his horror, little beads of light were coming straight at him, and he realised that the tail gunner of Harkins' ship was firing at the German fighter but the bullets were coming straight at him. A moment later he felt them go into the leading edge of his port wing. Before he could even switch on the radio to howl out his protest, the fighter was wheeling away, apparently unscathed. Harkins' tail gunner stopped firing at him, but from the back of his own ship the guns were chattering and the gunners were cursing and shouting to each other again. Magnified by the intercom, their shouts were only confusing. "Don't shout, guys!" J.B. tried to order them, but they didn't pay much attention.

Abruptly, accompanied by a loud boom, the B-17 was flung upwards. The tail came up and the nose was pushed down as if by a huge, invisible hand. J.B. had never experienced anything like it. He had completely lost control of the ship. It wasn't flying anymore. It was dropping like a stone.

"Jesus God! The ship behind us just blew up!"

Debris clattered onto the wings. Something fell right onto the roof of the flight-deck with a loud clunk and then rolled off backwards in the slipstream. The B-17 swooped upwards again, responding to the elevators as the effect of the blast wore off. J.B. regained control of the ship and headed back for his position, but the ship seemed to be sluggish and there was an unusual tremor coming over the rudder pedals. J.B. felt in his gut that something wasn't right, but he didn't know what it was.

"Pilot! Do you hear me?" It was the excited voice of the left waist gunner. "Something has happened to Olds!" That was the tail gunner.

J.B. tried his intercom. "Olds? Are you okay back there?"

"He's *not* OK! I just told you that!"

"Olds, report in!"

"He's been hit, I'm telling you, goddamn it! If you don't do something, Lieutenant, I'm gonna go back there myself—"

"If you leave your post, I'll have you court-martialed! Sergeant Roach" (that was the radio operator), "take the first-aid kit and go back and see what's happened to Olds."

"Jesus! Here they come again!"

The chattering of the guns started up instantly. The ship shuddered. She was vibrating much worse than before. Worse: now there was a gap behind them and their tail gunner was out of action. With a punching sound that would follow Jay the rest of his life, cannons punched along the side of the B-17. And then the fighter darkened the cockpit again, flying right over them.

"Number Three's on fire!" Tony screamed at him—not using the mike.

J.B. leaned forward to see around Tony and saw to his horror that the wing was perforated, fuel was streaming out of it, and smoke was pouring out of the cowling of the inboard engine.

"Lieutenant! Olds is bleeding to death back here and the tail's wide open!" The voice of the radio operator was so high and raw it was almost unrecognisable.

"Cut the fuel to Number Three!" J.B. ordered Tony.

"Did you hear me up there? The tail's half blown away!"

Well, that explained why she was flying so funny, Jay reasoned, but the first priority was getting the fire out. He feathered the engine and engaged the fire extinguisher, but it was still smoking dangerously. What the hell was he supposed to do now? J.B. stared at the smoke streaming back from his inboard starboard engine and felt utterly hopeless.

Sergeant Roach was screaming at him again. "Can't you hear me up there? Goddamn it, Lieutenant! Olds is full of shrapnel back here!"

J.B. pressed the mike button: "Yes, I hear you. What the hell do you want me to do about it?"

Off to his left J.B. could see a B-17 silhouetted against the sky as it stood on one wing-tip and then started to slide down the sky; flame completely engulfed the lower wing and was starting to eat at the fuselage. Little dots started to drop out of it. "Dan, watch that B-17 going down!"

"I've got it, Jay. Two parachutes so far." Now J.B. noticed them too. In a blossom of white another parachute opened. The silk touched the flames and went up in a flash of yellow. The dot fell away faster, flailing its limbs helplessly.

J.B. was sweating from every pore of his body. Their inboard starboard engine was still smouldering. The B-17 was shuddering and vibrating unnaturally from damage to the tail. The tail gunner was wounded and out of action. The next wave of fighters was coming in—and they hadn't even reached the target yet!

Part of J.B. wanted to drop out of formation and turn for home, but part of him was ashamed of even thinking of it. He couldn't very well write home about going to Berlin and back if he high-tailed it before he'd dropped his load. They were still holding their position, after all. The B-17 could fly pretty good on three engines. If the fire was really out…He leaned forward to see around Tony again. The engine cowling around the dead engine was charred black, but there didn't seem to be any more smoke coming out. He wouldn't be able to write home about it if they crashed, either. But if they left the formation, they'd never stand a chance against fighters. Jesus! What was he supposed to do? On the intercom: "Roach! How bad is Olds shot up back there?"

"He's goddamned bleeding to death, that's what! He's got bits of shrapnel in his face!—His arms and chest, too."

"Can he make it at all?"

"How the hell should I know? I ain't no doctor!"

"Five minutes to bomb run!" Dan called up.

That did it. They were going on in. Dropping their load would lighten the ship, and make them less vulnerable to explosion, too. A forced landing with a full load of bombs was not a good idea.

"OK, gang, this is the pilot. We're going to stay in formation where we've got the most protection. We're going to do what we came over here for—drop that belly-load of high explosive on Adolf Hitler's head—and then we're going to beat it back for home as fast as we can fly. Got it? Roach, bring Olds as far in-board as you can carry him and fix him up as best you can."

Below you could see big blocks of buildings with sloping red tile roofs built in squares around courtyards. There were chimneys belching smoke out into the dirty air, too. A dull, gun-metal grey river wound its way purposelessly between grey warehouses. Barges lined the river's edge. There were some parks with trees farther off to the south, but the formation was wheeling slowly around and sinking lower still, although the flak had opened up again and was cracking all around them.

Harkins' ship had its bomb-bay doors open, and a moment later Buzz demanded control of the ship. There was nothing J.B. wanted to do less at that moment than to go on autopilot. But that was what he had to do.

It seemed to take forever, and the flak was reaching for them again.

"Jesus God, Olds is bleeding to death back here! Would you bastards just drop that load of shit and get the hell out of here!"

"Keep off the intercom!"

"Bombs away!"

The last remark wasn't really necessary. The plane lifted as if with relief as the weight dropped away from her. J.B.'s heart lifted with her—and then he saw the sky in front of him. It was a filthy panorama of bursting flak. The whole sky was polluted with the stuff, and added to the bursts of flak were great billowing columns of grey-black smoke coming up from the ground. Against this churning grey-black panorama were the tiny aircraft, several of them trailing white or black smoke.

J.B. was pulling hard on the controls, trying to take them back up towards the protective layer of cloud, only the damned plane wasn't responding very well at all. That was when the next burst of flak went off. It wasn't close really but it shook them a bit, and Tony called out an octave too high. "Number Three's loose!"

The situation was now so bad that J.B. did not even swear out loud. He just clung to the control column, aiming for the clouds that were inching ever so slowly nearer. At least the formation was now so spread out that there was little immediate risk of collision. He let out his breath as they disappeared into the fluffy white camouflage. The sound and feel of flak receded. They came out into the sunshine. Up here that ugly city and the ugly flak seemed to belong to a different world. Here was blue sky, fluffy white clouds, and sprinkled about above them hundreds of tiny aeroplanes.

If only their tail weren't trembling, sending vibrations through the whole ship. If only their burned-out No. 3 engine wasn't hanging down at least two feet out of alignment and causing a serious drag that he could feel more and more clearly on the controls. If only they weren't still losing aviation fuel. J.B. was sweating again. They were hundreds of miles from home in a badly wounded ship, and the fighters might be back at any minute.

Try to deal with one problem at a time, he told himself. First thing to do was see if he could reduce the vibrations. They were clearly shaking the damaged engine looser with each minute. He started playing with the mixture, power, trim—trying everything that might reduce the vibrations. After about five minutes he thought he had found the optimal settings—only they were at a cruising speed of just 170 mph. That wasn't what the other B-17s were flying as they beat it for home. They were flying at something between 200 and 210 mph as they formed up again into a loose formation. Helplessly J.B. and Tony watched the other aircraft grow steadily smaller and then disappear in the distance.

They were utterly alone in the sky.

"Dan. Do you know where we are?"

"Roughly; I'll give you a fix in two minutes."

After a pause, Dan came back on the intercom with their position.

"OK. Plot us a course for home—just straight back. No dodging around anything. Got it?"

"OK."

After what seemed like an interminable time, Dan came back on the intercom with a new course. J.B. turned onto it, and turned the controls over to Tony again. He hooked up to an oxygen bottle and scrambled back down into the nose to look at where they were. At 170 mph it was going to take them almost 4 hours just to get home—if their fuel held that long. Then he worked his way back inside the ship to where Roach was holding Olds on his lap. Olds was shaking violently and there was a bloody bandage over one eye. Roach wordlessly pointed out other bloody holes in his leather flying suit. It was hard to know if any of them were potentially fatal, but J.B. noted to himself that Olds hadn't followed orders and put on his flak suit. This wasn't the moment to comment on it, however, and it seemed obvious that they had to get Olds up to the nose of the ship where there was heating of sorts. Here the wind was blowing in through the hole in the tail section, so that even though they were flying at 'only' 18,000 feet, it was bitterly cold.

J.B. called for Buzz to come back and give him a hand, and the three of them somehow managed to drag/carry Olds forward to the radio shack. His teeth were chattering. They packed their kit-bags around him, and Dan, who had come back to help, handed over his mittens as well.

J.B. went back down the catwalk to try to get a look at the damage to the tail itself. The left horizontal stabiliser was half gone, the elevator on that side in rags. There were probably chunks missing from the rudder as well. As he crawled back to the waist on the catwalk, J.B. could see the controls moving as Tony tried to keep the ship in trim and on course. The controls made loud clanking noises, audible even above the whistling of the wind, the rumble of the engines and the rattling of the empty shells all around him.

As he dropped back into his seat, Tony looked over at him. What you could see of his face around the oxygen mask was drenched in sweat. "Have a nice trip?"

"Yeah," J.B. answered.

"Good, then get this: we got headwinds, and they ain't weak."

The sun was getting lower and shining in their eyes. Far worse, the cloud just didn't stop. According to Dan they were far over the North Sea by now, but as far as you could see, that slightly rumpled blanket of white lay out in front of them. England, it appeared, was also under cloud. Well, if it was as high as it had been over Berlin, no sweat.

If it was low cloud, they were in deep shit.

Fuel was gradually running out on them. Quite aside from the stiff head-winds, the No. 3 engine was sinking ever so slowly lower, causing more and more drag. The more drag it caused, the more power it took from the other engines to keep them aloft. The more power the others required, the more fuel they consumed and the more they caused the ship to vibrate. The more the ship vibrated, the more the No. 3 engine was shaken loose and the more it dragged.

J.B. gradually let down to just 8,000 feet, where the headwinds seemed less powerful and they could go off oxygen, but the cloud was still below them.

"Dan? Where do you make us?"

"We should be approaching the English coast. We must be about 110 miles from home. J.B. asked Roach to try and get a weather report from base. Five minutes later the Sergeant squeezed his way forward to the flight deck and handed J.B. a message: "Cloud down to 500 feet. Rain and squalls. Winds gusting to 30 knots."

Did God hate them or what?

"Ask about diverting."

Roach disappeared. A few minutes later he was back. "Conditions better to the west. Try Winslow."

Great—that was *a lot* farther away. J.B.'s eyes wandered to the fuel gauges that were dipping nearer and nearer to the red zone. "See if you can raise this Winslow place, alright? If the weather's better, have Lieutenant Vernon plot a course for it, and then have him call it up to me. Got that?"

Roach nodded and disappeared again.

After another eternity, Dan's voice came over the intercom with a new course. J.B. turned onto it blindly and trustingly, but his left leg (the one he'd injured playing football) was starting to tremble, too. His shoulder muscles were completely cramped. He needed to relieve himself. "What's our ETA, Dan?"

"25 minutes."

J.B. turned the ship over to Tony again, and went back to the "pee-hole" to relieve himself. Feeling somewhat better after that, he returned to the cockpit. He took a deep breath, flexed his hands on the controls several times, and then nodded to Tony that he was taking over. Then with another deep breath, he started to drop them down through the murk. It was now more than seven hours since they had taken off in the bright morning sunshine.

Above the cloud it was still a bright, sunny day, but with every second, as the ship sank deeper and deeper into the muck, the darker it became. "Pilot to Radio! What was the weather report at this place?"

"Ah. Cloud ceiling 1,000 feet, Sir. Winds gusting 20 knots."

Great. The winds that could be felt tugging at their damaged engine and buffeting their open tail were unpleasant enough at altitude, but when landing they could be a real bitch. In fact, the ship seemed to be handling worse already. J.B. looked in alarm at Tony. Tony's face was chalk white and sweat was glistening on it. His oxygen mask dangled beside his face as he pointed agitatedly out his window and shouted against the howl of the engines. "Number Three's trying to tear loose!"

J.B. couldn't afford to take his hands off the controls long enough to really see what was going on—but he could feel the way the whole ship was lurching about the sky. Just then they broke through the cloud and into a drizzle that at once hissed on their windshield. Tony switched on the windshield wipers and shouted at the same time, pointing ahead. Like a miracle, there was a long runway running diagonally across their path not more than a mile away. Hangars lined it on the far side and a wind-sock stood stiff, barely rippling, showing a sharp wind coming out of the west.

J.B. called for gear and banked about as hard as he dared in order to line up with the runway. The big bird was wallowing through the sky and J.B. was sweating blood as he tried to haul her around. She just wasn't responding right. They were skidding off to the right. There wasn't going to be a second chance! He had to get her lined up on that runway.

"Should I fire a flare for—AAAAAAHHH!!" Tony's voice changed to a terrified scream. The next instant the cockpit darkened and the world closed around them. The landing gear of an aircraft passed what seemed like inches in front of them, and then its black wings filled their view, blotting out all else. It was screaming under full power, trying to pull up again, and J.B.—more from instinct than thought—jammed the wheel forward and so pushed the nose of the B-17 down. In a second it was all over.

The other aircraft was climbing up and away while J.B. was heading straight for the runway at excessive speed. There was no need for communication; instantly both Tony and he hauled up on the controls.

"Full flaps!" J.B. screamed, and throttled back. Only seconds later they hit the tarmac with a resounding thump, bounced up into the air like a kangaroo, and smashed down again with such force J.B. thought for sure the gear would collapse under them. A new but smaller bounce followed, and then a third. Then they were on the ground and J.B. was struggling to keep them straight on the wet runway, the B-17 fishtailing half the way.

When they finally came to a stop just short of a low brick building, J.B. just sank back in his seat and tried to breathe again. After a moment, the wail of sirens penetrated his brain, and he realized the ambulance was approaching. J.B. unstrapped himself and stumbled-crawled off the flight-deck to drop out of the aircraft by the fore hatch. He landed on the wet tarmac just as the ambulance screeched to a halt. "My tail gunner!" he explained. "He's back here." J.B. indicated the after hatch, which opened nearer to where Olds was stretched out. The RAF medical orderlies nodded and pulled the stretcher off the back of the ambulance. They moved efficiently toward the hatch, which was opened from the inside by Roach.

The sound of another aircraft coming in to land attracted J.B.'s attention. He looked over his shoulder. It had to be that bastard that had nearly killed them during the final approach! Sure enough, it was a black Wellington with RAF roundels on it. Suddenly J.B. was furious with that pilot. He must have been able to see that they were in trouble—the engine was dead, hanging down below the wing and charred black, not to mention the tail being half blown away. It was obvious they were making an emergency landing.

There was such a crowd around Olds, helping to gently ease him out of the B-17 toward the waiting stretcher, that there was nothing J.B. could do to help. He turned and strode out across the wet grass of the large, strange field toward the Wellington that had nearly killed them all. It had just come to a halt, turned about and cut its engines. All very proper—as if nothing had happened. The bastard!

J.B. reached the aircraft just as the pilot backed down the little ladder out of the hatch. He was dressed in white overalls, an ancient and very dirty Irvin jacket, and a leather flying helmet rather than a peaked or overseas cap. J.B. burst out with all his pent-up fear converted into fury: "What the fuck did you think you were doing back there! You nearly killed us all!"

The pilot turned around to face him and J.B. registered at once he was just a little wimp: slight, at least 8 inches shorter than J.B., and he had soft, delicate, almost girlish features. The RAF pilot opened his mouth and said in a girlish high voice: "I don't know who was trying to kill whom. I had a green from the tower and was on final approach. You cut straight across in front of me."

Then, leaving J.B. gaping after her—because by now J.B. realised it was a *girl*—she walked toward the Watch Office, with her parachute over her shoulder.

CHAPTER 9

▼

RAF Little Horwood, England
Late May 1943

The Duty Pilot was ever so nice. He took the chit from her and said he'd see that the crew chief signed for the delivery and bring it over to her at the Mess. What she needed just now was a good, hot cup of tea. He asked another officer to take her over in his car. No need to get wet and it was quite a walk, after all. He'd ring the Mess when the taxi Anson arrived to collect her.

Emily's hands were still shaking and she was grateful that all the RAF in the Watch Office made a point of not noticing. Still, she needed one last reassurance. "I did have a green, didn't I?"

"You did. Absolutely no question about it. Don't give it another thought."

She dropped her parachute into the boot of the car and settled gratefully into the passenger side of the dilapidated Morris. The rain was falling steadily now and the ceiling appeared to have dropped even lower. Very likely the taxi Anson wouldn't be able to get in at all. "Been flying with the ATA long?" the Flying Officer asked, in a kindly gesture to distract her from the near miss that had nearly killed her.

Emily had never been so close to death before. When that massive American bomber had suddenly dropped out of the cloud and cut right in front of her, she had thought simply: 'this is it.' She took evasive action entirely instinctively, trying to pull up and over the Flying Fortress that was clearly sinking down rapidly. For a split instant it had flashed through her mind that Robin had come to collect her to him. A second later, when she realised that by some miracle beyond comprehension she had survived unscathed after all, she was just as certain that Robin had saved her life. She couldn't possibly have had the strength to yank that Wellington up and over the Fortress on her own. He must have been at the controls with her. But after the relief at surviving had faded a bit, the thought that Robin had saved her life depressed her, because it meant he was dead.

She chatted with the kindly Flying Officer with only half a mind. He understood and didn't take it amiss. With a smile he dropped her at the Mess, suggesting she see about spending the night at the Waafery. The weather was only getting worse, by the look of it.

She thanked him for the lift, dragged her parachute out of the boot, and went into the Mess to report at reception. They agreed to look after her parachute for her, and directed her to the visitors' ladies' room. She got out of the overalls she was wearing, changed into her ATA uniform skirt, stockings and pumps, and combed out her hair. Her hands had at last stopped shaking enough for her to apply some lipstick as well. She was beginning to calm down, but she could hear Robin saying, "I think you could use a Scotch," and she thought to herself that she was becoming a regular alcoholic ever since he had gone missing. Worse: she had really let Colin's idea of spirits communicating across the grave get to her! She was becoming positively "spiritualist"!

The Lounge was quite crowded. The weather having closed down entirely, all flying had been cancelled. Apparently a show scheduled for tonight had also been cancelled, and the crews that had been scheduled to fly on it—and so not drinking up to now—were making up for it.

As she stood hesitantly in the door, a Flight Lieutenant caught sight of her there. He stood, came over to her and invited her to join him and some other officers seated in comfortable leather chairs around a low coffee table. "You must be the lucky lady that bounced a Wellington off a Fortress."

Emily felt herself blushing. So they all knew about it.

Of course they were being nice, saying 'good show' and 'you must teach me how to do that sometime' and the like.

"What can I get you?" the Flight Lieutenant asked as a Mess steward appeared attentively. "Pink gin?"

"Oh, no—maybe a hot toddy?"

The steward nodded and withdrew. Emily was introduced to the other officers. The Mess steward returned, "Mrs. Priestman?"

"Yes?"

"Number One Ferry Pool has just called to say the taxi Anson won't make it in to collect you. You'll have to take ground transportation home."

"Thank you."

"Is that very far?" One of the officers asked, seeing Emily's face fall. Even though she'd been half expecting it, ground transportation meant spending hours in the pouring rain waiting for busses and trains that were always late and always over-crowded. It would be long past dark before she could get home, probably with wet feet and aching shoulders from lugging 40 lbs of parachute with her everywhere.

"I live in Windsor."

"Maybe we can put on transport for you," the Flight Lieutenant offered. "I'll see what I can do. But, first, here's your hot toddy."

The Mess steward handed it to Emily with a smile, and she took it gratefully. For some reason, she was feeling chilled. She was grateful that her companions were quite cheerful—not that forced joviality of men living on nerves that she knew all too well from many evenings spent with Robin's officers. This cheer seemed quite unaffected, and she soon gathered that the Squadron had been engaged mostly against targets in Italy of late. The Italian flak and night-fighter defence did not compare with the German variety, and casualties had been comparatively light. In fact, only one aircraft had been lost in well over a month, and there had been at least five parachutes, so one assumed the crew had survived.

"Have you had any word?" Emily asked a touch too anxiously, and the others looked over at her with a knowing flicker.

"No, it's too soon. Missing someone?"

"My husband. Since March."

"Bad luck. Where did he go down?"

"Northern France."

"The French Resistance is quite well organised there. We had a chap in here the other day, who managed to *fly* out of Northern France in a Junkers he borrowed."

"He was being hidden by some friendly natives," another officer took up the narrative, "in a town with an airfield on which, one day, a Junkers 52 landed. It was carrying some dignitaries, all of whom climbed out and rushed off to their important meeting, while the pilot rushed to the local café, leaving only a pair of bored German sentries to look after the aircraft. Our chap talked some French school-boys into baiting the sentries with taunts and various unpleasant missiles. While the soldiers angrily took after the school-boys to teach them due respect for the Master Race, our chap rushed the Junkers, climbed right up into the cockpit, and got the engines going. By the time the sentries came running back, he was already revving up for take-off. He says their faces were priceless. He—"

A commotion at the door distracted them. Four Americans in their tan uniforms and leather jackets were being led in by a Squadron Leader, apparently the Station Adjutant. He was graciously leading the Americans over to the bar.

Jay was acutely aware that they were inappropriately dressed—being still in flight jackets, turtlenecks and the like—while the English officers were all in proper uniform. He was even more aware that his face was still chapped from the oxygen mask, and that both Dan and Buzz had blood on their sleeves from helping hand Olds down to the ambulance. The Station Adjutant was graciously assuring them that they should make themselves at home. Their group commander had promised to send transport to collect them and a crew chief to check out the damage to the B-17. "We have no spares for the Flying Fortress," the RAF explained apologetically, "and our fitters and riggers aren't trained on their maintenance, either. I'm sure you'd rather have one of your own crews do the repairs. Should be fixed up in a day or two, by the looks of her," he added cheerily.

J.B. found that hard to believe, but he was too polite and too shocked to contradict. He thought their beautiful new B-17 looked like an absolute wreck. At least the base medical officer seemed to think Olds would make it. J.B. and the rest of the crew had waited in the lobby of the Station infirmary until the first medical examination had been complete. They had been assured that Olds had no mortal injuries; he had lost a lot of blood and would probably lose sight in his right eye, but that was 'all.' The RAF promised to 'patch him up' enough to transport him to the nearest US Army hospital.

Only after that was settled did J.B. accept the invitation to dinner issued by the Station Commander via his Adjutant.

"Now, what are you drinking?" their host asked.

"Um." J.B. knew enough not to ask for an English beer, and besides, he could do with something stronger than that, so he asked hesitantly, "Do you have bourbon?"

The bar steward answered, "would Scotch do, sir?" and J.B. agreed. Dan and Tony joined him, but Buzz wanted a highball.

"Dinner will be in a half hour," they were informed.

"Thank you."

"Your first time at an RAF station?" the Adjutant inquired. He was a short, slight man who appeared to be in his mid-thirties, with thinning blond hair and very sharp features highlighted by deep-cut lines.

"Well, we dropped in unintentionally on another station during training, but continued as soon as we found out our mistake," Jay admitted.

"Lost in the weather?"

"Yes—just like today, it changed pretty suddenly."

"I'm terribly sorry about that. It catches us out all the time, too. Had a terrible incident this past winter when ground fog closed most fields after the squadrons had gone out. Several kites crashed on landing, and other crews ran out of fuel circling their own fields waiting for a chance to get down. Half a dozen crews had to bail out."

J.B. thought to himself that he hoped he'd be home and safe in the good old US of A by the time winter rolled around again. Nothing in the world sounded better to him at that moment than the thought of going home.

"Have you been over in this country very long?" the Adjutant asked next, still trying gallantly to get his guests to relax a bit.

"We barely got here," J.B. admitted, rubbing his face absently because he couldn't get over the way the oxygen mask had rubbed his cheeks, chin and the bridge of his nose almost raw.

Dan smoothly took up the burden of conversation, telling about their trip across the Atlantic, saying how impressed they had all been by the courage of the crews of the cargo ships. "We never did get back to pick up the lifeboat we lowered," he told their host; "fortunately one of the escorts found them the next morning. We heard later that they had managed to rescue just eleven of the crew of that capsized freighter they had gone to help."

The adjutant nodded earnestly, "The Squadrons here have made repeated sorties against the U-Boat pens on the French coast to try to catch them in their lairs, so to speak. Can't say we've been terribly successful, though. The Germans keep their U-Boats in vast concrete bunkers. None of the ordnance we have is sufficient to crack them."

"What about the bombs you used on the Ruhr Dams?" Buzz asked, professional interest awakening in him. The sensational attacks on the Ruhr Dams had made the headlines shortly after Jay and his crew arrived. Everyone was still talking about them. "Surely anything that can bust a dam, can crack a U-Boat pen?"

"Well you would think so, wouldn't you?" the Adjutant agreed. "But I must say, it's all way beyond me. Leave it to the boffins, is what I say."

A burst of laughter from the lounge drew Jay's attention, and with a start he realised that an attractive young woman in an elegant dark blue uniform with golden wings was at the centre of it. He started. It had to be the woman who had been flying the Wellington that nearly landed on top of them!

"Excuse me," he interrupted the conversation about bombs. "Who's that woman over there, and—if you'll pardon my French—what the hell was she doing flying a Wellington?"

"Oh, she's an ATA pilot. You know, Air Transport Auxiliary. They ferry all our aircraft from the factories or stations to Maintenance Units for final fitting or repairs, and then back to our Squadrons when they're ready. Very remarkable group of chaps. Had a pilot in the other day, who had only one arm and one eye! Don't know how he does it! Fighter pilot from the last war, you see, when the Hun had done a rather nice job on him, but it didn't stop him from volunteering to do this ferrying work in this show. Another chap is really quite blind, but he has prescription lenses fitted in his flying goggles and zips around in Spitfires and Hurricanes as well as anyone. ATA used to have quite a few American chaps, too. Came over before you were in the War, you see, and they chose to join the ATA, which—being a civilian outfit—didn't cost them their citizenship as flying for the RAF would have done. Unfortunately, most of them have returned to America now, one presumes to help out with the war effort in their own country."

"But isn't that a *woman*?" Jay pressed him.

"Well, yes, they have quite a number of women pilots. You've heard of Amy Johnson, surely? First woman to fly alone to Australia and then to Tokyo? Broke all records to Cape Town and back, too. She was with the ATA, but unfortunately crashed in bad weather quite early on in the war—January 1941, if I'm not mistaken. I think there are almost 100 ATA girls nowadays."

"It's bad enough letting women drive!" Tony groaned in protest. "Letting them *fly* is madness!"

"Oh, I wouldn't say that," The Adjutant's voice suddenly had an icy edge to it—the way the Brits did when they seriously disapproved of something that had been said. "They fly the four-engine bombers these days, and have delivered our Wellingtons for years without a single mishap."

"It was a damned near thing today!" Tony pointed out hotly.

"Now, *whose* fault was that?" answered the Adjutant coldly, looking them straight in the eye with raised eyebrows.

"Jesus! We've been to Berlin and back!" Tony insisted, getting angry. "Our tail was blown away and our No. 3 engine burnt out—"

"Which is all in a day's work, I should have thought," the Adjutant cut him off.

"A day's work?!" Tony protested. "What the hell do you know about it?!"

"I've done it once or twice."

Jay's eye checked the Adjutant's left breast. He hadn't paid enough attention when they were being told about British medals, but Jay noticed that this man had several ribbons between his wings and his pocket. The Adjutant was not just a pilot, he was a decorated pilot, and Jay lay a restraining hand on Tony's sleeve. While Tony turned on him in outrage, the Adjutant was continuing, "You dropped out of the cloud and cut in front of that Wellington. You *ought* to be grateful that the ATA pilot was skilled enough to prevent a collision by pulling up at the last minute."

"He's right, Tony," J.B. told his co-pilot before he could say anything more.

"Are you Brits really so hard up for pilots you have to use women?" Buzz asked, trying to see around people to the woman pilot half-obscured by officers moving in and out, and standing about the bar.

"I don't know that 'hard up' is the word. These ATA pilots are doing a very vital job that otherwise our own chaps would have to do. Because of their efficient service, over 500 RAF pilots, who would otherwise be tied down with ferrying, are freed for operational flying. Surely you have a similar organisation?"

"We have the Ferrying Division in Air Transport Command. Most of the pilots there are Army, but there are a bunch of civilian pilots too old for the Army Air Forces that help out. But we sure as hell don't have any *women* flying military planes!" Buzz explained emphatically.

The Adjutant shrugged eloquently, "Well, no doubt you *do* have an excess of manpower reserves and don't need to draw on support from your women in the same way we do in this country. But I must say, our chaps rather enjoy seeing the ATA girls now and again—just as we appreciate the WAAF. Women have a decidedly civilising influence on just about everyone—I'm told, even on the Hun."

Jay had been watching the woman pilot while the others talked. She fascinated him, because here she looked lovely and feminine in her tailored, dark uniform, but he could still see in his mind's eye the way she'd looked in that beat-up Irvin jacket and helmet. He'd always thought that women who tried to do men's jobs were—at best—like his sister Barb, overgrown tomboys, and at worst pushy bitches. But this woman with her soft, brown hair, clutching a mug of something hot in her hands and smiling shyly at the men around her, looked almost timid—and very attractive.

"Excuse me a minute," Jay said to the others, and went across the lounge to the circle around the ATA pilot. The RAF officers fell silent and glanced up as Jay approached. Emily followed their gaze and saw it was the American pilot who had verbally attacked her before her feet even touched the ground after landing. She felt herself stiffen with resentment.

Jay saw her stiffness and the flashing of indignation in her eyes. "Ma'am, I just wanted to apologise for what happened—and for my rude language earlier." That took her by surprise. Her eyes widened. "It was our first mission and we got shot up pretty bad. My tail gunner was wounded. Then we got diverted from our own base, and—" he took a deep breath "I guess I wasn't paying attention to anything but getting the ship down on the ground as fast as I could."

"It's quite alright, Lieutenant" (she pronounced it Leftenant), "we are both an experience richer."

"You can say that, Ma'am." He touched his cap, and started to withdraw. She turned back to her companions. Then, before he really knew what he was doing, Jay stopped, turned and stepped back towards them. "Excuse, Ma'am, but I forgot to introduce myself. I'm Jay Baronowsky, 81st Squadron, 110th Bomber Group, based up at a place called Beauchamp Rodding—or, I guess you pronounce it *Beecham* Rodding." He held out his hand to her.

She hesitated, but it would have been rude to reject his hand, so she held out her own to him and dutifully introduced herself. "Priestman, Emily Priestman."

"Nice to meet you, Ma'am. Gentlemen." He nodded to the RAF officers, who had all been watching the little exchange guardedly, and retreated again.

Soon afterwards they all went in to dinner. It was a sit-down dinner at tables with tablecloths and linen napkins served by airmen and airwomen. The remark about 'civilisation' went through Jay's head, since this was a very different scene from what he was used to in the Army. Meals at USAAF establishments tended to be in huge cafeterias echoing with the sound of voices, chairs scraping, cutlery clattering, and the banging of doors as men constantly came and went.

The Americans were asked to join the Station Commander at his table with the Adjutant and other staff officers. It was a rather awkward affair, with the Americans on their 'best behaviour.' Jay's eye kept wandering over to the woman pilot, however. She was sitting with a half-dozen RAF officers and seemed to be having a good time. From their gestures it was clear they were talking about flying, and they laughed frequently. Sometime before dinner was over, however, an airman stepped up behind the woman, bent and whispered something to her; she excused herself to her companions and went out.

After dinner, most of the RAF officers set out for the local pub of their choice, but the Americans were expecting transport back to their own base to arrive at any minute and so stayed at the Mess. In the bar, some of the RAF were having a quiet drink, and the Americans joined them. Jay recognised one of the men who had been sitting with the woman pilot. "Where did that woman pilot go all of a sudden?"

"Oh, we organised a lift for her with a chap who had to run into London anyway. He had a meeting there and couldn't delay his departure any longer."

"She was a great sport about what happened," Jay found himself admitting. He couldn't get over the way he'd nearly killed her and then chewed her out, and she'd just accepted his apology and carried on as if nothing had happened. He couldn't picture Kathy being so calm after something like this—or his sisters, either. Barb would have been hissing and spitting mad, and Mary or Sally would have been in tears. Kathy—well, he wasn't sure, but he thought Kathy might have been angry in that cold, self-righteous way she got. She certainly made him feel like shit if he even came close to using a bad word. Then she made him feel like he was beneath her, not good enough for her. When he thought of what he'd said to this woman pilot, it made him blush inside, because after watching her through dinner it was clear that she was a real lady, at least as much a one as Kathy was.

"Yes, she's a very fine pilot," the RAF officer was saying. "Pity about her husband."

"She's married?" It surprised Jay that a married woman would be doing something as dangerous as ferrying military aircraft—but then again, until 3 hours ago, he had never imagined women flying military planes at all.

"Yes, but her husband was shot down over France at the start of March and they still have no word about what's happened to him. Apparently it was a pretty bad prang and he didn't get out, but the crate didn't catch fire so there's some hope. That's always the worst, hoping against one's better judgement that maybe, just maybe, he's alright. Poor girl."

"Her husband was a pilot, too?"

"Yes. Wing Commander, Fighter Command."

"And she's been doing this ferrying business all along?"

"Oh, I don't know. I didn't ask, but she's with No. 1 Ferry Pool at White Waltham, that's the Headquarters, and does a variety of flying. I should think she's been at it for a while. She was taught to fly by one of the best instructors we have up at Central Flying School, a German-Canadian chap, who got singed a bit during the Battle of Britain."

The conversation moved on to flying training, the Battle of Britain and more. By the time a bus arrived from base to collect them, Jay was sorry to leave. Everyone exchanged names and addresses and then went out into the rain for the long trip home.

Emily dumped her parachute inside the door, and squatted down to calm a frantic Penny, who was clearly distressed by her late return. "It's alright, girl. I'm home safe and sound. You mustn't get this upset, you know. I can always get stuck out in bad weather. Nothing to worry about."

Penny snorted and sneezed and licked out at her in reproachful affection.

Philippa emerged with a drink in her hand. "Oh! Hello! I wasn't expecting you so soon. Your Adj. called earlier and said you were stuck out and coming in by British Rail."

"I was, but the RAF at Little Horwood managed to find me a lift."

"Do you need dinner?"

"No, I had some at the Mess." Emily paused and then asked directly, "Are you alone?"

"No, Teddy is with me. Do join us."

Emily resented it, but there was nothing she could do about it. She followed Philippa into the drawing room where the black-out curtains were firmly drawn on this rainy night, and soft lighting and soft music gave the room a cocoon of romantic cosiness. Something about the way Teddy was fussing with his jacket and hair suggested to Emily she had interrupted more than mere talk. She sighed inwardly. "I won't disturb you for long. I'm quite exhausted. Had a near miss today."

"Oh dear. You mean a crash?"

"No, just some American returning with a beat-up Flying Fortress dropped out of the clouds smack in front of me and cut me off while I was on final approach. I had to pull up and go around again. I don't think I missed him by more than inches. Too close for comfort, really. Then he had the nerve to insult me verbally as soon as I landed."

"Good heavens! What cheek!"

"To be fair, he apologised to me later in the Mess. His first sortie, apparently, and his tail gunner had been wounded."

"I don't see how that excuses rudeness to a lady," Teddy insisted disapproving.

"He didn't realise I was a lady until it was too late," Emily admitted, accepting the brandy offered her by Teddy.

"You look done in," Philippa remarked observantly.

"I am," Emily agreed. "I think I'll go up and have a nice hot bath. You'll excuse me?"

They murmured their agreement, and Emily retreated up to the floor above with her brandy in hand and Penny in loyal attendance. She started running the bath, changed into her bathrobe, and then settled into the bath with her glass of brandy and the steam rising around her. She had a splitting headache, and knew she was close to tears. It was hard to explain. Everyone at Little Horwood had been so pleasant and cheerful that she had managed to suppress her feelings. But here alone, with Philippa downstairs in the arms of a man, the hopelessness over-whelmed her. Robin was dead. He had to be. No matter what Colin said about telepathy between living people, Emily just couldn't get herself to believe it. But she did, strangely, believe in ghosts.

Ghosts were a well-recorded phenomenon, actually, common to every culture in the world—even Asians and Aboriginals and Africans. The spirits of the dead *did* still walk the earth, and they could influence our lives in mysterious ways. Emily was absolutely certain that she could not have avoided the collision this afternoon without the help of something supernatural. Since she did not believe in God, much less guardian angels, it seemed certain that Robin's spirit must have been with her in the cockpit. Who else would have cared about her enough to even try and help?

Emily broke down and started sobbing so miserably that Penny jumped up and rushed to stand with her front paws on the edge of the bathtub, sniffing in distress. Emily only cried harder.

The mail was waiting for them in their hut. Jay eagerly tore open the letter from Kathy and flopped himself on the cot to read it. "Dearest Jay," it started as always. "Today I had a nice wedding shower. I know it's a bit early and all, but my Aunt Pat always goes up north during summer vacation and wanted to have it before she left for Travers City. Besides, a girl can *never* have enough wedding showers!" There followed a lengthy description of who was there, what they wore and what gifts they had brought.

Jay supposed Kathy still hadn't received any letters from him and so couldn't respond, but somehow it still seemed so petty—worrying about the colour of shower curtains and complaining about getting three rolling pins and no egg-beater. He'd seen at least one B-17 go down in flames this morning. He'd seen a parachute go up like a torch and the man attached to it fall to certain death. The B-17 directly behind them had blown up with its full load—10 men gone in an instant. His tail gunner had chunks of aeroplane embedded in his chest and was going to lose one eye—at 19 years old.

Jay put the letter aside wearily. Even the three X's at the bottom couldn't cheer him. He was feeling rotten. He remembered Roach shouting at him that Olds was bleeding to death, and his answer had been "What the hell do you want me to do about it?" That was a pretty lousy answer—even if it was true.

Jay had always pictured his first mission being more heroic than this. They'd go in, give the Krauts hell right on their god-damned heads, they'd shoot the squarehead fighters clear out of the sky, and come home like John Wayne—silent and strong and calm. No need for big words and gestures.

The reality was bitterly different. They'd all been scared shitless out there. They'd been shouting at one another. Logan threatening to leave his gun in the midst of the attacks to look after Olds. Roach coming on the intercom in the middle of the run into target telling them to just dump 'em and go home. Tony screaming in terror rather than giving a proper warning about the imminent mid-air collision. And he hadn't done anything right. He hadn't calmed them down. He hadn't even got them home. He couldn't figure out why he hadn't radioed in during their approach. And how could he miss seeing that Wellington? How could he just turn in front of it like that? All he'd seen was that runway, and he'd gone for it without a thought to whether there might be other aircraft anywhere in the sky. How dumb can you get?

Jay sat up and propped his elbows on his knees.

Dan had already turned in. Buzz and Tony were getting changed to go out for a drink. "You coming, Jay?"

"Naw. Too tired." He headed for the showers.

Returning to his bay, all was dark except his table lamp, lighting up Kathy's open letter. He folded it up, stuffed it back in its envelope, and closed it in the drawer of the bedside table. He crawled into bed, but he couldn't sleep. He lay staring at the ceiling, listening to the groaning of the trucks bombing up the air-craft for tomorrow's mission. At least they weren't going to be on it: *Halifax Hooker* had to be patched up first.

One down and just 24 to go.

Just 24?

Surely they weren't all as bad as this one had been. Berlin had to be the worst. And the weather couldn't always change for the worse. Not every mission could be like that.

They'd never make it, if they were.

Think of something pleasant, he told himself. Kathy. Think of how pretty Kathy looked the night he proposed to her—like a movie star with her auburn hair in a cascade of curls and her pearly-white shoulders bare above her tight-fitting bodice. But the magic didn't work.

Jay tried to compose a letter to her in his head. "We flew our first mission yesterday. Berlin…" But what could he tell her? He was too ashamed to tell her the truth—about being scared and not knowing how to calm his crew and nearly killing them all landing. He couldn't lie, either. He just couldn't, that wasn't like him. But he had to say something to make her understand. If she didn't understand what it was like over here, she wouldn't understand why he didn't care if she had three rolling pins or ten.

A chill of alienation sent a shiver down his spine. He resented her chatty letter about gifts and gossip when he was over here risking his neck—when he had come within a hair's breadth of killing himself and his whole crew. But that wasn't Kathy's fault. She just didn't know what it was like.

It crossed his mind that that woman pilot, Emily Priestman her name was, *did* know what it was like. She must—or she wouldn't have accepted his apology like that. Her husband had been a pilot, and she probably spent a lot of her time in RAF Messes, talking to pilots who were doing just what he was doing. The image of her at dinner, making flying gestures with her hands and laughing with the RAF, floated across his consciousness as he drifted into sleep, mixed with the certainty that she did understand.

CHAPTER 10

▼

White Waltham, England
June 1943

"Well, someone has to take the Airacobra!" the exasperated Operations Officer pointed, out after the second pilot had made excuses about it not fitting in at all and it really didn't make sense for this-that-or-the-other reason.

The Airacobra was a vicious little beast. It was an American-built fighter, which had its engine behind the cockpit, giving it an unnatural feel. More to the point, it had a reputation for blowing up. One of the ATA's most experienced and competent pilots had been killed flying the very first one they had to deliver—before there had been time to develop Handling and Pilot's Notes for it. Although there were now very precise instructions on how to avoid the over-heating of the engines which caused the explosions, it was still one of the least-loved aircraft of the more than 140 types the ATA had to deal with from time to time.

Fortunately, the RAF had not liked them, either. Both squadrons that had been equipped with the Airacobra had complained about excessive maintenance and unserviceability. After only one operational sortie, it was decided that performance was only marginally better than older, more reliable aircraft. The only solution seemed to be to give the rotten things to the Russians. While this meant that in the future the ATA would have little need to worry about them, in the short term a number of the beasts had to be flown up to Glasgow to be put aboard freighters bound for Murmansk. As it happened, today two of these had to be taken by No.1 Ferry Pool as far as Hawarden, where the Pool there would fly them onwards to Prestwick.

Emily, overhearing the unusual debate with the Operations Officer and the word Hawarden, spontaneously offered, "I don't mind taking one of them."

The others looked over at her, surprised.

"Anything coming back which I can't handle?"

It was quickly decided that nothing spoke against Emily swapping her own daily chits with that of one of the pilots who did not want to fly the Airacobra. After checking with the Maps and Signals and Met Officers, Emily set off in the taxi Anson to the Maintenance Unit where she was to collect the Airacobra. On the trip over, rather than looking out the window at the glorious summer day, she read up on the Airacobra in the comprehensive Handling Notes.

The Maintenance Unit at which she was to collect the Airacobra was one of those from which Emily's Ferry Pool flew many aircraft day after day, and all the staff knew the ATA pilots well.

"Got stuck with the Airacobra, did you, Mrs Priestman?" the Flight Sergeant commiserated with her as she signed for the aircraft.

Emily smiled rather weakly. She was not feeling at all happy about this. She had never flown an Airacobra, and its reputation did not exactly fill her with confidence. She had never been one of those pilots who particularly liked flying something new and different.

She would never forget the way Robin had been madly keen to fly a Me109 that had crash-landed near his Station. He hadn't cared that he couldn't read the instrument panel, or that the aircraft had clearly been shot up somewhat and there might be damage they had not yet located. He did not care that he had no Handling or Pilot's Notes. All he wanted to do was get his hands on the controls, take it up, test it out, put it through its paces, *fly* it. Two Air Vice Marshals had tried to talk him out of it, saying they could wait for a test pilot, but Robin wanted to fly it so badly and so obviously that they had given in to him. AVM Park had the final word, remarking laconically, "Let him have his fun. Where would the country be if our pilots weren't keen?"

Emily did not share any of that fascination with the unknown. She had her distinct favourites: the Spitfire leading the list, followed by the Hurricane, the Anson, and she was starting to like the Hudson and even the "Wimpy." She thought she would have been quite content if she did not have to fly any other type of aircraft, much less one with such a terrible reputation. But the temptation of flying back to Hawarden had been too much for her.

Hawarden was where Robin had been stationed when they met. At the time it had been an RAF station, an Operational Training Unit (OTU) to be exact, rather than an ATA Pool, and Robin had been an instructor there. Her very first trip in an aeroplane had been from Hawarden, when Robin took her up for a joy-ride in the Station Miles Magister. That had been the day she fell in love with flying—she was *already* head-over-heels for Robin at the time.

Returning to the present, she admitted to the friendly Flight Sergeant, "Well, someone has to fly the wretched thing, and the sooner we get rid of them the better. Was this one here with a serious problem?"

"The flaps were a bit sticky, but not to worry. We've fixed that up. You're a mite short for this aeroplane, Mrs. Priestman," the Flight Sergeant noted, as she sank into the seat and could no longer see a thing in front of her. Emily at once started looking for a way to adjust the seat, but the Flight Sergeant knew better. "Don't bother, Ma'am, the ruddy Americans think all pilots come from Texas and are six feet tall or some such thing. I'll fix you up with some cushions. You can bring them back next time you're here." The Flight Sergeant dropped back off the wing to go get some cushions, and Emily took the opportunity to carefully re-read her Ferry Pilot's Notes. Given the reason this particular P-39 had been in Maintenance, it was not comforting that the Handling Notes specifically referred to the difficulties of landing without flaps. The Notes ended by advising that it was only wise to do this at "a large airfield with runways." What a useful tip for an emergency landing! She put the Handling Notes away disgusted.

The Flight Sergeant was back with the cushions, and he helped Emily slip them under and behind her until she felt reasonably comfortable.

"Don't forget not to let her overheat," the Flight Sergeant reminded her with evident concern. "If you see the needle approaching the red zone, just pull right off the taxiway and shut down. Wait 'till the engine cools, and then start again."

Emily nodded her thanks, unconsciously biting her lower lip. She also pulled her helmet tighter, feeling like one of the Black Prince's knights facing the final French onslaught at Poitiers ('my lords, your helms make fast'). She had no excuse for delaying further, however, and so with a sigh she leaned out of the cockpit to see if the fitter was ready. When he gave her a thumbs-up, she called for contact and started up.

As the Handling Notes had warned, the Airacobra had a very vicious vibration below 1,000 rpms, and so revs had to be kept above this almost from the start. The problem was that the engine also had a tendency to overheat on the ground. And if it overheated, it exploded. Since the pilot was virtually sitting on top of the engine, this was an exercise with no future in it.

Emily had not reached the head of the runway, and already she felt as if the horrid beast was more in control of the situation than she was. But she mustn't let it get away from her, she warned herself, as she was given the green and throttled forward, committing herself to take-off.

The instructions were very explicit: this was an American designed and built aircraft with no safety cut-off system on the boost. She must *not* exceed the specified take-off boost. At least in the air the problem of over-heating took care of itself, she thought with relief, as at last the aircraft left the earth behind and started climbing up into the morning sky.

Once in the air, the Airacobra was a very nice little aeroplane, Emily decided. It was almost as light on the controls as a Spitfire. It was eager and willing and obedient—in the air. But she still had to get it safely down again. Well, she would worry about that later.

She had plotted her course very carefully—to take her directly over Ludlow. A trip of double nostalgia. While reading History at Cambridge she had done a paper on the Battle of Ludford Bridge and spent a weekend in Ludlow. It was because she knew and loved the castle and town so well that she had been so thrilled when Robin innocently flew her over both on her first flight. They had then gone for lunch in Ludlow afterwards and she had shown him the Castle from the ground. It had been a wonderful afternoon, sunny and breezy with cotton-wool clouds. As the castle came up again now, she circled over the ruins of the great medieval fortress as slowly as she dared in this over-charged aeroplane, indulging her memories.

With her memories still vivid in her mind's eye, she gingerly landed the Airacobra at Hawarden and taxied over to the Watch Office. In 1940 Hawarden had been an improvised RAF station, with the Mess located in the former home of the factory owner. The result was a curious mixture of floral wallpaper, chintz and pastels providing a background for youths in RAF blue who could talk of nothing but Spitfires, Spitfires and Spitfires. Emily, visiting an RAF Station and mess for the first time in her life and on her first weekend with a young man, had been very nervous. For a girl who had never had a serious boyfriend in her life, being the guest of a good-looking RAF Flight Lieutenant in the summer of 1940 was very intimidating. But it had been a lovely weekend—flying with Robin and then dining and dancing with all those high-spirited young men…

Now everything had changed. The factory had expanded beyond recognition and even the ATA had a sprawling brick building, specially designed and built to house this important Pool. There was not a Spitfire anywhere in sight. And all those boys with their excited laughter, silly pranks and boyish blushes were gone. Emily felt a hundred years old. She shouldn't have come.

Lugging her parachute, she made her way over to the Watch Office, to get someone to sign off her delivery chit.

It was at Little Rissington that Philippa's call caught up with her. Just as she was about to go out to the taxi Anson a WAAF came chasing after her, "Mrs. Priestman? Telephone call!"

"Blast. I'll miss the taxi. Is it urgent?"

"I assume so, Ma'am; it was from a Flight Officer."

"Oh." Emily guessed at once it was Philippa—but then again, what if it wasn't? She could hear the taxi Anson starting up its engines and glanced over to it. The last of the other ATA pilots was climbing aboard. But they knew she was scheduled to fly with them and would surely wait for her? She turned and followed the airwoman back to a telephone box. "Second Officer Priestman here. Can I help you?"

"Emily, darling. Teddy has arranged for us to spend the weekend at his cousin's. You have the next two days off, after all, and it would be a pity to spend them around here doing nothing—or rather, moping, as you're inclined to do. So I've packed your things already, and we'll collect you at Little Rissington in about an hour. That's alright, isn't it, darling? Teddy says there's a wedding on at a neighbour's and we're all invited. It will be such a jolly change. Just what you need!"

From the airfield came the unmistakable sound of the Anson revving its engines threateningly this time. Emily could picture the remaining 7 pilots, all tired after the long day of ferrying and looking forward to a quiet beer and a hot meal at home.

"What about poor Penny," Emily protested, "we can't just abandon her for the weekend—"

"Of course not! She's right here with me now, and she'll be thrilled to be in the country with lots of rabbits to chase—"

"But I haven't anything suitable to wear for a wedding, besides—"

"I found two absolutely divine evening dresses in your closet, and I've packed them both so you can choose whichever one you prefer. I've put in a couple of cocktail dresses and high heels, too. You can't back out, Emily! Without you it would be so awkward arriving with Teddy. People might get ideas. If he brings two guests it's entirely different. Surely you see that? Be a sport, Emily, and I'm sure you'll thank me for it before the weekend's over."

Emily found it very hard to say 'no'—seeing as she had no particular reason to—so two hours later she found herself in the back of Teddy's luxurious Bentley. Teddy and Philippa were in very good spirits, apparently from a cocktail or two. For once Teddy was driving himself, and he drove very fast and very aggressively. He was clearly showing off for Philippa, trying to prove he was still a dashing, daring man. Philippa, although she clung to the door handle and occasionally gave little cries of alarm, appeared quite impressed and invigorated by the experience. She cast Teddy ever more admiring glances, which he met with a smile tossed in her direction whenever he could take his eyes off the road. Emily sat cowering in the back seat, with a panting Penny in her lap, hoping they wouldn't have an accident. Might as well have crashed the Airacobra as die in a silly road-accident, she thought to herself.

It was long after sunset, although a luminous light still hung over the western horizon, before they pulled up at a large stone gatehouse. Emily hadn't the faintest idea where they might be. In the dusk on unmarked roads, all that was certain was that they were somewhere southwest of London. Teddy leaned out and pulled a cord. A moment later, the barking of what sounded like a whole pack of hounds split the silence of the countryside. Then an old man tottered out to open the gate, knuckling his forehead as he waved Teddy in before closing the gate behind them.

The drive twisted and turned its way through woods and pasture and over a hump-backed stone bridge across a stream. At last they came to a stop upon crunching gravel before a large, stone manor house that Emily mentally dated as late 15th/early 16th century. A detached chapel was considerably older, possibly Norman.

As the motor cut off, the door opened and another ancient man, this one in livery, came down the moss-covered and cracked steps to open the doors of the car for Emily and Philippa. He bowed as he welcomed them. Behind him other figures appeared and Teddy went forward, shaking hands with the men and kissing the ladies' cheeks. Then he took Philippa on one arm and Emily on the other and introduced them to everyone.

Everyone was dressed in tweeds, woollen cardigans and solid, no-longer-new country clothing. They exuded that rather pleasant provinciality that one expected from *Country Squire* or *Memoirs of a Fox-Hunting Man*, Emily thought. At least the war seemed far away and irrelevant in a society so apparently untouched by events beyond The Hunt. As a crowd they went up the steps into the manor, and here one of the elderly ladies took charge of Emily and Philippa to show them to their rooms.

It was impossible not to be impressed. The room was as large as the entire ground floor of her parent's terraced cottage in Portsmouth. It had a large casement window over looking the park. Heavy carpets, antique furniture, a four-poster bed, and shaded brass lamps completed the furnishings. Everything was old, a little rundown, faded, and threadbare, but solid and gracious. Emily did not think she had ever stayed in such a stately room in her life—not even on her honeymoon. On the bed-stand was a vase with fresh flowers.

The aunt, who had shown her up to her room, also showed her the bath she was to use. She pointed out the hot-water boiler that had to be lit by match a half-hour before the hot water was needed, and reminded Emily not to fill the tub above the eight-inch mark. "A nightcap will be served in the solar in a half an hour," was the woman's parting remark, as she left Emily to 'freshen up.'

Emily went to the door at which Philippa had been deposited and knocked. She wanted guidance on what to wear for a 'nightcap in the solar.' Philippa opened at once smiling. "Isn't it divine! Have you seen the window-seats? It's 15th Century, did you hear? It was built by a knight who was killed fighting for Richard III at Bosworth. Tudor gave it to one of his supporters, but they remained Catholic when he divorced Catherine of Aragon—oh, I must show you!" She pulled Emily deeper into her room and led her over to the corner of the room. A small, semi-circular tower jutted out into the park from here, and the wall adjoining the tower was panelled in dark oak. Philippa showed Emily that in fact there was a door cut in it. She opened this, revealing a stairway plunging down into the darkness in the thickness of the wall. Philippa closed the door again. "This was used as a private chapel and that was the way the priest came and went. Isn't it thrilling?"

Emily had to admit it was, actually. After all, the 15th century had been her period at Cambridge, and she had made an effort to visit houses from the period that were opened to the public. She had shuffled along behind the other tourists to peer across the ropes keeping her out of rooms like these. 'Do not touch!' had been the most common instruction during such tours, and everything had been seen only for a passing second. Now she could take her time touching and even sitting down on the chairs and sleeping in the bed. Yes, it was very thrilling, and she was glad Philippa had dragged her here, so she admitted it. "Thank you, Philippa. It *is* wonderful to get away from our daily lives, and very kind of Teddy to invite us. When is this wedding?"

"Tomorrow early afternoon. We must hurry now to change for that nightcap."

Emily excused herself as early as possible, and retired to her spacious chamber. Penny was 'billeted' with her, of course, and seemed rather unnerved by her strange surroundings. She sniffed about in all the corners and under the furnishings, sneezing frequently, then came and kept very close to Emily as if she didn't like what she had discovered. "What's the matter, Pen? Too many ghosts?"

Penny gazed at her with her big, intelligent eyes but she could not answer in a language Emily understood.

Emily washed, brushed her teeth and hair, and changed into her nightgown. Then she carefully turned off the lights so she could open the black-out curtains to get a look at the park. It was spread out before her in the moonlight, landscaped meticulously: stands of trees, fish-ponds glistening silver, undulating pastures dotted with grazing sheep. Emily perched herself on one of the window seats, her bare feet curled up under her, and gazed across the peaceful countryside, indulging in fantasies of belonging to a different time and age. Anne Neville, perhaps, awaiting word of Barnet Heath...Or—

From far away came the rumble of engines. The scores of windowpanes in their lead casings started to rattle. Emily's heart tightened, and she searched the sky. But the sound was definitely growing, the vibrations increasing; there was a plaintive, desperate note in the whining. Something was wrong with one of those engines, Emily noted professionally. She stiffened, craning her neck now to locate the bomber. It was coming home, but it was wounded. You could hear that, feel it in the very trembling of the air. And it was low. Very low. She found it at last. A Halifax. Flying at not more than 1000 feet, and although it was hard to see in the darkness, Emily thought that the starboard outboard engine was still. That meant that the discordant note came from another engine, and only two were functioning properly. At least it had a clear, moonlit night for a landing, she comforted herself, as she watched it drag itself across the night sky until it was out of sight, praying inarticulately to nobody that they would make it.

Then she shivered and realised her feet were cold. Anne Neville could be conjured up no longer. She went over to the bed. The heavy, embroidered covers had been removed and the bed-covers turned back for her. Because the bed was too high for Penny to jump up, she lifted the dog onto the foot of the bed and slipped in under the cool, starched sheets. She lay back in the vast feather pillows and sank far down into a deep sleep.

She awoke with a start.

It was difficult to tell how long she had been unconscious. The room lay still and unchanged—except for the angle of the shadows cast by the moon. But Emily did not know how to measure them, and was aware only that she did not appear to have moved. But Penny was standing up, snorting in her agitated way, and staring at the far wall.

Emily sat up. "What is it, girl? Have you seen a ghost?"

Penny gave a low, guttural grunt that was the closest she came to barking. Emily, beginning to get frightened, stared at the blank wall the dog was staring at. It was the wall that separated her room from Philippa's. A slight cry penetrated it. Again, louder now, higher pitched. Not a cry for help or a scream, but a cry that was intense, desperate, inarticulate—ecstatic.

Embarrassed, Emily lay back, rolled over on her side, curling herself up into a ball, and pulled the covers over her head. That secret passage! It was all so obvious now. Why had she agreed to be an accomplice to this? She felt hot and humiliated. She nearly suffocated as she kept the covers up so she would not hear.

But she couldn't forget what she had already heard, and she found herself thinking of her wedding night. She had gone to her marriage bed not only a virgin, but a rather sheltered virgin at that. Her knowledge of sex had been very vague, to say the least. She knew the mechanics of reproduction only in the cold biological way that they had been communicated to 14-year-olds at a girl's school. She had overheard conversations at the Salvation Army Mission once or twice, but they had only been snatched, incomplete hints, often in a language or using phrases that meant absolutely nothing to her. She had always planned to read *Lady Chatterly's Lover*, but somehow never found the time.

Then the wedding had gone so terribly wrong. First there had been that interminable waiting at the church, with the time ticking away and her parents insinuating that Robin had stood her up. It was so obvious that she was too plain and too poor and insignificant for a man like him, they whispered among themselves just loud enough for her to hear. They had never believed he'd really marry her...

By the time Robin arrived, the next wedding was assembling and her photographer was gone. The priest kindly asked the next wedding party to wait, and they had generously agreed. It was September 1940, after all, and a request on behalf of a Squadron Leader from Fighter Command was not something to be scorned. In fact, the next couple and their guests had been quite excited by it all. Their guests had all crowded in, and the only photographs Emily had were from the other couple's photographer, who had taken a dozen shots of Robin and herself totally free of charge and sent them to them as a courtesy.

So they had married in front of a church full of strangers, and then when they got to the part about the exchange of rings, Robin didn't have hers! Of course not. It was in the breast pocket of his best tunic back at Tangmere. His grandfather had come to the rescue. He was widowed and wore both his wife's and his own wedding rings on his left hand. He removed his wife's ring and handed it to Robin. Since Robin's hands were bandaged, however, Emily had not been able to put the ring she'd bought him on his finger at all. He pocketed it instead.

The ceremony over, Robin insisted on going back to Tangmere to change into his best blues and collect the suitcase he had packed. Although it meant they were late for dinner, it was actually fortuitous. The Station MO had insisted that Robin would not be fit to fly for at least two weeks, and Robin's leave had been extended accordingly.

But by the time they got to the restaurant for their dinner, they were so late that their table had been given to someone else. They would have let it go, but the manager was outraged that a Squadron Leader of Fighter Command (with bandaged hands, no less!) had been done out of his table, and there was a terrible fuss made. The champagne was on the house after that, and somehow it was terribly late before they finally pulled up at the posh hotel Robin had booked for them.

Emily had never stayed in a hotel like that before. (She'd had very little opportunity to stay in hotels at all.) She felt completely intimidated by the plush carpets, the gilt and crystal and the liveried staff. She found herself whispering and feeling completely out of place—like an impostor. Even more intimidating was the way Robin took everything for granted—and even found this or that to complain about. She couldn't remember what it had been anymore, something minor and to her completely acceptable, but he'd rung the desk almost as soon as they'd reached the room and complained. A maid had come dashing up with profuse apologies. Oh, yes, it was a light bulb that was burnt out. In the morning they were told the entire bill was on 'the House.' "We wouldn't think of charging a Squadron Leader of Fighter Command…"

But between arriving in their suite and checking out the next morning had been the wedding night. It was really only after they were alone together in that strange, luxurious room that Emily had had time to recover from the tension of the day enough to realise she was about to *go to bed* with the semi-stranger beside her. The day they wed, Robin and she had known each other less than four months.

They had an en-suite room, and Emily had taken refuge in the bath-room in a state of near panic. She had never in her life undressed in front of a man, nor ever seen a man completely naked. The closest intimacies she had exchanged with anyone up until that night had been one evening when Robin had unbuttoned her blouse and caressed her breasts with his hands and lips. He himself had remained fully dressed except for removing his tunic and tie. Even after that innocent exchange, Emily had been unable to sleep for hours afterwards. She had been too excited and embarrassed by the incident.

In the fancy bath with its gilt-framed mirrors, marble basins with gold fittings, and chintz-covered stools, Emily had been overcome with sheer terror. She knew she didn't have a pin-up figure. The sight of herself in that vast, well-lit mirror filled her with despair.

She had bought a negligee at considerable expense—cream-coloured satin. She put it on and discovered that she didn't look at all like the movie stars looked in such attire. (It was obviously made for a woman with much larger breasts.) Somehow she still looked like 'plain' Emily Pryce.

And *Robin* was no virgin! Aunt Hattie had warned her that Robin had had a 'serious' affair with a Hungarian Countess while he was competing in air shows internationally—a Jewish Hungarian Countess, whose husband was a notorious gambler but fabulously rich.

Emily had no idea how long she spent in that bathroom, combing out her hair, re-applying make-up, trying to get up her courage, but it had been inordinately long, she knew. At last she could delay no longer. She turned out the light in the bathroom and timidly emerged. Robin lay sprawled out on the double bed in his shorts—sound asleep.

Emily had felt guilty at once. If the day had been difficult and exhausting for her, it had been much worse for Robin. He'd gone on readiness at 6 am, flown a sortie against German bombers at 10.30, bailed out during a dogfight at about 11 am. Gone to hospital. Had to escape from hospital to get to the wedding. It was hardly surprising that he had fallen asleep while waiting for his bride to emerge from the bathroom sometime after midnight on that fateful night. But it was also a bit anti-climactic.

Emily turned out the lights and slipped between the sheets, trying not to disturb Robin, who was snoring lightly. She had lain awake uncertainly for some time after that—but eventually, feeling confused, cheated, guilty, relieved and exhausted—she had fallen asleep.

Robin woke her in the darkness. He was naked. He said nothing, but he removed her expensive negligée and made love to her. She had been very passive and a little bewildered by what was happening to her. She had been a little frightened, too. She wasn't at all sure she was doing everything 'right.' She had felt awkward and inexperienced and even a bit silly. She had not been able to relax, really, and she most certainly had not cried out in ecstasy.

Not that night. It had taken Robin almost the whole of their extended, fortnight honeymoon before she had been uninhibited enough to make a sound.

Robin had been quite pleased with that, almost triumphant—which made her realise how disappointed he had been at first. Poor Robin.

Suddenly Emily was sobbing miserably. She'd never been good enough for him. Never.

It was a beautiful wedding. The bride was not a beauty in herself, but she was radiant in her grandmother's lace and satin gown from the turn of the century, and her groom, a Lieutenant Commander, lit up the whole church when he turned to smile at her as she came up the aisle. Emily felt tears pricking her eyes, but was embarrassed only for a moment, because she noticed the woman beside her was also blinking back tears. Suddenly they were sharing a smile. As they stood to follow the bridal couple out of the church again, the strange woman remarked to Emily, "Isn't it lovely that people can fall in love again? To think that it's just three years since Anne lost Don at Calais. We thought she'd never recover. Poor thing. She was *so* in love. She gives her whole heart when she loves and after losing Don like that, she was utterly shattered."

There was dancing, of course, at the bride's own manor, which had a ballroom large enough to accommodate the hundred guests or more. Music was provided by a local NFS band. By now Emily was feeling morose. She had seen enough of other people being happy: particularly the bride and Philippa. She'd had enough of watching other women dancing with their respective young men. Emily didn't feel like dancing. She didn't want to dance with anyone but Robin. She wanted to get very drunk and cry herself to sleep, but she had no way to get back to the house she was staying in; she had been brought over by Teddy, of course.

And Teddy and Philippa showed not the least interest in calling it a night. Emily didn't understand how they could be so obvious about being seen with one another. First all that nonsense about needing her as a chaperone—or had Philippa only said that to convince her to come along? Maybe that was it, after all. Philippa had just wanted her to get away for these two days. But could she have been any more unhappy alone at home?

"So that's the way the wind is blowing?" a bitter masculine voice said close beside her, causing her to jump. Emily glanced up and was astonished to recognise Wing Commander Yves 'Steeplechase' Gorrel, DFC. He was sipping something alcoholic, and his eyes were riveted on Philippa as she waltzed dreamily in Teddy's arms. His eyes were sunken in his face and the skin around his nose and mouth was red and chapped. Emily caught her breath; he must have been over last night.

"Oh, hello. Where did you come from?" Emily tried to sound light-hearted.

"I live here," he snapped back. Then he seemed to remember his manners and turned to look at her. His eyes looked at her very hard, as if looking for something, and then the corners of his lips curled up, but he did not smile. "Sorry. I guess you didn't know. This is my sister's wedding."

"No, I had no idea. Philippa, or rather Sir Howard, asked me to come along for the weekend, and as I had nothing else going…" She felt very foolish knowing so little about the people whose wedding she was attending, but she was sure the bride's name had not been Gorrell.

As if reading her thoughts, Steeplechase remarked, "it's her second wedding. Her first husband was killed at Calais—subaltern in the Queen Victoria Rifles. We slaughtered them, you know. Orders were to 'Defend Calais to the last.' The bitter defence of Calais was what pinned the Germans down long enough for us to get the bulk of the Army out at Dunkirk, but it was a rotten deal for my 23-year-old brother-in-law. He'd been married six weeks."

"I think it's wonderful she's found someone new," Emily said firmly, focusing on the present and the positive.

"Undoubtedly," he said, without sounding as if he meant it in the least. Emily found herself sympathising with Philippa's preference for the ever polite and charming Teddy.

"So how long has *that* been going on?" Steeplechase wanted to know, nodding toward Philippa and Teddy with his chin.

"I don't know what you mean by 'going on,'" Emily started rather defensively, noting too late that her very defensiveness had given too much away. Steeplechase's gaze was now so penetrating that she felt she was being stripped naked right here in front of everyone.

Then he knocked back whatever it was he was drinking and told her bluntly, "She's a fool. He'll never give up his wife for her. I'm amazed he'd even go this far." Then he was gone as suddenly as he'd come.

Emily was left on her own again, but later she caught sight of Steeplechase filling up with alcohol again, and a shiver went through her.

It was very late before Teddy and Philippa finally took their leave and drove Emily back to Teddy's cousin's place. "A nightcap?" they asked, but it was obvious to Emily that they just wanted to go to bed—together. She excused herself and left them to it.

That night the image that plagued her was the haunting face of Steeplechase pumping himself full of alcohol.

CHAPTER 11

---------------- ▼ ----------------

London, England
June 1943

J.B. was footsore and weary. He sank onto one of the wooden benches facing the Thames and leaned his elbows on his knees. The brown waters of the great river slapped against the embankment and undulated as they oozed toward the invisible sea. It looked just like any other river, J.B. found himself thinking—the Detroit River or the Hudson. He made himself turn around and look back toward the Houses of Parliament. A part of him still couldn't believe he was here. A part of him wished he wasn't. And another part of him didn't care.

Bold pigeons started pecking around at the concrete not far from his feet. They nervously risked getting closer and closer, tipping their heads and greedily eyeing the crushed crumbs of a cookie beside his left foot. With jerky movements they stalked the crumbs, but when Jay sat up straighter they fled in a flutter of wings.

How instinctive it was to fly away from danger, Jay thought. How crazy it was to do what they were doing—fly right into it: 210 mph, 28,000 feet, course whatever. Straight and steady. Wing-tip to wing-tip, tail to tail. Madness!

The RAF had been right about the damage to *Halifax Hooker*, and she'd been patched up and back in the air just three days after that first mission. Since then they'd been to Hamburg, Antwerp and Bremen twice now. So far, Berlin had been the worst. At least they hadn't had serious damage on the other missions, just some shrapnel in the fuselage on one of the Bremen runs. They had been able to keep with the formation all four times. No casualties either. Olds had been replaced with a young kid from Kentucky with the thickest 'Hill Billy' accent Jay had ever heard. But he was a cheerful kid, full of beans really, always claiming he shot down German fighters that hadn't even been in range (according to the other gunners). Still, J.B. liked him, liked the way he'd start off each flight by saying, "Y'all take care of yourselves up there, y'hear!?"

Jay decided to go for a walk. He dragged himself to his feet. God, did he feel old! How could you get feeling this bone weary at just 24? He thought back to all those nights at college, staying up all night to cram for an exam, or the parties they used to have after winning a football game. He never got tired back then. A shower after the game, and then booze at one bar after another, and eventually some girls who were anxious to go all the way with a football player. Now he could hardly drag himself along the streets.

He crossed over the Thames, still lost in thought about how de-energised he was. It was two days since the last Bremen run, and what had that been? Seven hours in the air at the most. Why did he feel as if he was still completely drained of strength and energy?

There wasn't much traffic on the south bank of the Thames—except those bright red busses that towered and swayed their way along the roads. There were hardly any army trucks, and no dark cars with military drivers taking VIPs around, and certainly no private cars left on the street, either—just a lot of bicycles. Jay couldn't get over the way people over here really used the things for *transport.*

Jay noticed that this side of the river had a different feel to it, too. He didn't know what it was, but it was rougher and dirtier and more monotonous. The people looked more run-down, too. The men wore old dungarees and shirts without collars, while the women were in cotton dresses with aprons and scarves, and socks rather than stockings. Men and women were down at the heel, their faces grey. Jay was reminded that this was what he'd expected all of Britain to be like before he came.

A gang of young kids, boys of 8 or 9, sighted him. They came running up—bare knees, plastic sandals, dirty socks. "Got any gum, chum?" "Got any sweets, Mister?" "Chocolate, mate?" Jay emptied his pockets for them and continued.

The streets all looked the same: houses crammed together with no front lawns or gardens or trees. Brick and concrete dark with the grime of what looked like a hundred years of coal-dust. It wasn't even as if the war were to blame for this gloomy scene. J.B. was reminded of a Charles Dickens novel. And then he came to a dead halt. In the middle of a row of identical houses with their monotonous brick facades there was a heap of rubble fronted by a deep hole. Two houses were just gone—like a missing tooth in a smile.

He'd been over to St. Paul's earlier and stared awe-struck at the damage all around it. But that had been different. That had been a vast field of ruin from which the great Cathedral rose up defiant and proud. That had been war: a violent struggle between two fierce and proud nations, a struggle between good and evil—with the sombre grace of Wren's cathedral symbolising God and Good. This was so much more—well—personal. And a little pathetic, too.

After he'd recovered from his surprise, Jay edged closer to the bombsite. It was roped off and a hand-painted sign warned 'stay clear.' But he was fascinated. You could see into a cellar where a toilet basin lay on its side, cracked but intact. You could see broken pipes pointing into nothingness. You could see rusted tools and bits of clothing so tattered they weren't worth salvaging. Broken pottery lay scattered about, but one cup with a flower painted on it sat undamaged, as if waiting for someone to take it in her hand again. The head of a doll stared up at him with blank eyes in its dirty, round face. Jay turned and walked away, his hands in his pockets.

J.B. had agreed to meet up with Dan, Alan Pearson and Patrick Brown at Covent Garden to go to a play together. Since that day they'd both been lost together, the pilots and navigators of the *Hooker* and Pearson's ship, *Buckeye Betty*, did a lot together. Because J.B. had wandered too far into Southwark, he was the last to arrive.

The others hailed him with a cheer. Pat said, "Hey, we were beginning to think you'd stood us up!"

"Yeah, like maybe something better had come along." Alan winked at him.

J.B. shook his head. "What could be better than being with a bunch of good buddies? Have you decided what we're going to see?"

"Well, sort of. A lot of shows are sold out. The only things we could get tickets for were some Shakespeare play—"

"*Macbeth,*" Dan supplied.

"Yeah, *Macbeth,* or *The Importance of Being Earnest* or *HMS Pinafore.*"

Jay sat on the vacant stool they'd saved for him. He thought he ought to go see *Macbeth* so he could write to Kathy about it. She'd be impressed if he saw a Shakespeare play here in London, but already Alan was saying, "I don't want to

go to something heavy like *Macbeth*. Let's go to either the comedy or the musical."

"Let's do the musical," Pat urged. "There'll be more girls in it."

"Maybe even lightly clad." Alan suggested grinning.

"*HMS Pinafore* is fine with me," Dan agreed, so it was settled.

It was a great performance. J.B. was sure he'd never seen such wonderful cos-
tumes or dancing nor heard such clear singing in his life. The one night he'd
spent in New York City, they'd gone to Radio City Musical Hall rather than a
real show. With the rest of the audience, they gave the cast enthusiastic applause
for at least five minutes, and then went out into an evening that was still not
completely dark. The black-out was already in effect, however, and so the city
was dark against the luminous blue sky.

Patrick had 'got the dope' about where to go after the theatre and they ended
up in a restaurant with dance band where, according to Pat, "all the starlets come
after a show—just as soon as they get changed out of their stage make-up and
stuff."

The restaurant was fairly crowded and they had to wait twenty minutes for a
table, but except for being hungry they didn't really mind. It was fun watching
the people coming and going, because the female guests were turned out in their
finery. "There sure are some great-looking dames over here," Alan declared,
watching appreciatively as a slender woman in a well-fitted evening dress which
left her back naked to the waist was escorted by a Naval officer into the dining
room. She wore a mink stole looped over her arms and long gloves. The men in
the room were almost without exception in uniform—at least the men under 40
were.

The American airmen were taken to a table with a good view of the dance
floor, and that was entertainment as welcome as the musical had been. There
really were a lot of attractive women here, Jay admitted to himself. The menu was
less satisfying. There seemed to be an awful lot of innards and other oddities on it
that J.B. didn't even want to try. He finally settled on ox-tail soup, followed by
something with a fancy French name that the waiter said was a kind of wild
'fowl.' When it arrived it was the scrawniest bird Jay had ever laid eyes on, and he
had his work cut out for him trying to scrape scraps of flesh off its many, tiny
bones.

"Pigeon is what I'd call that," Patrick decided, and J.B. was inclined to agree.
They laughed.

"So where are all these starlets you promised me, boy?" Alan complained to his
navigator.

Pat jerked his head toward a table on the other side of the dance floor. "Don't you recognise those four girls over there? They were all in the chorus."

"They were?" J.B. and Alan looked over harder. It was hard to tell. But then again, maybe Pat was right. After all, they were sitting together as a group without any escorts to be seen—as if they'd just come over as a group from the theatre. They were also all very attractive and meticulously made-up and coifed.

"So what are we waiting for?" Alan wanted to know.

"The blonde's mine," Pat told him, straightening his tie and starting to get to his feet.

The others followed him. Alan made a bee-line for the black-haired beauty opposite the blonde, and J.B. took the red-head. "Hi," Alan opened in best American tradition. "I'm Alan Pearson from Pocahontas, Iowa, and I was wondering if you'd care for a dance."

It was one of the other girls, who appeared a bit older than the others, who answered. "We're rather tired and thirsty, actually," she said, "but if you can find some extra chairs, why don't you join us for a few minutes?"

They learned that the girls were part of an organisation called ENSA, Entertainment National Service Association. They weren't performing in *HMS Pinafore*, but rather in the process of practising and perfecting their variety routine before being 'deployed' by the government to various locations to entertain the troops or war workers. The girls could all dance very well, and they were smooth professionals when it came to small talk and being charming.

All in all, it was a nice evening, but it wasn't like being with Kathy, Jay thought wistfully after they'd seen the girls back to their hotel just after 1 am. Patrick and one of the girls exchanged addresses and promised to try to meet up again, but J.B. was content to just say good-bye. Just ships passing in the night…

They pulled the curtains back. It was Berlin again. Jay hated himself for it, but his stomach turned over and his hands started sweating. Bochanek was droning on and on about something, and Jay couldn't concentrate. He didn't want to go back to Berlin. He was *afraid* to go back to Berlin. That's how bad it was, he was afraid. His mouth was dry.

This time he was one of the guys who decided to go to the latrine again before going out to the ship. Not that he needed to, really. Silly, this feeling of nervousness that confused even your most fundamental functions. At *Halifax Hooker* he went through the ground check with Fuentes. Tires, fuel vents, pitot head, the patches over the holes in the fuselage…The air stank of aviation fuel, dope and something else J.B. couldn't put his finger on—rotting hay, maybe, from the field beyond the fence? His own sweat stank, too, as he slow-boiled inside all his flying clothes here on the ground.

Up into the cockpit. Tony had the checklist ready beside him. The rest of the crew was still restless, moving about in the fuselage. Jay was late. Other ships were starting up. "Number One engine."

"Contact."

It backfired badly—like a pistol shot—and smoke gushed out of it. For a second Jay thought it wasn't going to start. For a second he thought they were going to have a mechanical problem and have to scratch. For a second he was relieved. Then he was angry at himself. "Goddamn it!"

On the second try the engine caught and roared into life. He throttled back a bit, watched it out of his window. It settled down and ran smoothly. "Number Two."

When all four were running smoothly and the ship trembled in that contented way it did when all was well, Jay pulled his head-set over his cap and pressed the mike. He called to each of the crewmen in turn. They all checked in. "OK, Gang, here we go. Number six—good ol' Berlin."

"Y'all take care of yourselves up there, y'hear," the Kentucky Kid replied cheerfully.

They eased out onto the taxiway and fell in behind another B-17 rolling heavily toward the start of the runway. Jay glanced at the sky: scattered cloud at 8,000. The windsock showed a gusty wind that was quartering the runway. He turned onto the runway and paused, watching the B-17 ahead very slowly lift off the concrete. It seemed to rise hardly at all, its left wing a little low as if it wasn't trimmed quite properly. Tony looked over at Jay questioningly.

OK. OK. He eased the throttles forward, and they started to roll forward, gradually gaining speed. The faithful ship trembled more and more intensely. The tail became light. The trembling was almost unbearable. And gently and almost imperceptibly, they left the two-dimensional world behind.

The good weather held all the way this time. The coast of Holland, Jutland, the Baltic Coast of Germany were spread out like a map below them. The sun glinted off the rotating propellers of a thousand engines, and off the little panes of glass on the cockpit windows and the bombardier's bays.

Today they were flying right beside Alan Pearson in his ship, *Buckeye Betty*. There was something reassuring about that. Once or twice, Jay looked over and saw Alan's co-pilot, Bill Howden, look back. He gave Bill a thumbs up. Bill turned to Alan, who leaned forward and returned the gesture to J.B.

Perfect visibility. For fighters, too, of course. Jay kept looking for them, almost wishing they would come just to get it over with. Looking about made it impossible to hold perfect formation, and the *Hooker* floated up and down and drifted to the left or the right in response to her pilot's unease.

This time they came in from head on. There seemed almost no warning. Suddenly one of the lead planes seemed to leap up, then settle down again—but with flames shooting out of its starboard-outboard engine. The next second J.B. saw two fighters coming straight at them and heard Tony call it out: "Fighters 12 o'clock level!" They were firing as they came. The ships ahead of him were firing back at them, but they didn't get much of a chance. The fighters were coming flat out. For a horrible instant, Jay thought they were going to crash. Jay shoved the control column forward and put the nose down. Bullets ripped along the roof of the B-17 just behind the top of his head.

A cry of surprise came from the upper turret and then silence. Well, not really. The right waist gunner was cursing and the tail gun was chattering, while the engines were grumbling as they always did. But the upper turret was silent.

"Logan! Are you OK?"

No answer.

"Goddamn it! Logan! Answer me! Are you OK?"

The Germans were sure to come back again. They never stopped their attacks until they were out of ammo or fuel.

"Roach! Get up to the Upper Turret and see what's happened to Logan."

"Yes, sir."

Ahead, more of the small dark 'beetles' were curving around for a frontal attack. Buzz was calling them out: "They're at 10 o'clock. Turning. Coming in at 9'oclock."

"OK. I got 'em!" the right waist gunner called out.

Jay opened and closed his hands on the control column, trying to uncramp them. God, he hated this. His mouth was dry; the oxygen tasted absolutely horrible—metallic.

The next two fighters were further off to the left. J.B. could follow their progress down the length of the formation.

"Radio to Pilot! Logan's—ah—Logan's dead, sir."

"Are you sure?"

"Ah—yes, sir. He's sort of blocking the way into the turret."

"Is the gun operable?"

"Ah—I don't think so, sir. I can't get to it."

"Well, find out, for God's sake! It's the most powerful gun we've got, and we haven't even got to Berlin yet."

What followed was not words, but sound—like someone being sick. Tony and J.B. looked at one another. J.B. gestured with his head for Tony to go back and find out what was going on. Tony unstrapped himself, took bottled oxygen and climbed over his seat. J.B. watched the next pair of fighters rake the length of the formation just to the right of them.

This is crazy, just plum crazy, Jay thought as he sat there, unable to do anything else but hold his course and speed, waiting for the next blow. For some reason it didn't come. As suddenly as they'd come, the fighters were gone.

Tony climbed back into his seat. He looked very pale. Jay looked at him hard. Tony held up his arms. His sleeves and gloves were soaked in blood. Apparently Logan's. Tony looked pointedly out his right-hand window.

The flak over Berlin was as bad as the last time. It straddled them laterally and vertically. They were shaken, slammed up and down. Several times the air that held them up seemed to have been sucked away and they dropped like a stone. A ship off their starboard bows took a direct hit that severed the tail off it. The tail fell away, a 'chute blossoming out of it as it tumbled down, but the fuselage flew on as if oblivious to what had happened to it for a moment or two. Then the nose went down into a dive and Jay lost sight of it.

The formation was now sinking down toward that ugly mass of concrete, brick and tiles. On this bright sunny day, Jay was aware of more green in the city and some pretty big lakes, but the houses and streets were grey, the roofs a dirty red-grey. Smoke was pouring out of factory chimneys, and soon the first bombs started sending up little puffs and then great gushes of black smoke. Buzz took command of the ship as they went into their bomb run.

Now the flak was really bad. Jay found himself gritting his teeth and clenching his hands hard to keep himself from taking evasive action. He glanced to his left looking for reassurance, and saw it happen. He saw a burst of flak explode right beside *Buckeye Betty's* nose. Pat was obliterated instantly. The B-17 flipped up onto her starboard wing, and the port wing caught fire at once. Jay was looking straight into the cockpit. He could see that Alan was slumped forward over the control column, a hole blown into the cockpit on his side, and he could see Bill struggling valiantly, trying vainly to regain control of the ship. Jay could *see* him reach forward and try to drag Alan off his control column, but the dead weight of his captain was too great for the co-pilot. Then Jay could see no more because they had slipped under the *Hooker*, and the smoke from the wounded bomber seemed to engulf him.

"Jesus Christ!" Buzz screamed, and at the same instant Jay felt a thud and the *Hooker* bucked violently.

J.B. and Tony both grabbed the controls in panic. They regained control of the aircraft, but you could feel something was not right.

"What happened? What was that?" The voices came in from all around. J.B. pressed his own mike. "Pilot to Bombardier, what happened?"

"Bombs away!" It was Dan, not Buzz's voice.

"What happened down there?" J.B. shouted into the mike as he started pulling them up.

"*Buckeye Betty's* wing-tip hit us. The glass is bashed in. Buzz is hurt."

"How bad?"

"I don't know yet. The Norton bombsite is gone too."

"OK. Report to me when you know."

They were still flying through flak, of course, but they were gaining altitude again and turning for home. Jay throttled forward, and with gratitude felt the great bomber respond. The wind coming through the open nose disrupted the aerodynamics somewhat, made it harder to keep course and altitude and trim, but it was not a mortal injury, Jay could sense that. If nothing else happened, they should make it home. That was all he dared think about at the moment: getting them home.

As they came onto the circuit, Tony fired a flare to indicate 'wounded on board,' and they were given priority landing. J.B. lined up with the runway and eased down to earth. The wheels touched with an audible screech and they were down, rolling forward at almost 100 mph. Jay gently applied the brakes and slowed them down to turn off the runway at the end. Overhead a score of B-17s circled, awaiting their turn to land.

They rolled to a halt at their own hardstand, and an ambulance wailed up to greet them. J.B. unstrapped himself and tore his headset off. He clambered stiffly over the back of his seat. He was completely exhausted. He didn't have an ounce of energy left. He could hardly find the strength to drop down and check on the damage to the nose or crawl back to see the damage to the upper turret. Below the turret, Logan's body was laid out on the floor with his flight jacket covering what was left of his head and neck. Jay didn't lift the jacket; he just glanced up at the hole in the turret and noted the dried blood that covered everything. Then he dropped out by the aft hatch and joined the rest of the crew, watching as the stretcher with Buzz on it was shoved into the waiting ambulance.

Dan had diagnosed broken bones. Buzz had flung himself over to the side when he saw the wing-tip was going to hit them. This or the collision itself had knocked him so hard against the side of the plane that he'd apparently smashed his shoulder, upper arm or collar bone in the process. He was in pain and unable to move his right arm or shoulder, but he was conscious. Dan and Roach had fixed him up in a sort of sling, and given him a shot of morphine. He'd make it.

Alan and Patrick…

J.B. couldn't grasp it. Just two nights ago they'd been in London together—*HMS Pinafore*, dancing with those nice girls.

The crew truck pulled up. "All aboard who's going aboard," the driver called out.

Numbly the crew of the *Hooker* climbed aboard. No one spoke. Roach was hugging himself as if trying to hide the bloodstains left from pulling Logan out of the turret. The smell of vomit came from his flying boots.

They had to debrief. The Intelligence Officer wanted to know exactly when the fighters had struck. Dan answered that one. What tactics had they used? Head-on attacks in pairs, J.B. told him. Tony nodded assent. What was the flak like over the target?

"Fucking awful! What the hell do you expect?!"

"How many ships are back?" J.B. countered the questions with one of his own.

"15 have landed here. Two elsewhere. Three are still missing."

"*Buckeye Betty* didn't make it. You know that, don't you?"

"No. It's missing in my books."

"Yeah, well you can scratch it." J.B. heard himself speak and didn't even recognise his own voice. It was as if someone else was speaking, as if he was listening to someone else speaking. Someone who was hard and cold. It hurt to talk, too. His throat and mouth were so dry.

"Do you want to report what happened?" the Intelligence officer asked softly. He was a Major. Not really a bad type, just too old and fat for flying in this war. In fact, he wasn't a pilot at all. J.B. thought he'd heard he'd been a high-school teacher before the war. Something like that.

"Flak during the bomb run. Blew the nose off her. Killed the bombardier and navigator instantly. Probably the pilot, too. Tore open the cockpit and put the wing on fire."

"Could someone have got out?"

J.B. shrugged. "Maybe the guys in the tail." Maybe Bill, too, J.B. told himself. But not Alan. Not Pat.

They were released. Mission dinner. Steak and French Fries and corn on the cob. They shuffled along the cafeteria line, taking what was handed out to them. Coke or Orange Squash. They sat down at their table—and there were only three instead of eight of them. Dan, Tony and J.B. looked at one another, their faces still red from the oxygen masks.

"Jesus," Tony said for all them, and then they ate in silence.

CHAPTER 12

▼

Windsor, England
June 1943

Philippa had brought two other WAAF officers with her, and they were all out on the terrace. You could hear the faint, high-pitched tinkle of frequent volleys of laughter from anywhere in the house. It was a happy sound and drew Emily like a moth to a light. She'd spent most of the day waiting on an A-1 Priority Wait aircraft that *had* to be delivered at the first opportunity, but which had been undergoing some kind of top-secret modification that had evidently taken longer than expected. Because the pilot of an A-1 priority aircraft had to wait on the aircraft and could not do anything else until the aircraft had been delivered, Emily had eaten both dinner and tea at the Maintenance Unit before finally being able to take off with her delivery. As a result, she had not been terribly hungry on arriving home, and had gone up to nap instead. The sound of Philippa and her friends' laughter drew her back downstairs and out onto the terrace.

"Emily! I'm so glad you've joined us!" Philippa declared with every evidence of sincerity. "In fact, I was going to wake you, if you didn't come down on your own soon. You remember Grace and Eileen?" She referred to her two companions, and the three young women exchanged smiles and greetings. But by now Emily's attention was drawn to the fourth woman.

She was wearing a scarf over her head like the pictures you saw of East European refugees. She wore a faded cotton print dress that might well have come from charity, as it did not fit her well. She was very thin with claw-like hands.

Her colouring was dark and her skin was leathery. Her black eyes looked very hard at Emily from a face gouged with deep lines. They were very alert eyes.

"This is Madame Rose," Philippa introduced her to a suppressed giggle from the other girls. "She's a Gypsy and she's come to tell our fortunes. You must ask her about your husband."

Emily felt herself go rigid at once. It was bad enough living with the uncertainty and Colin's silly notions about telepathy without letting herself get roiled up by some charlatan with vague and mysterious—but undoubtedly fictional—predictions of everything turning out alright in the end. She did not believe in this kind of nonsense, Tarot cards and crystal balls! Such things were so obviously cheap tricks that she was genuinely shocked to think Philippa would waste her money on it. In fact, she was rather irritated to have such a dubious character in her house—even if the woman didn't look like the usual fat, oily Gypsy they portrayed in the films.

Emily was never very good at disguising her feelings, so Philippa had already seen the look of disapproval cross her face and started urging her "not to be a spoil-sport."

But before Philippa could say very much, 'Madame Rose' herself said in a low, melodic and yet guttural voice, "The man who waited for you all day is back safe."

"What do you mean?" Emily snapped, utterly outraged. How could this woman *possibly* know that there had been an Army commando waiting all day for the delivery of her Priority aircraft with its special equipment?

"He has made the delivery to his friends and he is back safe." The Gypsy insisted solemnly.

Emily sat down in confusion, staring at the woman. She *couldn't* know about it. Had she read Emily's mind? But Emily herself didn't know if he was *delivering* something rather than being dropped over enemy lines on a mission of his own. Maybe he had been. How could she know that what the Gypsy said was true? But the very fact that she had known about the *waiting* shook Emily's self-assurance enough to silence her; she hadn't even told Philippa about it.

"You see?" Philippa declared with evident satisfaction. "Madame Rose is very good. She's been telling us all sorts of fascinating things."

"I'm going to marry a tall, blond foreigner," one of the other girls declared enthusiastically, but Emily saw the Gypsy woman drop her eyes hastily. It was irrational, but Emily sensed instantly that she had been lying—or, more kindly, simply saying what the WAAF wanted to hear. But it had been different about the Commando. Emily had not wanted to hear that; she had not asked about it or expected it. How could she have known?

"And I'm *not* going to marry my Danny, it would appear," the other WAAF sighed, but without appearing too upset about it.

"And what about you, Philippa?" Emily asked.

"We were just about to start," Philippa declared happily, full of anticipation.

Madame Rose was staring at Emily. "Please. May I see your hand?"

"My hand?"

"She reads palms," one of the others explained.

"No, no. I'm not interested." Emily shook her head vigorously and folded her hands in her lap to underscore the point.

"Here!" Philippa eagerly held out her own hand for the palmist, but the Gypsy was still gazing at Emily. "Please. I charge *you* nothing. Let me see your hand."

Emily shook her head. "Read Philippa's hand. She wants you to."

The Gypsy woman's expression was pained. She took Philippa's hand and gazed into the palm, but she shook her head several times. She glanced up at Emily. "I have a message for you. Please, just let me hold your hand."

"No, I'm not interested." Emily was now clutching her hands together.

"Do mine!" Philippa insisted, beginning to get annoyed. "I'm the one paying you, after all."

The Gypsy woman sighed and stared long and hard at Philippa's hand. "I see a boat on waves. No. It is an aeroplane. Yes, a large, heavy aeroplane with wings, but it is lying on water. There are large waves, and the aeroplane is half submerged. There are two men clinging to it. One of them is wounded badly."

Philippa jerked her hand away and stood up all in one motion. She stood for a second staring in horror at the Gypsy, and then turned and fled. The other two WAAFs gazed after her in astonishment.

Emily just gazed at the Gypsy woman.

The Gypsy dropped her eyes again and her cheeks were flushed.

"That was cruel," Emily commented after a moment, very softly. She did not understand how this woman could know about Philippa's brother, but she was now sure that she did.

The Gypsy woman raised her head and met Emily's eyes. "I have a message for you. I cannot concentrate on other things when that happens. It does not often happen—a clear message, in words."

"Alright." Emily gave the Gypsy her hand. She was very tense now.

The Gypsy held her hand, but she did not make any pretence of reading the lines in it. She just held it and looked straight into Emily's face. Her black eyes were intense but they looked inward rather than outward. When she spoke it was in a different voice; that is, it was her voice, but the intonation and inflection were different—slower and more precise—than for her natural speech. She said: "The field is lost in fog. I must go on. Where I can safely land, I do not know. Perhaps no more on earth. My thoughts fly on—to you. Wherever you may be, I will be, too—always." She stopped speaking. The look in her eyes changed. She was looking at Emily again, watching for a reaction.

Emily was still holding her breath. Then she shook her head sharply, and pulled her hand back, a little roughly. "No. That cannot be. It doesn't make sense," she told the Gypsy categorically. "There was no fog. He crashed. The whole wing *saw* him crash. He did *not* have to fly on."

The Gypsy looked disappointed, but she took a deep breath and declared: "That is the message. I cannot change it. It is very, very clear—clearer than almost anything I have ever received. Perhaps the message is from someone other than you think?"

"Who else should it be from other than my missing husband? Who else would want to be with me always?"

The Gypsy shook her head. "I do not know. I never know where the messages come from. I am only a medium—like a telephone wire. I know nothing about who or why."

Philippa was back. She returned to her seat with great dignity. "I'm sorry. You took me by surprise. Can we continue?"

The Gypsy gave Emily a little, sad smile, and then—willingly—took Philippa's hand. "I see two men in your life."

"Two?"

"Yes, two. One old, one—I cannot say 'young.' He is young in years but he is old, too."

"I see," Philippa quipped; "two old men are in love with me. Is that all?"

The Gypsy laughed at that—a real laugh. Emily saw her eyes flicker with amusement, and the creases around her eyes deepened for a second or two. Then she looked into Philippa's hand again and declared: "No, that is not all. You have many admirers. Many who wish you well. But love…love is from the famous man."

The other WAAFs at once started congratulating Philippa, calling her Lady Philippa. Emily thought they were being hasty—after all, Steeplechase was a famous man, too, arguably more famous than Sir Howard. Philippa herself also looked quite pleased, however, and asked eagerly, "Do you see a wedding?"

The Gypsy frowned. She turned Philippa's hand this way and that. Emily, watching her very intently, thought she was playing for time. At last she shook her head and replied, "A wedding, certainly, but not soon. Not before the man in the floating plane is back."

"What?"

"The man on the plane in the water."

"My brother is dead," Philippa declared harshly, suddenly stiff again.

"Yes, but the other man, he will come back."

"I don't understand."

The Gypsy shrugged. "I cannot explain what I see. I only see it."

Not long afterwards, the Gypsy woman stood to leave. Philippa and the other two WAAFs each paid her a guinea, but she did not ask for money from Emily and Emily did not offer it. Emily was still confused by what had happened. She saw the Gypsy out.

At the door, Emily went to shake hands, but the woman held her hand and wouldn't let it go. She looked up into Emily's eyes (she was much shorter than Emily). "You will be happy again. You will travel halfway around the world and see much. You will have children."

Emily was disturbed and confused. She wanted to believe the Gypsy, but at the same time was rather ashamed to do so. It made her no better than all the other silly girls who read their horoscope or played with Tarot cards. These 'fortune tellers' always promised only good.

Seeing the doubt in her eyes, the Gypsy put her second hand over Emily's and declared with still greater intensity, "Truly, you will be happy again, and deeply loved—far more than your pretty, rich friends." She indicated with a little jerk of her head the women they had left behind.

Emily shook her head in confusion and drew her hand away. She did not want to be happy at Philippa's expense. She just wanted Robin back.

RAF Wattisham
June, 1943

It had been a very wearying day because morning fog had delayed everyone getting started, and they had spent the rest of the day trying to catch up, skipping all meals in the process and living off chocolate bars instead. Then Emily's last delivery, an Oxford, developed an engine problem on take-off. She circled around and brought it back immediately. The ground crew had heard the engine as she circuited and were waiting for her. They set to work on it at once, at first very cheerily, certain they knew just what the problem was. An hour and a half later they admitted the problem was apparently much more serious than they initially thought and repairs were going to take some time. It was by then 7 pm and since this particular aircraft was not an A-1 Priority Wait, Emily didn't have to wait for it overnight. But she also had no transport home and was stuck out in the middle of Cambridgeshire.

Lugging her parachute with her and calculating that it was going to take her at least 4 hours by train to get home, she went to the Operations Room to place a call into White Waltham and explain her predicament. Maybe, just maybe, someone else was flying by and could drop down and collect her?

"Oh, dear," the Operations Officer declared solicitously, "I'm afraid there's nothing we can do for you. You'll just have to find your way home as best you can. But, Mrs. Priestman, I do have a message here for you. Do you have something to write a number down?" Emily found pen and paper and told the Operations Officer to go ahead. "You've been asked to call a certain Lieutenant Baronowsky at the following number."

"Baron what? I don't know any Barons."

"No, no. Not Baron Ovsky, Baronowsky—all one word."

"Oh."

"He's called three times. Most persistent, actually. He seemed to think we might not pass on the message to you" (the Operations Officer was obviously offended by the insinuation), "so you will call him, won't you?"

"I suppose I will. Baronowsky, you say?"

"Yes, Polish name, but an American, presumably—by his accent and rank, I mean."

At last it dawned on Emily who it must be. What could he possibly want with her? She thanked the Operations Officer and after a moment's hesitation, decided to get the call to Baronowsky over with—otherwise she'd spend the whole evening wondering what it was he wanted. She *certainly* wasn't going out with him, if that's what he thought. But that couldn't be it, or he would have called shortly after they'd nearly killed one another.

She put a call through to the number given her and heard a harsh, twangy voice on the other end rattle off a bunch of letters and numbers that meant nothing to her. She answered with as much authority and dignity as she could muster, very anxious to convey that this was NOT a personal call: "This is Second Officer Priestman of the Air Transport Auxiliary calling from RAF Wattisham. I was requested to return the call of a certain Lieutenant Baronowsky. Can you connect me?"

"Yeah, just a minute, Ma'am."

After what seemed like a very long time, a young male voice asked: "Hello? This is Lieutenant Baronowky. Who's there?"

"This is Second Officer Priestman. You left a message for me at White Waltham, asking me to return your call."

"Yes! Yes! Ah—Geeze. I'm sorry. Ah—" Jay was completely flustered. After calling three times and getting nothing but a very proper British brush-off, he'd never expected Emily to call. Certainly, not when he was summoned to take a call from the RAF. "They said you were calling from RAF Wattisham, so I thought it must be about something else," he blurted out.

"I *am* calling from RAF Wattisham, but I have to take ground transport back home, so I'm in a bit of a hurry. What can I do for you?"

"You're at Wattisham? But that's just a couple miles away. Look, let me come get you. I'll drive you home." Jay couldn't believe his luck. Wattisham wasn't more than 20 miles away. All he had to do was get a jeep out of the motor pool and the gas coupons.

"Good heavens, that's halfway across the country, and quite unnecessary. Just what were you calling about?"

"I wanted to take you to dinner or something—just try to make up for what happened—"

"That really isn't necessary. You apologized and it's all forgiven and forgotten."

"*I* haven't forgotten." Jay insisted, desperate to keep her from hanging up. The sound of her voice—her proximity—filled him with a desperate need to see her—though he couldn't for the life of him have explained why. He simply felt he *had* to see her again. "You don't know how often I think about you—"

"You shouldn't. I'm married. Find yourself another girlfriend—"

"I have a fiancée at home in Michigan, and those RAF guys the day we met told me about your husband. Look, I'm not trying to put the moves on you or anything. I don't expect you to start dating me or whatever. I just want to take you out to dinner and then, if it helps you, drive you home. What's wrong with that?"

Nothing, Emily's brain said. There was absolutely nothing wrong with going to dinner and letting him drive her home. How many, many times in the last two years had she had lifts (by air and land) from men she'd never met before? What difference did it make that this one happened to be American? And she was ravenous. She really, really could use dinner and then being driven home right to her doorstep, rather than dragging her parachute on and off trains and busses and trying to snatch some awful, cold food in a WVS or Sally Ann canteen. Part of her still resisted Jay's offer, but not strongly enough to stop her. "Are you sure you can drive me all the way to Windsor? It will take hours."

"I can do it," Jay declared firmly, not knowing how he was going to get a jeep or gas or find his way around on unmarked roads or anything else.

"I must warn you that I'm very, very hungry. I haven't had a thing since breakfast and it would be good to have a hot meal before we set out."

"I'll pick you up in 30 minutes."

"You know the way here?"

"Yes, no problem," Jay lied.

"Alright. I'll wait out at the gate house," Emily said in a tone of voice that suggested she wasn't at all sure she would really go through with this.

"Wait for me!" Jay urged desperately. "I'll be there as soon as I can."

"Alright. Cheerio." Emily hung up and stood biting her lower lip in confusion. Then with a little shrug she went and changed into her skirt, stockings and shoes, and stuffed her flight jacket, helmet and flying boots into her tote bag. After that she went out and waited at the gatehouse, chatting to the duty Sergeant and getting suggestions on a place for dinner.

At last Jay arrived. He drove up at a ridiculous speed, screeched to a halt, jumped out and ran up to the gatehouse, apologizing even before he said 'hello.' "I'm sorry I'm late. I got a little lost. I had to ask for directions twice. I'm sorry."

"It's quite alright," Emily assured him, giving him her hand to shake. "I didn't really think you could be here in half an hour. The Sergeant has kindly suggested the *Pig and Whistle* as the best place for a nice meal." Emily indicated the Sergeant on duty, and with a 'thanks' and a wave, she started for the jeep.

Jay leaped to open the door for her, and then ran around to the other side. "Remind me to keep left, please. Otherwise, I might drive on the wrong side of the road. I came close to killing myself at least three times on the way here," Jay admitted, aware that he was talking much too fast and much too loosely. How the hell was he ever going to impress this classy lady if he admitted he got lost and didn't know what side of the road to drive on?

"Maybe I should drive?" Emily suggested, simply out of a strong sense of self-preservation.

Jay stopped just as he was about to turn the key in the ignition and looked over at her. God, she looked good! Ever since she'd called he'd been frantically running around changing into his best uniform and shaving while Tony got the jeep organised for him. (Tony knew all about pulling the right strings and had done it in 10 minutes flat with only one comment: "You owe me one, buddy.") Jay knew he was going to be late and so he'd driven like a madman, and it was no joke that he'd nearly had three accidents on the way over—and the whole time he'd been half-certain Emily wasn't going to wait for him. He kept thinking she would probably change her mind, and be gone when he arrived. He knew he'd never have another chance like this—when she was near to Beauchamp Rodding and in need of a meal and a lift.

And now she was there next to him in that trim, dark-blue uniform with the golden wings and the thin gold rank rings, and he couldn't believe it. His heart was battering at his chest—and it wasn't all from rushing or the adrenaline of the car-crashes he'd barely avoided. Jay was suddenly aware that he'd never been attracted to any woman like this in his life. What was Kathy compared to this?

With cruel clarity he saw Kathy as a spoilt little girl. Kathy would never, *never* have offered to drive. That would have been beneath her dignity, and she would have looked down on him for not being 'man' enough to do 'what was right.'

Emily, seeing only his hesitation, thought she had offended his masculinity and cajoled gently. "It really does make more sense for me to get us both safely where we want to go, than for you to get us both killed. We've tried that once already, after all."

"We sure have, Ma'am." Jay opened his door and jumped out, walked around the front of the jeep while Emily walked around the back. She got in and quickly ascertained her feet couldn't reach the pedals.

Jay leaned forward to help her adjust the seat, but she was still reaching. "No problem. Just stuff my parachute pack behind my back," Emily ordered, and Jay obliged. Then she familiarised herself with the jeep as if she were in a cockpit. "Let's see. Headlights? High lights? Windscreen wipers? Turn indicators? Horn?"

Jay responded to each question as if they were doing the cockpit checklist before take-off. They both fell into the roles without thinking about it, and yet all the while Jay felt his admiration for her growing. He liked the competent way she went about it. Some girls, Barb for example, would have just roared off to show they were as good as any man—and cracked up at the next corner because they hit the wipers rather than the lights.

At last Emily decided she was as ready as she was ever going to be, and after one last squiggle to get as comfortable as possible, she reached for the key to the ignition.

"Contact," Jay said.

She tossed him a smile—the first she'd ever given him—and they started off.

Emily had been given careful directions to the *Pig and Whistle*. They found it readily, and pulled into the nearly full parking lot. Inside most of the guests were in Air Force blue. They glanced over curiously at the ATA and USAAF, but then went back to their own discussions. Emily, more familiar with pubs than Jay, led the way toward a more secluded and quiet room at the back. She settled herself onto a sofa under the window with a little, unconscious sigh of relief. She really was very, very hungry, and the scents from the kitchen here were mouth-watering.

After the bustle of getting drinks and ordering their meal, Jay at last found himself sitting opposite Emily in the soft light of the shaded electric lamps on the wall and a flickering oil-lamp on the table. A Benny Goodman record was being played in the next room, and the gentle rhythm filtered in to them across the murmur of the other voices and the occasional bursts of laughter.

Emily, who had been contentedly allowing the tension of the whole long day to drain away, suddenly realised that she was sitting opposite an attractive young man. Jay was *very* good-looking, shaved and combed as he was now. He'd removed his tunic (after asking her permission to do so) and sat in his starched shirt, with his tie tucked in between the second and third buttons the curious way the Americans did it. The uniform with all its metal bits and pieces was more military, somehow, than the RAF one. Emily was far too fond of the RAF to admit the uniform opposite was more *attractive*, but its very strangeness was also just a little bit exciting. It was, Emily thought quite irrationally, almost like sitting at a table with a Luftwaffe officer.

Jay saw Emily stiffen after he'd accidentally knocked his knee against hers, and at once he shoved his chair back and asked, "Have you heard anything new about your husband?" He wanted to reassure her that he hadn't forgotten she was married, that he really wasn't trying to seduce her or anything.

"No. Tell me about your fiancée," Emily countered defensively.

Jay nodded, thinking that was fair enough. And in some odd way he didn't even mind talking about Kathy. Maybe it would do him good. He'd never talked about her to anyone, really. He'd bragged about her to the other cadets and pilots, proudly showing the glamorous pictures she'd sent him. He'd told his mother and sisters about her—but only to say 'this girl is special. Don't disgrace me.' He'd told his Dad about her, too, but his Dad didn't understand about girls like Kathy. His parents had met at church. They both came from immigrant families where the men worked in the auto factories and the women worked as seamstresses (as his mother had done) or were in domestic service until they married and settled down to be housewives and mothers. So his parents had 'walked out' every Sunday and gone to a dance or two, and then they got married just as everyone expected. His Dad's only question about Kathy was when they were gonna get married and what they were waiting for?

"I met Kathy—actually Kathleen, but she doesn't like that—at college. I was a junior, and she was a freshman. She was the prettiest co-ed on campus—or one of them, anyway—and all the guys were pretty hot for her. She didn't pay me much attention, though, if you want to know the truth of it. Not then, anyway. We didn't go out together more than a handful of times the whole year. You know, she'd only go out with me if she didn't have any better offers going."

"That's very unkind."

"Why? I don't blame her. It was probably good for me. I was a varsity football player and pretty popular with the girls that like sports—or should I say, 'athletes.' I never had any trouble getting a *date*. I guess that's why Kathy fascinated me so much."

"Ah, the intoxication of the chase," Emily commented with an amused smile. She found it disarming the way Jay so disingenuously talked about his love life. Robin had never once told her anything about his affair with the Hungarian Countess—or any of the others, for that matter. He'd simply asked if they mattered. Since Emily had been too embarrassed to admit that, well, yes, they *did* matter to her *in a way*, but then again not *really*, she had said 'no' and that had been the end of it.

"Yeah, in a way it was that, I guess," Jay admitted, wondering to himself for the first time if that was *all* it had been? "I mean, she made it so *obvious* that she wasn't interested in 'meat'—that's what she called football players because she said we were all muscle and no brain. She wanted someone with, well, you know, *class* and taste and brains."

"I see." Emily commented, leaning back and sipping her wine. "Is she *very* rich?"

"Well, a whole heck of a lot richer than I am. Her Dad's a super-successful lawyer. They belong to a country club and have a coloured cleaning lady. My Dad works in an auto factory. My grandparents were Polish peasants, see, and they immigrated to America with *nothing*. I'm the first person in my whole family that ever got a college education or a commission." Jay had been raised to be proud of how far his family had come in such a short time, but then he remembered that in England things were the other way around: you were proud of being from a good, *old* family. He looked sharply at Emily, apprehensive about her reaction.

"Well done," Emily answered, meeting his gaze steadily. "And this Kathy, she comes from an old family?"

"No, not really. Her grandparents were immigrants, too—but they came from Ireland, and I guess that's a whole lot finer than Poland, isn't it?" Jay gave Emily a little, tentative smile that was already conspiratorial.

Caught by surprise, Emily laughed, before asking, "Is that what she thinks?"

"Oh, yes. Ireland has one of the very oldest civilisations in the world. They were reading and writing and building great churches there while the English lived like wild men and the Vikings raged all over the seas and there were nothing but heathens hanging from the trees in Poland."

"Ah ha," Emily remarked, asking: "Just what subject is your Kathy reading?—Obviously not history."

"That obvious, huh?" Jay was strangely pleased—his grandparents would be, too. "No, she's studying theatre—drama, I guess you call it."

"She wants to be an actress?"

"Yeah. She's very good."

"You mean she has all the right curves?" Emily raised her eyebrows a touch condescendingly.

Jay hastened to defend Kathy, "No, no, I mean, *sure* she's got all the right curves and a face like an angel, but she really can act, too—serious stuff. She was just in *Hamlet*."

"A professional production?" Emily was impressed despite herself.

"No, the University players, but she had one of the leads."

"Ophelia?"

"Maybe. I don't know. I didn't see it. She wanted me to, but I had my orders and had to get to Halifax. She was pretty mad at me for that."

"That was hardly your fault." Emily could not imagine being angry with an officer for doing his duty. The closest she had ever come was when she learned Robin had put himself on readiness the morning of their wedding, but a wedding was certainly more important than a play and Robin hadn't been *under orders*, he'd *volunteered* for readiness.

"No, but she was disappointed," Jay answered; but even as he defended Kathy, he was glad that Emily saw things differently. He was certain Emily would never have made a fuss. "Kathy takes her career very seriously, you see, and, as I was saying earlier, it took me a long time to get her to even give me a chance."

Emily, who had always been a wallflower, could not really identify with women who had lots of admirers and could take their pick. Philippa still baffled her, for example, and she certainly didn't approve of the choice *she* had made. "When *did* she give you a chance?"

"As soon as I got these!" Jay patted his wings proudly.

"That's just as bad as being interested in a football hero or whatever," Emily declared indignantly.

Jay looked at her admiringly. She was particularly pretty when she was flushed and her eyes flashed with emotion. "Yeah, it is, sort of, isn't it?" He'd never thought of it that way. All he'd cared about was winning Kathy, it didn't matter how. Hadn't someone said, 'all's fair in love and war?' "So why did you fall in love with your husband?" Jay asked conversationally.

Emily reacted very defensively, her cheeks flushing even more than before, and her eyes turned brittle with indignation. "Not because he was Flight Lieutenant or Fighter Ace! I didn't even know he was a pilot when I met him." No, not when he walked in, her conscience reminded her, but when he walked out. And when he called for the first date, and when he invited you up to Hawarden...

"Tell me about him," Jay urged her in a low, serious voice. His elbows rested on the table and his eyes fixed on hers solemnly.

Emily caught her breath. She opened her mouth to say 'no,' and then changed her mind. Maybe it would be better to talk about him. Maybe then Jay would understand better what she was going through. "Practically the first thing he ever said to me was: 'Can I help?' At the time, I was trying to serve dinner to about a hundred thousand starving sailors at the Seaman's Mission in Pompii. You have to understand, he was not in uniform and he was on crutches, his leg in a cast. I mistook him for a Conscientious Objector sent to help out. It wasn't until later that I learned he was an RAF Flight Lieutenant who had broken his leg bailing out over France during the evacuation of Dunkirk."

Jay whistled in admiration.

"You also have to understand that my life was rather grim at the time. I was living with my parents in their little flat behind the dockyards, working days at an insurance company and doing volunteer work for the Salvation Army evenings. I had never dated anyone in my life, and suddenly I was being taken to nice restaurants and dancing in Officer's Messes. Robin came from a much better family than I. Not rich. His mother had to live on a Navy Lieutenant's widow's pension. Nevertheless, Robin had gone to public school and then to Cranwell. He'd been posted to Singapore and then competed in international air shows in the last year and a half or so before the War. He'd dated socialites and been introduced to the Duke of Windsor. That was a totally different world. It was," she paused, trying to find the right words to describe it, "it was as if an angel had come down from heaven, reached out his hand, and pulled me out of—if not hell, then at least purgatory."

"He must have been some guy," Jay agreed.

"I'd like to think he still is," Emily reminded him firmly, the pain more intense for having talked about him.

Jay hastened to agree with her. "So do I." And then, because he could see how upset she was, he added, "Hey, what do you say I get you another glass of wine, and see if I can't rustle up dinner. They seem to be taking forever." He got up without waiting for an answer, so she would have time to compose herself.

It was almost midnight before Jay found his way to Emily's house in Windsor, and she was very tired and had to keep stifling yawns. She also had a bit of a guilty conscience. "You're sure you'll find your way home?" she enquired for the umpteenth time as he cut the engine and pulled the hand brake.

"Oh, yeah, sure. Eventually. If I get too lost, I'll just pull off the road and wait 'till dawn. My squadron's stood down tomorrow."

Emily held out her hand to him. "Thank you very much for a very pleasant evening."

J.B. took her hand and shook it with a sense of rising panic. He didn't want this to be good-bye. "Look, can I call you again? I mean, if you had a good time, why not do it again sometime?" Why did he sound so gauche and unsophisticated? "I could come take you for dinner somewhere around here, so you don't get in so late."

"Oh, that's *much* too far for you. I really shouldn't have taken such shameless advantage even tonight."

"I'm not complaining."

"No, but it was very selfish of me. I knew how far it was, and you didn't. It would be quite impractical for you to come all this way just for dinner. But thank you for the invitation anyway. It really was very kind of you to feed me and bring me all the way home. I can't thank you enough."

"Sure you can. Let me take you out again another night."

Emily laughed at his persistence. "You're terribly gallant, Jay, but by the time you get back to your Station sometime in the wee hours of the morning, I'm sure you'll see what I mean. But thank you again, and good night." Emily opened the door of the jeep and stepped down. Before she could even reach back in to collect her parachute and tote bag, Jay was beside her to help. He insisted on carrying them for her to the front door.

From inside the house came the scratching and coughing of a frantic Penny.

"What the dickens is that?" Jay asked in alarm.

"Oh, not to worry. That's my bull-dog. Well, she's not mine really, but my lodger's, but she seems to have adopted me. She thinks I need looking after."

"I get it. She bites the pants off any impertinent suitor."

"I don't have any suitors, Jay. I'm already married."

"I know, I know," he dismissed the subject irritably. Sure she was married, but no one had heard anything from her husband in four months. Everybody he'd talked to about it said the Germans were more efficient than that. If her husband had survived, they'd know by now. Of course, if he was dead they should have heard by now, too. Damn it! Why did things have to be so complicated? "Look, if you don't mind, I will give you a call again, OK? I mean, here I am living in England and except for one 48-hour pass to London I haven't seen anything of it. I hear Cambridge is real nice, and I'd really like to see it before I go home. I mean, it's famous and all. Oxford and Cambridge." Why was he running on like this? He was babbling like a fool for fear that she was going to go through that door and they would never see each other again.

"Cambridge is lovely," Emily admitted wistfully. "Arguably the happiest years of my life were spent there." It had been before Robin, of course, but also before the war.

"Gee! That's great. Then you know it! You can really show me around. I mean, really give me the grand Cook's tour, so to speak."

"Oh, Jay, I don't know. I only get two days off a fortnight, and you never know when you can get off—"

"So next time you have two days off just give me a call, OK? If I can make it, than we can meet there and you can show me around. If not, then no big deal, we wait for the next time. Eventually, it will work out. You wouldn't want me to go back to America without having seen it, would you?"

"Well, I don't know that it's *that* special. I'm sure you have much bigger, more impressive universities in America."

"Yeah, well, big maybe, but not so old. And I can't tell if they're more impressive 'till I've seen Cambridge to make a comparison. Please, Emily, wouldn't you like to spend an afternoon showing a poor American boy around Cambridge?"

Emily was too tired to resist. "Alright. I'll call next time I have a day off, and see if you're free and still so keen on seeing Cambridge."

"Great! Thanks! I'll be looking forward to it!" He held out his hand again. They shook hands and Emily unlocked the door, while Jay stood to one side, his hands in his pockets watching her. Penny danced and jumped about Emily's feet in greeting, and Emily bent down to pat her before glancing over her shoulder to wave goodbye to Jay. Something about the way he stood there, hands in his pockets, with his cap pulled low over his eyes, sent a sharp pang through her heart just as the door fell shut.

Emily felt such a pang of pity for Jay—an inexplicable pang given that he wasn't really a lost little boy—that she almost reached out to open the door again. She didn't know what she would have done then, but it wasn't necessary. She heard the jeep door crunch shut and then the motor start up.

The moment was past, and Emily made her way upstairs to her bedroom. As she got ready for bed, she debated with herself whether she should give him a call or not when the time came. She had had a nice time and she trusted Jay. He wouldn't pressure her to do anything she didn't want; she was sure of that now. He really seemed to want nothing more than someone to talk to. He'd told her about having three sisters. Maybe that was what he saw in her? Well, there was no harm in that. She really had had a lovely evening, and it was refreshing being with someone whose life had been so different from anything she knew up to now.

As she climbed into the double bed, she wondered how she would ever explain about Jay to Robin. But Jay would be gone long before Robin came home. If he ever came home…

As she drifted off to sleep, the Gypsy's words came back to her. Maybe the message was from someone else. Hadn't Jay said he'd been thinking about her all the time? And what was all that that the Gypsy had said about going halfway around the world? What if she were to be happy again—but with someone else? Like Steeplechase's sister…

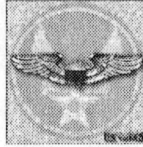

CHAPTER 13

▼

Beauchamp Rodding, England
July 1943

"Look at it this way," Tony argued, lying flat on his back, his eyes closed and his arms hanging off the side of the narrow bed. He was stark naked, having just stripped off his flying kit and underwear. The sweat was slowly drying in the sticky air in the Nissan hut. "It was one Fourth of July we're never gonna forget."

Someone had decided that the 8th Air Force should celebrate the Glorious Fourth of July by launching the biggest raid ever. Maximum Effort and all that. But because of weather Berlin had been ruled out as a target (which was just fine with Jay) and they had been sent against Essen instead. That looked OK on the map. A whole lot shorter than Berlin. Of course, they'd been warned about the 'concentrations of flak,' but there seemed to be so little relationship between the terse, dry phrase 'concentrations of flak' (accompanied by Bochanek's pointer cracking the map) and the murky, trembling sky that had tried to crush and swallow and blow them apart all at once.

Jay had never in his life (this was, after all, his 10th mission, and he was moving slowly up into the position of an 'old hand') experienced anything like it. The sky had been filthy with the smoke and debris that surrounded them, and the shaking had been like an earthquake that went on and on and on. More than once he'd lost control of the ship. Tony and he had shouted themselves hoarse as they tried between them to keep her halfway steady, and then there was the bombardier.

Buzz was in hospital, of course, and they'd been given a bombardier whose previous crew had finished their tour of duty and gone home before him. Since then he'd been filling in wherever needed, and the mission with Jay had been his last. Unfortunately, he was also a nervous wreck. Dan had had the worst of it, down with him in the nose. Apparently he'd kept saying out loud: "This is it. This is it. I'm never gonna make it. This is it." It was so bad, even Dan lost his patience and told him to shut up. But apparently he couldn't.

When they went into the bomb run and Jay went on autopilot, he felt like no one had control of the ship. Jay was sure they were wide of the mark by more than the usual margin of error. And then the guy clammed up and said not another word—just held onto himself, Dan reported.

They had been lucky. Flak had nicked the tip of one wing, but otherwise they came out of it unscathed—but very glad to say good-bye to their dazed substitute bombardier. He had hardly seemed able to believe he'd survived his last mission after all, and had hurried off to start packing without so much as a word of thanks or good-luck to the others.

"I hope whoever they dig up next is more reliable than that crazy guy," Tony remarked.

"I hope we aren't all *like* that by the time we've flown 24 missions," Jay countered, as he grabbed a towel and started for the showers.

He washed in hot water and then turned off the warm water and showered cold for a few seconds. He found it restorative, and feeling better he stepped out of the shower, rubbed himself dry vigorously and then went back to the hut. He was surprised to find Sergeant Roach waiting for him.

Roach was wearing nothing but his trousers and his hair was standing on end, still sticky from dried sweat. He was red in the face and breathing hard. "Lieutenant, you gotta come quick. The Kid's gone crazy."

"What?"

"The Kid! He got some kind of news in the mail and he just plum went crazy. He started screaming and ripping things up and smashing things. He hits everyone who tries to stop him and the MPs are going to get him, if you don't come quick."

Jay grabbed his own trousers, pulled them on and followed Roach at a trot to the Enlisted Men's quarters. Behind the enlisted men's huts a large crowd of heckling, cheering men surrounded his tail gunner. The boy would lunge one way or the other, trying to land a fist on any obliging body, but the men generally sprang back just in time.

"What's going on here?" Jay demanded, trying to sound authoritative.

Several men turned to see who was coming, and the Kid got in a good blow. You could hear it connect, and the victim let out a loud grunt of pain. Then he got angry and shouted, "you fucking son of a bitch" and hit back at the Kid.

The Kid was undersized and underweight. Naked from the waist up as he was now, you could see just how skinny he was—all ribs and sharp shoulder blades— and he looked more like 15 than 18. He'd been on the receiving end of more than one fist already, too. His right eye was starting to swell up, and his lips were broken and bleeding. He stood a little crooked as if a blow to his side had hurt him, too. Jay made a split-second decision and launched himself in a once well-practised tackle. Even if it had been a couple years since he'd played football, he hadn't lost all his skill. He knocked the Kid down and away from his assailant. Then with his superior size and weight he pinned the Kid down until his frenzied resistance ended in broken sobs for breath. Or was he really crying? Jay saw something glisten on his cheek, and he released him to stand up and shoo the crowd of spectators away. "Show's over, guys. Break it up. Go find something else to amuse you."

The crowd started to disperse with shrugs and murmurs and some curious backward glances. Meanwhile, Roach was helping the Kid to his feet—or trying to. The Kid kept shaking him off, his head turned away.

"Leave him to me, Roach. And thanks."

Roach looked up at him with a frown, then he asked the Kid. "You OK, Kid?"

"Leave me alone!" the Kid shouted at him, his head still turned away.

"OK. See ya later." Roach cast J.B. an unreadable look and then withdrew.

"Come on, Kid. I want to have a word with you." Jay turned away, so the Kid could fall in beside him without feeling he was being looked at. He did.

All around the edge of the airfield, the planes were being worked on by the ground crews, so Jay led the Kid away from all that bustle of activity. Away, too, from the Mess Halls, where another meal was being prepared to the loud clatter of pots and pans and the curses of the cooks. He led the Kid toward a baseball pitch someone had scratched out in the English grass. Jay had never seen anyone play a game on it. It just sat here growing more and more weeds. Deserted as it always was, it was a good place for a private talk.

"So, you gonna tell me what that was all about?" He asked his tail gunner.

"Do I got to, sir?" the Kid asked sullenly.

"No. I guess you don't have to, if you mean do I have a legal right under the Articles of War and all that. But you're going to be in a heap of trouble for brawling, and if I can't speak up in your defence, it's going to be a whole lot worse."

The Kid was kicking at the dirt of the pitcher's mound with his bare feet. His feet were big and bony like his hands—too big for the size of his body, like a puppy that should have grown into his paws but somehow never had. "You reckon I'm in big enough trouble to get sent home?" he asked hopefully.

"No." Jay almost had to suppress a smile, before asking as seriously as he could: "Is that what you wanted? To be sent home?"

"I *gotta* go home, sir!" the Kid countered with fierce conviction, and for the first time he looked up and met Jay's eyes. He really was an ugly kid, with big, crooked teeth in a face that was much too narrow.

"You had bad news from home, didn't you?" Jay remembered what Roach had said.

"Yes, sir! I gotta go home and fix things up!"

"Just what is the problem? I'm not promising anything, but if you've got a serious problem, you might get special leave. You could hitch a ride on one of the Ferrying Command transports, and be home in 3 or 4 days."

The Kid's expression cleared rapturously. "Could I get there that quick, sir? That'd be great! Nobody'd expect that! What I got to do?"

"Start by telling me what the problem is," Jay suggested.

The Kid looked down and kicked at the pitcher's mound. His jaw was working too, thinking hard. At last he said, without looking up, "It's my kid sister, sir."

"What about her?"

Silence.

"If I don't know what the problem is, I can't help you."

The Kid seemed to consider this, weighing the advantages with the disadvantages. Then he took a deep breath and announced in a rush, "It's my kid sister. She's been knocked up by one of them McGilvery bastards, and I gotta go home and *kill* him!"

Jay was taken so by surprise he wanted to laugh—but he could see that the Kid was deadly serious, and he caught himself in time. He bit down on his tongue and took a deep breath. The Kid looked up a him anxiously. "You understand now, sir?"

Jay drew a breath but couldn't decide on the right answer. Then he shook his head. "I'll be honest with you, Kid. The United States Army Air Forces is not going to give you leave to go home and kill somebody. That's against the law."

"But he banged up my sister, sir!" The Kid was outraged. "She ain't barely 15! She couldn't do nothing about it. Those McGilvery bastards are all a bunch of animals! My Ma says she's in a real bad way. Tried to hide it and tried to get rid of it on her own. She's real ashamed, but it ain't her fault, sir! I know it ain't. She's not like that!"

"Well, at 15 it's statutory rape whether she was willing or not. All your folks have to do is file suit."

"Go to the sheriff, you mean?"

"That's right."

The Kid shook his head violently. "He's a McGilvery! He'll never arrest one of his kin. Do you see now, sir? I got to go home and kill that bastard!"

Jay tried to be more forceful. "No one is going to give you permission to go home and kill someone!"

"Well, sir, I won't tell them *that* part, if you won't." He looked hopefully at Jay.

"No one is going to give you special compassionate leave to go visit your sister just because she's pregnant unless she's your legal dependent, which she's not, is she?"

"Oh, no, sir. She's living with Ma and Pa."

"Well, can't your Pa take care of this for her?"

The Kid shook his head. "Pa lost both legs down the mine. He's no match for the McGilverys, and my older brother's in the Marines—somewhere in the Pacific."

"I see." Jay thought for a moment, trying to find some way to help—or at least appear to help. "I've got an idea. Dan—Lieutenant Vernon—he's a lawyer, or he was studying to be one when the Japs hit Pearl Harbor and he quit law school and volunteered. Maybe he'll know some way we can bring suit against this guy without going through the sheriff. Let's go talk to him, OK?" Jay was very pleased to have thought of Dan.

The Kid seemed to hesitate. "Lieutenant Vernon, sir," he licked his lips and added very solemnly, "he's related to General Lee."

"What?"

"General Robert E. Lee, sir. On his mother's side."

"What's that got to do with this?" Jay asked bewildered.

"Well, sir, my family was Rebel, and I wouldn't want a descendent of General Lee to know how my sister got disgraced by them Yankee McGilverys!"

"Kid, in case you haven't noticed, the Civil War ended almost a hundred years ago. Besides, the rest of us are all Yankees, too."

"That's alright, sir. You can't help it. You was born that way."

Jay gave up trying to figure it out. "Look, wouldn't you rather talk to Lieutenant Vernon about this than let this McGilvery guy get away with what he did?"

The Kid bit his lip and thought about that. "Maybe you're right, sir—or why don't you tell him about it for me?" He looked up hopefully. "That'd be a whole lot more tactful like?"

Jay drew a deep breath. "Alright, I'll talk to him about it, and ask him to see you if he thinks he can help, OK?"

The Kid nodded, looking much happier already. Jay gave him a quick punch on the arm and a smile, and they returned to their separate barracks.

Back in his own Nissan hut, Jay found that Dan had already left. He'd gone, as he usually did after a mission, to a nearby manor with good riding horses. Riding seemed to be a catharsis for him, and the elderly lady of the manor welcomed his help with exercising her difficult horses. Tony was sleeping flat on his back, still naked, and snoring. A heap of letters had been dumped on Jay's bed. Dan or Tony must have taken them at mail-call for him.

He picked them up and sorted through them. Two from his mother. One from Sally. One from Barb—that was great! The first she'd written since she'd joined the WAAC. And four from Kathy. Jay sighed and stared at the latter. He almost wished they weren't there. He didn't feel like he had the energy to deal with them just now. He was emotionally drained, and it took such an effort to summon up what he was supposed to be feeling about Kathy. He was engaged to her, after all. She expected him to answer each and every one of her letters. He put them aside and started with the other letters.

His mother and Sally told him all the mundane news from home, and it was comforting to think that things went on just they way they always had. Barb's letter, in contrast, was like a breath of fresh air. She wrote to him in her candid way, complaining about all the "bullshit discipline" like standing at attention and marching "even to the John—I swear!" But through it all, he could tell she was loving it. She was quick to learn, to test the limits, learn exactly what she could get away with, and then take as much leeway as she could without getting into serious trouble. She proudly told about how she filled Scotch into coke bottles, re-capped them, and sold them on base to the male enlisted men. "Easiest twenty bucks I ever made in my life!" she bragged, asking: "Why did they repeal Prohibition? I would have made a great bootlegger!" She'd already finished 'boot camp' and was in training as an MT driver. She ended the letter by saying she had volunteered for overseas duty, and thought she had a good chance of being sent to England. "Just think, I could be driving your jeep one of these days—when you make Colonel or whatever it takes to rate a jeep and driver. When are you finally going to make Captain, by the way? There are too many WAACs around here with lowly Looeys as brothers and lovers. A Captain would improve my status buckets." She finished off in haste with love, but then added a postscript. "PS: Don't do anything silly to get promoted, OK? I'd rather have a live Looey than a dead Captain. Lots of Love. Barb."

Good old Barb. Smiling unconsciously, Jay put her letter aside and gazed at the four from Kathy. He considered putting them off again. Looked over at the wall clock. It was only five o'clock. Another hour 'till dinner. Might as well get it over with. He sorted the letters by date, and opened the oldest one first.

The first of the four letters was focused on the china again. Although she was sure he had her first letter, he had completely failed to comment on it. She needed his opinion because it was <u>so</u> important…Jay went on to her next letter. This letter was an outraged lament about not having been cast in the part she thought she deserved. "That b—Sheila Huxley was given the part. It is such a miscast! It will ruin the whole production!!! I don't like to be catty, but there is no question that the <u>only</u> way she could have gotten such a <u>difficult</u> part was by sleeping with the director…"

Jay unconsciously rubbed his forehead. He had a headache. Actually he got them a lot, but particularly after being on oxygen for a long time. He didn't notice either the headache or that he was rubbing his head, however, as he went on to the third letter. This continued in much the same vein. Rehearsals were 'torture' because Kathy had to watch "that b—Sheila massacre Shakespeare's lovely language." Then one of the actors had said something "<u>*unforgivable*</u>!" The letter made no reference to anything he had written. It was as if she'd had no mail from him.

When he opened the fourth letter, however, it was obvious she had indeed received mail. The entire letter was a diatribe about his style of writing. He could almost hear her wailing out of the pages at him. Didn't he love her "<u>*at all!?!?!?*</u>" Why didn't he ever say so? And why did he take so little interest in her life? What did she care about what the houses were like in England? She certainly didn't ever want to go—much less live—there! And, of course, the English were snobby. She had warned him about that.

Jay couldn't think what he could have written to make her think he was complaining about English snobbishness. Quite the opposite. He'd been pleasantly surprised by how polite and kind the English were. A little reserved, maybe, but not snobby at all. And how on earth could she "warn" him about a people she had never met, a place she had never been? It struck him as intolerably arrogant.

She still treated him like he was just the 'dumb football player' who needed to be 'educated and refined' by herself.

But he was getting hung up on a side issue. Most of the letter was a teary, self-pitying complaint about his lack of *romantic* intimations. And the problem was that she was right on that score. He couldn't bring himself to write sugary stuff. It sounded fake. What did she want from him? Well, she answered that, too: something like Shakespeare's sonnets, apparently. Well, that really *was* unreasonable. He was just a dumb football player/engineer/pilot, not a poet!

But she was so obviously miserable that he was going to have to think of something. With a deep sigh, Jay got out his paper and pen and grimly set himself up at the only writing desk in their bay. He smoothed the paper, addressed the envelope, and generally took as long as possible to get ready to write in order to delay the actual writing. He kept hoping it would be time for dinner before he actually started. But no such luck; at 17.40 he could think of no way to procrastinate any longer.

"Dearest Kathy," he started and then stopped, already stumped. The clock ticked loudly. He decided to start with the easy things. He loved the china she'd chosen. (In fact, he couldn't even remember what it looked like, but he didn't care.) He didn't find the English at all snobby and liked it here very much. Now the difficult part: how could he reassure her about his feelings?

The sound of his name being called over the intercom made him jump clean out of his skin. Jay grabbed his cap and ran out of the Nissan hut to the main Admin building like it was an emergency. Maybe it was? Why else would he get called like this? Or did it have to do with the Kentucky Kid? He clattered into the main reception. "I was just paged?"

"Yeah, you've got a call." The Corporal pointed to one of the phone boxes.

The word Emily flashed through his mind instantly, but he hardly dared really hope. "Hello? This is Lieutenant Baronowsky."

"It's me. Emily Priestman. I have the next two days off. Do you still feel like seeing a bit of Cambridge? I'd quite understand if—"

"Yes, yes, yes, a thousand times, yes. When can we meet and where?"

"You're quite sure you wouldn't rather spend your time with a woman who's not already married?"

"Yes! I'm engaged, remember? Where and when can we meet?"

"Well, if you're sure." She sounded very doubtful, but continued, "I've looked at the train schedules—of course nothing ever runs to schedule these days, but according to the schedule I could be in Cambridge by 11.20 tomorrow morning.

If you met me at the Station that would probably be easiest all around, don't you think?"

"Whatever you say."

"You're sure you're free?" She sounded rather surprised by his ready acceptance and Jay wondered if she'd been hoping he'd say no? No point thinking about that.

"Tomorrow's OK. I don't know about the day after. Maybe it will pour rain or something."

"Well, we'll meet up tomorrow then and see what happens. Alright?"

"Great!" They said good-bye and hung up. Jay could have leapt into the air for joy. All his exhaustion was gone. He felt invigorated and alive. He was grinning so widely, that even the corporal at the desk asked, "Good news, sir?"

"The best. I've got a *great* date tomorrow."

The corporal grinned back at him. Jay trotted back to his hut in high spirits. Tony was sitting up on the bed yawning and stretching. "What's happened to you? Did you just get laid, or did Hitler surrender?"

"I've got a very special date tomorrow," Jay told him contentedly.

"You're right; anticipating the lay is almost as good as re-living it. Only actually doing it is better. So where did you pick up this English rose?" Tony asked lazily as he stood, scratching himself half-heartedly here and there. "You didn't seem so hot for that actress, not the way..." He didn't finish, because one didn't talk about the dead unnecessarily.

"Nope. This gal's a whole lot better than that." Jay knew he was misrepresenting his relationship to Emily, but Tony wouldn't understand about a platonic relationship. The only kind of relationship Tony had (or admitted having) with women were erotic ones.

"Hey, this must be the chick you rushed over to that RAF station to collect and take out to dinner, right?"

"You're slow, sometimes, Antonio, but you get it right in the end."

"You said you needed a jeep quick 'cause she was stuck over there. She was some kind of officer, wasn't she? A WAAF or whatever, right?"

"Better, Buddy, she can fly the little bombers."

"Not that woman that tried to kill us after our first mission!?" Tony gasped in amazement.

Jay nodded smugly. "Um hum."

"Holy Shit!" Tony gaped at him. Then he nodded respectfully. "Not bad, buddy. Not bad." But then something occurred to him. "Wait a minute! I thought those RAF guys said she was married?"

"Yeah, and her husband ran into flak at 1,500 feet, crashed, and over-turned several times. Nothing's been heard from him since. Probably incinerated so bad they couldn't read his dog-tags and that's why he's officially 'Missing.'"

Tony whistled now in admiration. "A widow, huh? A *flyer's* widow. No wonder you're so sure of yourself. She must be terrific stuff!" Tony was really envious. Then he added, only half playfully, "Ask her if she's got any friends—you know, other women pilots with her whazit outfit. Didn't they say there were over a hundred of them? Must be one or two others who have been widowed and are desperate for another pilot. The war's been going on over here for ages."

"Yeah, yeah. I'll ask," Jay assured him with a smile, and they both knew he wouldn't. Meanwhile, it was time for dinner, and Jay hastily collected the letter to Kathy he had (foolishly) left on the desk. He'd finish it tomorrow or after Cambridge. Whenever. She'd never know it wasn't just the lousy mail. It would give him time to think of what to tell her, too.

Cambridge, England
July, 1943

Emily was an excellent guide. It wasn't just that she knew Cambridge well, it was that she loved history and she could bring it to life. There wasn't a college, a church, or a bridge that she didn't have a story about. Jay had never been much interested in history—until he heard Emily telling stories about Kings and Mistresses, heretics and rebels. Of course, the fact that it was the first time Jay had seen her out of uniform might have added to his enthusiasm. She looked trim and pretty in her neat, dark uniform, but in a summer dress with short sleeves and fluttering skirts she was more enchanting still.

Emily then introduced Jay to 'Creamed Teas' with scones and strawberry preserves (if you could produce the ration coupons for the cream, that was), before letting him take her punting on the Cam. Jay had seen a couple of youngsters doing this and had been eager to try. As most beginners do, he underestimated how difficult it was, and nearly fell into the water two or three times when his pole got stuck. But he was a natural athlete and soon got the hang of it. Before long, they were gliding along on the tame waters with the ducks escorting them and the sun glinting.

"You said you went to college here?" Jay asked enviously. "I used to think Ann Arbor was a nice town, but this is the nicest place I've ever been in my whole life." Jay meant every word of it. "I'll bet you did this every day with a different beau!"

Emily started, surprised. She had been trailing one hand in the cool water and glanced up at Jay rather sceptically. He had removed his leather jacket and was wearing his so-called 'pinks'—khaki shirt and trousers. He wore a forage cap rather than his peaked cap. His blond hair caught the sunlight and his face was tanned. But what struck her most was how muscular and powerful he looked. He was very, very masculine—as her friends from University had not been.

"I didn't have any boyfriends then," Emily answered his remark simply.

"You're putting me on!" Jay countered with a grin as he caught the punt with an increasing skill that pleased him subconsciously. At that moment there was literally nowhere on earth he would have rather been, and Berlin was a million, million miles away.

"No. I'm quite serious. I was here on a scholarship, you see." No, it was obvious he didn't see. "That means my parents could never have afforded to send me here," Emily explained. Jay still looked rather blank, so she went on. "There are two classes of students here, you see: the scholars, who are here on merit only and must work very hard to keep their places and work even harder when they leave, and the rest. The rest come from families that can afford to let them study whatever and for as long as they like. Studying for them is a tradition and a rite of passage and a life-style—not training for a future job."

"Rich kids; I know the type," Jay assured her, although Emily did not really think he did. Things were reputedly so different in egalitarian, money-grubbing America.

"Well, you see, I got in with the wrong crowd—that is, I moved in a rich and privileged crowd. Maybe I should tell you that my parents were Communists—"

"What?!" Jay's jaw dropped and he stared at her in shock so sincere, he nearly fell off the punt. Jay had rarely heard the word "Communist" used without the adjective "God-damned" in front of it. He had certainly never expected to meet a Communist—unless it was some visiting Russian officer.

"It's not illegal over here, you know," Emily reminded him, a little annoyed by his reaction. "And if you knew anything about the working and living conditions of the lower classes in this country in the last century, you would understand about the Communist Manifesto."

"Are you crazy? Communism is an oppressive, brutal dictatorship, and I don't care if they are our allies now or not, they were Hitler's allies until he invaded and they'll turn on us again the minute it suits them!" Jay felt strongly about this.

Emily sat up in the boat and clutched her knees in her arms. Then she answered calmly. "You are talking about Leninism, or even Stalinism. Communism has nothing to do with dictatorship. But I don't want to argue with you about it. I came to resent the Party because it was so consuming, demanding, uncompromising, but there is nothing inherently wrong with the ideology—"

"Yes, there is!" Jay insisted indignantly. "Communism makes everyone poor. It takes away from people everything they earn and work for! It robs hard-working people of the fruits of their labour. My grandparents came over to America with nothing, but now they have a house of their own and a car and a washing-machine! And my parents have more, and I'm going to have even more than them, and that's the way it should be! Making everyone equal is just another way of penalising people for working hard and rewarding people for doing nothing!"

Emily had never encountered anyone with such vehement anti-Communist views, and it baffled her somewhat. All her upper-class, intellectual friends had been tolerant of Communism, if they hadn't outright flirted with it from time to time. It struck her as odd that this young man who, from her parents' point of view, ought to have been more receptive to Communism, was so hostile. She found herself trying to imagine how her parents would have reacted to Jay, if she'd brought him home as her fiancé instead of Robin.

They had hated Robin before they even met him, just because he was from the 'wrong' class—the son of privilege rather than labour. (Her parents had always had more class prejudice than her friends at Cambridge.) They were outraged that a child of theirs, who had been 'properly' educated in Marxism-Leninism since the time she was weaned, wanted to marry a man who 'hob-nobbed' with royalty and cavorted with debutantes. They had argued that Robin 'couldn't possibly' be serious about a 'plain, working-class girl' such as herself, and insinuated that he was only playing with her. The only times Robin and her parents ever met, the air had crackled with mutual hostility. But Robin had never been overtly anti-Communist.

And here was a young man who came from humble origins, who had worked his way up from nothing just as her parents had done. Jay even fit the image of the healthy young worker that had so enraptured her father on his one and only trip to the Soviet Union in 1936. Emily's father had returned home with hundreds of photos of factories and Collectives, his camera focusing again and again on the tanned, broad-shouldered youth, which he contrasted to the 'sickly, pale, bent' workers in England. She knew that her parents, particularly her father, would have welcomed Jay into their humble home like the prodigal son. But what would he have done with his opinions?

Jay, mistaking her silence for displeasure, was trying to think what he could say to set things right again. What did he care about her politics? Emily was the most important person in his life at the moment, and he didn't want to offend her in any way for fear of losing her. "Look, I'm sorry," Jay blurted out in a kind of panic, not entirely sure what he was going to say. "I guess I shouldn't have said those things. I mean, heck, what do I know about Communism?—except, you know, what my Grand-Dad says. He's got two brothers and three sisters still living in Poland, see, and they—well—when Stalin invaded in 1939—"

"It's alright, Jay. I quite agree with you. I had a terrible fight with my parents about the Molotov-Ribbentrop Pact. Bigoted as they were, they swallowed the Party line, and hated Hitler one day and praised him the next. It was the last straw for me. I'm really not a Communist now; I just wanted you to understand something about me and where I come from."

Jay felt worse than ever for going off like that and lecturing her. He hastened to assure her earnestly, "It doesn't matter to me who your parents are. Where do they live? Are you from around here?"

"No. I was born and raised in Portsmouth, on the south coast," she added, guessing correctly that he had no idea where Portsmouth was.

"Why don't you show me around your home town on your next day off? I'll bet it's beautiful."

"Good heavens, no!" Emily answered horrified. "It's the principal seat of the Royal Navy, and His Majesty's Dockyards are there. It's a horrible, filthy city built on mud-flats. It is nothing but a lot of docks, pubs, brothels and row-upon-endless-row of working-class housing."

Jay nearly choked when he heard her mention brothels so casually. Kathy would have made a big show of dropping her voice and cupping her mouth and whispering loudly, "houses of ill-repute." Dramatic delivery, he supposed she would have called it, but it only served to embarrass everyone by drawing so much attention to—and so focusing one's thoughts upon—the object of contempt. The way Emily said it, it was just a fact of life. As, he supposed, they were. In answer, Jay said: "I'd still like to see it. I'd like to see where you grew up."

"It was in one of those horrible terraced cottages without any front garden— red brick, grey with grime, narrow, dingy and very run down. It was not the kind of place I could ever bring guests—not my friends from school, much less my friends from University or Robin's fellow officers."

"Are you saying you're ashamed of your parents?" Jay couldn't help himself. He disapproved of someone being ashamed of their parents just because they were poor. He thought that was wrong.

Emily heard the reproach and disapproval in his voice and met his eyes. "Yes, but not because they were poor—because they were cold."

Jay frowned. "I don't get it."

"Well, you described your family to me last time we met. You described a family where everyone cared about one another and tried to help in any way they could: your grandmother helping look after you and your sisters and brothers, your father working extra hours to make sure you could afford football equipment or your sister could take piano lessons, and your sisters helping you with your homework. I can't remember all the details, but I could tell by the way you talked about your family that they not only mean a lot to you, but they earned your love by giving it."

"You can say that, yeah," Jay agreed, unsure where she was going.

"Well, my family wasn't like that. I was an only child, but I can't remember my mother ever kissing or hugging me. Nor did I ever see any sign of affection between my parents. They never kissed, nor held hands nor hugged. They never fought like our neighbours did, either. There wasn't enough passion in their relationship for even that. The marriage was nothing more than a rational alliance for the benefit of the Party. I always suspected that even I was part of some Five-Year Plan. No doubt my parents received a Directive to contribute to the Party's future strength by producing offspring. If they could have done it without intimacy, I'm sure they would have."

Jay was staring at her, more horrified than ever, but now he was feeling sorry for her, too. He couldn't imagine a more dismal childhood. Even being an orphan wouldn't have been worse. "I guess you aren't very close to them," Jay surmised.

"No. I have a better relationship with Robin's family than I ever had with my own, although—"

"Yeah?" Jay prompted.

Emily sighed. "It's just that his mother has given up, that's all. She's a widow and lost her husband in the last war. She's convinced Robin is dead, too. She's got black ribbons draped over his portrait and goes around in black. She's even had a memorial service said for him. I don't understand that. It's as if she's glorifying in him being dead. I can't stand to visit her because of it. I call once a week, but it's always a very strained and unpleasant two minutes. The Admiral's better."

"Who's the Admiral?"

"Robin's grandfather…why are we talking about my husband's family?"

"Because you want to," Jay told her simply.

Emily was taken aback. Was that true?

Seeing her chagrin, Jay offered, "Besides, last time I did all the talking. I must have talked your ear off. But right now, I've got to admit I'm getting mighty hungry. What do you say we park this thing and go get changed for dinner?"

Emily readily agreed.

Jay told the concierge at his hotel that he wanted to take a lady out for a very special dinner, and he stressed the word lady. "I don't care what it costs me," he told the elderly man, who looked so fragile he might fall apart if the wind blew too hard.

"I understand, sir," the concierge replied stiffly, and then offered to make reservations at the restaurant of his selection. "They have an excellent menu of game, which is not rationed, and if you're lucky they may have some champagne."

Jay changed into his dress uniform and Emily appeared in a stunning evening gown—like nothing Jay had ever seen. No off-the-shoulder-low-décolleté-and-puffy-skirt affair as Kathy would have worn. It was a modest, elegant, sophisticated burgundy gown with one bare arm and one arm encased in sheer silk.

The restaurant was small, unassuming on the outside, but meticulously decorated within. The carpets were thick and the only lighting came from candles. Even the chandeliers burned real candles, something Jay had never seen before. The candlelight, being unsteady, made the cut crystal of the glasses, the gilding on the ceiling mouldings, and the silverware glint. There was a woman pianist providing very discreet background music. The other guests seemed to be predominantly elderly couples in dinner jackets and evening gowns. It was very respectable, almost too respectable. Jay would have felt more comfortable if there had been at least one or two younger couples.

They were taken to a table near a magnificent fireplace with a huge carved marble mantel. Over the mantel hung a heavy oil painting with a landscape of Cambridge from the distance. The waiter held the chair for Emily, helped her get settled and then handed Jay a menu (with prices) and a wine list, while Emily was given a menu without prices and no wine list. The waiter rattled off a number of wine suggestions, which left Jay feeling dizzy, and then withdrew. Jay felt the perfect fool, and licked his lips uncertainly.

Emily came to his rescue with a smile. "I'd like the Sauvignon Blanc, if that's alright with you?"

"Yes, of course."

"It's usually one of the cheaper wines, Jay," Emily hastened to assure him.

"You can have the most expensive wine there is, if that's what you want," Jay told her bluntly. The way she looked right now, he thought he would have sold his soul for her to be happy with him tonight.

"It's not what I want, Jay. I'm not a connoisseur at all. In fact, I was raised a teetotaller, and have only started to learn about wine since my marriage. The Sauvignon is a very nice wine that I know I like. I'd much rather have it than some fancy wine that is too sweet or too strong."

There it was again, that straight-forward practicality that made it so easy to be with Emily. Keeping Kathy happy always required an effort: watch your manners, watch your language, impress, impress, impress. Jay tried to picture Kathy here in this restaurant, and he could do so all too well. He could picture her preening and then holding her glass with her pinky extended and sitting very, very straight in her chair—acting. That was it: Kathy would only have been play-acting, whereas Emily belonged here—even if she had been raised in the slums.

Emily was already studying the menu, and he followed her example. He got a bit of a shock. It was all in French.

"Do you want any help?" Emily asked without even looking up.

"You speak French?"

"Enough to get me through the menu."

"Okay."

When it came to ordering, however, Emily chattered to the waiter in French, who brightened at once, and the conversation became quite lengthy. At the end, the waiter withdrew with a bow and a smile, and Emily turned to Jay and announced, "I hope you don't mind, but the waiter said the hare is not good, and he talked me into trying the venison. Oh, and the frog legs."

"Frog legs?!" Jay looked rather green.

"Try them, you'll like them—and they're not rationed so there will be plenty. The waiter, by the way, came out with the BEF at Dunkirk. The limp he has is from his leg getting crushed when the first transport he was on was bombed and capsized. He was fished out of the wreckage by some civilians in a whaler, who brought him to one of the paddle-wheel excursion boats taking part in the evacuation. He hasn't heard from any of his family since he left France."

Jay didn't know what to say. It was all so matter-of-fact. But it reminded him of why he was here, too. To bomb Hitler back to where he came from—Hell. If only it weren't so hellish up there.

"Jay?" He started at the sound of her voice, and looked over guiltily. She had noticed his thoughts wandering. He could tell by the way that she was looking at him that she suspected what he was thinking about. "I really must introduce you to one of my colleagues, Anna Leska. She flew liaison aircraft for the Polish Air Force and managed to get her aircraft across into Rumania just ahead of the German panzers. Then she escaped from the internment camp on false papers and got to France and from France to England."

"Wow. That must be some story."

"It is—and she's a lovely girl, much prettier than me."

"I'm not after just a pretty face," Jay told her intently.

Embarrassed, Emily persisted on talking about her colleagues. "We have quite a few Polish pilots, actually. Two women, but twenty men as well. And we used to have lots of American men, but most of them went home when America entered the war. We still have 25 American women, though. I must introduce you to them. I could have a little party at my house and you could bring some of your mates from your squadron." Emily was warming to the idea the more she spoke about it. She liked Jay, but it would undoubtedly be better for him to find an American girl for him to spend his time with. Robin might not be dead.

"That'd be terrific," Jay agreed, sounding less enthusiastic than his words suggested. Jay didn't want the others to meet Emily or want them around when he was with her. He didn't want to waste what little time he had with her in the company of a bunch of other officers. But he knew he couldn't tell Emily that. She might think he had the wrong intentions. So he tried to sound positive: "The others would get a thrill out of meeting so many women pilots. I don't know if you ought to trust them, though. Some of the guys only have one thing in their heads when it comes to women."

"No doubt, but I trust you to invite only men who can be trusted," Emily countered.

"Yeah. OK. You tell me when, and—God and the 8th permitting—we'll be there." But Jay hoped it would never happen.

Their appetisers arrived and then their dinner. They talked about food and cooking. (Jay thought his mother's was the greatest. Emily admitted she wasn't particularly good.) They talked about the rationing, and wartime shortages and all sorts of other non-personal things, until it was very obviously time to leave. Jay saw Emily to the friend's flat she was staying in, and then wandered back through the dark and seemingly deserted streets alone.

He could not ever remember feeling so lonely in his whole life. Cambridge was so very different from any place in the States that he was very conscious of being a stranger in a strange land. But that wasn't the problem, really. The problem was that he was conscious of not belonging anywhere. It wasn't just Cambridge that was strange, it was America, too. Jay couldn't imagine going home to that little world his mother and Sally lived in and just fitting in again. More important, he was separated from Kathy, because he began to see that she would never understand what he was going through. She couldn't understand because he couldn't describe it to her, and he had the feeling she didn't really want to hear, anyway. If she didn't even care about what he was seeing and doing, why should she care about what he was thinking and feeling?

He didn't get it. She was mad at him because he didn't write her long, romantic letters, but she didn't even ask him about what he was thinking, or seeing or doing. She wanted to hear his feelings for her—but not his feelings generally. He couldn't have put them into words either, of course, but Emily seemed to understand them intuitively.

The weird thing about it was that he felt so comfortable with Emily. Despite the different accent and all the little mannerisms that were so different, he still felt completely at ease with her. He was less worried about making a fool of himself with her than when he was with Kathy—which was why he kept shooting his mouth off sometimes. But the moment of embarrassment never lasted very long because Emily blew it away with a word, a smile, a gesture.

Damn it! Jay stopped dead in the middle of the street. He knew what had happened to him, and he knew it wasn't good. He was head-over-heels in love with this woman, and she was married to someone else and he was engaged to Kathy. And only God knew if he'd live to see Christmas.

So just take it one day at a time, boy. He told himself. And with a deep breath, he went up the steps of his hotel. The lights had been dimmed, and only the night porter was behind the desk. "Room 12," he requested his key in a low voice.

The porter reached for the key in the little wooden box, and brought out an envelope with the key. "A message was left for you, sir."

Jay stiffened as he tore open the envelope. It was what he feared. Report back immediately. He was flying tomorrow.

CHAPTER 14

▼

Beauchamp Rodding, England
July 1943

"How the hell can they get the weather so fucking wrong?!" Tony burst out, giving voice to what they were all feeling. For three days in a row they had been alerted, leaves had been cancelled, aircraft bombed up and crews briefed—and then the whole thing had been called off due to 'weather.' A murky, wet low-pressure system with fits of rain and squalls of wind had settled over the British Isles, turning the airfields into shallow lakes and the skies into cauldrons of dark, pregnant cloud. Today the mission originally scheduled for 6 am had been postponed twice. Now, at 2.30 in the afternoon, when it was almost too late to reach the target in daylight anyway, they had been ordered to take off yet again. The crews had been transported out to their ships, even though anyone who bothered to stick his head out of his office would have noticed that it was still drizzling from low cloud.

As *Halifax Hooker's* crew dropped off the back of the truck, rain was running off the wings of the big bomber and splattering onto the concrete hardstand. Inside the aircraft it was damp and gloomy, making Jay shiver despite his flight jacket as he settled into the damp leather seat on the flight deck. Rain rolled down the windshield in large rivulets.

Tony picked up the check-list and they started to go through it. "Lieutenant?" A voice came over the intercom; it was the new upper turret gunner, a young man from Maine.

"Yeah, Webber, what is it?"

"Well, I'm not a genius or anything, just a lobsterman" (he pronounced it "lobstahman"), "but I *do* see a lot of weather." (said: weathah)

"Get to the point, Webber."

"Well, sir, doesn't weather generally move from west to east?"

"Yes, it does."

"Well, sir, I might have got this wrong and all, but isn't Germany east of England?"

"Last I heard."

"Well, the way I figure it then, the weather we had yesterday must be just about over the target by now."

"Look, Webber, I don't give the orders to fly. 8TH Air Force does. So just do as you're told. Got it?"

"Yes, sir. Just thought I'd warn you, that's all."

Tony rolled his eyes expressively at J.B. and they continued with the pre-flight check. Then J.B. tested the intercom to the others.

"I can't believe they're really gonna send us out in this shit," Tony protested, turning on the windshield wipers. The inside of the cockpit was already steaming up and Jay cracked his side-window to let in some cold, fresh air. It made him shiver.

This was 13. If they could just put this one behind them, they'd be more than half finished—over the hump, so to speak.

They started their engines, but Number Two seemed to be running rough, and J.B. cursed heartily. He couldn't stand it. The other ships were starting to ease out onto the taxiway, one after another, starting to line up. After waiting for this damn mission for three days, the last thing he needed was mechanical difficulties that kept them on the ground while the others took off. He shoved back his window and shouted out to the crew chief. "What the hell have you guys been doing the last three fucking days?"

Fuentes cast him a furious look, but the crew was already swarming over the engine, opening the cowling, tinkering with this and that with their oily rags hanging out of their pockets. You could see their overalls turning dark from moisture as the rain sank in more and more.

The first of the other ships turned onto the start of the runway, awaiting a green from the tower. The sound of scores of engines idling at slightly different pitches and speeds filled the air with an ominous, nervous humming that made the whole world seem to vibrate. One of the mechanics dropped down off the wing and ran back toward the maintenance hangar. Still the first bomber had not taken off.

"They're going to call it off again," Tony speculated watching the first bomber in line. He could clearly see that the pilot of that plane was moving about uneasily. He saw him shove his window back, thrust his elbow out and lean out into the rain, his cap low over his eyes. It was Major Rutgens, one of the other squadron commanders. A jeep was speeding around the perimeter toward the lead plane.

The mechanic was back, scrambling up onto *Halifax Hooker's* left wing. It looked to J.B. like he had a new sparkplug with him. Then the crew closed over the engine and he could see nothing but them bending over and fussing.

A red flare soared up over the airfield.

"Fucking hell!" Tony flung his gloves at the windshield in exasperation. The rain was hissing more fiercely now, shortening visibility. Through the grey mist the other bombers docilely started to roll back to their respective hard-stands.

"OK, Gang, looks like it was another false alarm. We've just been stood down again," J.B. informed the others over the intercom. A lot of groans, curses and impolite remarks followed.

With a clang the cowling was shut, and Fuentes turned and gave J.B. a gesture to start up again. J.B. warned the crew over the intercom that he was just going to run up number two engine to be sure it was firing correctly. After this operation was successfully concluded, they shut down and one after another dropped out of the ship again. A truck was coming to collect them and take them back to the Mess, but for a moment they stood in a miserable huddle, their collars turned up and their caps pulled down against the drizzle and chill. Nobody spoke, silently sharing the same mixture of frustration and relief for a minute or so. Then Tony burst out, "If only they'd let us off this fucking base for 24 hours! If I have to sit around in that goddamned hut another day, I think I'll start shooting holes in it."

"What a brilliant idea," Dan countered sarcastically. "Aren't we wet enough already without you making holes for the rain to come in?" On account of the rain, Dan wouldn't be able to ride, either, and that always put him in a bad mood. Furthermore, Tony and Dan had never really liked each other but over the last couple of weeks relations between them had noticeably deteriorated.

Tony at once flared up. "Wet? You're wet as a baby's bottom!—"

"Cut it out!" J.B. tried to stop it before it went any further. He couldn't stand the way they were bickering all the time, and they were setting a bad example for the enlisted men. Besides, there was the new bombardier to consider. He was a First Lieutenant like J.B. himself, who had just been released from hospital. His name was Rick Orloff, and he had 19 missions behind him with another crew that had since gone home. He also wore the Air Medal—which was sort of intimidating. Although released from hospital, he was recovering from shrapnel in the thigh and calf and still walked with a limp. "Alright, Rick?"

"Fine."

J.B. hadn't been able to coax more than monosyllabic answers out of the man yet, and it was beginning to get on his nerves. Everything was getting on his nerves. "Look, what do you say we all go down to one of the pubs around here and play a game of darts. Officers against the enlisted men. Five dollars says we can beat you guys."

The response wasn't exactly enthusiastic. The others just sort of shrugged and muttered things, but no one protested outright, so J.B. held them to it. A couple of hours later, right at opening time, they were shaking water off their caps and brushing it off their leather jackets as they shuffled into the *Black Horse*. There was a fire going in the open fireplace and the whole pub smelled of wet wool, smoke and damp coal. The mood was pretty gloomy here too, J.B. thought, but then he bought a round for his whole crew, and that started to cheer them up a little—or at least some of them.

The Kentucky Kid brightened at once. "This is sure one hell of a moonshine, Lieutenant," he declared almost ecstatically, savouring the taste of the Scotch J.B. had set in front of him. J.B. had heard no more about the Kid's sister since the incident two weeks ago, but Dan had written a letter for him to a lawyer he knew in Lexington. J.B. figured there might be trouble again when he got more news from home, but mail came very irregularly and usually after long delays. For now the Kid seemed satisfied.

"It sure doesn't take much to please you, Kid, does it?" the ball turret gunner, Brier, remarked rather contemptuously. Brier was from Georgia, but he was no hick. In fact, he made sure J.B. knew that he'd gone to some fancy private school. It was pretty obvious he thought he was better than the rest of the enlisted men. God only knew why he was still just a corporal, but J.B. suspected it was his attitude and a tendency to laziness and sloppiness that did not endear him to drill sergeants. It was a wonder, sometimes, that he hadn't been sent back to the infantry.

The Kid grinned back at him, apparently oblivious to Brier's contempt. "No, siree! I ain't never had it so good as I got it here. Hell, the first pair of shoes and socks I ever done owned was given me by the Army. Warm, dry feet even when it rains! Now that's something!" The Kid proclaimed this in all sincerity, pointing at his boots proudly.

Most of the others laughed, but Brier was in a bad mood, it seemed. "You can't beat that for dumb, can you?!" he declared, speaking pointedly to the others. Then he turned back to the hillbilly. "Bare feet can't kill you, Kid. German flak and fighters can!"

"Ain't killed me yet," the Kid answered, still grinning, and J.B. called everyone over to the dart board, distracting them.

It took them a bit to get into things, but after the first couple of rounds they started to have fun. Roach, otherwise so introverted and 'booky' (as the others complained), turned out to be the best, followed by the new bombardier. They kept increasing the range and everyone (now on their third round of drinks) was feeling pretty happy when some RAF arrived and made derisive remarks about the Americans' dart game. This led to a challenge—which of course the Americans accepted—only to be soundly defeated. Generous in victory, the RAF bought the next round. Outside it was pouring rain again.

J.B. noticed that his bombardier was standing alone at the bar and went over to join him. "Can I get you anything?"

Rick held up his glass to show it wasn't empty.

"We haven't had much chance to get to know each other—you living in another hut and all. Where are you from?"

"Indiana. Small town. Place you've never heard of."

"Try me."

"Candice."

"You're right. Never heard of it."

For the first time since they had met, Rick cracked a smile. Their eyes met for a moment. Then Rick looked away again, but remarked, "it was a good idea to come here."

"I got the idea from the RAF," J.B. admitted. "You often see their crews together here. Got separate messes just like we do, so the best place for a crew to be together is in a pub." Rick nodded. "Would you mind telling me how you got that medal?"

Rick glanced down at it, and shrugged. "I was too dumb to tell the pilot I was wounded and did the run anyway. When he found out about it, he got all excited and put me in for the medal. All I cared about was getting rid of the load and getting home."

"I know what you mean," J.B. admitted with a grin, and Rick smiled for the second time.

The door to the pub opened and the sound of feminine voices came through the door. All the men looked over expectantly. A bevy of young women, chattering happily together, came inside with a whiff of cold, damp air, and then started taking off their caps and shaking out their hair. They were all WAAF, all with chevrons and stripes on their sleeves, and dressed not in the going-out uniform of skirt and grey stockings, but still in battle-dress top and trousers. The Americans all looked twice, and the first wolf-whistles split the room.

The girls glanced over, but then gave them the cold shoulder and went in the direction of the RAF, who evidently knew them, welcoming them with cheery 'hellos' and greetings by name. J.B. turned back to Rick. "What did you do before the war?"

"Me?"

"Yeah," J.B. insisted.

"This 'n that. I'm no college boy, like the rest of you guys, if that's what you mean. I was lucky to finish high school." He paused, and then added almost aggressively, "Not bad grades—I got straight A's—but my Dad was out of work and I had to get a job to help out at home. It was my Mom that made me finish school. She took a second job herself, night shift, so I could at least graduate. She wanted me to have it better than she and my Dad."

J.B. nodded understandingly. "That's like my folks. I'm the first in my family to go to college, and my Mom and Dad had to make a lot of sacrifices for it. I'm going to make sure it wasn't for nothing, either."

"Yeah, that's what I tell myself, too," Rick agreed with a wan smile. "Then I go and do something dumb like get myself shot up. I haven't dared write home about it."

"I'll bet your parents would be proud."

Rick shrugged with one shoulder and looked down in his glass. "Yeah, when my Dad's sober enough to notice." Rick let their eyes meet only a second, and then knocked down his drink. He pushed his glass across the counter. "Apple juice."

"Sir?" the bartender asked.

"Another apple juice, please. What are you drinking, J.B.?"

Jay never got the chance to answer because there was a loud outcry from the other side of the room. A female voice had been raised first, but by the time J.B. looked over, two RAF sergeants had sprung to their feet, and facing them was Brier. There was a WAAF between them. J.B. saw Brier reach for the WAAF and one of the RAF sergeants slugged him hard in the face. Very effectively too. Brier staggered backwards, his nose gushing blood. Nisley and Howe, the two waist gunners, leapt to their feet and started forward with raised fists, while Brier let out a stream of filth, apparently directed at the WAAF rather than the sergeant who'd hit him.

J.B. and Dan sprang in between their own men and the RAF at almost the same instant. Rick followed a step behind Jay. "Get out now!" J.B. ordered his gunners.

"You mean you're going to let them just get away with this, sir?!" Nisley started to protest.

"Get out, or I'll throw you out!" J.B. cut off the protests. It was a definite advantage being taller and stronger than most of his crew. Dan took Nisley and Howe each by an arm and shoved them before him out into the rain. That left Brier, who was standing in shock, the back of his hand dabbing in disbelief at his bleeding nose. He kept looking down at the blood on the back of his hand as if he couldn't believe it was his.

"This isn't fair, sir! Look at me! These bastards—"

"Don't you call us bastards—" one of the RAF started, but one of his mates silenced him.

"We're leaving," J.B. decided simply, and grabbed a still dazed Brier. "Can you make sure our bill is settled up, Tony? I'll reimburse you." With this he firmly pushed Brier out of the pub, while Tony with a little shrug went to settle the bill with the bartender. The Kid, Webber and Roach trailed behind J.B., the Kid grinning, Roach grim and Webber unreadable.

Outside it was still raining, but J.B. was met by a greater storm of protest from his gunners. J.B. had to shout at them to shut up. "But you don't even know what happened, sir!" they pointed out indignantly.

"Alright, tell me." J.B. looked pointedly at Brier.

"You saw those sluts come in—"

"What sluts?"

"The girls in slacks!"

"WAAFs, you mean."

"WAAFs, sure!" Brier sneered, curling his blood-smeared lip derisively. "We know what *they're* there for! Service the RAF, don't they, sir? Well, why not us? What's the big deal? Just because we're American, we're not good enough for them, or what? Since when are whores so fussy? I'd told her she could have a pair of nylons! You would have thought I'd spit in her face."

"Worse," J.B. told him bluntly. "Where have you been hiding the last three months? Those WAAF all out-ranked you, corporal!"

"Out-*ranked* me?! What the hell are you talking about, sir? I don't give a shit how the RAF pays them! No decent girl walks around in slacks in public places! Where I come from, girls who wear slacks in public get locked up, and that's just where they belong! In jail or in bed, that's what I say!!"

Tony burst out laughing. "You're barking up the wrong tree, Brier. Our captain is head-over-heels for a girl who wears pants everywhere she goes."

The remark caught Jay off guard, and the tone and implications were enough to make him lose his own temper. He was within a hair's breadth of punching Tony in the nose, when Rick stepped in. "Those girls were aircraft mechanics. They probably know more about engines and airplanes than you do, corporal. And if you think that a woman's virtue is defined by whether she wears a skirt or not, you truly are as dumb as you look!"

J.B. was reminded that Kathy thought like Brier. She'd been outraged when she'd seen a couple of the women workers from Willow Run come into a drug store for a soda. She'd whispered loud enough for everyone to hear that it wasn't right to let women '*like that*' into a store where 'decent women' came to shop. 'There ought to be a sign out front,' she'd declared with righteous indignation: 'Dogs and women in slacks not allowed!'

Meanwhile, the others were responding to what Rick had said about the women's qualifications. "Mechanics? Aircraft mechanics?!" the others protested incredulously. "Are you kidding, sir?" "I wouldn't set foot in a ship serviced by women!" "Is it any wonder they're losing this war?!"

"Who's losing the war, mate?" This last question came belligerently from an RAF sergeant in the doorway. J.B. groaned with a sense of despair, certain that they would now have an open brawl on their hands.

"The Germans," Dan answered, quick off the mark.

"Yeah," J.B. agreed, with relief for Dan's fast thinking. "The Krauts are losing the war, but they'd lose it a lot faster if it would just stop raining for a day or two."

The RAF sergeant wasn't fooled, but in recognition of the good will of the American officers (and inbred respect for a man holding a commission), he let it pass with a grunt and a glance at the grey over-cast that was still pouring water on all of them. He turned up his collar and walked away. J.B. immediately started herding his own crew in the direction of the two jeeps they had used for transport. As he turned the key in the ignition, he glanced over at Rick, who was in the seat beside him, and remarked wearily, "I guess it wasn't such a great idea after all."

"Sure it was. Even a good brawl is better than just waiting."

J.B. wasn't so sure, and they still hadn't flown Number 13. They would probably go through the whole damn thing again tomorrow.

RAF Honeyborne

Emily, too, had been caught out by the weather. She'd managed to deliver a replacement Pryce Page Harrow to the OTU at Honeyborne just as the weather closed down. In fact, it had been a nightmare flight at the end, with the visibility deteriorating by the minute, so she had had to lose more and more altitude in order to keep in contact with the land. Meanwhile, the wind picked up and started to buffet the tired bomber, making it harder and harder to manage. The fact that it was the first Harrow she had ever flown didn't make her feel any happier, although it was behaving relatively well given its age. She had rarely been so relieved to finally sight the flares on the runway and feel the solid earth under her feet again. As she taxied in toward the Watch Office, the clouds opened with a vengeance and rain pelted down. A gallant RAF corporal dashed out from the Watch Office with a rain cape over his head and ducked under the wing to receive her.

"Glad to see you made it, Miss," he greeted her. "Your Ops Officer has been calling every few minutes to see if you got in safe."

"Oh dear," Emily answered. She wasn't so much embarrassed about causing worry as afraid that they must have lost a pilot somewhere. It was when they started losing pilots, that Operations realised the weather had closed down abruptly and started worrying about all those still in the air.

The corporal kindly carried her parachute for her, while she lugged her tote bag, and they dashed back to the Watch Office under his cape. She signed over the delivered Harrow and then asked about accommodations. "I'm afraid there isn't much we can offer you here," the Duty Pilot admitted. "The Waafery is under re-construction, you see, and all the WAAF are billeted at private homes in the meantime. There's a nice country inn just up the road, however. I could have someone ring up and see if we can get a room for you there, if you like? I'll lay on the transport."

"Yes, thank you."

Emily would have preferred a mess where there were other people about. An RAF mess always offered at least company, conversation and distraction, and at best entertainment, wit and warmth as well. If she were stuck out at some 'nice' country inn, it would mean being utterly alone in a cocoon of genteel silence. She had nothing to read with her, no evening clothes suitable for dining in a nice restaurant, and since she was uncomfortable going into a bar alone, she would be reduced to just sitting alone in her room feeling sorry for herself. She wouldn't even have the comfort of Penny!

She was also feeling chilled through and damp. She looked forward to a warm meal and a change into dry clothes, but it hardly made sense to put on the only dry things she had now. RAF transport might well be wet and draughty and public transport likely to be even worse. But she couldn't go into the Mess in trousers, either, so all she could do was wait here in the gathering gloom feeling sorry for herself.

After about 45 minutes, a Pilot Officer stuck his head into the Watch Office and called out: "Second Officer Priestman?"

Emily jumped up with relief, grabbing her parachute.

Their eyes met, and he smiled at her. He was very young and wore the wings of a navigator, not a pilot. "Lewis, Ma'am, I understand you need a lift down to the *Sommerset Arms?*"

"Yes, if that's not too much trouble."

"We're heading that way now." He took the parachute from her kindly, although he was slight of stature, in fact an inch or so shorter than Emily herself.

As they stepped outside into the rain, he smiled shyly at her sidelong. "You're a pilot, are you, Ma'am?"

"Yes, I just delivered that Harrow," she pointed to it, as it had not been moved and still waited outside the Watch Office.

"Jolly good." Lewis nodded toward a rather battered-looking old Ford, and indicated she should get in while he tossed her parachute and tote bag into the boot. Emily noticed there were two men in the back seat already, and as she settled herself in the car she introduced herself, turning around to offer her hand over the back of the seat. Both were young-looking Sergeants, one an air gunner and the other a bomb aimer.

Lewis got in behind the steering wheel, and announced, "This is the rest of the crew—'Jamie' Jameson and 'Red' Royce."

Red (who did have red hair and a freckled face) leaned forward to address Emily, while Lewis started up the motor with a horrible racket. Red had to raise his voice to be heard over the back-firing and revving of the engine. "You're a pilot, Les said."

"Yes," Emily agreed, trying not to get annoyed; but it really was getting tiresome, this having to confirm it over and over again. It wasn't *that* unusual, and she'd made deliveries to this OTU at least 3 times before.

"We're missing a pilot," Red continued; "wouldn't you like to be our pilot—for the evening, I mean."

"Oh," Emily was taken aback and ashamed of her annoyance of a moment before. Her tongue was running on rather foolishly to cover her embarrassment, saying: "Well, it's not exactly flying weather."

They laughed. "No, we meant at dinner. We're going out for dinner at the *Arms* and thought you might want to join us. But, of course, if you have other plans—"

"No, not at all. I'd love to join you for dinner! I was just feeling sorry for myself for being all alone in some genteel hotel where no one talks to anyone else."

They laughed. "Done, then!" Red grinned at her and leaned back.

Les Lewis drove very fast and rather unsafely given the wet, winding roads and the fading light. Emily was almost as glad to get to the hotel safely as she had been to land. It was, exactly as she had expected, a large old manor converted into a posh hotel. This particular manor was Georgian, with a great semi-circular portico, and was set in its own deer park. The drive was gravel, and a doorman came down the steps to open the door for her. He also took her parachute pack and tote bag without batting an eye, and led her to her room with a "this way, Mrs. Priestman." She was obviously expected; the RAF must have called ahead.

As so often in such establishments, the room was very elegantly appointed, but it was also chilly and damp on a night like this. The only fire was a small gas unit fitted into what had once been an open coal fireplace. It took coins. At least the room had an en suite bath, and Emily found the towel racks were heated. Gratefully she removed her flying clothes and hung them over the towel rack to dry, then changed into her skirt, stockings and shoes. She also brushed out her hair and put on lipstick, before going back down to the lounge where she'd agreed to meet the others.

The three young men all got to their feet at the sight of her. They looked so *very* young—and awkward, too. She began to wonder if they had really intended to come here, or if they had been ordered to escort her. If they had been ordered to do so, they were being very gracious about it. In fact, they made quite a fuss over her, escorting her to the reserved table before the fire and holding her chair for her. "You're our guest for the evening, Ma'am," Lewis announced, "so have whatever you like."

"Oh, that's really not necessary," Emily hastened to assure him. "We ATA women just got a raise in pay. In fact, since June, we're now being paid exactly what the men pilots of equal rank earn." This was a major coup by Pauline Gower, since the government had a blanket policy of paying all women 20% less than their male colleagues. Granting the women pilots of the ATA equal pay for equal work was therefore a dangerous precedent; it would cost the government millions if the women in the services—WAAF, ATS and WRNS—started to demand the same treatment. Emily almost felt guilty mentioning it, but at the same time she hated to think of these young airmen, who certainly earned less than she did, paying for her meal.

"Well, that's only as it should be," Les insisted firmly. "But we'd still like you to be our guest."

"That's extremely kind of you." Emily felt it would be impolite to insist further.

"Would you like an aperitif?"

"A little sherry would be warming."

The waiter had only been waiting for a signal, and now bowed as he took their order.

"Are you celebrating something?" Emily asked. They looked at her with startled faces. "I mean, to come to a place like this? Most of the RAF I know prefer places that are, shall we say, a touch livelier." Emily had expected a laugh of agreement, and was met with awkward silence.

So they *had* been ordered here, she thought. Then Les drew a deep breath. "Actually, Ma'am, we were all given 24 hours leave because we were supposed to come here for a wedding. We rather expected to get very drunk and spend the night here and sleep in long tomorrow. There was a wizard band hired, too, and some first rate-popsies invited and all. Only the wedding got cancelled."

"Oh."

"It was our pilot's wedding, you see. Only he went up on a check flight yesterday," Red explained, "and crashed along with the instructor. They were both killed."

Emily couldn't grasp it. The day before his wedding. On a routine check flight. The poor girl. "His bride…"

"I'm told she took it very bravely, Ma'am. The CO called her."

"I'm so sorry. My husband managed to get himself shot down the morning of our wedding, but he bailed out in time and made it anyway—three hours late, but safe and sound."

"Then your husband is a pilot too, Mrs. Priestman?" Red asked.

She heard herself say: "He was shot down over France four and a half months ago. I've heard nothing since."

"Sorry, Ma'am."

There was a moment of silence, and then Red pulled himself together. "Well, let's not sit around moping. I say we order a bottle of champagne and drink to absent friends."

"Good idea!" Les agreed, and at once turned and signalled the waiter rather more vigorously than was expected in places like this. The waiter responded rapidly but with a look of open disapproval. "Yes? Is there something I can get for you, sir?"

"We've changed our minds. Rather than the other drinks, we want champagne."

The waiter raised his eyebrows.

"Put it on my bill, please," Emily intervened in a tone of voice she had unconsciously picked up from Robin, and the waiter's glance suggested a sudden re-appraisal of her as he bowed and withdrew. "You can pay for dinner, if you insist," Emily told her companions, "but the bubbly is on me—he wouldn't have given it to us otherwise." (Emily calculated that the champagne very likely cost a Sergeant's monthly wage, and the RAF was not considered good credit. But a married woman—even one in uniform—might still be the wife of a peer or an industrialist or an investment banker; there was thus no way of knowing what her income was, and her credit was better in any case; she was less likely to die tomorrow.)

They laughed, probably from embarrassment, but it didn't matter. The champagne came chilled, and watching the way Jamie sipped it, Emily very much suspected it was the first time he had ever had the stuff. He seemed to be the youngest of the three, and didn't look more than 18. They had all just been school-boys before the war.

She started asking each of them about their families, schools, what had made them volunteer for aircrew—anything to get them talking. The champagne started to have its effect too, and Emily signalled for a second bottle discreetly. She didn't care if it cost *her* a month's wages. What was she saving her money for, anyway? A home she would probably never have?

They were all very drunk by the time they started for bed (because the three young men still had their rooms booked and 24 hours' leave), but it was a happy kind of drunk. In fact, they were all silly, and Emily could not remember *ever* having been so uninhibitedly drunk and silly in her life. When she'd been up at Cambridge, she felt very daring to have so much as a beer, coming as she did from a teetotalling family. She'd only really started to drink more potent alcohol after she met Robin, but she'd always been very anxious not to disgrace him by getting tipsy. Tonight it didn't matter at all. She would probably never see any of these young men ever again.

They insisted on escorting her to her room. There she gave them each a long, passionate kiss in the hall, and then scuttled into her room, closed and locked the door, and sank down with her back against it giggling. She heard them retreating rather loudly down the hall, and curled herself up where she was to sleep for a bit. An hour or two later she got up, undressed, washed and brushed her teeth, before settling into the large bed contentedly.

She was astonished to be awoken in the morning by a loud knocking and a male voice announcing from the far side of the door, "Skipper! Church parade in 20 minutes." Skipper? Skipper was what Robin's squadron had always called him. It was also what a bomber crew often called their pilot.

From somewhere a church bell was indeed tolling. It was Sunday. Not that it was sunny. The awful weather still held and it was pouring rain; she could hear it hissing on the windowpanes and gurgling down the gutters. But the bell was tolling for church nevertheless, and she couldn't disappoint her 'crew' by failing to arrive. No need to mention she was an atheist.

Fifteen minutes later she emerged, still a bit bleary-eyed, from her chamber and was greeted by three grinning young men in their best Blues. They looked much fitter than she felt. Ah, the virtues of youth! They were also very slicked down in their best, and Les ceremoniously offered her his elbow. The other two fell in behind like footmen to the King and Queen, and so they went to church.

After church (having checked with the airfield that there was still no flying for Emily), Red suggested they could go to a matinee at the nearest cinema. They all piled into Les' car and drove to Bristol. After the film they had tea together and then selected a place for dinner and dancing. Emily was wilting by now, and protested that she had nothing suitable to wear for dancing. "You wouldn't want to be caught dead dancing with me in this old skirt," she told them.

"Skipper, I wouldn't want to be caught dead with you *anywhere*," Red told her bluntly, "because I don't even want to *think* about you being *dead*. But I wouldn't mind being seen *alive* with you anywhere, even if you were wearing an erk's overalls."

Emily went on tip-toe to kiss him on the cheek. "Thank you."

They went dancing.

At about 10 pm, Emily remembered they only had 24 hours' leave. "Shouldn't you be back at the Station by now?"

"We're all AWOL, Skipper," Les told her, unconcerned. "Let 'em hang us from the yardarm until dead!"

"Les! I don't want you to get in trouble."

"Look outside, Skipper. Even the birds are walking."

"I know, but, Les…"

If Les had driven dangerously while sober, he was a positive menace when drunk, but Emily was far from sober herself that night and didn't notice it as much. They left her at the *Sommerset Arms* at about 2 am and then continued on to RAF Honeyborne. She kissed them all good night in the drive, the rain soaking them slowly, as they kissed lingeringly and hungrily.

"Take care of yourselves," she begged.

"We are invincible!" Red assured her as he fell back into the car, raising his hand in the 'V' for Victory.

"Are you sure you can't *really* be our new skipper?" Jamie asked wistfully.

"I'll ask the Air Minister next time I see him," Emily promised.

"Do that!" Les urged her and honked once as he careened back down the drive.

Emily felt very foolish as she staggered up the steps of the hotel and let herself in with her key. She was sure there were dozens of disapproving eyes looking out from behind the black-out blinds, shaking their heads in disgust. She was also in urgent need of a loo. But when she had gained her room, locked her door and found herself in the bathroom, she knew she did not regret a minute of it.

CHAPTER 15

▼

Windsor, England
August 1943

As they pulled up in front of Emily's house, Tony whistled, and gave J.B. a look of sceptical re-appraisal. Dan seemed unimpressed, but as Rick climbed out of the back he looked at J.B., straightening his tie unconsciously, and asked bluntly, "You're sure they want me around here?"

If there was any one of the three of them J.B. had doubts about it was Tony, but he answered Rick honestly. "Yes, I am. She asked me to bring the other officers of my crew."

"Yeah, but British officers are *real* gentlemen—not my kind, by Act of Congress only."

"Come on in and meet her. She said she'd have some of her colleagues over, too." As he spoke, Jay reached down and pulled from the floor of the jeep a bag full of 'contributions.' It contained a bottle of Bourbon, a bottle of rum, a tin of Virginia ham, two tins of pineapple and lots of candy bars.

"All pilots, right?" Tony wanted confirmation.

"That's what they do in her outfit, Tony: fly."

"OK, let's go get 'em, boys." Tony started for the front door, and Jay cast an appealing look to Dan.

"I'll make sure he doesn't get out of line," Dan promised.

Tony was already ringing the bell, rather too long and too insistently, making J.B. cringe and wish he hadn't brought him along. He was going to ruin everything, make an ass of himself and confirm everyone's worst prejudices against Americans.

The door was opened by a middle-aged woman in a black dress with a white apron and white hat, a proper maid. Tony took a step back in sheer astonishment. With one leap J.B. was on the doorstep beside Tony and removed his cap fast. "My name's Jay Baronowsky, and these are my friends. We were invited—"

"Of course, sir," the maid said, backing up to let them into the house. The maid took their caps and Jay's bag full of food and drink, indicated the downstairs bathroom (in case they wished to 'freshen up') and the entrance into the parlour, from which music and voices were spilling out into the entry hall. The first maid disappeared, but from the left, another uniformed maid emerged from what was evidently the kitchen, carrying a silver tray laden with little sandwiches. J.B., who had never crossed the threshold into the house before, was starting to get intimidated. Kathy's family had a black cleaning woman, but only one.

"I thought you said this was your girlfriend's house?" Tony remarked, as he watched the maid disappear into the parlour in wonder. They were waiting for Rick, who had slipped into the bathroom.

"It is," J.B. answered. He was tempted to add the question: 'What did you expect? A brothel?' but he was afraid someone might overhear him and get the wrong impression.

"You never said she was some sort of duchess or whatever."

Dan hissed irritably, "Try not to embarrass the rest of us, would you, Tony?"

"Me? Embarrass *you*? That'll be the day! I'll have you know—"

"Shut up." J.B. cut him off, and went for the bathroom himself as Rick emerged with his hair slicked down.

Rick fell in beside Dan, wriggling his shoulders nervously as his eyes swept around the hall taking in the chandelier, the parquet floor covered with a small Turkish rug, and then focused on the room beyond. He ran his finger around the inside of his collar uncomfortably. Tony started to pick a fight with Dan again, but Dan brushed him off, and J.B. re-emerged, also slicked down.

J.B. then started for the parlour, the others a little behind him. As they entered, J.B. searched the room for Emily, but he couldn't find her. Instead there were at least a half-dozen other girls, all in pretty cocktail dresses, two male ATA pilots in their smart dark-blue and gold uniforms, one RAF officer and one elderly civilian in a three-piece suit—all strangers to Jay. A slender, dark beauty was coming towards him with a smile and a bold look in her eye. She wore a sleek, well-fitted raw-silk dress with a bolero jacket in velvet, and pearls. "You must be

Lieutenant Baronowsky," she proclaimed, holding out a perfectly manicured hand highlighted with red nail-polish. "I'm Emily's lodger, Philippa Wycliffe."

"How do you do, Ma'am. May I introduce my co-pilot Tony Costino, my navigator, Dan Vernon, and my bombardier, Rick Orloff."

"A pleasure to meet you, gentlemen." Philippa shook hands with each of the others in turn, smiling graciously. "Do come in and make yourselves comfortable. I'll send Graves to take your drink orders," she promised, "and tell Emily you're here."

She withdrew with a last smile, and Tony turned demonstratively to follow her with his eyes. She had very shapely legs. He was still looking the wrong way when a voice boomed out in a very broad Texas accent, "Well, if it ain't the 8th Air Force—late as usual."

That got Tony's attention, and he turned around so fast, he almost tripped himself. A tall blonde woman with shoulder-length hair was coming toward them in an off-the-shoulder, tight-bodiced, printed gown of rustling chiffon and silk petticoats. She was smiling broadly. Although she was not a real beauty, she was a girl sure of her charms nevertheless—with every right to be. She had an hourglass figure, long legs, bright red lips, and that wonderful mane of blonde hair in big curls hanging down at the back of her head, but looped up fashionably and piled on top of her head from the sides.

She reached the American officers and held out her hand, "Hey-ah, fellas, I'm Mary-Lou Bennett of Dallas, Texas. Where'd y'all come from?"

"Tony Costino from New York City," Tony told her, up-grading his Hoboken home without batting an eye. "But I did my flight training in Texas. Don't tell me you're a pilot, too?" Tony hadn't let go of Mary-Lou's hand and he was looking deep into her eyes.

She laughed at him, answering, "You can bet your booties on it, Sugar." Then she firmly took her hand away from him and offered it to J.B. with a smile.

"Jay Baronowsky of Detroit," he told her, adding quickly, "I'm the one who nearly killed Mrs. Priestman in a mid-air collision."

"Oh, of course!" She grinned and offered her hand to Dan.

"Dan Vernon, Ma'am, Richmond, Virginia."

"What a *pleasure* to hear that accent, Mr. Vernon! We *must* talk. And I don't care a *thing* what you say, Honey, just so *long* as you sound like molasses in sunshine!" Already she had turned her attention to Rick, however.

"Rick Orloff, Candice, Indiana."

"Now *where* in the *world* is that?"

"No place special, that's for sure, Ma'am."

"Well, don't be a hog, Mary-Lou," a second girl came up beside the Texan beauty. She was dark, a little plump but in a pleasant way, and she spoke with an accent off the Great Plains. The introductions started again; the girl was Cindy Caldwell from Idaho. A moment later two more American women joined the little group, Alice Leonard from Los Angeles, and Rita Domoulin from Chicago. They were all lively and attractive and self-assured—as you would expect of girls who had braved the U-boats in the North Atlantic to come and fly in and for a foreign country. J.B. admired them all, but they weren't Emily.

Looking around the room, he spotted Philippa sitting with the grey-haired civilian and went across to her. "Excuse me,"

"Oh, don't you have a drink yet?" she asked, springing up. "I'm so sorry. We had a minor catastrophe with the oven, and Graves has been trying to trouble-shoot, I'm afraid. I'll fetch you something myself. What are you drinking?"

"Thanks, but I was looking for Emily. Didn't you say you would tell her we were here?"

"Yes, but we had this little emergency in the kitchen. I'm sure she'll be right out. Meanwhile, sit down and talk to Teddy, and I'll get your drink. What did you say you were drinking?"

"I don't suppose you have rum and coke, do you? I mean, I brought along a bottle of rum, but I know coke isn't g.i. around here—"

"But, of course! Emily's American friends wouldn't *come* to a party without coke! So they brought their own. I'll go mix it for you." Philippa was gone, and J.B. was left with the elderly civilian. Jay held out his hand and introduced himself, receiving the unnerving reply that he was talking to *Sir* Howard Edward Downs. J.B. was certain he'd never shaken hands with a knight before. "Do you fly fighters or bombers?" the Englishman asked.

"B-17s, sir," J.B. answered uncomfortably, wishing Philippa or Emily or anyone would come and rescue him.

"Ah, yes, and have you been over here long?"

"Since the beginning of May, Sir. Beautiful country."

"Well, you have seen it at its best weather-wise, I dare say, but of course the war has done terrible damage to our cities and infrastructure. How long have you known Mrs. Priestman?" The way he said it, with just a hint of disapproval, made J.B. wonder in panic if this man was a relative of hers. But he couldn't be. Her father was a Communist, and her husband's family name was Priestman. "We met on my first mission, sir." J.B. told him honestly, omitting the embarrassing circumstances. He got the feeling this man thought he was dirt anyway. Why make matters worse?

Philippa was just returning with Jay's drink when another late guest entered the parlour. It was Steeplechase, and Philippa stopped short in her tracks. "Where did you come from?" she demanded without prelude.

"Through the front door, to be precise," Steeplechase snapped back.

"Yes, but I mean what are you doing here?"

"I was *invited* by the hostess." They were glaring at each other. "I gather I'm in the way as far as you're concerned," Steeplechase added, with a pointed look in the direction of Teddy in conversation with an American officer.

"Well, *I* certainly didn't ask you," Philippa told him. "Emily's in the kitchen at the moment. We had a little accident with the dessert."

The maid with a tray of sandwiches was already beside Steeplechase, discreetly offering him a choice of cucumber or liver-paste. He took a sandwich while Philippa tried to escape him, continuing to J.B. to deliver his drink. Steeplechase followed in her wake.

J.B. saw him coming, recognised that he was a fairly senior officer with more than one ribbon on his chest, but for the life of him he couldn't remember the RAF ranks. Three rings meant he had the same seniority as a Commander in the Navy, he calculated, and that was a Lieutenant Colonel in the Army, but what did the RAF call them? "Lieutenant," Steeplechase held out his hand.

"Sir!" Jay drew himself up to attention, omitting only the salute in the absence of a cap.

"Oh, forget all that, old chap, we're off duty. I'm Yves." Steeplechase held out his hand.

"J.B. Baronowsky," Jay introduced himself.

They shook hands, but Steeplechase was gazing fixedly at the civilian as if he wanted to kill him. "Sir Howard," the RAF officer greeted the civilian without holding out his hand.

"How are you doing these days, my dear boy? I heard you'd racked up another new gong the other day. DSO, was it?"

"No, just the bar to the DFC."

"I'm quite amazed you weren't on that Damnbuster's raid thing, you know. Thought you were the type for that kind of work. Hedge-hopping and hush-hush and all."

"Gibson and I can't stand each other."

"Understandable," Sir Howard answered with an icy smile. If looks could have killed, they would both be dead, Jay thought, and decided it was time to excuse himself.

"If you'll excuse me, sir, I'd like to say hello to our hostess."

"Of course, of course," Sir Howard dismissed him with an absent smile. Steeplechase just nodded without taking his eyes off Sir Howard.

J.B. went in the direction of the kitchen. The air definitely smelt burnt the closer one got to it. The door opened in front of him and he caught a glimpse of smoke-filled air, a man in livery bent over an open oven, and a cluttered table. Emily was coming out, trying to brush her hair out of a red, sweaty face. She caught her breath and drew up at the sight of Jay.

"Everything alright?" he asked with a smile. She was out of uniform again, and the very way her hair was falling in her face made her look more fragile and vulnerable than usual. Each time they met, he discovered a different side of her, it seemed, from that first meeting under the Wellington when she was in an old, beat-up Irvin jacket, to the dinner in Cambridge in evening gown, to this: the somewhat flustered housewife.

"I'm so sorry I haven't greeted you and your friends. I'm afraid I've ruined the dessert. The oven appears to be over-heating and then we couldn't get it to turn off at all. But I think everything is alright now—except that we have no dessert."

"We brought a bunch of candy bars. Maybe you could hand those out instead. Not the same, I know, but—"

Emily did something she'd never done before. She reached out and touched his arm in a spontaneous gesture of gratitude rather than a formal handshake. "Thank you, Jay. That's very kind, and just what I *will* do. Just let me fix myself up and then I'll come and meet your friends. I do hope you'll all enjoy yourselves. Is the hotel alright?"

"Fine," Jay assured her. In anticipation of a late night, the four American officers had taken two rooms at a hotel Emily recommended. Tony had objected, complaining that it was a waste of money when they were supposed to be meeting 'hot chicks,' but the others had ignored him and he'd checked in like the rest of them, sharing a room with Rick.

"Have you met the other girls yet?" Emily asked.

"Swell bunch. Really great. Got to admire all of them." But he was gazing at her, and Emily understood perfectly. He wasn't about to let himself get distracted by them. It made her feel more self-conscious than ever.

"Please excuse me. I must wash up." She showed him her sticky hands. Without awaiting his consent, she hurried up a flight of stairs.

J.B. stood for a moment at the foot of the stairs in indecision. He had no desire to go back into the parlour where all the others were. He could hear Mary-Lou's loud voice above all the others, and now and again Tony's laugh cut through the rest of the din. No, he couldn't face that.

He noticed another door leading off under the stairway and wandered hesitantly in that direction. He found himself looking into what was evidently a study. There was an open secretary cluttered with papers, book-cases, a reading chair with a standing lamp behind it, and a rack full of newspapers. On a little table placed between the two windows shielded by floor-length damask curtains, there was a vase with roses. Several petals had fallen off.

J.B. stepped cautiously into the room, conscious that he was snooping and trespassing, but his curiosity exceeded his sense of guilt. He scanned the room looking for clues about Emily. There were the newspapers that suggested her interest in current affairs. And lots of books. Many history books, of course, and the complete works of Shakespeare (a much nicer edition than what Kathy had), and several plays by a G.B. Shaw. There was a collection of Conrad and Kipling, too. That surprised J.B. for a moment, and then he noticed that the next titles were all sailing books, and suddenly a creepy feeling ran down his spine as it occurred to him that these were *her husband's* books.

J.B. shuddered and stepped back guiltily—irrationally expecting the absent man to suddenly appear, to challenge him for trespassing into this private space—to challenge him for being here at all. The feeling was so strong, that J.B.'s whole body tensed and he held his breath. He looked about himself again, and then he saw it. The silver-framed photograph on the secretary. How could he have missed it earlier? It was gazing straight at him.

Jay forced himself to take a step closer, and leaned forward to get a better look. A solemn young man with dark hair and dark eyes stared back at him accusingly. He was very good-looking, J.B. had to concede. Good-looking and he had the DFC and three rings on his sleeve, too. J.B. sighed and straightened.

There were two other photos on the secretary also. One showed the same young man, this time with only one stripe on his sleeve, at what appeared to be a garden party. Ladies in big-brimmed hats and white gloves stood around in the background while the young RAF officer shook hands with a man even Jay recognised: King Edward VIII. The photo was striking because there was a tension between the two men that the camera had captured—a flash of anger in the King's eye and defiance on the face of the young officer. Jay found himself wishing he knew the story behind that picture. It certainly wasn't your standard celebrity with unknown-member-of-the-public shot.

The third photo at last contained Emily as well as her husband. It had not attracted Jay's attention at first because it was taken from farther away, so that the people were shown at full length and their faces were very small. Now J.B. picked it up to look at it more closely. It showed Emily in an elegant, high-waisted wedding gown with a veil down her back and a long train arranged in a fan at her feet. She held a bouquet of flowers in her right hand. She looked lovely, fragile and yet proud, but not radiant. Not at all. In fact, she wasn't really smiling. J.B. thought a bride ought to look *much* happier than that! Her left hand was hooked in the elbow of an RAF officer, and J.B. had to lean closer to convince himself it really was the same man as in the other photos. The man in the wedding photo was dressed in a rather ill-fitting uniform, with a turtle-neck rather than shirt-and-tie, and was still in flying boots. J.B. was offended. How dare he marry Emily in old flying clothes rather than dress uniform?! It was an insult. But he had hardly thought it, than he noticed the bandages on the bridegroom's hands, and an inkling of what must have happened sent a shiver down his spine. He noted, too, that Emily's husband's unkempt hair was falling over his forehead, his eyes were sunken in his face, and there were very dark shadows under them—but *he* was grinning from ear to ear. J.B. recognised that look. It was the look of slap-happy disbelief at things having turned out alright after all. It sent another shiver down his spine. He put the photo back and retreated in haste from the little study, regretting that he had ever gone into it.

Back in the parlour he avoided the Americans, who were still clustered in a loud, happy group in the centre of the room, and slipped over to where the two male ATA officers were standing together. He introduced himself to them.

"Ah, Baronowsky!" They broke into smiles. It seemed they were both Poles, and vigorously shook J.B.'s hand as they introduced themselves effusively.

J.B. was at once delighted. "How did you get out? Get over here, I mean?" he asked eagerly, looking from one to the other.

"Anna's story is much better," one of the men insisted and turned to signal a young woman, who was talking to the other RAF officer in the room—a Flight Lieutenant. The young woman responded to her colleagues' gestures, bringing the RAF officer with her. The sight of the latter gave J.B. a jolt. His face was stiff and vaguely discoloured. In fact, there was something entirely artificial about it, as if someone had pasted it on. Even as he realised what it was, the other man answered his look of horror. "Too slow getting out of a burning Hurricane in September of '40. David Goldman."

"That an American accent?" J.B. asked, amazed. There had only been a handful of Americans who had risked their citizenship—not to mention their lives—to fight in the RAF during the Battle of Britain, while the US was still neutral. He felt privileged to meet one of them.

"Canadian," the RAF officer corrected him, and pointed to the Canada patch on his shoulder.

"But born in Wilhelmshaven," Anna announced.

"Isn't that in Germany?" J.B. blurted out, confused. "At least I hope it is! I've bombed it twice!"

Wrong thing to say, J.B. noted from the stunned reaction. But then the Canadian RAF officer recovered and answered simply, "Yes, Wilhelmshaven is in Germany. My family left shortly after Hitler came to power."

J.B. suddenly felt very small and very stupid. On one hand, it occurred to him that he might have been dropping bombs on this man's friends and relatives, and on the other that this man was probably a Jew. His grandfather hated Jews, and Kathy was anti-Semitic too, claiming that the only bad thing about the University of Michigan was that it admitted so many Jews. "Jew-U" was what Kathy called it sometimes.

J.B. didn't know what to say to this German Jew in RAF uniform, and was relieved when suddenly Emily re-appeared—until she looped her arm through David Goldman's elbow and leaned against him with every evidence of affection and ease. J.B. nearly dropped his glass. Surely she hadn't been playing the faithful wife all this time while actually having an affair with this German-Jew whose face was wrecked?

"How are you all getting on?" the hostess asked. "Can I be getting anyone anything?"

They shook their heads and Anna explained to everyone, "Flying Officer Goldman was explaining to me about plastic surgery."

From the looks of the others, J.B. gathered that Anna had some reason she wanted to know about that very badly.

"What do you hear of Micha?" Emily asked gently.

"He is now in 'stable' condition. That is better than 'critical,' no?"

"Yes, it is better," Emily assured her, and then, leaving David, came and took J.B.'s arm. "Let me introduce you to Steeplechase," she said as she moved them away from the Poles.

"You seem rather fond of that Kraut," J.B. heard himself saying, heard how jealous he sounded, and he knew he shouldn't have said it—but it was too late and it was the truth. He *was* jealous.

Emily looked up at him sharply and her eyebrows shot up. "He's a very old friend. He was in my husband's squadron, and he spent a lot of time with us while he was recovering. He has no family here."

"Oh, would your husband approve of him more than me?"

"Jay!" She turned and faced him in shock and outrage.

"I'm sorry, but you've been pretty stand-offish to me for hanging on him like that."

"You have no right to judge me, Lieutenant," she told him in a low, cold voice, and left him standing in the middle of the room.

Jay could have torn his own tongue out, or at least kicked himself in the gut.

Someone thrust a drink in his hand. "Not an easy nut to crack, our dear Mrs. Priestman." It was Steeplechase.

"Have you known her long?"

"I hardly know her at all. It's Philippa I've been chasing for the last two years, and you can see where it got me: eating the dust of some old bugger with a title, a fortune *and* a wife and kids."

J.B. gaped at the senior officer. "That Sir-something-or-other over there?"

Steeplechase nodded, not displeased by J.B.'s look of absolute shock.

"Women!"

"Yeah." Steeplechase raised his glass and downed it in one go. "I'll go get us another."

They had been drinking together for quite a while before J.B. got up the courage to ask, "I guess you've flown quite a lot of missions, haven't you?"

"Oh, a few."

J.B. waited expectantly.

"82, if you insist."

J.B. whistled and shook his head in admiration. "I honestly don't know how I'm going to get through 25."

"One at a time," came the answer, with a wry, understanding smile.

"Yeah. Sure."

"How many have you flown now?"

"Sixteen." Jay paused and then asked, "Does it get easier at some point?"

"In a way. You see, eventually, you get addicted to it."

"*Addicted?*"

"I suppose it's the adrenaline or some such thing. Your body adjusts to these regular doses of sheer terror and if you go off ops, you crave them again. They've put me in desk jobs twice, and both times I became a nervous wreck. I got to the point where I couldn't sleep at all, and then I hung around airfields and made such a nuisance of myself that they had to put me back on ops. Admittedly, when I'm up there, I usually swear to myself that this is the last time ever, and I never want to set foot in an aircraft again, much less fly it somewhere hostile. But it doesn't last. You land, wash away the sweat, and there it is again: that anticipation, that hunger for the next flight."

J.B. could only stare at him, uncomprehending. He couldn't imagine begging to go on missions—not now that he knew what they were all about.

Steeplechase continued, his gaze fixed across the room on Philippa, who was now dancing with Teddy. "Maybe it would be different if I had a wife to come home to—to live for, I mean."

J.B. followed his gaze. Philippa would certainly be something to come home to—particularly if she clung to you the way she was clinging to that old man. J.B. didn't get it at all. Steeplechase was a real hero, and not bad-looking either. How could Philippa throw herself at a married man like that? It offended him, and he hoped Tony didn't find out that Sir-Whatshisface was married. If he learned that Emily lived with a woman who was having an affair with a married man, he'd automatically assume that Emily was a slut, too. Which reminded him, what had become of Tony and the others?

Rick and Dan were both dancing with a couple of the American girls, but Tony was nowhere to be seen. At last J.B. spotted him in a dark corner with Mary-Lou. Well, no harm in that if they were both happy about it. Kept him out of everyone else's way. So Jay relaxed and had another drink.

The Poles left first. Then the Kraut. By the time Dan came over to get the keys to the jeep so he could drive the American girls home, J.B. noticed that Tony and Mary-Lou were no longer around, although he hadn't any idea when or where they'd gone. The other three American girls waved good night and went out with Rick and Dan. Rick only saw them out to the jeep, however. Rather than crowd them, he came back and joined J.B. on the sofa.

"Have a good time?" Jay asked him.

Rick perched himself on the arm of the sofa and stared into his drink for a moment. At first Jay thought he wasn't going to answer at all. But then he declared. "Well, you know, those are about the nicest bunch of girls I've ever met. But what's the point?"

"What do you mean? The way that girl from Idaho was dancing with you, I'd say she'd be more than happy to see you again."

"Sure. But she's a nice girl. She'd want to fall in love and get serious. You can't knock up a girl like that."

"Is that all you want to do with a girl?" Jay asked angrily.

Rick didn't even get riled up. He just swished his drink around in the bottom of his glass and declared as he stared into it, "Nope. But, you see, what's the point in falling in love with a girl like that? I couldn't ever take her home—not to the shack we live in with no running water and a stinking outhouse out back. Or can you see me introducing her to my Dad? The old man stinking drunk."

Jay was stunned into silence.

Rick looked at him hard. "I can't offer her anything, either. I mean, even if I pretended my folks were dead and all, and just said: come on, let's build a future together. What sort of future do you think that would be? What sort of job do you think I can get? You can fly for an airline after the war, but they won't need bombardiers when the war's over, will they? So what good am I?"

"You can't look at things like that, Rick!" J.B. was genuinely unsettled by so much pessimism. "Look at my folks. They started out with nothing. They couldn't even speak English. But by working hard and saving and sticking together, they've built a decent life—and it's getting better generation to generation."

"Right. And what about my Dad? He lost his job in the Depression, became a drunk, and we've only gone from bad to worse."

"You don't have to be like your Dad. You aren't even drinking, are you?"

"Straight Coke!" Rick held up his glass.

"See. You're a better man than me, buddy. I hope you at least got that girl's telephone number. I'll bet she'll be broken-hearted if you don't give her a call tomorrow."

A loud crash followed by a groan interrupted before Rick could reply. On the far side of the room, Steeplechase had fallen down, apparently dead drunk, knocking over a little side table and spilling glasses with their contents onto the floor. Everybody who was still present rushed over.

The butler emerged and started issuing orders to the two maids. The table was righted, the glasses and glass-pieces were collected or swept up, and a cloth soaked in hot soapy water was brought to dilute the stains in the carpet; but while the staff dealt with the things, the hostess was left to deal with the person. Emily was on her heels beside the Wing Commander, shaking him gently. "Steeplechase, are you alright?"

"Come now, Mrs. Priestman," Teddy said from a great height above her. He was looking down on the RAF officer with Philippa hanging on his arm. "It's perfectly obvious the boy can't hold his liquor. Really quite an appalling commentary, but there you have youth nowadays. All talk and no substance."

"Yeah, like 82 missions!" J.B. flared up furiously. He didn't care if this was a Sir-Somebody, it was the first time since he'd got over here that he'd ever found an Englishman to be absolutely insufferable.

"My, my, aren't we defensive," Teddy purred contemptuously.

"*We* aren't anything, because I wouldn't want to be associated with the likes of you in any way, shape or form. Now why don't you clear off and keep your unwanted opinions to yourself." Jay had his hands on his hips, and his pose was increasingly hostile and aggressive.

"How dare you! In case you've forgotten, this is my country—" Teddy was starting to get offended, too.

"And you are *both* guests in *my* house!" Emily reminded them pointedly from the floor.

"Yes, Teddy, don't make a scene," Philippa urged, tugging at his elbow.

"You know, I don't see what right these Americans have coming over here and—"

"Stop it, Teddy! You know perfectly well we desperately need them." Philippa was still pulling him away firmly.

"*Desperately*, did you say? You think we need *them* desperately? My dear girl—"

"Teddy, please," she had him to the door, and the others could turn back to Steeplechase.

"He is out cold, Ma'am," Rick declared professionally. "The best thing would be to just let him sleep it off. Is there somewhere we could put him for you? A sofa or a cot or something?"

"There are two extra bedrooms, but I could never get him upstairs."

"We can manage," J.B. assured her, slipping his hands under Steeplechase's shoulders and getting a hold under his arms, while Rick took his ankles. They heaved him off the floor and Emily guided them up the stairs and into a small, neat, sterile room that looked like it was never used. J.B. and Rick got Steeplechase onto the bed and removed his shoes, tunic and tie. Then they left him there, closing the door behind them, and retreated back down the stairs. J.B. had only a glance into what he presumed was Emily's bedroom. It was a bit messy, with her uniform still flung over a chair by the bed.

Back in the parlour, the music and lights had been turned off. The only noise came from the kitchen, where the maids were evidently washing up. "Thank you both, so much," Emily said sincerely. "Is there anything I can get you? A coffee perhaps? Not that I have any real coffee."

"Rats!" J.B. declared, angry with himself. "I forgot to bring it. Next time, I'll bring coffee."

Emily looked at him a little oddly. "What makes you think there will be a next time?"

"Emily, I'm sorry about what I said earlier. Honest, I am."

"Maybe I should go for a walk around the block," Rick volunteered.

"There's no need for that, Lieutenant. Lieutenant Baronowsky and I have nothing to say to one another that we can't say in front of you."

Rick looked from one to the other, and then said, "Yes, you do. Thank you for a wonderful evening, Ma'am. I'll be waiting for you out front, J.B. Good night." He got half-way to the door, stopped, turned back and asked, "Excuse me, Ma'am, but do you think you could give me a number where I might reach Miss Caldwell?"

"Of course. Just a moment." Emily disappeared to get a paper and pen.

J.B. mouthed to Rick, "Thanks."

Rick shrugged and mouthed, "Good luck."

Emily returned and handed him a note with the number he'd asked for. Rick shook her hand, thanked her again and was gone.

They were alone together in the darkened room. Neither spoke.

"I didn't know you had servants," J.B. remarked just to break the silence.

"They aren't mine. Philippa's mother lent them to us for the evening."

"Oh. I can't say much for Philippa's taste in gentlemen friends."

"No." Emily hesitated. "And thanks for defending Steeplechase like that. He only drinks because he's so miserable. It's seeing Philippa with Teddy that makes him like that. I shouldn't have invited him, I suppose…"

"Why did you?"

"Because I think he's the better man and I didn't realise that Philippa had invited Teddy. I thought she'd be without an escort and that Steeplechase would have a chance…I feel terrible now," Emily admitted, adding a bit plaintively, "The whole evening was a disaster, really, from the ruined dessert to Teddy rubbing Steeplechase's nose in it."

"And me not taking the bait, right?"

"What do you mean?"

"You wanted me to take an interest in one of those American girls."

"Wouldn't that be better for both of us?"

"Why?"

"I'm a married woman."

"I noticed. And what if your husband really is dead? Is that Kraut next in line?"

"Honestly! You don't understand a thing!" she told him, anger flashing in her eyes. "David taught me to fly! Without him, I'd probably still be serving tea and sandwiches at a Salvation Army canteen! I'd never even been up in an aeroplane before the war started, and after it did there was no commercial flying anymore. Robin realised how much I wanted to learn, but he didn't have time to teach me.

He gave me the odd lesson when he could squeeze it in, but it was only when David showed up—released from hospital after almost two years of skin grafting and other forms of medicinal torture—that he found a way to arrange everything. You see, David had been rated 'unfit for flying duties' and was desperate to prove to the RAF that he could fly despite his injuries. He begged Robin, who was a Station Commander in 10 Group at the time, to let him fly the station trainer until he was up to a standard to pass a flight check. Robin said he would let him do that *only* if he'd use the time to teach me to fly. They were both risking I-don't-know-what for my sake. I can't thank David enough for what he did for me."

"Meaning, he's first on your list to replace your husband, or what?"

"That's ridiculous! Why do you say things like that?"

"Because—" What could he say? That he was in love with her? It might be true, but the implications of it still frightened him. If he was in love with her, he had to break off with Kathy, no matter what. Didn't he? And how could he be so sure he was in love with her? Maybe it was just like with Kathy. Maybe he was only so fascinated by her *because* she rejected him? The thought caught him off guard and he laughed shortly.

Emily cocked her head, frowning.

"I was just thinking, maybe I'm only so fascinated and ardent because you keep rejecting me. What did you call it? The intoxication of the chase?" Emily continued to gaze at him. "Well, don't you see? If you want to get rid of me, all you have to do is start being interested. You know, turn the tables on me. If you get interested, maybe I'll turn tail and run."

Emily gazed at him uncertainly. "That sounds a bit risky to me," she concluded at length.

"Nothing in this life is without some risk," J.B. countered with a crooked grin. When she said nothing, he got serious again. "Look, Emily, I'm sorry for what I said earlier. I know I don't have any right to be jealous or possessive and all that, but it's the way I feel. I concede the field to your husband. He was here first and he's got all the legal rights to you, but you can't expect me to give anyone else precedence graciously. I mean, you didn't even say anything about him."

"That's because he is just a very dear, old friend, to whom I am very grateful. Nothing more."

"OK. Maybe I saw something that wasn't there. And what am I?"

There was a long, pregnant pause. Emily could hear her own heart beating wildly. Since that weekend with Les, Jamie and Red, she realised how desperately she wanted to be in a man's arms again, to kiss and be kissed, to laugh and dance and just plain be in love again. She was ashamed of herself, but it was true. Finally she asked softly, "What do you want to be, Jay? I thought you were engaged to a girl in America."

"Yeah, to a selfish, immature little bitch, that's what. To a girl who doesn't give a damn about me at all—except that I'm a feather in her cap at the moment, a pilot in the 8th Air Force. Emily, if I thought I had a chance with you—presuming your husband is dead—then I'd give Kathy up in a second."

"It sounds to me, Jay," Emily answered softly and very seriously, "like you should give her up regardless of anything I say or feel. You should never marry a woman you think is a bitch, much less one who doesn't care for you."

J.B. thought about it and then admitted, "Yeah, you're probably right, but it doesn't answer my question. What *do* you feel about me?"

Emily took a moment to answer, trying to sort out her own feelings. It was foolish to pretend that she felt nothing for him. Quite the contrary. She felt much more than she thought she ought to. She liked him. She liked his refreshing openness, his unabashed optimism, his almost childish enthusiasm for everything she showed him. He made her laugh and it was fun to be with him. She was flattered by his ardour, his attention. Robin had never courted her. It hadn't been necessary and there hadn't been time for it. Emily was certain she had loved Robin more than he loved her; with Jay it was—rather flatteringly—the other way around.

And standing here in the darkness with him, there was even a part of her that would have welcomed it if he took her in his arms. She could imagine cuddling against his broad chest. But she didn't love him. She knew that too. He flattered her. He made her feel special, but he didn't make her pulse race as Robin had done. He couldn't put her in a state of utter confusion with a look or a remark. Then again, maybe that had less to do with him than with the fact that she had grown up in the last three years?

"I like you, Jay. I like being with you. If I *knew* Robin was dead, things might be different between us. Harder at first, because I'd really grieve, remembering all the good times and mourning my loss more intently than I can do now because I won't let myself. But I think, once I accepted it, I would want to get to know you better and want our relationship to be become deeper and closer."

"And what about that Canadian-Kraut?"

"Oh, Jay, try to understand! I knew David before he was half incinerated in a Hurricane. I remember visiting him in hospital when he looked more like an Egyptian mummy than a person. I saw him limp into Robin's office and beg to be allowed to fly. He said: 'I don't care if I crash. I don't care if I kill myself flying, but if they ground me I'll kill myself for sure.' Robin's solution was to have him teach me to fly, 'killing two birds with one stone,' as he put it. How can I not be kind to David? But much as I like him…" She bit her lip, a little ashamed to say it out loud, but then forced herself. "I find his company gloomy. I'd rather be with you."

Jay was more relieved than he could fully fathom. He held his breath for a bit, just to get control of himself, to make sure he didn't do or say anything dumb. Somehow it meant the world to him that she wanted to be with him, because that was what he wanted more than anything just now. Steeplechase had been right about that: a girl to come home to made life itself worth living in a very tangible way. Jay wanted to sweep Emily up in his arms and kiss her—really kiss her—but he was afraid that might make her take fright again. So instead, he forced himself to say just, "Thank you." Then he looked around at the darkened parlour and remarked, "I guess it's pretty late, and Rick must be getting cold out there. I'll give you a call in the morning, OK?"

"Fine, Jay." She saw him out to the front hall, took his cap from the clothes closet and handed it to him. He set it on, and hesitated. He was still terribly tempted to kiss her, but he kept control of himself and managed to just touch his cap in a kind of salute and leave.

CHAPTER 16

▼

Yarmouth, Isle of Wight
August 1943

The sight of the square, red-brick house with its widow's watch, neat hedge and large garden ending in a private pier out into the Solent filled Emily with heart-stopping memories. She had first come here on her honeymoon. Robin and she had rented a cottage nearby for the fortnight, and they had been invited to tea here by his grandfather, Admiral Priestman. Emily had been quite nervous about it. She had met the Admiral for the first time the day of the wedding itself. He had seemed a very intimidating figure in full-dress uniform, masses of gold braid and a chest full of ribbons, ramrod straight and gruff of manner. He had seemed to incorporate all that was the British "Establishment," "Tradition," "Wealth & Privilege"—not to mention calcified concepts of Honour and Duty. She was very worried what he might think if her.

She had good reason to fear his opinion. The Admiral had objected so to Robin's mother that he had cut off all contact with her the moment his son was dead. In fact, Robin's mother had never set foot in the house here at Yarmouth, and the Admiral had returned the compliment by not crossing her threshold in Southsea. But the Admiral had paid for Robin's schooling, and from the age of seven Robin had been required to spend his summer holidays with his grandparents. Later, the Admiral had also tried to force Robin into the Royal Navy, refusing to pay for Cranwell. This had caused a short breach between them, but not one which had lasted.

Indeed, with the sharpened powers of observation that her own insecurity gave her, Emily had soon sensed the affection that bound Robin and his grandfather, although at first she had been somewhat baffled by the tone that ruled between them. The Admiral, although dressed in casual flannel trousers and a blue blazer, had still managed to look the Admiral to the core. Robin addressed him as 'sir' more often than not. The Admiral's voice was as gruff as ever, and he flung remarks at Robin that sounded almost insulting. Things like: "It was in weather like this that Robin managed to wreck my 16-footer!"

But Emily noted that Robin was more flattered than offended, and gave as well as he took. To the remark about the boat, Robin had laughed and countered, "Not at all. It's not blowing more than Force Five out there at the moment. There was a Force Six blowing the day I wrecked the *Stormbird.*"

"Only makes it more reprehensible!" the Admiral retorted. "I never thought my own flesh and blood would be so lacking in judgement as to take an open boat out into a Force Six."

"Maybe I'm not your flesh and blood?" Robin quipped back, with such amusement in his eyes that Emily was completely bewildered—until she saw the Admiral's reaction.

He bristled with outrage and pointed his cane at Robin. "Don't start that preposterous nonsense with me again! I've stuck my neck out for you a dozen times! You had damn well better be my flesh-and-blood!"

Between these bouts of mutual provocation, which they both seemed to enjoy immensely, they laughed a great deal about shared memories—often at the expense of Robin's grandmother and cousins. Unable to relate to either the people they were talking about or the events they recalled, Emily had felt a little left out of things, but not unkindly so. In fact, she found it wonderful to be able to sit back and just watch her husband of only five days. Seeing him with his grandfather was to see a side of him she had never seen before.

Among his fellow officers, Robin was relaxed but reserved; he rarely thrust himself to the forefront or dominated a crowd. Robin was the last man who 'pulled rank' on anyone, and his habit of going around with one hand in his trouser pocket made him distinctly 'unmilitary' in posture and manner. Emily had been astonished, therefore, to observe that an apparently casual suggestion on his part could cause men to spring to comply as readily as a drill sergeant's shouted command. With his grandfather, however, Robin was far less retiring and understated. For the first time Emily glimpsed a wit and mischievousness that she had never previously suspected.

That afternoon, a blustery October day in 1940, had been refreshing for them both. Emily had learned that Robin had an impish, carefree and sometimes still very boyish streak to his personality, and Robin had managed to utterly forget the Battle of Britain and his command for an entire afternoon.

Over the next three years, Robin and Emily had rarely found the opportunity to visit the Admiral. Altogether, they had seen him perhaps a half-dozen times in that period. Yet with each visit, Emily had come to feel more comfortable with the irascible old man. She had learned that his bark was worse than his bite, and increasingly learned to appreciate his bone-dry humour. But she had always come with Robin up to now. This was her first trip to see him alone.

At his wife's death in 1937, the Admiral had gradually become more and more reclusive. He had also closed down more and more of the house. The 2nd floor, with its nursery and maid's rooms, had been disused for some time in any case. By the time the war started and the staff had been reduced to just one man-servant and a housekeeper, who came in to cook one meal a day and clean, only the ground floor of the house was really in use. The Admiral had set up a camp-bed in his study, and only ventured up to the floor above to bathe, dress and shave at the start of the day. Emily felt the whole house was beginning to feel like a ghost-house.

Not that the Admiral was letting *himself* go in any way. He greeted Emily at the front door dressed in a debonair blazer with ascot, and he was as straight as ever. But Emily noted he walked with a bit of a limp as he led her into the conservatory with its palms and view of the Solent, and his cane was clearly no longer the 'affectation' Robin had claimed it to be.

"It's very kind of you to take time from your busy schedule to visit an old man, my dear," the Admiral proclaimed as he led the way.

"I had to deliver a Walrus to Cowes," Emily admitted, "and when I realised there was no return delivery, I asked for the afternoon off so I could come see you."

"Very kind of you, my dear. I trust the Fleet Air Arm was courteous to you?"

"They were, as always, a model of generosity, Admiral. They let me leave my parachute and overnight bag there and drove me to the bus-station."

"Well, that is at least reassuring." He sounded as if he had sincerely doubted it, and then announced, "Mrs. Hayes has made tea for us, you see." He pointed with his cane. "Sit over there and pour."

Smiling to herself at his tone of command, Emily did as she was told, finding a silver tray laden with a china tea-service and a plate of unidentified, rather dry and unappetising cakes. The Admiral lowered himself into an armchair opposite her with careful movements suggesting stiffness or pain. Emily pretended she hadn't noticed and asked: "Milk and sugar?"

"Milk and two sugars."

It was rare to see cubes of sugar anywhere these days. Emily supposed the Admiral had placed his whole month's rations on this tray—or more likely, the sugar came from ancient, pre-rationing reserves that had still not been depleted in this one-man household.

"I've put that album there for you," the Admiral continued in an irritable tone, gesturing peevishly with his hand toward the table on the other side of her. "I thought you might want to see some photos of Robin when he was younger."

"Oh, yes!" Emily agreed readily, looking over at the heavy leather album with interest. After a moment's hesitation and a glance toward the Admiral, she put her own tea aside and took the album on her lap. She opened to the first page, which contained only a single photo of a squinting, fussing dark baby in christening robes being held by a plump young woman dressed in black. "His father was lost at Jutland just days before his birth, you know." The Admiral commented without actually being able to see the photo.

"Yes, his mother told me," Emily confessed.

"Did she also tell you *why* my wife refused to have her in this house?" He asked belligerently.

"She said you disapproved of her."

"Little conniving strumpet, that's what she was! She set her cap for Neil and snared the innocent boy with feminine wiles she must have inherited from *her* mother. You know, don't you, that *her* mother was a French can-can-girl—to put it politely, that is."

Emily had heard all about this family 'skeleton': Robin's maternal grandmother had been the mistress of his maternal grandfather and the cause of a great scandal that ended in the old man being ostracised by society. After the death of his first wife (of grief, the family claimed) he had further offended good society by marrying his already pregnant mistress. What she said now was simply: "Robin always said that's where he got his looks."

"Hmpf!" the Admiral snorted, casting her a severe look—but then a twinkle of amusement lit his eyes. "He would say that, wouldn't he? The rascal!" Then reflectively, he added, "But there's no doubt a grain of truth to it. I never saw the woman, of course. She abandoned her daughters when they were both infants, you know. One presumes she returned to France. Neither of the girls were particularly striking, but looks often skip a generation. Robin always did have something slightly apart about him. You'll notice it in the next pictures." He waved his hand at her to turn the page.

There followed a bunch of photos of boys and girls in summer clothes (sailor suits predominated) having ice, sitting on beaches or in boats. At first Emily wasn't sure which one was Robin, but then after looking at the pictures more intently, she noticed that one of the older boys was indeed always a bit apart. He was darker than the rest, too, and he usually looked at the camera in the pictures—unless there was a boat in it. If there was a sailboat, the dark boy was invariably fussing with it in one way or another.

"He took to boats like a duck to water," the old man commented, as if he could tell what she was gazing at. "I hardly had to show him anything about them. Most remarkable, and I'll never understand why he insisted on this flying nonsense! Most ridiculous decision! Worse than his father wanting to be an engineer! What a splendid deck officer he would have made." The old man's voice softened abruptly, and Emily looked over at him uncertainly. The Admiral was gazing into his tea, which he held over his lap primly as he said: "He was always my favourite—despite my best efforts to resist him. My dear wife, you know, did not really want him in her house at all. She was convinced he would be an insufferable brat, seeing that he was the spoilt only child of a widowed mother and all that. She expected him to be badly behaved, and warned me that she would send him home at once if he proved too 'unmanageable.'

"It must have been very hard for him, coming to a strange house to live among complete strangers. I know he was frightened, but he faced me at the front door with a doggedness that was tangible. I could tell from the first moment that he intended to show me that he was his own man. At age eight!" Then as if he realised he was rambling on, revealing too much, the Admiral looked up and gestured to her impatiently. "Go on! Look at some of the other pictures!"

Emily turned the pages slowly, scanning the pictures. There were pictures of Robin in school uniform, pictures of him rowing, pictures of him looking uncomfortable in evening clothes with one of his female cousins. Finally, the first picture in flying helmet and overalls next to a Gypsy Moth. Then graduation from Cranwell in dress blues. Next a picture of Robin in tropical kit standing beside his cousin, Kevin, at the rail of an ocean liner; Kevin wore the rings of a Fourth Officer, Merchant Navy.

Emily's eyes lingered over that photo because she had briefly known Kevin, too. "Kevin was a lovely young man," Emily remarked to his grandfather.

"Yes." The Admiral hesitated and then confessed, "I underestimated him. His courage was subtler than Robin's. I could intimidate him and so I bullied him. I didn't notice until too late that he was strong and tenacious without being defiant. I regret that I did not get to know him better...I've lost three of the five of them now. The best."

Emily looked up, alarmed by his tone of voice. She had never heard the Admiral sound defeated before. She followed his gaze, and saw that he was looking toward the mantel, on which six photos in identical frames were lined up neatly. One was of a girl, Robin's cousin Amanda. The other five were in uniform: three in that of the Royal Navy, Kevin in that of the Merchant Marine and Robin in Air Force blue.

Emily felt a shiver run down her spine and then confronted the Admiral. "You don't think he's coming back, do you?"

"My dear," the Admiral turned his head to look at her squarely. He sat very straight and dignified. "Sailors are used to men being lost without a trace. No one ever brought me Kevin or Jimmy's bodies either."

"But the Germans should have reported him dead."

"Even the Germans make mistakes—forget to file something, get a name wrong, send things to the wrong address. It happens."

"It could happen if he were a prisoner, too."

"Yes. Of course. I don't mean to take that hope away from you. If you can bear the hoping, then it would be a crime to take it away from you. Keep faith with him as long as you can. Is there any more tea?" He held out his cup.

Emily set the album aside, and poured for the Admiral.

"Tell me about this Air Transport Auxiliary thing," he ordered as she handed him the tea-cup, and Emily knew that he did not want to talk about Robin anymore. So Emily talked about her work willingly. She liked it, and she was pleased by the Admiral's intelligent questions and apparent approval. After two hours, however, Emily could tell that the Admiral was weary and she rose to leave.

The Admiral saw her to the door. Here he grasped her hand in both of his and thanked her again for coming to see him. "I know writing is quite out of fashion, but it would be kind of you to drop me a card now and then." He suggested it in a tone that was almost petulant, but Emily sensed that he was just trying to hide the fact that he was, in fact, asking a favour of her. Emily could imagine that a man so used to command found it hard to ask for favours.

"I will," she assured him, and with a smile started to withdraw her hand and turn away.

Admiral Priestman stopped her, holding her hand in such a firm grip that she turned back to meet his eyes, almost alarmed. "Dearest child," he told her in a low, urgent voice that was devoid of all pretence, "if he *is* dead, you must go on living. You are young and your whole life is ahead of you. It would be quite wrong for you to bury yourself in grief and memories. Don't be like his damned fool of a mother: revelling in her grief! You must try to love again, give all that you have in your fine heart to another deserving man, and so make a new life for yourself."

This said, he let go of her hand and nodded firmly and imperatively for her to go.

Beauchamp Rodding, England
August 1943

"But she's not 'enlisted'; she's my sister, for crying out loud!" J.B. argued with the Adjutant. "You can't be serious that just because my sister happens to be a WAC, I can't take her into the Officers' Club? Do you realise that we are both five thousand miles from home and in the middle of a God-damned war and that I could get killed tomorrow?"

"Don't be melodramatic, Baronowsky. If the weather turns bad, you won't even be flying tomorrow."

J.B. threw up his hands. "Great, then it will be the day after tomorrow before I get killed!" Then, abruptly changing his tactics, he leaned over the Adjutant's desk and pleaded pathetically, "Look! My sister's got her first pass in 3 months. She's blowing it all to come see me. She's an innocent, small-town American girl in a strange country for the first time in her life, and she wants to see her big brother. It's really not asking a lot of the f—" he cut himself off "of the Army let her into the Officers' Club."

"The answer's 'no.' Do you know how many other officers on this base have sisters who are enlisted WAC?"

"No. How many?"

"I haven't any idea, but *maybe* it's hundreds or thousands."

"Right, and all of them are here in England! Come on, Adj, this is crazy. I'm not allowed off base, and my sister's not allowed into the Officer's Mess or Club. What are we supposed to do? Stand out in the middle of the tarmac? Come on, Adj, be human."

"That's not my job, Baronowsky. You want sympathy, go talk to the chaplain. That's a good idea anyway; I'm sure you could meet with your sister in the Chapel."

"Yeah. Great. Last I heard, all they had to eat and drink over there was wafers and wine. The wine might be okay, but wafers are a bit thin on calories. My sister's going to have been bucking trains and busses for hours by the time she gets here. She's got a right to a decent meal, at least."

"She can eat in the enlisted men's mess."

"One girl among all those wolves?! She'd never come out of there alive! Do you want to be responsible for an American casualty, Adj? I can see the headline now: "Beautiful young WAC killed on USAAF base in England!""

"What is this all about?" The question came from the open door into the Colonel's office, and J.B. and the Adjutant, both taken by surprise, sprang to attention. "Sorry, Sir. I didn't see you come in."

"Just what is this all about, Baronowsky?" the Group Commander repeated.

"My sister, sir. She's a WAC. She's just been assigned over here and she's got a 24-hour pass and is on her way to see me. I just came in here to get permission to take her to a pub or something, and the Adj says we're all confined to the base. So then I asked if I could take my sister into the Officers' Club with me, and—"

"She's enlisted personnel, is she?"

"Well, technically, I suppose she is, sir, but she's still my sister, you know, and we're five thousand miles away—"

"Spare me. You're both adults and you're both in the Army."

"Don't I wish I weren't..." J.B. muttered.

"What did you say, Baronowsky?"

"Oh, nothing important, sir."

"Good. When your sister arrives, bring her here and report to me."

"Sir?"

"Did I speak in a language you don't understand, Lieutenant? I said report to me with your sister as soon as she arrives."

"Yes, sir!" J.B. saluted and retreated, cursing the Army under his breath and swearing he was going to get out the day the war ended.

He waited for Barb at the gatehouse, and saw her get off the green double-decker bus at the stop, looking around herself uncertainly. He dashed out and swept her up into his arms before she'd oriented herself. She had never looked better to him. He was used to women in uniform after four months in England, and Barb looked slimmer than he'd ever seen her. Her shorter hair suited her, too—made her look like the vigorous, self-assured young woman she was rather than a girl trying to imitate a glamorous style that she could never live up to.

"You look great!" he assured her, holding her at arms length.

Barb giggled and broke free of him to salute smartly. "PFC Baronowsky reporting, sir!"

"Come on," J.B. pulled her through the gate with him. Barb was happy to show the guard her orders and ID, but the guard waved her through. Beyond, J.B. explained they had to report to the Group Commander.

"To Group CO? Why?" Barb balked.

"I don't know. I don't understand most of what they order us to do."

"You either, huh? And I thought my big brother was finally going to explain it all to me. I mean, can you believe it? I'm a great driver and I can fix a tire or change a spark plug better than half the guys in the motor pool. They send me over here, which I thought was because I was so good. But when I get here I find out I've been assigned to the motor pool, alright—as a *clerk*! I'm not allowed to drive anything! Just sit in the office and keep track of who's driving what. It's crazy!"

"Well, they do drive on the wrong side over here, you know."

"Yeah, I noticed. So what? I can learn to do that, if they'd let me. I'd sure as heck learn to do that faster than I'm gonna learn all the gol-darned forms the army's got for their darned jeeps and trucks!"

"Well, maybe it's only until they get used to you, you know. How many women are there on your base, anyway? We haven't got any here—as you can tell."

As they made their way to the CO's office, they were causing a minor sensation as soldiers stopped and turned to watch Barb as she walked past, showering her with wolf-whistles and cat-calls.

Barb was obviously used to it, because she ignored it all. "There are just 15 of us at the moment, but more are supposed to follow. All cooks and clerks, would you believe? They don't want to let us do anything fun."

They had reached the admin block, and J.B. straightened his tie and re-set his cap before mounting the steps. Barb also rather nervously tugged at her uniform jacket and straightened down her skirt. "Are my stockings straight?" she asked Jay, and he glanced down the back of her legs.

"Fine," he said uncritically.

They went in together and reported to the clerk. He checked with the Colonel by intercom and then waved them in.

Colonel Bochanek stood behind his desk, and the two Baronowskys saluted smartly—Barb better than her brother, because she was more recently out of boot camp and more nervous.

"Alright, at ease. Your orders, Private Baronowsky." The Colonel held out his hand, and Barb, with a little sidelong glance at her brother, took them out of her breast pocket and handed them over. The Colonel read them very carefully, then handed them back. With a gesture he indicated some wooden chairs around a battered wooden table under the window. "Have a seat," he ordered. They moved over to the table in a group. The window offered a view of the runway and Watch Office and Tower beyond. You could see some of the dispersed B-17s as well. J.B. and the Colonel didn't even glance out, but Barb found it hard to tear her eyes away.

"So, Private Baronowsky. Your brother tells me you just arrived over here."

"Yes, sir, we landed in Liverpool 10 days ago."

"And you've been given a pass already?"

"Yes, sir. It's in lieu of home-leave, which I didn't take on finishing training, sir. I wanted to see my brother more than my folks."

The Colonel met her eyes as she said that, and Barb looked back at him unabashed. Jay sensed that she had scored. Bochanek nodded once. "Alright, and why did you join the WAC in the first place?"

"For the same reason you joined the Army, Sir. Because I love my country."

J.B. looked down so the Colonel wouldn't catch him smiling. The Colonel looked over at him suspiciously anyway. Then he turned back to Barb. "That's all very well, Private Baronowsky, but a lot of girls who love their country are helping it by working in factories, on farms or in hospitals. Why did you want to be in the Army?"

"I wanted to build B-24s at Willow Run, sir, but my Dad wouldn't let me. He thought 'nice' girls didn't do things like that."

"Do 'nice' girls join the WAC?" Bochanek asked back.

"Are you suggesting my sister isn't a 'nice' girl, Colonel?" J.B. had it out faster than Barb could react.

Bochanek looked from J.B. to Barb and then back again. "No. You've satisfied me—but one does hear rumours, you know. I just wanted to see for myself." Then turning to Barb he announced, "I'm promoting you to Lieutenant for the next" (he looked at his watch) "9 hours and 25 minutes. That's until 10 pm tonight. By that time, I want you off this base. Until then you can go anywhere your brother goes—as long as he's with you." He added in an aside to J.B., "You'll have to stand guard outside the toilets for her, Baronowsky."

"Yes, sir!"

"Dismissed!"

"The first thing I get to see is your ship!" Barb told her brother as soon as they were back in the open.

Jay was more than happy to comply. As they started over, they heard an announcement over the PA that WAC Private Baronowsky was visiting for the afternoon and would be treated with the courtesy due a Second Lieutenant of the USAAF. Anyone in non-compliance would face disciplinary measures.

Barb hooted. "Did you hear that? That guy's alright. What's he like to fly with?"

"I don't know. He usually doesn't fly. When he does, he's up somewhere in the front of the formation."

Barb let the subject drop, and they continued across the grass and the taxiways, past the rows of battered bombers. Barb looked at them with open interest, and finally remarked, "Geez, they look pretty run-down."

"Why? Do they look better in your Group?"

"Oh, we're just forming up. The airfield isn't even finished. They haven't got half the buildings up yet. We WAC are part of the advance party to get things ready for the planes and aircrews. There aren't any bombers there yet—or crews."

J.B. wasn't listening anymore. He pointed, "That's her there."

"*Halifax **Hooker**?*" Barb made a face. "Mom would *love* that!"

"Yeah, so don't tell her, OK? The crew chose the name in a secret ballot, and *Hooker* won hands down."

They continued toward the big bomber that waited patiently but expectantly, her nose pointed skyward. Barb looked up as they walked under the wing, and her expression was one of rapturous awe. "God, I'd love to get my hands on those engines! Cars are so boring! Aircraft engines—now they're something else! I've been reading up on them."

J.B. shook his head in bemusement. "You're crazy, Barb."

"Why?" she asked indignantly, her hands on her hips.

"You don't want to be a grease monkey, for Christ's sake."

"It takes more brains than just driving these things!" He jerked her head toward the nose.

J.B. just shook his head and automatically started toward the fore hatch, then stopped himself. Barb wouldn't be able to haul herself up into it like he did—not in a straight, fitted skirt. To get a ladder, he'd have to go over to the hangar, which he didn't want to do. He led her to the aft hatch near the tail instead, and they climbed inside the airframe. J.B. started forward, pointing things out to her, and Barb followed, tense with excitement as she tried to take it all in. The mixture of smells from oil, aviation fuel, metal and cordite was unique to bombers and Barb breathed it in consciously; J.B., unconsciously. They worked their way past the navigator's table, all the way forward to the very tip of the nose: the bombardier's "office" first. After Barb had oohed and aahed a bit there, J.B. led Barb onto the flight deck and told her to slide into the co-pilot's seat. Sitting side by side, he went over the controls with her. Technically, of course, that was a serious breach of security, but no one but a fanatic would have taken it seriously. Barb was, if anything, more patriotic than J.B. himself.

"What's it like flying a mission, Jay?" Barb asked abruptly, turning to look at him.

Jay shrugged and avoided looking back. "The rudder pedals are down there, see." He pointed forward and then played them with his feet, so that the rudder could be heard clunking far behind them.

"That bad, huh?"

"Some are worse than others. Hey, aren't you getting hungry? I'll take you over to meet the ground crew. They always have coffee, coke, sandwiches and candy bars in their workshop. You can talk to them about engines."

"OK. Great!"

Jay clambered over the back of the seat and offered Barb a hand, but she ignored it, scrambling awkwardly over the seat and showing the tops of her stockings in doing so. J.B. caught himself thinking how much more practical and modest trousers were, and resenting for the 100th time the remarks Tony had made about Emily always wearing pants. They returned down the incline of the fuselage and dropped off the bomber into a circle of grinning men. J.B. groaned.

"You weren't really going to try to hide her from us, were you, Jay?"

"Alright. Might as well get it over with," J.B. conceded, and started with his co-pilot. "That's Tony, the bane of my existence. Can you imagine? I've got to sit up there with him next to me for hour after hour."

"That ain't nothing to watching your brother fly, Miss, let me tell you. Makes you want to cry half of the time," Tony retorted and Jay ignored him, pointing to his navigator instead. "That's Dan Vernon, my navigator."

"Ma'am," Dan offered his hand.

"That's Rick Orloff. You may not have heard about him yet. He's only been with us two weeks."

"Bombardier, Ma'am." Rick touched his cap.

"Sergeant Roach is our radio operator."

"How do you do, Ma'am."

"Those two jokers, Nisley and Howe, are the waist gunners. Brier there mans the ball turret. Corporal Webber just came on board three weeks ago, so you won't have heard about him, either: engineer and upper turret gunner. And that puny little kid over there tries to keep our tail clear, don't you, Kid?'"

"Yessir, sir!" The Kid grinned, turning to Barb to explain, "They all call me The Kentucky Kid, 'cause I'm from Kentucky, see?"

"Not all of us from the South are as dumb as that, Ma'am," Brier hastened to assure her, rolling his eyes in disgust at the Kid.

"I ain't dumb," the Kid told Brier with a rare frown. "I just ain't got much schooling, Ma'am, that's all. The Lieutenant didn't tell us he had a kid sister," the Kid continued in his candid fashion. "I got a kid sister too. She's real fine, Ma'am. I know you'd like her, if you got to know her, only she's still in Kentucky."

"Is she a WAC, too?" Barb asked.

"Oh, no. They wouldn't take her. She's just 15, see."

For a moment Jay thought the Kid was going to spill out the whole sordid story about his sister being pregnant, and he prepared to open his mouth and intervene, but fortunately the Kid cut himself off.

Barb looked around the circle with an amused smile. They were all staring at her, and used as she was to wolf-whistles and cat-calls this was a more intimate and intense kind of observation. She half turned toward the three officers and her eyes swept them, meeting Rick's for a split second. "I say, don't any of you fellas have a fag?"

"Since when do you smoke?" Jay asked indignantly, while the others all started patting pockets and competing to comply first.

"Don't be a bore, Jay. I've been smoking for years," Barb countered with a toss of her head.

Tony was first off the mark, and shook a cigarette out of his pack at her, but Rick had the match ready. He stepped forward, the flame protected by his cupped left hand, and Barb leaned forward to touch the cigarette tip to the flame. As she drew back, she glanced up with a smile of thanks, and then she exhaled, lifting her head and blowing downwind. J.B. found the entire gesture excessively affected, and he rolled his eyes in disgust. Barb saw his gesture and frowned slightly, but also stopped posing.

"Come on. I promised to introduce Barb to the ground crew. She's got a thing about engines."

"Engines?" Rick asked, falling in beside her, and shoving his hands in his trouser pockets. His leather jacket bulged upwards, which had the effect of making his chest and shoulders seem broader while also adding a jaunty, non-regulation touch to his appearance. Jay frowned.

"Yeah, I happen to be a great mechanic, only the Army is too stupid or whatever to recognise it and has me working as a clerk. But as I was just telling J.B., cars are dead boring. I'd love to learn about aircraft engines. I've been reading up on them. You've got Wright 'Cyclone' 1,200 hp radials on your ships. They are some of the most reliable engines ever built."

"Yep. Or rather, they g—" (he intercepted Jay's look) "sure the heck better be. We've got enough problems with flak and fighters without the engines conking out on us."

"Rick's flown more missions than the rest of us. He was with another crew," J.B. explained.

"Isn't that the Purple Heart?"

"Yeah."

"And the Air Medal?"

"You don't have to rub it in, Barb," J.B. told her with a groan.

"Just asking," she told her brother. If they had been alone she would have stuck her tongue out at him.

They reached the maintenance hangar, and J.B. introduced Barb around to all the ground crews. She was offered coffee, cokes, sandwiches and chips from dozens of oil-stained, eager hands, but she bowled them all over when she started asking technical questions about the engines. J.B. laughed aloud at the dumfounded expressions that greeted her. Fuentes angrily told her he had better things to do than answer a lot of "dumb questions" and stormed off. Most of the other mechanics were not so bigoted, however, and eagerly started explaining everything they could to her.

J.B. got himself a coke from the machine and helped himself to a sandwich and just watched it all—with Rick waiting beside him. The little huddle of men crowding around Barb went around the hangar from station to station, jabbering and pointing, and Jay shook his head. Then he glanced over at Rick, who was lighting a cigarette beside him. "And you watch your moves, Bud. She's my sister, remember."

"Oh, aren't I good enough for your sister?" Rick shook out the match, dropped it and stepped on it.

"That's not what I said."

"Nope. Just what you implied." He met J.B.'s eyes with his own narrowed in defensive hostility.

"I just don't want her to get hurt." J.B. looked away first.

"So, who does?"

"Look. She may act like she's some sophisticated dame, but it's all a put-on. She hasn't been kissed."

Rick laughed, and then added, looking hard at J.B, "Want to bet?"

"No, I don't! Just keep your paws to yourself."

"You don't out-rank me, Baronowsky, and I don't have to take orders from you when we aren't flying."

"No, but I'll beat the shit out of you, if you get out of line with her."

"You can try."

"What the hell are we talking about?" J. B. asked suddenly, as he realised what a ridiculous exchange they had just had. He was almost as bad as the Kentucky Kid, threatening to beat someone up!

Rick threw back his head and laughed. When he finished, he took a deep drag on his cigarette, and then said in a low, serious voice, "You're alright, Baronowsky—and so's your sister."

Jay followed his bombardier's gaze across the hangar to his sister. She was in seventh heaven—not because of all the guys crowded around her, but because they were taking an engine apart for her. Jay shook his head. "I don't get it, really. Barb should have been born a boy."

"Oh, no she shouldn't. She's got great legs."

Jay looked again. "Yeah, she does, doesn't she."

They laughed together.

"Where did Tony and the others go?"

"They gave up. She's not their type. Too tough. Too independent. Too smart."

"You really like her." J.B. was amazed.

Rick shrugged and concentrated on his cigarette. "I'd like to get to know her better. We could do some double-dating with your English dame, if that makes you feel better about it."

"Yeah, that would be okay. Then I can introduce them to each other too."

Eventually Barb was finished with her introduction to the 'Cyclone' engines and she contentedly rejoined her brother and his bombardier. They jointly took her on a tour of the rest of the base, and Jay was half-annoyed and half-amazed that she paid more attention to Rick than to himself.

Dinner was a public affair. Barb was invited to the CO's table, and so they ate with the Staff and the Squadron Leaders. J.B. was proud of Barb because she managed to act polite and correct. Not once did she make a smart-ass remark that embarrassed him. Not that Barb compared to Emily. Emily knew how to stimulate conversation, to charm and entertain, while Barb just answered questions and kept up her end of the conversation when directly addressed. But for a kid from a trailer home in Ypsilanti, Michigan, J.B. thought that was pretty good.

After dinner they went over to the Officer's Club for drinks. Barb didn't get much chance to drink; she was on the dance floor most of the time. J.B. only got one dance with her himself and then gave up. Guys kept cutting in. Just after nine o'clock, however, he firmly led her off the floor and escorted her back off the base and out to the bus stop.

Barb glanced at the schedule. "Hey, the next bus isn't due for at least 40 minutes!" she protested.

"Yep—and they're usually late," Jay agreed, leaning back against the little post that supported the roof over the bus stop.

Barb laughed. "Well, at least give me a fag, would you?"

Jay found his packet of cigarettes and lit one for his sister. She sat with her legs crossed and gazed out across the road at the hedge opposite. The late summer night was laden with the smell of moist earth and decomposing leaves. There was a slight chill in the air, and wisps of mist were hovering over the field beyond the bend in the road. The crickets were chirping.

"Sometimes I just can't believe I'm really here—in England, I mean. Europe. Can you believe it? I never *dreamed* I'd ever get to Europe. But you know what it's like on an Army base. Seen one, seen them all. I was kind of disappointed at first. It'd be fun to go to London, though. Rick suggested it. He said we could go there together—you, me, him and some girl he says you're seeing over here…That true?"

"Yeah," J.B. agreed, taking a drag on his own cigarette so the flame glowed brighter for a second. "I broke off with Kathy."

"Hot dog! You did? Congratulations! I never could stand the snotty little bitch!"

"*Now* you tell me," Jay told her sarcastically, but not displeased really.

"Hey! Would you have listened to me if I'd told you I hated her six months ago? Not on your life! You were soft-in-the-head over that bitch. She couldn't do anything wrong in your eyes, but I wish just *once* you could have heard the way she talked down to Mom! You would've thought Mom was the cleaning lady in the toilet the way she talked to her!"

Jay gazed at Barb, dumbstruck. How could he have been so dumb, so blind? Then he tried to picture Emily and his mother. Somehow he couldn't. He tried to picture Emily coming through the back door of the trailer house into the kitchen, or sitting in the cramped little living room, but he just couldn't. She didn't fit in.

"So tell me about this new girlfriend," Barb prompted.

J.B. shrugged awkwardly. "She's not really a girlfriend."

"Uh huh," Barb retorted, gazing at him unbelieving.

"She's married, you see, and—"

"Married! Holy shit! Mom would have a fit! Dad too! Are you saying—"

"Would you shut up and listen to me!"

Barb snapped her mouth shut and waited expectantly and resentfully. Jay felt very uncomfortable. "Her husband was shot down six months ago and they haven't heard anything from him since."

"MIA."

"That's right. She still hopes, of course, but the chances aren't very good. Still, it would help if the f-darn Germans would at least send word."

"Rick says she's some sort of fine lady."

"Yeah. She is that."

"So it's Kathy all over again! Why can't you fall in love with girls who look up to you rather than down on you?"

"What the hell is that supposed to mean? Emily doesn't look down on me."

"Are you sure? Kathy sure as hell did—'till you got those wings, that is."

"Yeah, well, don't judge someone you don't even know! And speaking of being a bad judge of character, watch out for Rick."

"What's wrong with Rick?"

"He's not serious, that's all."

"Just because he's one heck of a cute-looking guy, you think he couldn't be serious about me, huh?" Barb's inferiority complex about her looks made her hyper-sensitive, and Jay could tell she was already boiling with indignation and hurt.

"No! It's got nothing to do with that—just Rick *told* me he's not interested in anything serious. Besides, he'll be heading stateside soon. He's only got three more missions, then it's bye-bye England."

"OK. So who's getting serious? All I said I wanted to do was go to London with him—and you and this la-di-da English lady." Barb pursed her lips and made a silly pretence of an English accent, her pinkies extended in a parody of snobbishness. Jay hated it when Americans made fun of English accents, and he hated Barb's childish jealousy, too. He got to his feet, pulled his cap down, and announced, "I'm not supposed to be off base. You're old enough to wait for the bus on your own."

"Oh, God! Here we go again. Now I can't say anything against this *new* girl-friend!"

"No, you can't. You haven't met her." Jay relented enough to lean forward and give Barb a quick kiss on the cheek. "Let's not fight. Thanks for coming, and let's try to get to London together before Rick leaves."

Barb caught him as he started to turn away, and gave him a fierce hug. "I'm sorry, Jay. I didn't mean to upset you! Take care of yourself, OK?"

"Yeah, no problem. See ya later, Alligator."

"See you in a while, Crocodile."

Barb watched her brother walking back to the gate and watched him go through it and keep on walking toward the row of Nissan huts in the darkness beyond. She was mad at herself for quarrelling with him and mad at him for being so self-righteous, and she was frightened for him. Overhead came the first throbbing hum of the British bombers outward bound for the night.

CHAPTER 17

▼

Beauchamp Rodding, England
Late August 1943

"Y'all take care of yourself up there, ya' hear!" the Kid called over the intercom as always, and J.B. took a deep breath as he nursed the rudder and throttles to line up at the start of the runway. Ahead of him Harkins' B-17 was growing smaller and smaller as it lumbered down the runway. Very gradually it started to lift upwards, straight and level, climbing steadily. Text-book take-off for a fully loaded Flying Fortress. The green light flashed at him.

"Here it goes, Gang, number 19."

He eased all four throttles forward, toes still pressed hard on the brakes. The big ship started to vibrate at a faster pitch, and the faithful Wright 'Cyclone' engines roared at him, each in its almost identical and yet distinct pitch. Then he eased back on the throttles and let up on the brakes very carefully. Keeping the heavy plane on a straight line was both difficult and vital. Bombed up and fully loaded as she was, any veering could easily get out of control. A ground loop with the wing-tanks loaded to the gills and 6,000 pounds of explosives on board would be the end of them.

J.B. gradually increased power as they picked up speed. Slowly the ship started to feel lighter. All 55,000 lbs of her wanted to fly. Poor old girl, Jay thought to himself, doesn't know where we're taking her. The end of the runway was rushing towards them. Jay felt Tony look over at him with a query in his frown, his hands itching to jerk the steering column back. Tony's impatience made Jay hold off another second or two. Then he pulled the controls toward himself firmly and they left the earth behind.

They climbed slowly, painfully slowly. The ripe fields skimmed by just under their heavy wings; they cleared a hedge and then made the trees dance in the wash of their engines as they lifted over them. Beyond was the road, and Jay saw a girl on a bicycle stop, drop one foot to the ground and look up, the bicycle tilting. She shaded her eyes against the early morning sun to watch them climb eastwards. She was wearing a printed cotton dress and practical lace-up shoes. She looked vaguely familiar, but J.B. couldn't place her. The wash of the engines made her hair dance wildly around her head.

"That was Bunny! Did you see her?!" Nisley called excitedly over the intercom.

Now J.B. realised who she was, the girl who worked down at the *Unicorn* most evenings, helping her Dad. Days she had a job in the kitchen of the hospital a few miles away. There was a spate of teasing and slightly off-colour remarks from the others, from which J.B. gathered Nisley had been putting the moves on Bunny—how successfully was a matter of lively speculation. Eventually things settled down again.

Gradually, they were gaining altitude. Over the radio came the coded and staccato communications from the various Groups thrown into today's 'Maximum Effort' raid as they started to form up. J.B. didn't like it when there were so many aircraft up here. They were all wheeling around clumsily, and here and there were laggards trying to catch up. They were all heavy, somewhat sluggish, and J.B. knew from his own Group just how many rookies were up here. It would be so easy to misjudge speed or height or just get distracted for a second and—bang—20 men dead for nothing.

Jay didn't like it at all, and he was glad they were flying in the high formation. Slowly but surely, his Group was climbing above the chaos below them. *Halifax Hooker* was assigned the Number Two slot in the Squadron just to the left of Harkins today—the 'privilege' of increasing seniority. The flak batteries usually hadn't found their range when the lead bombers went over, and that improved the leading planes' chances of surviving the bomb run and of the lead bombardier getting his load right on target. On the other hand, the Kraut fighters knew perfectly well the role of the lead bombardier and so tended to concentrate on the leading planes. The privilege was therefore a little dubious.

As the confusion gave way to ordered flight, J.B. risked looking about. He could see the names and emblems of the closer ships, and the way the gunners were swinging their guns this way and that as they practised taking aim against the sun; the pilots were looking about themselves just as he and Tony were. Since Alan Pearson's ship had gone down before his eyes, J.B. hadn't let himself get close to any of them. It wasn't anything conscious, really; he just hadn't made an effort to get to know the new pilots as they arrived. When he wasn't flying, he was either trying to see Emily or writing letters home or doing something with his own crew. The aircraft closest to him on his right was flown by a rookie, anyway. The replacement crew had only just arrived a few days ago, and J.B. couldn't even remember the pilot's name, if he'd heard it. This was their first mission, poor bastards.

It promised to be unpleasant. Maximum Efforts always were. It meant the brass was up-tight about something and didn't much care about losses. Not that they ever did, really. Or maybe that wasn't fair. Jay supposed that the generals shook their heads and felt real bad when the casualties were reported. All those expensive planes and crews! After all, it cost the Army almost $300,000 to build a B-17 and tens of thousands of dollars to train aircrews—and then half the bozos went and got themselves shot down on their first day on the job, taking their expensive toys with them. *That* was sure to upset the brass and politicians!

Jay didn't like the sound of his own bitter thoughts and started scanning the instruments to distract himself. 'Just concentrate on flying,' he told himself; 'that's what you're paid for.' Besides, he *did* love it, he reminded himself. He loved the sound of those four engines screaming furiously just beside and slightly behind him. He sometimes thought of them as four lions dragging a chariot through the air. He loved the way the control column vibrated in his hands when he held it loosely. He loved the slow way the altimeter wound itself up, the smaller hand hauling the thicker hand after it. He loved watching the ball as he banked. But most of all, he loved the sky-scapes that opened around him.

The golden morning sunlight was skimming across the top edges of the rumpled clouds below them. It set the peaks ablaze and left the valleys cast in grey shadow. It was a glorious morning that reminded him of the hymn *Morning Has Broken*—which he unconsciously started humming to himself.

Why did the Nazis have to go and start invading innocent countries? Why did the Japs have to bomb Pearl Harbor? The questions were so stupid that Jay would have been ashamed to voice them out loud, but they were there in his head all the same.

Then again, the more mature part of his brain reminded him: no war, no expansion of the Army Air Forces, no need to train 100,000 boys to fly powerful aircraft. J.B. knew that if there wasn't a war, he wouldn't be sitting up here at the controls of those four 1,200 hp engines, watching the English coast slowly recede under his port wing. If there hadn't been a war, he would never have learned to fly at all.

They were passing through 10,000 feet and J.B. ordered the crew onto oxygen, fitting his own oxygen mask in place over his nose and mouth. It tasted bad as always in the first minute, but then you got used to it. They were still climbing, heading up for the cruising altitude of twenty-six thousand today. Cruising speed 175 mph.

Where was the fighter escort?

Jay looked up, squinting in the brilliant morning sunshine, searching for the fighters that should have rendezvoused with them by now. "Hey, Dan, haven't we got fighter rendezvous?"

"Two minutes to go yet, Jay."

OK, then.

Jay kept scanning the sky until, with tangible relief, he caught sight of the first tiny fleck of black against the high overcast. There they were falling into place nicely. Jay had known a couple of guys back at flight school who had been desperate to fly fighters. They had always been sneaking off to practice aerobatics and generally made it clear to everyone that they were really hot stuff—much too good for regulations, or hanging around with 'dead-beats' bound for bombers and 'all that crap.' Jay had hated them—hated their arrogance, their irresponsibility and their immaturity. Now he was grateful that there were so many of those bastards.

The droning of the engines was numbing after awhile. You stopped hearing them—unless something went wrong. J.B. forced himself to concentrate on his instruments and scanned the dials with complacency. Everything was reading normal, or was the oil pressure on Number 1 too low? J.B. watched it for a moment, and then tapped the glass face of the dial with his gloved finger. The needle jumped a bit and settled, still a fraction below normal but nothing serious. Rpms, temperatures…

Jay became aware that Tony was nervously looking up through the skylight overhead, watching the fighters. Jay followed his gaze and noticed that the fighters were bouncing about more than normal. At first he thought they were just horsing around, but on second thought decided they must be bucking a fierce cross wind. "Dumb fighter-jockeys can't fly formation worth shit," was Tony's commentary. J.B. figured it was pretty tough holding close formation in a light aircraft in heavy cross winds.

The whole formation wheeled cautiously onto a new course, and now they started to feel the buffeting of those winds, too. The individual ships in the formation started to bounce and drop irregularly. Jay had to concentrate to keep his position. "That must be one hell of a wind out there!"

"Want me to take her for a while?" Tony offered at once.

"Yeah," Jay decided impulsively. He took a bottle of oxygen, climbed out of his seat and, with a warning shout to Webber, climbed up into the upper turret. He had the most spectacular view from here, and he marvelled at it for a moment. The whole armada of flying ships was spread out in every direction as far as the eye could see.

"Something wrong, sir?" Webber asked, dropping the mask rather than pressing his mike.

J.B. shook his head, waved, and dropped back down into the body of the ship. He worked his way back past the bombs, all swaying slightly in their racks as Tony struggled to keep them on course. The turbulence was really getting bad. He left his stomach in the air more than once, and had to hold on tight to one thing or another as he wormed his way back to the waist. The gunners looked over at him rather alarmed; J.B. made a calming gesture and continued on to the tail. The Kid nearly jumped out of his skin when J.B. tapped him on the shoulder. "What's the matter, sir?" he shouted, his mask in his hand.

Back here it was the sound of the wind, more than the engines, that made the most noise. Compared to the cockpit, the engines seemed far away, but the ship seemed a lot less stable back here, too. The rudder and elevator cables were so close you could hear them being worked, and it made J.B.'s skin creep. Back here the Flying Fortress seemed like a fragile shell that could be crushed by almost anything. It was bitterly cold, too. The Kid was wearing a thick, bright-red scarf over his face—a gift from his Mom—so that only his eyes were exposed. His hands were in home-made mittens. They seemed much too big and baggy, but J.B. didn't interfere with what his men did to keep warm. He figured it was their business.

J.B. gratefully made his way back up the cat-walk. He gave Roach a pat on the back as he came by. "Any news?"

"Turbulence is bad right up to 35,000 feet, sir. The fighters can't hack it up there. We're going down to 22,000."

J.B. nodded and continued on to Dan. He didn't need to speak. Dan pointed out their position. They were crossing into Denmark.

Rick glanced up at him and then pointed downwards through the great basin of glass that housed his bombsight. For a moment J.B. thought he was only indicating the outline of the coast below them, grey on grey, rimmed by a line of white that one presumed were breakers going onto the shore. But then J.B. realised that those little puffs of cloud weren't cloud at all but flak. It was a long ways off yet. Bad shooting.

He nodded and then started back up toward the flight deck. One glance at the instruments and it was clear they were indeed down to 22,000. The formation was also more spread out; whether that was due to the turbulence or to make it more difficult for the flak, Jay didn't know. He sank back into his seat, but he didn't take the controls. He scanned the sky above them instead, squinting into the glaring sunlight. The Kraut fighters were gonna find them sooner or later. It was just a matter of when.

The first indication that the German fighters had come up to play was the silencing of the flak. The flak hadn't been bad up here in the high formation, and J.B. hadn't noticed anyone being hit, but Rick, with his excellent view of what went on below them, had reported two ships dropping out of formation. Suddenly he called out: "Flak's quit. Must be enemy fighters about somewhere!"

The next indication that the German fighters had found them was the twisting contrails in the sky above and ahead of them. That was OK; it meant the fighter escort had engaged. Good boys, J.B. thought, and felt a little guilty when a few minutes later a billowing black streak fell out of the sky with something burning furiously at the tip. It was a fighter. J.B. could only hope it was a square-head and not one of their own. Still, it was a vivid reminder that the fighter-boys were vulnerable, too. It wasn't all fun-and-games and glory.

"Here they come! Five-o'clock level. Coming right at us!" the Kid called in the high-pitched, over-excited voice that he always used on such occasions.

"No need to shout," J.B. reminded him futilely, and was answered by the chattering of the guns. The ship shuddered.

"I got 'im. I got 'im!" the Kid crowed triumphantly.

"Then why the hell's he still coming!" Nisley snapped back.

The flight deck darkened as the FW-190 flew between them and the sun, not more than a hundred yards away. Webber was blasting away at him from the upper turret, and J.B. thought he saw bits of metal break off. If so, it didn't faze the German.

There was a lull. Silence. The Eye of the Storm, J.B. thought, and scanned his instruments. Everything was fine, normal. The engines droned so consistently, it was like they were part of his own brain, the sound of his blood in his veins...

"More fighters. Circling around. Must be two or three dozen of them," Webber reported from the upper turret.

"Where are our fucking fighters?" Brier asked.

"The P-47s have turned back. Dog-fighting consumes their fuel faster than level flight," Roach informed them, adding almost pensively, "lost five ships, too."

At least there was only one man per fighter, J.B. reflected, but it wasn't exactly reassuring to think the Krauts were so damned good they could fight the pants off even an American fighter. What chance did a bomber have?

"Here they come!"

The guns chattered away again, but there were no hits this time. The Germans were concentrating on someone else, apparently. J.B. kept his eyes on his instruments and his course. Another lull ensued, broken only by false alarms, curses and exchanged insults from the gunners.

"Approaching IP," Dan's voice broke through the nervous chatter of the gunners.

They were well into the run when the fighters struck again. They came in from astern as before, but lower this time, and J.B. knew they'd been hit by the way the ship lurched. Someone cried out sharply in surprise/pain and someone else broke in over the intercom and cried out: "Fire! We've got a fire back here! Fire!"

Immediately you could feel the crew moving around frantically, trying to put the fire out, upsetting the trim. Rick called out in alarm. "Goddamn it! Keep still! I can barely fly it in this turbulence as it is!"

"More fighters!" Webber warned and started firing at once.

"Jesus God!" Tony screamed. The plane on their right had just exploded. The nose catapulted into the air, completely severed from the rest of the ship, and they could see the pilots flung about like rag-dolls. For an instant the two wing-tips seemed to hang in the air just where they had been before—wing-tips to a great ball of black smoke and flame. An instant later the blast hit *Halifax Hooker*; she was flung sideways as if she'd just been broad-sided by a battleship. There followed the sound of hail on a tin roof as debris from the other bomber rained down on them.

"Jesus God!" Tony screamed again. "We're on fire!"

"No, we're not! We've put it out!" Brier screamed back.

"No! The wing! The starboard wing!" Tony answered hysterically.

"Extinguishers!" Jay ordered.

"Jay!" Rick's voice broke in over the intercom. "Fly this goddamned plane straight and level for me! I can't handle it down here!"

But J.B. stared transfixed at the flames, which were eating away at the surface of the starboard wing-tip. The extinguishers weren't working.

"We've got to get out of here before we blow up!" Tony declared, tearing his mask off and climbing over his seat. J.B. didn't even have a chance to grab him; he was gone too fast. With Tony gone, J.B. could see the flames better: they were small at the moment but spreading—spreading toward the outboard engine, the fuel tanks. They were still fully loaded. J.B. saw again the explosion that had killed the rookie crew on his right: the cockpit hurled through the air like a toy, the wing-tips flying on their own…J.B. pressed his intercom and ordered: "ABANDON SHIP! Everybody out! Out! Get out before we blow!" At the same time he hit the "Bail out" button.

From the waist of the ship, J.B. could sense frantic movement again. Tony had probably reached the others.

"Can't you keep this goddamned ship on course for five more seconds?!" Rick demanded furiously.

"Are you out of your mind?! Isn't one medal enough for you? We're on fire! Drop the goddamned bombs!"

"We're not over the target yet!"

"We're over fucking Germany, aren't we?! *Anything* down there is a target! Just drop the goddamn load and get out!" But he kept flying the course and altitude, unable to abandon the controls as long as Rick was at his post.

To his immense relief, just seconds later J.B. felt the ship bounce upward as the first bombs fell away, and then it drifted upwards as the others followed. From the waist came a burst of unsettled movements, before renewed calm. The others must have jumped by now. What the hell was he still doing up here? He looked toward the wing-tip; it was burning as brightly as ever, the flames still creeping inward leaving charred, black metal behind them. Time to get the hell out of here! J.B. let go of the controls and started to twist around and get out of his seat. Rick shoved him back down and dropped into the co-pilot seat. "Roach's legs are shot-up. He'll never make it jumping. Better try to put the fire out."

"The extinguishers aren't working!"

"Then you better dive hard. The wind sometimes puts the flames out."

"Are you crazy?"

"It's been done. Try it."

"Are the others gone?"

"The Kid refuses to jump and Webber's trying to patch up Roach."

"The others?"

"Gone. Will you dive this goddamned thing, or do you want me to try doing it myself?"

J.B. gave him an outraged look and then shoved the nose down hard. Rick was looking out of the side window. "Harder! Put the nose right down."

They tipped up on their faces, the G-force shoving them back against their seats and the engines screaming in protest.

"Steeper," Rick ordered, still staring out the window.

"She's doing 250 mph already! If I put her down any harder, God knows if I'll be able to pull out!"

"Want me to do it?" Rick asked again.

J.B. shook his head and increased the angle of the dive. The speed increased to 260, 270, 280. She couldn't go any faster and not start coming apart. J.B. took a second to glance at the altimeter, too: it was unwinding at an alarming rate, 12,000, 11,000, 9,500, 8,000, 6,000—

"OK! The fire's out! Level out!"

"You're one hell of a guy for giving orders!" J.B. shouted back at him, trying to haul back on the controls, but they were frozen. Nothing budged. The big bomber was completely out of control.

5,000, 4,000

Rick was fighting the controls beside him. Sweat ran down their faces.

3,500, 3,000

She was levelling off somewhat, but J.B. didn't think they'd make it. There just wasn't room. If they'd started the dive with a couple thousand feet more to spare...

2800, 2500, 2300, 2200 and then—miraculously—they had her level again. After the height they'd fallen, it felt like they were skimming the tops of the trees. They were at 2,100 feet and holding. J.B. felt himself trembling, but couldn't stop. He glanced to his right. From the tip to about one-third of the way back, almost to the outboard engine, the wing was charred black. The very tip of the wing was nothing but metal frame. But there was no flame. And all four engines were still howling at him in their usual, monotonous fury.

That was good, he supposed. But then again, here he was utterly alone flying over enemy territory, and he hadn't the faintest idea where he was.

"Did Dan jump?" J.B. found himself asking. There was no one he wanted more at that moment than his reliable navigator.

"Yeah," Rick told him as he removed his oxygen mask and tried to wipe his face dry on the back of his sleeve.

It was like being abandoned. Dan had jumped and left him out here all alone—lost in enemy airspace! How could he do that?! But he'd been ordered to jump, J.B. reminded himself. *J.B.* had ordered them *all* to jump. He'd ordered them to jump into certain captivity when it wasn't necessary.

The thought came to him then for the first time, but not the last. Now he only gave the thought a half a second. It flashed through his brain that he had ordered them to jump in a moment of panic, and it hadn't been necessary, and they were all going to spend the rest of the war in a German POW camp because of it. It was a horrible thought, so J.B. shoved it aside. He had more important things to think about. He had to think about how to get the rest of them home alive.

He searched the sky again in the forlorn hope of seeing other Forts somewhere. If only he could find one other friendly aircraft, Forts or better still, some of those P-47s. No, the fighters had already gone home, but surely somewhere in this vast sky there was one or another of those thousands of ships that had taken off with them this morning? How could they all be gone?

J.B. felt utterly helpless and vulnerable. He was alone out here in a hostile sky without any friends, much less protection. He didn't know where he was and he didn't know how to get them home. West. He had to fly west. If he could just get them over the North Sea, maybe they could drop the rubber dinghy and jump. And get washed up on the Dutch coast and spend the rest of the war in prison? With the rest of the crew that had jumped…Don't think about that. The war might go on forever at this rate.

Rick reached over and pulled down J.B.'s oxygen mask for him. "You can breathe better without it down here," he remarked.

J.B. gulped the air from the cockpit. It tasted of smoke. He reached and shoved back the side window to let in fresh air. After a bit he stopped shaking, and looked over at Rick. "Can you fly?"

"Not well enough for the Army. They washed me out of flight training."

"But you had some training?"

"A hundred hours or so."

"Can you keep her straight and level?"

"At least as well as you did back there."

"OK, OK. I want to go check on the damage." J.B. climbed out of his seat and dropped down toward the radio shack. It was blackened and smoky, despite the largish hole in the port side that was letting in a wind that made everything not tacked down flutter. Roach was stretched out under a blanket, pale and unmoving. Webber was sitting beside him. The Kid was sitting with his back crushed against the fuselage, clutching his knees. He was white as a sheet, and his eyes were wild as he looked up at J.B. He shook his head. "Won't jump," he muttered stubbornly.

"Not now. I'll try to get us home," J.B. assured him, and turned to Webber. "How bad is he?"

"Not good, sir. Legs shot to pieces, but I think I got the bleeding stopped." Webber showed J.B. his work with the bandages. "I gave him a shot of morphine," Webber added. Roach moaned slightly and his head rolled from side to side, but he wasn't conscious at the moment. J.B. didn't know any more about first aid than the rest of them and nodded. Then he wormed his way forward toward the navigator's cabin, hoping to find something useful to help get them home—like a chart laid out with their return course neatly pencilled in…Dan had always been a very meticulous navigator…

There was a hole in the side of the ship here, too, and it let the wind in. The charts had been blown off the table and flapped and fluttered against the far side of the cubicle. Dan's instruments were on the floor. There was blood all over the table. J.B. retreated rapidly. Dan had been wounded when he jumped. What kind of chance did he have?

"You two guys better go back to your guns," J.B. suggested to his only remaining gunners. It was bad enough being alone out here with just the two gunners; the least they could do was man the guns.

"Won't jump," the Kid muttered stubbornly, shaking his head.

"It's OK. No one's asking you to. Just go back and man your gun. God knows we haven't got much of a chance if they come for us again, but as long as we can, we'll at least shoot back."

"Won't jump."

"I got the message. Now—"

"Won't jump."

"Christ! Would you listen to me, Kid?! I said go back to your gun, not jump."

Webber touched his arm. "Leave him alone, Lieutenant. He saw what happened to Nisley, that's all."

"What do you mean, what happened to Nisley?"

"Nisley jumped, but he pulled the cord too soon. The chute caught on the tail-wheel and tore apart. Most of it's still out there. Nisley's not."

J.B. felt bitterly cold. He hadn't just ordered them to jump into captivity unnecessarily; one of them had died doing it.

"I'll go back up to the turret," Webber volunteered before J.B. had recovered from the shock. "Got the best view from up there, anyway. Hope I didn't give

Roach too much morphine." Webber glanced rather uncertainly at the radio operator.

J.B. didn't have any idea, so he just returned to the cockpit. He felt icy cold although they were flying so low the cockpit was getting hot like a greenhouse in the summer sun. Nisley dead. Dan wounded. The other three captives at best.

"Did you see how bad Dan was wounded?" J.B. asked Rick.

"Shoulder and upper arm. We got him in the chute and put his left hand in the ring. He should be OK."

J.B. had the horrible feeling Rick was just saying that to cheer him up. They fell silent. The drone of the engines enveloped them. The sun was in their eyes. They sweated in their fleece-lined flight suits. The minutes crawled by. Or was it hours? Flak was lobbed at them once or twice but only half-heartedly, as if the Germans didn't particularly want to waste ammunition on a lone ship. The air became smooth again.

"Isn't that water down there?"

They had made the North Sea.

Holy Mother of God, J.B. prayed silently, thank you. I swear to you I will never blaspheme again. I will light candles to you every Sunday for the rest of my life. I will name my first born girl-child for you...

The sea went on and on. It felt like they were flying over the Atlantic rather than the North Sea. J.B.'s hands were so cramped that it hurt to flex them.

"Why don't we try the emergency channel? Get a fix for an airbase." Rick asked.

Why hadn't he thought of that? "Can you work the radio?"

"Yeah, I'll give it a try." Rick climbed up out of the co-pilot's seat and J.B. waited tensely. His left leg was trembling again as he tried to balance the changes in trim. His head was splitting from the sound of those four engines screaming right beside his ears and the sun glaring into his eyes.

Rick's voice came clearly over the radio. He gave the call sign. "Do you read? Do you read?"

And suddenly it was as if Emily was sitting in the cockpit with him. A clear, crisp English voice, not too high-pitched, not too guttural. "DG-H reading you loud and clear. How can we help?"

"We've lost our navigator and haven't the faintest idea where we are—except it looks like we're over the North Sea—and have been for eternity. Can you give us a course home?"

"Is your aircraft fully serviceable?"

"We've got the fire out and she seems OK."

"What is your fuel situation?"

"Good question. Just a second. J.B.? What does the fuel look like?"

"Pretty low."

Rick relayed this information to the emergency channel, and shortly afterwards the young woman informed them briskly, "You are cleared to land at RAF Horsham. Vector 100. Do you have wounded on board?"

"How did you guess?"

"They'll be expecting you at Horsham."

"Thank you, Ma'am!" Rick said it with feeling.

The WAAF at last let a shimmer of personality break through as she answered, "Oh, you aren't rid of me yet, Yank. I'll be watching you all the way in."

"Can I take you to dinner tonight?"

"No. You should be seeing the Essex coast very soon now."

"J.B.? Can you see anything up there?"

"Not yet...Wait a minute. It's pretty hazy, but...yeah, I've got it."

The WAAF brought them right to the airfield, and as J.B. swung onto the circuit (very careful to do it by the book this time) he noticed the ambulance rolling out onto the taxiway. He lowered the landing gear and put on full flaps—only nothing happened.

"What the fuck—" But of course he knew. The gunfire that had wounded Dan and Roach and set the fire in the waist had apparently damaged the hydraulics as well. He was going too fast to land, and without flaps there was no way to slow her down without stalling. Jesus Christ. He circled around, easing back on the throttles until he was as close to stalling speed as he dared. Then he lined up on the runway a second time. Now the fire-engines were pouring out onto the taxiway, too; they could see he didn't have his flaps or undercarriage and was coming in too fast.

Holy Mother of God, you can't have brought us this far to abandon us now...

RAF High Wych

Emily was surprised by how delighted she was to get the orders to deliver an Oxford to High Wych. It was so close to Beauchamp Rodding that she was certain that she could meet up with Jay—and the thought of seeing him, even if only for a few minutes, made her feel cheerful and happy. Was that disloyal to

Robin in some way? It didn't make her love Robin—or was it just his memory?—any less. Surely he would want her to be happy? And it was a beautiful sunny day. If she was lucky and nothing got in her way, she'd have the Oxford to High Wych just in time for tea. She could call over to the US Base and—presuming J.B. wasn't away somewhere—they could surely meet for an hour or two. In fact, she told Operations not to worry about sending the taxi Anson to pick her up. She'd 'find her own way home.' Emily noted that she was being rather presumptuous, just assuming that Jay would again find some way to bring her all the way home no matter what it cost him in time and effort. But Jay made her feel like that—like he would do anything for her.

It wasn't at all fair to compare him to Robin in this regard, she told herself. She'd met Robin at the height of the Battle of Britain. He'd hardly had time to sleep or eat. It would have been unspeakably selfish to have expected him to wait on her hand and foot. She had never expected it—and he had once told her bluntly that it was the very fact that she *didn't* expect too much of him that had made him love her more. No, it was silly to make comparisons between them—but it was *nice* to feel that Jay would do anything for her, no matter what it cost him in time or money or effort.

Emily packed a clean blouse as well as her skirt, stockings and dress shoes. She was sure Jay would insist on dinner, and that always meant someplace nice with Jay. Emily even regretted not having washed her hair. It felt so good to have a reason to dress up and look your best.

The first two jobs of the day went off without a glitch, and by skipping lunch and rushing things a bit, she made it to High Wych even earlier than planned. It was just four-thirty in the afternoon as she made her final approach at High Wych. If Jay could get away immediately, they could have the rest of the afternoon and the whole evening together.

The smoke billowing up from beyond the orchard was unsettling, however. It was blowing across the field and it was black and oily, not an agricultural fire...It took some of the shine off her good mood. How could one be unrestrainedly happy when several men had probably just been killed in a crash?

As she turned over the paperwork on the Oxford she asked the RAF crew chief, "Who or what crashed?"

"American. They've taken a real beating today. They sent up what looked like everything they had this morning and they've been straggling in all afternoon." He shook his head knowingly. If the formation came back intact, it had met with little opposition. If it straggled in, then it had been badly chewed up.

Emily's stomach constricted, but she shouldered her parachute and took her tote bag and went across to the Mess to use the telephone.

The American sergeant on the switchboard at Beauchamp Rodding sounded the same as always, but the wait for J.B. seemed interminable. Emily kept picturing Jay's voice in her mind. She kept imagining him saying breathlessly into the receiver: "Emily? Is that you? Geeze! I wasn't expecting you! Where are you? Can we meet up?" She could hear it in her brain so clearly: his surprise, his eagerness, his gratefulness, his affection…

"Hello?" It wasn't Jay.

"Yes, this is Second Officer Priestman of the Air Transport Auxiliary. I'm trying to reach First Lieutenant Baronowsky."

"Yes, I'm sorry, Ma'am, but Lieutenant Baronowsky is overdue from a mission."

Oh God, Emily thought, I can't go through this again.

You should have thought of that earlier. What did you think? That Americans were immortal? Why weren't you expecting this? It's the most normal thing in the world.

She heard herself saying primly into the telephone, "I see. May I ask by how long he is overdue?"

"I'm afraid I can't say that, Ma'am…Ah…It is still possible he has put down somewhere else."

"I see. Thank you." She hung up. There was a loud click and then the ugly buzzing of the dial-tone. Why hadn't she left a message? She *should* have left a message in case he made it. Then at least he would know she had called and he could call her back, and…She reached for the receiver, but let her hand drop. She turned around and walked out of the Mess; the RAF watched her go. She could feel their looks of sympathy. And now she didn't even have the taxi Anson to get her home. She'd have to find public transport. It was going to take her hours. She might as well start now. No, she should get something to eat first. She'd had nothing since breakfast. *How can you think about food at a time like this?* Jay— maybe Jay had put down somewhere else.

Emily turned around and hurried back into the Mess. "May I please put a call through to Bomber Command?"

Raised eyebrows, but no one actually said no. She got through to Philippa in ten minutes. "Emily, darling, what's the matter?"

"Jay. He's overdue. Philippa, is there any way—"

"Of course, Love. Just a minute. Or better, where can I reach you?"

It was half an hour before Philippa called back. "An aircraft from Lieutenant Baronowsky's Group has put down at RAF Horsham. That's the best I can do."

"Philippa, I don't know how I can thank you—"

"Be nice to Teddy for a change. Must go."

The next thing she did, Emily had never done before in her entire career with the ATA. She went to the Station Commander and asked to 'borrow' one of His Majesty's Aircraft. He let her take the Oxford she had just delivered, provided it was returned 'expeditiously.' Emily promised.

As she made her way to Horsham, she found herself thinking that she had never done anything like this for Robin. But she *would* have, she told herself— and he would certainly have approved. Hadn't he broken regulations often enough for her sake?

As she circled the field at Horsham, she could see the B-17 lying on its belly and still surrounded by fire-engines, way out near the perimeter fence. It had overshot the runway by a couple hundred yards. The starboard wing-tip was clearly charred and the waist was blackened as well. Emily's eyes weren't good enough to read her name until she was down and taxiing past the wreck on her way back to the Watch Office. The relief at seeing that it was *Halifax Hooker* was dampened by doubts about whether the crew could have survived that landing unhurt, but at least the cockpit was intact...

She reported at the Watch Office and then asked: "Is the crew of that Flying Fortress alright?"

"What was left of it, yeah. They lost five men over Germany. The rest are over in the infirmary."

"I'll drop by then, if you don't mind. I think I met them once not too long ago."

Emily walked very slowly, consciously trying not to think. Five men lost over Germany but someone had flown it here, landed it.

The smell of the infirmary hit her first, that mixture of disinfectant and over-cooked food and sickness. Emily hated hospitals. Then she saw the four men in leather flying kit sitting on silly little wooden chairs crammed into the hall. They all looked over at her, and then J.B. sprang up with an audible but inarticulate cry. The next thing she knew she was clinging to him as he folded her into his arms. She pressed her head against his chest, her ear searching for the sound of his heart through all the leather and wool of his bulky uniform, and her whole body grateful for his warmth as the open flying jacket closed over her shoulders. He held her to him as desperately as she held him back. Neither of them said a word.

"Well, some of us are quite lucky, aren't we," a cool, sarcastic voice remarked, and Emily drew back sharply to find herself being observed sourly by a nurse of the Princess Mary's RAF Nursing Service. The woman had a pinched, unpleasant face with red patches from dry skin, but her veils couldn't have been more immaculate or stiff, and her cape stuck out around her shoulders as if it were stiffened with cardboard, not just starch.

Her tone and look put Emily on the defensive instantly. "I didn't know Lieutenant Baronowsky had survived until just this minute—"

"Yes, well, others have not been so lucky, you know!"

The words were designed to make Emily feel guilty and did—although there was nothing she could do for the others. "I'm sorry," she started to stutter, "I didn't—"

"Yeah, how could you?" Rick spoke up. He was standing now, as were Webber and the Kid, the latter hanging back shyly. "Don't let the bitch shake you—"

"I beg your pardon!" The Nurse drew herself upright indignantly.

"Just leave us alone, would you?" Rick told her roughly.

Emily winced and held her breath, but was relieved when the nurse stomped away in a huff. Emily held her hand out to Rick. "Are you OK? Where's Dan? And Tony?"

"Germany."

"Dan was wounded," J.B. murmured from behind her and Emily looked over at him, seeing his face for the first time. He looked five years older than the last time she'd seen him four days ago. All the youthful enthusiasm was drained away. He was grey except where the oxygen mask had rubbed his cheeks and chin raw, and his eyes were sunken. "Roach, too, but he's in there," he nodded with his head in the direction of a door leading deeper into the infirmary.

"The others jumped," Rick answered Emily's unspoken question.

"Sorry. That's Corporal Webber..."

"Ma'am..."

"And the Kid, I mean, ah—" J.B. tried to remember the Kid's real name, but it just wouldn't come to him.

The Kid didn't seem to notice. He was clutching his leather flying helmet in his hands and gazing at Emily with big eyes, but he stammered out in his rich hillbilly accent, "I sure am pleased to meet you, Ma'am." The Kid was shorter than Emily and his flying kit seemed much too big for him.

Emily smiled at him and held out her hand. "I'm glad to meet you, too," she told him.

He was evidently startled by her gesture, but then he grinned and shook her hand timidly. His hands were all bone, except where they were distorted and red from chilblains.

J.B. had finally recovered enough from the wonder of Emily's unexpected appearance to ask, "Where did you come from?"

"I had a delivery to High Wych and learned you were overdue. Philippa tracked you down here—but of course, I had no way of knowing you'd be safe. At least one of your aircraft crashed on landing at Beauchamp Rodding and was still burning when I left."

J.B. nodded numbly, but he reached out and took her hand at the same time. "We're waiting to hear the verdict on Roach. He's been in there for almost two hours."

"Can I get you something while you wait?" Emily asked. "Let me bring you tea and biscuits from the NAAFI."

"Haven't you got anything stronger than that, Ma'am?" Rick asked. "I could sure do with a Scotch!"

J.B. started and stared at him, but Emily didn't know that Rick was a confirmed non-alcoholic and simply answered, "Oh, I don't know about that, but let me see what I can find." Emily looked toward the other two.

Webber nodded, "Tea would be fine, Ma'am."

"Yes, Ma'am!"

Emily squeezed J.B.'s hand and let go. "I'll be right back," she promised and left them there, still standing.

She managed to get tea and biscuits for them, and they sat together unable to talk until a doctor emerged from the ominous door and announced that 'the patient' was now out of surgery. Two cannon shells had been removed, from his thigh and hip respectively. The hip had been fractured as well. There was extensive internal bleeding. But the patient was not in mortal danger.

The four young men nodded, thanked the doctor, and then stood there awkwardly, not knowing what to do next.

"Why don't you all go get something to eat at the Mess. I'm sure your unit will be sending transport for you shortly," the doctor suggested.

They filed out of the infirmary, but then stood about awkwardly in the long shadows of the dying day. "Surely there's a pub around here where we can get something to drink," Rick suggested. J.B. had his arm around Emily and she glanced up at him. He seemed completely numbed. It was Emily who answered for him. "I'm sure. We can ask at the gate."

They walked the half-mile to the nearest pub, leaving word at the gate where they could be found. The pub was smoky and crowded and loud, but that was probably just as well. The Americans were not in a very convivial mood. All Emily could do was sit beside Jay, letting him hold her hand, while they drank themselves into a still greater state of numbness.

By the time the jeep arrived to collect them, none of them could walk straight. They staggered and lurched their way out into the darkness, and the Sergeant driver had to help them get in to the jeep. "Can I give you a lift anywhere, Ma'am?" he asked politely.

"No, I'm fine. Drive carefully, Sergeant."

"Yes, Ma'am," he replied as he climbed in behind the wheel. As he drove off, Emily could see Jay's arm hanging off the side of the jeep as he lay more than sat in the seat. He was out cold, and it sent a shiver down her; she was reminded of Steeplechase.

CHAPTER 18

▼

White Waltham, England
September 1943

Emily moved fractiously around the mess. Four pilots were playing cards at one table. Several were reading magazines. One of the other women was knitting. The sound of the drizzling rain pervaded the whole room. Emily stood by the window and gazed out into the gloom. The ceiling was down to maybe 500 feet at most, and the pavement and grass were soaked. The aircraft sat dispersed around the field, wet and unhappy. Except for the smoke that drifted up from the chimney on the hangar and the half-hearted wriggling of the wind-sock, nothing moved. It was all such a depressing harbinger of the approaching winter.

The weather alone wasn't to blame for Emily's mood, however. She had heard nothing from Jay since the day he crash-landed at Horsham. She didn't know whether to be hurt, insulted or worried. She supposed he might be embarrassed or ashamed of having all but passed out in front of her, but it still seemed odd that he hadn't called. She would have expected him to apologise, if he felt he'd behaved inappropriately. In fact, she had all the phrases assuring him she understood and he had nothing to be ashamed of ready and waiting on the tip of her tongue—but the call hadn't come.

She began to wonder if he regretted being so affectionate to her. Maybe he felt he'd gone too far.

Or was it that he really was only interested in the chase? Had he lost interest, the minute she'd run to him like that, held him in her arms and let him hold her hand?

She found that answer plausible—but painful. It made all his gallantry and apparent ardour nothing but tactical tools for the pursuit of his prey.

Well, it was better to find out that he wasn't serious now than later, she told herself. After all, she had let things go far enough. There was still a slight chance that Robin had been found by the French Resistance, nursed back to health, and was even now trying to find his way home to her. You read about such miraculous escapes in the newspapers all the time. And there had even been that case of a pilot flying a Junkers over…

"The weather's lifting," someone called out, and with a start Emily made herself focus on the weather again. The rain had stopped, and the cloud cover appeared to be lightening.

"You're an optimist!" someone else replied from behind her.

"Or a pessimist," someone countered, and the card game resumed.

Emily concentrated on the cloud for a little bit. It did indeed seem to be getting lighter and lighter, as if it wasn't quite so thick anymore.

The Operations Officer entered. "I've got a Priority One Mosquito here that has to get to Wattisham today if at all possible. Anyone volunteering?"

"Yes, I'll take it," Emily found herself saying. Anything but this waiting about and brooding.

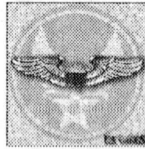

Beauchamp Rodding

Jay stared at the curving ceiling of the Nissan hut and listened to the metallic pinging of the rain on the roof. Rain was gurgling loudly down a drain somewhere, too. From farther away came the tinny sound of a radio or a gramophone playing band music. The mission today had been scratched, but it didn't matter to Jay. He was grounded anyway. He'd lost half his crew—he'd ordered them to jump when it wasn't necessary. Not one of the men he'd come over with was still with him. One by one they had been killed or wounded or—unnecessarily—jumped into captivity.

The Kid and Webber were flying with other crews now. Rick wasn't technically grounded, but he hadn't been assigned to a mission since that nightmare flight, either. He only had two more to go, and the inactivity was driving him crazy. He was in a bad way, anyway. The alcohol after their flight had opened the floodgates to a latent addiction. Now he spent every night in the Officers' Club, drinking until he couldn't stand. Jay had dragged/carried him back to his bed every single night since then. Jay felt he was to blame for that, too.

In his mind Jay went over those fatal ten seconds, when he'd first seen the other ship blow up and then realised their wing-tip was on fire and the extinguishers weren't working, again and again. If Tony hadn't panicked…But that was no excuse. He was the captain. He should have ordered Tony back to his post. He should have thought about diving to put the flames out.

If the Army court-martialed him, it would kill his granddad. It might even have repercussions for Barb. J.B. had images of himself busted down to private and put on KP, or would they make him fly as tail gunner or something? It didn't seem fair to give him a safe job, no matter how unpleasant. Surely the only fair thing would be to take him over Germany and then tell him to jump…

Rick groaned from the cot next to him, and turned over with a lot of squeaking from the bed-springs. J.B. glanced over and noticed the open letter on his bedside table. It was from his Mom. She was upset because she'd had a call from Kathy's mother. Kathy's mother claimed that Kathy was absolutely 'devastated' and called J.B. all kinds of names starting with 'cad' and 'gigolo.' J.B.'s Mom could take that, but then Kathy's Mom had started raving about all the money they'd spent on the wedding preparations. There was Kathy's $475 dress, her $17 veil, and her $35 shoes. There was also $105 for her 4-piece luggage set for the honeymoon (Jay couldn't remember planning a honeymoon, but supposed he would have gotten around to it eventually). And $99 for the engagement announcements (engraved) sent out to their friends and family. J.B. couldn't remember it all—just that Kathy's mother had sent an itemised list of all these expenditures and suggested that J.B.'s parents ought to pay half the costs *or more*, since he was to blame for everything. That upset his parents because they couldn't afford to do that, and it shamed them that they couldn't.

Worst of all, of course, Kathy's mother had told his mother that the real reason Jay had broken off the engagement was that he was "having an affair with an English slut." Kathy's mother said everyone knew that "the English girls throw themselves at our brave boys and could hardly wait to drag them into bed." Everyone knew that the English girls were all willing to hop into bed with anyone at all just for a couple of pairs of nylons. But she was "shocked to learn" that Jay didn't have the "self-control to resist such creatures." She had then gone on to warn his mother about the effects of VD on a man's mental and nervous state and sarcastically hope that it wouldn't so impact Jay's flying skills that he "made a mistake on a mission."

If Jay had ever had a moment's doubt about breaking off with Kathy, this letter had erased them forever. He would never forgive her or her mother for putting ideas like that in his mother's head. His mother had sounded angry in her letter, really hopping mad, but J.B. knew that the seed of doubt had been sown. They were there in her timid question, "You wouldn't ever have anything to do with a bad girl, would you?"

He supposed he ought to write an answering letter. He ought to tell his Mom that he'd pay *all* those goddammed expenses personally. He was sure the intent had only been to rub his parents' noses in their own poverty. Paying the debt would be the best way of spitting in Kathy's parents' smug faces. And as for having anything to do with "bad girls"…J.B. sighed.

What he really wanted to do was write his Mom about Emily. He wanted to tell her how Emily had come to him when he needed her most. How she had been there like an answer to his prayers. It was as if God wanted them to be together. How else could you explain all those coincidences? How else explain that on the very day of that disastrous mission she got her first and only aircraft delivery to High Wych? Or explain that she could find out where he put down and that the CO at High Wych let her borrow an airplane? It was too much to be just chance. It had to be the Hand of God. And if God was on their side, how could man be against it?

But his Mom *would* be, if she learned Emily was married. J.B. briefly considered saying she was widowed—but what if her husband showed up after all?

And what could he tell his Mom about their relationship anyway? That he was head over heels in love with a woman older than himself, who had only said she would "want to get to know him better" *if* her husband really was dead…?

But that wasn't the way she'd held him back there at Horsham. She had held him like she didn't want to lose him. She had gone to a lot of trouble to find out where he was, too. And she'd bent the rules—something that wasn't like Emily at all—to borrow an aircraft like that.

Nor could J.B. get over the way she'd dealt with the situation. She hadn't asked any stupid questions. She hadn't tried to get them to 'talk about it' or tried to get them to 'cheer up and forget it.' She hadn't even tried to stop them from drinking. The way she had just stayed with them, smiling at the Kid, listening to Webber talk about bandaging Roach, parrying Rick's impertinent questions calmly and humorously—and holding Jay's hand—filled him with awe and gratitude.

He knew he'd clung rather childishly to her hand, but it had been a life-line for him at that moment. Every other part of him had felt numb, dead, lifeless—except the hand that held hers. The feel of her soft skin, the fragility of her slender bones, the warmth that pulsed through the veins into her soft fingertips, had been his only hold on life. Whatever happened to them, even if her husband came back and they had to stop seeing each other, he swore he would always be grateful to her for giving him her hand that night.

J.B. wished he could talk to her. Sometimes he told himself that it would help if he could just hear her voice. He imagined calling her and when she answered, just not saying anything. She'd say 'hello' several times, and probably ask 'who's there?' or something like that. Maybe just that much of her would help ease the guilt.

But then he realised that that would only make him want to see her more, and his need to see her was almost unbearable as it was. But there was no way he could fulfill it. He couldn't, no matter how desperately he wanted to hear her voice, call her and tell her he was grounded, probably facing a Court Martial, and that he had killed Nisley.

RAF Wattisham

The entire Station appeared to have been awaiting the arrival of her Mosquito. Emily had not even cut the engine and already ground crew was swarming around it, a bowser rushed out and they started re-fuelling instantly. A staff car drove up and disgorged two very high-ranking officers. Oh dear, Emily thought. ATA had just issued some orders about personnel being expected to show military courtesy to senior officers, but no one had bothered to teach them how to salute. It was rather funny, actually, you watched other people do it all the time, but Emily felt absolutely silly doing it herself.

She folded her map together, stuffed it in her boot, and started to put the ladder down. "Do you intend to stay in that cockpit all day?" an annoyed voice called from the tarmac.

"I'm just getting my things collected," Emily answered, casting a last glance around to be sure she didn't forget anything. Then, with her tote-bag in one hand and her parachute over her shoulder, she let herself gingerly down the flimsy ladder.

A Group Captain and an Air Commodore were glaring at her as she emerged. She made her silly salute to one and then the other, and received rather surprised salutes in response. But that was all. The Group Captain himself saluted the Air Commodore and then grabbed the ladder and hauled himself into the Mosquito, followed by a Flying Officer. Emily had hardly had time to get out of the way before the engines were started up again.

They were definitely in a hurry, whatever they were about.

Emily went over to the Watch Office to get her chit signed. "You'll have to take my word for it that I didn't fly here on a broom," she told them as she handed over the chit. The Mosquito had already taken off again.

"I don't suppose you'd like something to fly home in," the Operations officer remarked, adding suspiciously, "would you?"

"Oh, have you got something?" Emily was rather surprised. They hadn't said anything about it at White Waltham.

"Well, I wouldn't want you to think you *have* to take it…"

"What is it, then?"

"Well, there's this rather awkward Hampden, you see…"

"No, what about it?"

"Well, a couple of chaps dumped it on us. That is to say, they landed it here not in the best of condition and then abandoned it. We've patched it up enough to fly, but it's very much in the way and of no use to us."

"Where does it belong?"

"Oh, well, that appears to be a rather debatable point. You see, it was written off."

"Written off?"

"Reported shot down."

"And then it turned up here?"

"Exactly."

"I don't understand."

"Well, it did go down, you see, in Holland. But somehow the crew and the locals managed to hide it from the Germans long enough to get it patched up and refuelled, and they took off again. They got as far as here before the pilot, feeling rather queasy on account of all the blood he'd lost in the meantime, put it down. But his squadron says they don't want it back, because they've already put in for and received a much prettier replacement."

"And where should I take it?"

"Well, one of the Maintenance Units ought to be able to do something with it—cannibalise it, I should think. Take it anywhere you like. We just don't want it here anymore."

Emily found the proposition very tempting. It would have been more tempting if it hadn't been a Hampden, but even so, the idea of having an aircraft she could just fly anywhere she wanted...Well, obviously, she *would* fly it to White Waltham and let the ATA find out from 41 Group where it belonged, but if no one was expecting it anywhere, what was to stop her from dropping by, say, Beauchamp Rodding, just for example?

Half an hour later, Emily was studying her Pilot's Notes in the cockpit of the Hampden. At least the weather really did appear to be clearing. The rain had stopped entirely, and the ceiling was up to at least 1,000 feet. Perfectly reasonable flying conditions, Emily told herself—not without a certain self-conscious bravado.

It was a little awkward sitting in an aircraft that was so obviously patched up, however. The bulk of the aircraft Emily flew were straight out of the factory, brand new and shiny. This poor crate was at least 3 years old, and it was covered with scratches, dents, dust and stains everywhere you looked. The leather on the seats was cracked and oily. What had the man said about the pilot feeling queasy from losing so much blood? Better not look at those stains too closely. There was an unfamiliar smell in the aircraft, too. It took more than one try to get the port engine started up, and it seemed to smoke unnaturally at first, but then it settled down and purred quite happily.

Just as Emily waved the chocks away, a bright beam of sunlight stabbed through a break in the clouds, and the low, slanting, afternoon sun lit up the still-wet airfield. Looking up, she could see the trailing edge of the weather front moving steadily eastwards. Behind it was clear blue sky. Yes, she really would hop over to Beauchamp Rodding and see just what game Jay thought he was playing with her. There was plenty of daylight left to drop in for a half hour and then continue on her way to White Waltham.

As the Hampden lumbered into the air, Emily was feeling rather smug. After all, it wasn't that long ago she'd been intimidated by the heavy twins. Maybe if she put in enough more time, she'd be selected for the real heavies. Only a very few women had been allowed to qualify on the four-engine bombers so far, but they had proved it could be done. Robin would be so proud of her if he came home and found her flying around in Lancasters and Halifaxes!

Beauchamp Rodding

The door banged open and the Kid shouted at him, "Lieutenant! You gotta come quick!"

J.B. was trying to write his mother, and he gaped at the Kid, completely confused.

"Come quick, sir. It's your girl! She just landed in a banged-up old bomber out there. Said she had engine trouble, but I'm sure she only come to see you."

"Emily?"

"Yessir!"

J.B. grabbed his cap, but his uniform jacket was in the closet so he grabbed his leather flight jacket instead—and ran. The Hampden looked very dainty among the Flying Fortresses and was obviously the centre of attention, with bowsers, fire-engines and ambulances all guarding it. The cowling was off the port engine, too, as mechanics looked it over. Bochanek was there, too—and Emily.

J.B. slowed down as he approached, not really wanting to draw attention to himself. There was enough of a crowd so that he could just sort of join the back of it. Emily was arguing with Bochanek. "I have a flight authorisation card and I decide if I can fly or not. I only landed because the oil pressure on the port engine was low and I thought I ought to have the engine checked, but I am *not* going to let you or anyone else ground me."

"Look, lady, I don't think you have any business in the cockpit of a bomber even if it's brand-spanking-new, but you sure the heck do not belong in the cockpit of that beat-up scrap-heap! If the oil pressure was low, then there's probably a leak somewhere—even if my mechanics can't find it in two minutes. So just settle down and let us handle this from now on."

"I'm sorry, we don't seem to be communicating very well, Colonel. I have the responsibility for delivering this aircraft to White Waltham, and that is exactly what I intend to do. You have no authority to stop me from flying—whether you like the idea or not."

"Well, Lady, I may not have the authority to stop you, but I'll let you in on a secret. Those trucks you see there and that ambulance and that fire-engine all take orders from me, and they ain't moving until I say so."

Since the Hampden was completely surrounded by these vehicles, this meant that Emily was effectively checkmated. If she couldn't fly out, she'd have to stay here—or at least nearby. Jay was beginning to imagine spending the whole evening with Emily, and his heart was lifting unconsciously.

He hadn't reckoned with Emily's determination. "Are you saying, Colonel, that you intend to confiscate His Majesty's aircraft?"

"What?"

"If you prevent me from carrying out my duty by physically seizing control of this aircraft, you are in effect expropriating His Majesty's property."

"What are you talking about!? I don't believe for one gosh-darned minute that that piece of scrap is your King's personal—Oh, I get it. They're *all* his, aren't they? OK. Well, don't get in a tizzy about it, because I don't want it blocking my runways anyway. I'll have one of my own pilots fly it wherever it belongs."

Jay didn't hesitate for an instant. It was a sign from heaven. God was very *definitely* on their side. "I'll take it, sir."

It was the first time the others noticed Jay. Emily and Bochanek looked over; Emily's glance seemed relieved and grateful, Bochanek's annoyed. "Oh, you," was his first reaction, and he glowered at Jay. His short grey hair seemed to all but stand on end. But then he shrugged and decided, "Why not? You aren't doing anything productive around here anyway. Yeah, get this scrap-heap off the runway and dump it wherever the Lady says. Just make sure you don't break it—got it?"

"Yes, sir!" Jay saluted smartly.

Emily turned and climbed right back into the Hampden as if she was angry. Jay waved to the mechanics to put the cowling back on and prepare for take-off, then followed her into the cockpit as fast as he could—before Bochanek changed his mind. He dropped down into the right-hand seat and Emily handed him her Pilot's Notes with just one smile and the remark, "I don't care what your Colonel thinks or says, I'm flying this crate."

J.B. answered with a mixture of amusement and annoyance, "Yes, Ma'am."

Emily was all business. She was clearly doing a pre-flight drill without any reference to a co-pilot—she usually didn't have one. She started to lean out of the window to call for "contact," but remembered herself just in time, and had Jay do it. A moment later the port engine started in a burst of smoke. J.B. didn't like the looks of it at all. It seemed to be quite rough as well, and he looked in alarm at the oil-pressure gauge. "There's no oil pressure at all!" he called out horrified.

"Yes, there is; it's just the indicator that's not working," Emily replied calmly.

Uncomfortably, Jay accepted her word for it, because the temperature reading was rather on the cold side and not increasing noticeably. Meanwhile, she had started up the starboard engine, and the ambulance, fire-engine and fuel tanker had withdrawn, leaving the way clear to taxi. Emily eased the two throttles on and they rolled slowly forward. Then Emily applied the brakes and, cutting back the port engine, used the starboard engine to turn them around to head for the top of the runway again. Once she reached the top of the runway, she swung the Hampden around neatly and ran up the engines, while Jay watched the temperatures, pressure, and rpms and found himself feeling very nervous. He knew Emily could fly, but he never liked being a passenger, and this old ship didn't fill him with any confidence. As they started down the runway, it seemed to be trying to shake itself to pieces.

Then again, it seemed to fling itself joyously into the air—at least compared to a loaded B-17. Emily climbed steeply and banked away sharply, too. "You didn't warn me that your CO was an insufferable pompous ass, who doesn't think women should fly!" was the next thing Emily said to him—without taking her eyes off the windshield.

J.B. grinned. "If I'd told you that, you never would have dropped by."

Emily glanced over at him, and suddenly she was smiling, too. It didn't make sense. J.B. still had a great of explaining to do, but just having him here sitting next to her made her feel good. Still smiling, she looked back out the windshield. "Well, we could have rendezvoused somewhere more hospitable."

"But then I wouldn't have had the pleasure of watching you chew out the CO. I liked the line about His Majesty's aircraft—especially applied to this old wreck."

"Don't be insulting. I'm getting very fond of this aircraft. In fact, I'm thinking about keeping it."

"Keeping it? His Majesty's aircraft?" Jay managed to sound shocked.

"Well, to be very precise, the King thinks it was lost over Holland, and the RAF finds it embarrassing to admit they wrote off an aircraft that is still very airworthy—as we both see. So it doesn't officially exist. I was just thinking that if I could hide it away somewhere until the end of the war, I could have my very own aircraft."

"Hm. Maintenance might be a problem. And gas, of course."

"Gas? Oh, petrol. Yes, I suppose that might be quite expensive, but think of all the money we'd save on train-fares?"

"Not very comfortable accommodation for passengers," Jay pointed out with a glance behind him.

"Oh, we would have to fix it up a bit—rather like a caravan, you know. Then we could fly about the country—or even to the Continent—and sleep right on the airfield in the back of our flying caravan."

Jay loved the way she was saying 'we.' Suddenly it was as if they were planning a future together—no matter how fanciful. He wanted to prolong the joint nonsense as long as possible. "The shower might be tricky."

"Well, sail-boats have them, don't they? Why not an aeroplane? And commercial airlines have galleys, too. I'm quite sure—"

With a horrible "boom" and then a crack and a violent swinging of the aircraft, an emergency was upon them. Jay was stunned for a second. They were over England. There couldn't be flak anywhere. Emily, on the left, saw or sensed the problem faster. "The cowling's just blown off the port engine!"

"Holy Mother of God! It must have hit the fuselage farther aft. Is the ship still—"

"No!"

Emily was struggling with the controls. There had obviously been damage to the tail-section. The aircraft was yawing to the left and starting down. J.B. grabbed the co-pilot's controls. With his greater strength, he could just hold it straight and level. "Where the hell are we?" he asked Emily desperately. "And where's the closest airfield?"

"Stansted," she replied without hesitation. Pointing, "just up there."

"Get us an emergency clearance," J.B. ordered, forgetting he wasn't in command of this aircraft.

"I can't. No radio." J.B. had forgotten, and it filled him with alarm, but Emily was reassuring. "Don't worry."

"What about a flare?"

Emily had never shot a flare in her life, and she didn't know where they might be stowed—presuming there were any. She shook her head.

"Try throttling back a bit," J.B. ordered next. He was sweating heavily and his arm and thigh muscles were already starting to hurt. He couldn't spare a hand for the throttles.

Emily did as he asked, adding, "She stalls at 82 knots without flaps or undercarriage and 68 with both flaps and undercarriage."

"Give me full flaps."

Emily did.

"There's no way I can do a circuit. We have to get it right the first time."

"Undercarriage?"

"Not yet."

J.B. was letting them gradually sink down toward the airfield, but it was still a continuous struggle to keep them on a straight course. If they swung too far to the left, there wouldn't be enough space to roll and they would crash into a line of trees running along the perimeter of the airfield. Some future they were going to have together…"I might be able to hold her long enough for you to jump…"

"No. I'd rather stay with the aircraft."

Jay felt a stab of disappointment that she had ended that sentence with "aircraft" and not with "you." But there was no time to think about that. "Are you strapped in tight?"

"Yes, of course."

"Landing gear!"

Usually Emily had a little trouble with the undercarriage on a Hampden, but that was because she had to lower it and fly at the same time; it was easier now. They could feel it catching the wind, noticeably slowing them down. Emily glanced at the air speed indicator; they were only ten to twelve miles an hour over stalling speed.

Even so, the ground seemed to be coming up at them very fast, and Emily's eyes started to wander back and forth between the compass and the horizon. They were yawing badly. J.B. was clearly aware of the problem; he was bracing himself hard on the port rudder and trying to keep the control column turned enough to keep them on course.

"Throttle back gently."

Emily reached for the throttles, and staring at the air speed indicator, started to ease them back.

"I'll try to level off just above the runway and then stall her, alright?"

"Roger."

They were wobbling badly now. He just couldn't hold course and descend in a controlled fashion at the same time. The grass was beneath them, the ambulance was in motion. They were too high for a proper landing, but it would have to do. J.B. nodded to her, and she pulled the throttles back further. They dropped like a stone; there was a horrible jolt, a bounce, then they dropped again unevenly, one wheel hit before the other. The tire burst and a split second later the wing-tip went in, spinning them around violently.

Emily cut the engines, and the sound of the ambulance and fire-engine sirens were louder and rapidly approaching. "That was my first ground loop. In fact, it was my first accident," she admitted mournfully. She was already imagining her dismissal.

"I was at the controls—"

"No, you weren't! If they find that out, I'm sure to be dismissed!" Emily was so upset that her voice was raised and pitched higher. She sounded almost hysterical, and that surprised J.B.

They stared at one another.

More calmly, she added, "It's bad enough I had you as a passenger, but I might just get away with that. Let me handle this."

The ambulance was already alongside, and the RAF medical orderlies were jumping down. Emily opened the hatch and dropped down to the ground first. "We're alright," she told the ambulance crew. A Flight Lieutenant in a staff car drew up next and got out. Emily addressed herself to him, "The cowling came off in flight and damaged the tail."

"I can see that. Everyone alright?"

"Yes, thank you."

"I'll take you over to the Watch office, then," he offered, and Emily knew she had no choice. His next question sealed her fate. "You have a passenger aboard?"

"Yes, he hitched a ride from Beauchamp Rodding." She called up into the cockpit, "Lieutenant?"

The sight of an American astonished the RAF, but there was no comment. Emily got in beside the Flight Lieutenant, and J.B. clambered into the back with Emily's overnight bag as if it were his own. They were driven to the Watch Office, and there the paper battle began.

Emily, of course, had to file the accident report, RAF Form 765C. She had the snag sheet on the aircraft to fill out, too, and she had to call White Waltham with her whereabouts and situation. Then she had to explain to the RAF what she was doing with an aircraft that didn't exist and an American passenger. Everyone was very polite about it, but Emily had the distinct feeling that no one believed a word she was saying. It was as if they thought she were an enemy agent or something.

If she had collected the aircraft at RAF Wattisham, what had she been doing at Beauchamp Rodding? So she had to explain about the oil pressure. But if the oil pressure were reading nil, why hadn't she stayed at Beauchamp Rodding until the problem was fixed? Because the American mechanics couldn't find a problem. Well, said the RAF, that was logical enough, since they had no experience with Hampdens—as evidenced by the fact that they hadn't even got the cowling on properly. Why had she been in such a hurry to leave Beauchamp Rodding? She was hoping to get home for the night, she told them rather sheepishly. Home? White Waltham? But why would an American officer want to go to White Waltham?

"I don't," Jay butted in for the first time. "I've never even heard of the place—but I was told it was near Windsor and I have a girl there. Surely you guys can understand that? Why are you giving this poor lady pilot so much flak? She did a great job putting that beat-up old crate down without doing it—or us!—more damage!"

"Please stay out of this, Lieutenant," Emily told him firmly. "The aircraft was my responsibility, and the RAF has every right to an explanation of what happened. Furthermore, I have every intention of answering everyone's questions to their satisfaction. It might help matters, sir," she addressed herself to the Station Commander who was conducting the interrogation, "if you would at least put in a call to Wattisham. The Station Commander there will be able to explain about the aircraft."

The Wing Commander raised an eyebrow at her and then withdrew into his office. After a moment or two, she could hear his voice but not what he was saying. A Flight Sergeant came into the Watch office and reported that the Hampden had sustained considerable damage to the tail-fin and elevators, and the wing-tip, of course, but that it could easily be patched up. Not U/S more than a day or two. The port engine was quite alright—just leaking a bit of oil, but that was nothing unusual in an engine that age, he assured them happily. The Flight Sergeant withdrew.

A burst of laughter came from the Station Commander's office, and Jay cast Emily a hopeful look. She continued to look prim and proper. White Waltham called up. They wanted the name and details of the American passenger. He would be wanted as a witness for the Accident Committee. Emily gave the details with a very dry throat, but Jay winked at her.

The Station Commander emerged from his office looking more relaxed than when he went in. "Alright, Mrs. Priestman, I understand now about the aircraft. We will take it off your hands here and now." It took a moment before they found the proper forms for that transfer, but at last Emily was able to sign the aircraft over to the RAF. "You'll be needing ground transportation; I'll see what I can do to get you to the nearest train station," the Duty Pilot suggested in a friendlier tone than before.

"Thank you."

Emily and Jay found themselves in a cheerless station without so much as a shelter. The sun had set and the air was getting very chilly. Darkness was creeping over the silent countryside around them. The only sounds were the birds and crickets and the wind in the trees. Emily started to shiver, despite her Irvin jacket, and Jay recognised it as the aftermath of the shock she had just had. He put his arms around her and started rubbing her back vigorously.

A whistle blew and they glanced up to see a train coming toward them. It was coming from the north, heading for London, but it was small, old and battered. "That's the stopping train, according to the schedule," Emily remarked. "It stops at every town and village all the way to London. We'll be in Paddington sooner if we wait for the fast train."

"Yeah, but by then you might have got your death of cold. Let's take it."

It squealed to a stop with the conductor standing on the step of the first wagon. The engine hissed. Jay reached forward and opened one of the heavy doors, and let Emily climb in first. It was one of the old type of cars where you entered directly into a compartment. Two long benches faced each other— ancient, worn, faded and threadbare seats that once upon a time had been red. Two elderly ladies occupied the seat facing forward, with a straw basket, in which a small, shaggy dog perched, occupying the seat between them. Jay touched his cap to them before lifting Emily's overnight bag and parachute onto the rack over the other seat. Emily settled herself as far from the window as possible. With a jerk and a loud hiss, the train started forward again.

A moment later the conductor was at the door, taking their fare. Jay paid for both tickets before Emily could stop him. Then he sat down beside her and put his arm over her shoulders, pulling her to him closely. Her teeth were chattering and she was shaking all over.

One of the women passengers was pretending not to notice, staring pointedly at her knitting but sneaking glances at the newcomers, while the woman with the dog looked at them with open hostility.

"I couldn't have held her myself," Emily murmured, avoiding the woman's harsh stare by turning her face into Jay's soft leather jacket.

"It's OK. I was there."

"I would have crashed."

"But you didn't. And, you know, I would have crashed it if *you* hadn't been there to handle the throttles and undercarriage. It was a team effort." He hesitated a fraction of a second and then added, "We're a great team, Emily."

Emily didn't answer, but she snuggled closer.

"I don't know what this country is coming to!" the woman opposite declared indignantly. "Don't you young girls have any self-respect anymore? In my youth I wouldn't have let a man so much as lay his hand on me in public! And don't start up about the war! There was a war on when I was young, too!"

Emily broke free of Jay's embrace, jumped up and fled from the compartment into the passageway that ran along the side. Jay glared at the woman opposite. "That young lady just flew a damaged Hampden into an RAF airfield; it almost crashed on landing, and she's got every right to be upset and every right to a little comfort."

"Oh, is that what you call it?" the woman sniffed at him with a sneer, but Jay was already following Emily out. He found her just down the corridor, holding onto the door as the train swayed and clacked its way through the darkness. Again he took her in his arms, and just held her until her shivering started to subside. "You shouldn't let old bitches like that get to you. She was only jealous."

Emily hiccupped. Then she risked looking up at Jay with a little smile. "I know." The next thing she knew they were kissing. It seemed so natural, and so inevitable that she didn't even feel guilty about it. Somehow it was the right thing to do. So they stood there in the darkness, swaying and kissing until with a loud squeal and hiss, the train started to slow for the next station. Then Emily drew away, muttering, "I'd better get changed."

She found her way back to the compartment, pulled down her over-night bag and took it to the WC. There she got out of her flying boots and trousers and into her skirt, stockings and shoes. She also brushed out her hair vigorously, but left it down. She applied powder and lipstick and a touch of rouge. By now the train was moving on again, but feeling more feminine, Emily carried her flight jacket over her arm and returned to the compartment. The look Jay gave her was reward enough. He put her bag back onto the rack for her and they sat side-by-side without talking. Just holding hands.

Neither of them knew where they were anymore. The blackout shades were drawn over the windows and there was no outside world. The light inside the train was so dim that it was impossible to read and difficult to see faces. The train swayed rhythmically and the wheels drummed out the monotonous clickety-clack, clickety-clack, clickety-clack. Emily consciously closed her mind to all but the present: she wanted to concentrate only on the feel of Jay beside her, warm and strong, and his hand holding hers. She didn't want to ponder whether it was right or wrong. She didn't want to ask herself what she was feeling. She didn't want to think about what she was doing or why or where it would lead her. She just wanted the train ride to go on forever.

Jay, in contrast, was feverish with thought. He had no doubts anymore about how Emily felt for him. She loved him. And that changed everything. To his own astonishment, he realised that he loved her more than ever. His sister was wrong. This was *nothing* like Kathy. Kathy had been a trophy. He had wanted her *because* she hadn't considered him good enough for her. He had wanted to prove that he was. He had wanted to show the rest of the world that he could win her. He had been proud of her—like wearing a class letter, Lieutenant's bars, and pilot's wings. But with the wisdom he had gained in the last six months he knew that he had never even come close to loving her. Emily was different. He loved her so much that he was suddenly afraid for her. He wanted what was best *for her*. He wanted to make *her* happy—and for the first time he had doubts about whether he could.

He thought again about the contrast between her house and his parents' trailer home. If he got a good job after the war, at one of the auto companies, for example, he ought to be able to afford something better than that, but that was a long way off. Would Emily even want to come to America? She seemed open-minded, but this was her home, after all. And she was an only child. Even if she wasn't close to her parents, she might not want to be that far away.

"Emily?"

"Um."

"Don't you think I should meet your parents one of these days?"

"You can't."

"Why not?"

"They're dead."

"Dead?" Jay was so shocked that he twisted to look her straight in the face. She opened her eyes and met his. "They were killed in an air-raid."

"My God! Why didn't you tell me?" Jay was trying to think how he could have missed the fact that Portsmouth had been bombed. Was he really that wrapped up in himself?

"December 1940."

It took Jay a moment to absorb that. "But then—they've been dead as long as we've known each other."

"Yes."

"But...We talked about your parents. Why didn't you mention it?"

"It sounded so piteous—poor little orphan girl and all that. I told you I wasn't that close to them, Jay. It's all history now." She closed her eyes again with a little squeeze of his hand.

Jay leaned back again and reflected that if she had no family ties to England, she should be all the more willing to follow him to the States. Maybe even before the war was over. After his tour of duty, he ought to get a posting in Training or Air Transport Command next. They could get married and move back to the States right away. Then it wouldn't matter how long the war lasted.

Of course, he had to get through his tour first. For the first time since he had seen Emily out there beside that Hampden, he remembered his current situation. He was grounded, facing an investigation, and God knew what was going to happen next. If he got busted to private, there was no way he could afford a wife— much less a lady like Emily. And if he didn't get busted and was given a new crew, then he still had 6 missions to fly. Not much when you compared it to that English Wing Commander, the one with the funny name, but any one of them could be his last.

The train had reached the outskirts of London now. The stations came quick and fast, which meant they were stopping every few minutes. People starting getting on and off the train more frequently. The two original passengers were long since gone, replaced by others who had come and already gone. At ten to ten they finally pulled into Paddington Station, and with a loud hiss the engine came to a last stop. The door was flung open and the echoing voice of the announcer and the chatter of the crowds poured into the compartment, shattering Emily's cocoon.

Jay stood first and got Emily's bag and parachute down for her. She stepped down onto the platform and they looked about. There were crowds hurrying every which way; trains were lined up on the tracks huffing and puffing. Conductors blew their whistles and from the exit came the honking of horns. Everybody else seemed to know where they wanted to go, but Emily and Jay didn't. They should have been finding out about connections back to their respective bases, but neither of them had the slightest inclination to do so. Jay certainly had no particular reason to rush back to Beauchamp Rodding. As long as he was grounded and had no crew, there was nothing for him to do there but hang around feeling guilty. Emily was only vaguely aware that returning to Windsor and Robin's house would be the end of this pleasant interlude. It would be a return to reality. She wasn't ready for that just yet.

"Look, I'm starving. Let's go to dinner," Jay suggested.

"Oh, yes, I could do with dinner," Emily agreed.

"Let's go to the Ritz." Jay suggested, set on celebrating and impressing, too.

"Heavens! I'm not dressed for that! Besides, they'd never let you in in a flight jacket. Someplace small and warm and friendly would be much better."

"OK. You know the town. Take me."

"Oh! I don't know London. I've hardly ever been here. I have a friend from College…" But how could she call up Grace and say she was with an American? It wouldn't do. "Let's just ask the taxi-driver. They always know of something."

A half hour later they were in a tiny Italian restaurant crammed into a cellar below a haberdashers' in St. James. There was hardly room for the six tables, and all of them were full. But it was warm and the food smelled divine. The waiters were really Italian, too, and one suspected they had avoided internment because someone powerful in the government liked to eat here. Jay ordered the house red wine, and first it warmed them and then it went to their heads.

Jay started talking. "Emily, there's something you've got to know."

She looked at him with large, expectant eyes.

"I've been grounded. They haven't given me a new crew. I guess you can understand why. I mean, you know what happened to the last one. No, that's right, you don't know." Only now did he remember that he hadn't told her about Nisley. "Oh, God," he murmured to himself and then he wished he were drinking something stronger than wine.

She was still gazing at him patiently.

He took a deep breath. "I ordered them to jump, you know that."

Emily nodded slowly.

"The right waist gunner, Nisley, he—he pulled the cord too soon. The chute got tangled on the tail-wheel and tore apart." J.B. paused to think how to word the rest, but he didn't have to. Emily understood about parachutes. She reached out and touched the back of his hand. "It's not your fault, Jay."

"I ordered him to jump."

"But not pull the cord too soon."

"He'd be alive today, if I hadn't given that order."

"Maybe. Maybe not. He could have been killed on the next mission, or walking home from the pub one night, or in an air raid. And you could have been killed today. Death is so close to all of us, really."

Emily was not looking directly at him anymore, but looking at something in her mind. Jay feared she might be thinking of her husband. He entwined his fingers in hers, drawing her attention back to him. "God was with us today, Emily. Just as he sent you to me after No. 19. He means for us to be together. Always."

Emily started slightly. She didn't believe in God—certainly not in a God who took an active role in the personal lives of insignificant humans like herself and Jay. But there seemed to be something miraculous about what had happened today, even to her. If Jay hadn't been in the Hampden with her, she would have crashed. (She didn't think about the fact that if she hadn't stopped to try to see him, the cowling would never have come off.) After such a long, frightening, tiring day and a half-bottle of wine, Emily was absolutely convinced that Jay had saved her life.

"I love you, Emily. You know that, don't you?"

Emily nodded slowly.

"I want to marry you, Emily. As soon as you're ready."

She remembered that Gypsy, saying she would be happy again and that she would travel halfway around the world, and she nodded.

By the time they finished with dinner it was almost midnight, and Emily was falling asleep on her feet. She could hardly keep her eyes open, and kept nodding off despite her best efforts. Jay excused himself, went to the back of the restaurant and consulted with the proprietor. Then he collected their jackets from the coat stand and helped Emily into hers. He shouldered her parachute, and took her tote bag in his hand and followed her up the stairs out of the restaurant. On the street again, he stopped and announced simply: "I want to spend the night with you, Emily."

They looked at each other, and then Emily tipped forward to lean on his chest and said, "I'm exhausted, Jay. All I want to do is sleep. I'm sorry."

"Then we'll sleep together," Jay told her softly as he put his arm around her and guided their steps back to Pall Mall. He flagged down a taxi, and gave the driver the address.

Emily went straight to the airfield the next morning, arriving just a little after nine. The others were still there; the taxi Ansons hadn't left yet. Somebody made a crack about ground looping, but Emily ignored him and hurried in to Operations to apologise for being late. She talked rather too much and too fast. She knew she was doing it even as she did it, but she couldn't seem to slow down. The Operations Officer considered her calmly, puffing on his pipe, and then told her to get herself a cup of tea and he'd call her. That wasn't normal and Emily had a very bad feeling.

Then next thing she knew, Pauline Gower was standing in front of her. "Would you mind coming to my office for a minute, Mrs. Priestman?"

Emily felt as if the floor had dropped out from under her. She was going to get the sack. She closed the door behind her, and Pauline Gower smiled her gentle, restrained smile and told her to sit down. "You look very tired," she observed as she seated herself behind her desk.

"I—I—I'm afraid I didn't get much sleep last night. After the accident—I just couldn't seem to sleep." Emily was so tense, she was unconsciously hunching over and clutching her hands together.

"Maybe the best thing would be for you to go home now and catch up on that sleep," Gower suggested softly.

"But I can fly—I've got to fly—" Emily started rather desperately and then cut herself off as she realised how nearly hysterical she sounded.

"Of course," Gower agreed simply—after a moment. She paused and then added, "I think it would be better, however, if you went home and got some sleep and just relaxed for a day or two." She glanced at her calendar. "Report for work again on Thursday morning, alright?"

"You're not grounding me, are you?"

Gower shook her head. "No. I'm asking you to go home and get some sleep. I'll have one of the girls drive you home." (ATA had a motor-transport pool with a number of drivers.)

"Alright. Thank you." Emily stood and left the office. No matter what Gower said, Emily was certain this was the first step toward grounding and dismissal. The ATA took accidents very seriously. They weren't combat pilots, after all, who routinely wrecked their aircraft due to enemy action, low fuel or weather. Their job was to deliver the aircraft briefly entrusted to them safely so the RAF could do what it liked with them. In consequence, every crash—no matter how minor—was carefully investigated and the degree of pilot responsibility was determined. If the accident committee decided that Emily had been to blame for the accident, she would get the sack. She was further certain that the fact that she had landed at an American base, was carrying an unauthorised (American!) passenger, and flying an aircraft that officially didn't exist could only count against her. She couldn't bear even looking at her colleagues, and she hurried out to wait for the car in front of the Mess.

When she let herself into the house, Penny flung herself at her with so much force it nearly knocked her down. In a frenzy the little dog jumped, turned and butted, gasping for breath. Emily swept her up into her arms and clung to her warm, soft body, sobbing miserably. She carried Penny upstairs and set her on the bed. Then she managed to get herself undressed while she ran a bath. Penny insisted on watching her solemnly while she soaked and washed her hair, and then padded after her as she lay herself down. Emily cried herself to sleep holding the distraught and sympathetic dog in her arms.

By the time Philippa arrived home, Emily had risen and dressed. She had made dinner for them both, and was sitting at the dining-room table waiting for her lodger. Philippa took one look at her, saw the swollen eyes and the red splotches on her face, and concluded, "You've been crying."

Emily answered with a stifled sob, and then managed, "I had an accident yesterday."

"They rang and told me. They said no one had been hurt."

Emily wasn't looking at her. She was fussing with the things on the table. Somehow she was too weak to pretend. She croaked out: "Jay was with me."

Philippa took a moment to absorb that. Then she sat down opposite Emily and asked quietly, "Was he hurt?"

Emily shook her head. "No, but—afterwards…"

Philippa waited. When Emily dropped her head in her hands and started sobbing again, Philippa got up, went around the table and knelt down at Emily's knee. "What happened?"

"It was a bad crash." Emily sobbed. "We could both have been killed."

Philippa just waited. She knew that wasn't the problem.

"I was shaking," Emily continued. "Jay was so good about it. He—he just held me. Nothing improper! Just held me. Until I could calm down."

Philippa nodded. "And then?"

"I don't know!" Emily cried out in anguish. Then she calmed herself enough to explain, "We went to dinner. I don't know. One thing just seemed to lead to the next…"

Philippa waited.

Tears were streaming down Emily's face and from her nose, and she couldn't be bothered even wiping them away. "And then, Philippa, I found myself staring at myself in the bathroom mirror and—and—" She couldn't even say it calmly. She wailed it out in a rush of agony, "and-wishing-Robin-was-dead-so-I-wouldn't-be-an-adulteress!" As soon as it was out, she pressed the heels of her hands to her eyes again and let herself cry uncontrolled.

Philippa laid her arms on Emily's lap and let the gush of misery abate a little. Then she reached up and pulled Emily's hands away from her face and held them tightly in her own. Emily turned her head away, and Philippa insisted: "Emily, look at me."

Sobbing, Emily turned and looked at Philippa uncertainly, the tears still running down her face, her lips trembling from her effort to keep her mouth closed. "Emily," Philippa spoke in a soft but urgent tone, "whether you wish him dead or not, *doesn't make any difference.* Just as all your wishing he were alive, couldn't bring him back."

They gazed at one another, and gradually what Philippa had said started to sink in, and Emily felt some of the tension receding. She pulled one hand free of Philippa's and reached up to try and wipe some of the tears away. Philippa produced a handkerchief, and gave it to Emily.

"If he's dead, he's dead. Nothing you do or think or wish will change it." When Emily didn't contradict her, Philippa continued gently. "Did you make your American happy?"

For a moment Emily just sat there staring at the handkerchief, and then she nodded. "I think I did, yes."

"And did he make *you* happy?"

"Not like Robin—but—but—"

"Emily, stop comparing them! Did he make you happy?"

"I don't know—it felt good to be in his arms, Philippa. It felt so *good...*" Emily sobbed once and then blew her nose.

The telephone started to ring, but Philippa ignored it. She waited until she was sure she had Emily's attention, and then she urged: "Let the dead bury the dead. You have to concentrate on the living."

"But what if he's *not* dead?"

"Cross that bridge when you come to it." Then, because the phone was still ringing insistently and Philippa was expecting a call from Teddy, she said: "Let me just get that phone. I'll be right back." She pushed herself back to her feet and hurried into the parlour.

Emily wiped at her face with the soaked handkerchief. The worst was over. She could sense it. Philippa was right.

Philippa was standing in the door. "It's your young man."

Emily gaped at her. How could she possibly talk to Jay now?

"Come on," Philippa urged with a smile. "Don't keep him waiting. He sounded like he's been trying to reach you for at least a century."

CHAPTER 19

▼

Beauchamp Rodding, England
Late September 1943

The air seemed to bite. You could see your breath like dragon's smoke, and the tarmac was a glaze of silver frost in the darkness. Their boots left big, sloppy footprints on it as they crossed toward the Mess. It was hard to believe that being 30 degrees colder down here wouldn't make much difference at altitude. Jay paused and looked up at the sky. It was still too dark to see properly. You could just barely make out the silhouettes of the various buildings around the airfield against a dark grey sky. There were no stars up there, however, so the sky was probably overcast high up. J.B. stared at the greyness for a moment, trying to guess the ceiling, but the chill got to him first. He shook himself and continued to the Mess Hall.

Inside, the artificial light was garish and cruel after the soft darkness of the fading night. The clatter of trays and cutlery seemed harsh, too. The smell of the 'mission breakfast' made Jay's stomach turn over. He could no longer disassociate it from what was to come afterwards. He wondered vaguely if he'd associate the smell of bacon and eggs with flak for the rest of his life.

Yeah, very likely, since the 'rest of his life' might not be more than a few hours.

Even as he thought it, however, he didn't believe it. He was *reminding* himself that it could happen, but he didn't believe it. He believed that he was going to survive all his remaining six missions. He believed that he was going live long enough to marry Emily and take her home with him.

They had met twice since that night he'd proposed to her and made love to her for the first time. Each time had been better than before. Each time she had opened up a little more to him, and allowed herself to love him more. He knew that it was hard for her to forget her husband, and he loved her for that—for her loyalty and the fact that when she loved she loved deeply. He'd already promised himself that they would name their first-born son for her first husband. It was only fair. He would never be jealous of a dead man. He would never do anything to belittle or besmirch the man's memory. Christ, he'd been a real hero, Battle of Britain fighter pilot, DFC and Bar and whatnot. Jay didn't mind acknowledging all that, just so long as Emily was his.

And Emily *was* his. Just as she had been loyal to her husband even after he was dead, she was loyal to him now. She was on his side, no matter what. She'd been as happy as he had been to learn there would be no charges against him, and when he told her he was flying again, she had been happy for him—even though he could tell she was worried. She was a pilot; she understood about being grounded. She knew that, crazy as it was, he was happier flying wherever in hell they were sending them today than being left behind on the ground. Jay was even beginning to understand what that English guy had said about getting addicted to it…

If only they'd given him his own ship. Not that he deserved it, Jay reminded himself. No, he'd killed Nisley and four men were *probably* prisoners—if they were lucky. But more and more horror stories were making the rounds about how Allied airmen were being lynched by German civilians. Lord Haw-Haw made it sound like the German authorities were doing all they could to restrain their vengeful people, but they weren't always fast enough. Some of the other guys claimed that the Gestapo was killing the crews and blaming the civilians. One way or another, it looked like it was getting more and more dangerous to bail out over Germany. Even if Jay's crew had escaped the lynch mob and the Gestapo, Dan's fate lay in the hands of some Kraut doctors who might or might not have his recovery truly at heart. All because Jay had panicked.

Jay still hated himself for that, but he also wanted to prove he'd learned his les-son. Jay had begged Bochanek for a second chance, another ship and crew. It didn't even have to be a new ship. He'd volunteered to take any beat-up old wreck that could halfway fly. He offered to take all the remnants of crews that had been decimated by injury, death and returnees. Bochanek had said 'No.' Instead they had put him in the 'dummy seat.' He was flying co-pilot to a man with less experience.

Jay looked across the echoing Mess Hall for his pilot. The man's name was Rawlings; he was a plump, round-faced man from Florida. He'd joined the Group almost two months after J.B., and he had now flown 11 missions to J.B.'s 19. That wasn't a lot less, J.B. supposed, but then again it was. *Eat crow*, J.B. told himself, as he spotted his new commander shovelling eggs into his face with both elbows braced on the table, reminding himself: *You killed Nisley.*

Jay did not go over to the table where his new captain, navigator and bombardier sat together. He didn't dare. They were a little, self-sufficient group. You could tell. One of them stole something from the other's tray and got his hand slapped, and then the other dropped something down the first man's collar. Kid's stuff. They could have been in a Jr. High School cafeteria. Jay didn't belong with them—not in the place that the dead co-pilot should have occupied.

Jay couldn't remember the guy's name, but he'd developed a case of appendicitis on a mission, and no one had believed he was really sick at first. They just thought he was fooling around. By the time they realised he was serious and aborted, it was too late. He died in hospital.

Jay sat at the end of a table that wasn't full. The other officers glanced over at him, nodded politely, and went on with their own lives and thoughts and conversation. He wasn't so much a pariah, Jay figured, as a ghost. The crews around him probably couldn't even remember Dan and Tony—much less Buzz or Logan or Olds. They saw him as a forgotten left-over from some dead ship that didn't really belong here anymore. The sooner he either finished his tour or just didn't come back, the better.

Jay forced himself to eat. He was going to need his strength. He drank coffee to help keep himself awake, but no orange juice. Keep the caffeine high and the fluids low. He hated the pee-hole.

Briefing. The usual bullshit. The target was vital to the Nazis. It had to be obliterated. At the same time, it was likely to be a milk-run; there would be fighter escort the whole way. The only trouble was that it was located in the middle of Antwerp, which happened to be in Belgium, which meant that lots of innocent people were going to get killed—or at least have their houses levelled—if they missed the target. Of course they would miss the target—some of them would, Jay thought. You couldn't help it. Flak would be throwing the ship around, and just a little cross wind and—oops, you missed the factory and smashed a five-story apartment house. At least when they bombed Germany you could comfort yourself that they were all just a bunch of Nazis anyway, but Belgians?

God, why did you curse me with this imagination? J.B. asked himself, with a glance at his new skipper. The man was nodding unconsciously like he thought it was all peaches and cream. What was it about plump men that always made them look complacent? J.B. supposed that was better than flying with a guy who looked like he thought he was riding into the Valley of Death like the captain of the *Little Red Riding-Hood* (who was sitting next to him). He looked like he had no hope of return—and crossing himself as the briefing ended didn't exactly dispel that impression.

Jay took a deep breath, put his cap back on, and shuffled with the others back outside. Now the bottoms of the clouds were dusted with bright pink. Almost like burning embers.

J.B. donned his heavy flying clothing, and dragged himself onto the back of the truck with the others. He was dumped beside the unfamiliar ship, *English Rose*, and paused to look up at the nose painting. All the ships were painted by the same artist—one of the cooks from the Sergeant's mess. All the girls looked the same—buxom, big-lipped, and promiscuous. Jay found it all rather tedious. This one was wearing nothing but roses, which covered her crotch and her nipples only.

Jay pulled himself up through the fore-hatch and with a twitch of sharp humiliation, sank into the right-hand seat. He took out the check-list.

Rawlings sank heavily into the commander's seat on his left. He burped once, and then cleared his throat. "Everything set?"

"I'm just checking, sir," Jay answered him levelly. J.B. could feel the man looking at him, narrowing his eyes suspiciously or resentfully, Jay didn't know which. Then Rawlings took some Doublemint gum out of his pocket, shoved a stick into his mouth, and crumpled up the paper. He just tossed the paper over his shoulder onto the flight deck behind them. J.B. glanced over his shoulder at it and saw the silver paper shining against the grimy metal floor. He'd been raised not to do things like that. His mother had to pick up after him, after all. If he'd been captain and his new co-pilot had done something like that, he would have given him a head-washing. But he wasn't captain...

"Ain't you never seen a gum wrapper before?" Rawlings asked belligerently.

"Not just thrown on the floor of the flight deck," J.B. answered as evenly as he could.

Rawlings again narrowed his eyes at Jay, but he said no more. They started the pre-flight check, J.B. calling out the items and Rawlings reporting back the settings. J.B. felt the humiliation intensely, and he started to understand Tony for the first time—really understand him, that is. Forgive me, Tony, he prayed silently as he finally put the check-list aside, and Rawlings, with a lot of squirming and squiggling, started to flip the switches for the engines.

They taxied out behind the other ships, bouncing and waddling their way to the start of the runway. Just ahead of them was *Card Shark;* the nose art showed a girl (half naked of course) playing cards. The Kid was tail gunner in that ship now, and no sooner had Jay remembered it than he saw the Kid was waving at him. Jay automatically—gratefully—waved back.

"What the hell are you waving at?" Rawlings snarled, his gum smacking loudly when he opened his mouth to talk.

"That's my tail gunner up there."

"He ain't *your* gunner no more, he's Harvey's."

Too true. J.B. refrained from replying.

Card Shark turned onto the runway, and they waited. J.B. looked back along the line of waiting B-17s, wondering which one was *Emerald Eyes;* Webber was serving in her now. Rick had finished his tour and gone home, so Webber and the Kid were the only members of his old crew on this mission with him.

Card Shark started to roll forward slowly, and Rawlings at once shoved the throttles forward to roll onto the runway. He used his port engines to swing them around, then revved up all four until the ship was shivering and trembling. "That Number Three sound funny to you?" Rawlings asked, smacking his gum as he talked again.

"No, sir," J.B. told him—but then what did he know about this Number Three engine? J.B. cocked his head toward it and tried to listen more carefully, but he still couldn't detect anything wrong. He automatically checked the dials recording Number Three's oil pressure, oil temperature, rpms, looking for some indication of trouble, but everything read normal.

"Well, what the hell." And with that, Rawlings released the brakes and started rushing down the runway in a frightfully careless manner. A minute later, J.B. noted that they weren't going straight down the runway but weaving back and forth, almost fish-tailing, as Rawlings applied uneven pressure on the pedals. It was as if he didn't have full control over the Fortress, and J.B.'s instinct was to grab control before they careened off the runway and exploded. He gritted his teeth and his hands cramped as he restrained himself. At last he felt the Fortress leave the earth, and he let out a long, slow sigh of relief. They lifted off on a slight side-slip, but it didn't matter.

Rawlings, however, at once started to bank around much more tightly than was necessary. J.B. started to wonder if he always flew like this, or if he was just trying to put J.B. off, or provoke a remark. J.B. decided to keep his mouth shut. He didn't even remind Rawlings that he had forgotten the intercom check.

A moment later he decided it wasn't necessary. This was a very talkative crew. In fact, their chatter drove J.B. crazy before ten minutes was up—and it didn't stop. They were telling jokes to one another, competing for the dumbest or the dirtiest or some such thing. They certainly weren't very funny. Rawlings was grinning, however, and looked over at J.B. after a while. "What's the matter with you? Can't you even laugh at a joke? Christ, you're a real tight-ass!" J.B. had evidently spoiled his mood, and, scowling at the sky ahead of them, Rawlings concentrated on flying after that.

J.B. directed his attention to outside the ship, trying to tune out all the jabber in his headphones. He tried to listen to the engines. Was Number Three running just a little rough? *Card Shark* was flying on their right and ahead of them, leading the section. The Kid waved at him again. J.B. just nodded his head in reply. He didn't want to give his new 'boss' any more excuses for rubbing his nose in it. Just get it over with.

Four hours later it was indeed over. A real milk-run. The Kraut fighters had been kept at bay by the P-47s. They had been routed around coastal flak, and the flak over the target had been OK. The Germans didn't seem so hot about defending Antwerp as they were about Essen or Berlin or Bremen. Rawlings had even let J.B. fly most of the way back while he ate the half dozen sandwiches he'd brought with him and talked (with his mouth full) to the bombardier, who came up onto the flight deck to chat. They were making plans for the evening. There was a night-club in London they were anxious to visit.

J.B. started to calculate that he had time to get to Windsor and be waiting for Emily when she got home—surprise her. He could take her to dinner somewhere nearby. He might even have time to visit the Castle while waiting for her. Of course, if she got stuck out somewhere, he'd wait for her in vain. Maybe he ought to call in to White Waltham first and see what her schedule was like. They usually could guess whether a pilot was likely to get stuck out or not.

They touched down at just 12.14 on a beautiful sunny day. All ships were back safe. No one was wounded. They were all in the best of spirits—until the word came down that they were confined to base. They would be flying again the next morning.

Bochanek stood in front of the still-closed curtain, and the pointer waved behind him as he waited impatiently for the aircrews to settle down a bit more. "Well, I hope you enjoyed your milk-run yesterday. I had to go to a lot of trouble to get it for you. Today we get back to business." He turned around with a nod to the corporal at the curtain-ropes, and the curtain parted with a swish to reveal a long red line stretching almost due south. It ended on the French coast, at town on the Bay of Biscay. "La Rochelle!" Bochanek cracked the pointer on the target (or near enough). "One of the lairs of Hitler's treacherous U-Boats. They sank over 100 ships last month, keeping a strangle-hold on the vital lifeline of supplies and materiel coming from the good old US of A. What we of the USAAF are doing to Germany's war effort with our air assaults, the U-Boats are effectively doing to our industry. It doesn't do any good to produce the stuff only for it to end up at the bottom of the ocean before it can do anyone any good. And don't forget every gallon of aviation fuel that your big ships guzzle up there" (he pointed toward the ceiling with his pointer) "is being hauled across the Atlantic. Twenty of the ships we lost last month were tankers. Now…" He got down to the details: start engines, take-off time, formation (same as yesterday), rendezvous with fighters, cruising altitude, departure of fighters, concentrations of flak…

The right-hand seat seemed a little more familiar already. J.B. settled into it and picked up the clipboard for the pre-flight check. He spared the gum wrapper only a glance. The question about the Number Three engine appeared routine. He answered as before, that he couldn't hear anything wrong with it. Even the take-off was better. They were so heavily loaded that even Rawlings decided to be careful, but it took them a long time to climb.

J.B. was prepared for the silly chatter this time, too. He managed to ignore it, concentrating instead on the scenery below him. They crossed out over the Thames Estuary, then were back over southern England. J.B. looked down and with a start saw a smaller aircraft far below the Fortresses. It was all by itself, darting along under them heading northwest. Very likely an ATA delivery, J.B. thought, and imagined it might be Emily at work. She needed to fly as much as he did, and he was glad that his testimony before the ATA Accidents Committee had been helpful. He'd told them that Emily flew the Hampden throughout, only giving orders to him for throttles and gear. The results had been a "pilot not responsible and commended"—which completely embarrassed Emily. She insisted it was quite undeserved, but at least it had also cleared her name and banished any hint of dismissal.

They crossed the south coast of England, and J.B. took a moment to admire the chalk cliffs. They really were spectacular—sheer and tall like nothing he'd ever seen before. All his previous missions had taken him east over the North Sea. The most southerly route ever had been the one yesterday running southeast to Antwerp. But now they were flying just a little west of south at 195 degrees. Maybe one day he and Emily could see those cliffs up close from the ground. She'd said Portsmouth was on the south coast, after all; it must be somewhere close by…

The next landfall was the French coast, and J.B. found himself anticipating it with a touch of excitement he hadn't felt in a long time. France was someplace he'd always dreamed about visiting. Well, Paris, anyway. You heard so much about it. From up here, of course, France didn't look very different from England. Maybe the fields were bigger, flatter.

"Hey, Toby, you hear about that guy that bailed out over France someplace and got taken in by a bunch of Frenchie girls? A real cat-house it was, and they were so thrilled he wasn't a German, see, they didn't want to help him escape, just keep him as a kind of pet, see?"

"You're welcome to jump any time you like, Charley!" Rawlings answered over the intercom. "It'd give me a chance to get a ball-turret gunner who can shoot something down."

"I've shot things down!" came the indignant reply. "It ain't my fault the rest of you are too blind to confirm it!"

They were off again, arguing about claims and counter-claims. A couple of them sounded seriously angry. J.B. tried to distract himself from their childish bickering, but he had nothing to do. J.B. glanced over at Rawlings, wishing him to want a break, but no such luck.

Suddenly the aircraft shuddered slightly.

"Hey! What was that?!" Rawlings asked in alarm, staring straight at J.B. as if he were in some way to blame.

"Flak," J.B. answered, pointing to a little puff of black smoke below and to the right of them. A moment later they were shaken again. Nothing really bad. The Krauts hadn't found the range yet.

"What the fuck! I thought this was going to be another milk-run!" Rawlings declared in outrage.

That didn't make sense to J.B. You only had to look at the map, see the distance, calculate that half the flight would be without fighter escort, and throw in the fact that Hitler's U-Boats were one of his most precious and effective weapons, and the answer was: this was *not* going to be a milk-run. J.B. didn't like the look of alarm on Rawlings' face. Had he looked like that every time they ran into flak?

Rawlings shouted into the intercom (nearly bursting J.B.'s eardrums): "Shut up, you guys! We've got flak out there! Start watching for fighters."

Start? J.B. started to feel helplessly scared.

Flak was jarring them incessantly now, but the lead bomber had altered course and they moved out of the flak quickly. About a half hour later, the fighter escort waggled their wings and then curved gracefully away, turning back to the north and home. Now they were in for it, J.B. thought with an attempt at resignation he didn't feel. He tightened his straps in an unconscious attempt to gird himself for the coming battle.

"Listen!" Rawlings shouted, taking his right hand off the controls long enough to grab J.B. by the arm and shake him.

J.B. turned and looked at the pilot, completely baffled. "Don't you hear it?! Number Three! It's running rough!" Rawlings was shouting at him like he were an idiot, and his eyes were wide over his oxygen mask.

J.B. frowned and looked out his side window at Number Three. Just then he heard it, too. A hiccup. A short, unnatural throbbing, then it started to whine. J.B. looked in alarm back at the instruments. The engine was over-heating. He looked back out the window in disbelief. It was clearly starting to smoke. Before he could even open his mouth to say anything, Rawlings shouted, "Number Three's on fire! We've got to get out of here."

No sooner were the words out of his mouth than he banked the Fortress hard to the left and dropped out of formation at increasing speed. J.B. couldn't believe what was happening. The engine was not yet on fire, and Rawlings had done nothing to try to prevent it. J.B. at once reached out, cut the fuel and feathered the prop, but Rawlings was still diving away hard and banking steeply. What the hell was he doing? So long as they were in formation, they were one of three score of aircraft, protected by the guns of the nearest Fortresses as well as their own. The minute they left the formation, they were cold meat, and there was no way they could outrun—much less out-dive—a Messerschmitt on three engines.

"What the hell are you doing! We're safer with the formation."

"We can't keep up with it on three engines," Rawlings insisted.

"Of course we can. The fire never really started, and it's out now. And the ship's still flying fine. Besides, we're fully loaded."

"So what?" came the astonishing answer. Then Rawlings called to his navigator for a course home, and turned onto it. J.B. just sat there feeling rather sick and guilty—and tense. He searched the sky for fighters.

They had almost made it to the French coast when the fighters struck. Just two of them—but that was more than enough. The gunners were shouting over the intercom enough to make his head split. Rawlings started to dive—an idiotic manoeuvre since a Messerschmitt could easily out-dive them—and there was nothing—absolutely nothing—Jay could do. He would have given anything for a gun at that moment, but there wasn't one fitted for the co-pilot as there were for the navigator and the bombardier. No wonder the Brits didn't have Second Pilots, J.B. thought; they were worthless.

The first burst of cannon fire hit them somewhere astern. Jay felt the ship shudder and heard one of the crew screaming—not from pain but fear.

"Jink, Goddamn it!" Jay shouted at Rawlings. "Take evasive action!"

"If you're so goddamn smart, fly it yourself!" Rawlings shouted back, and then as Jay grabbed the controls, Rawlings leaned forward and pressed the starter on Number Three. The engine started up flawlessly. It didn't even smoke.

Jay was too busy trying to out-fly the agile team of fighters to do more than cast one glance at Rawlings. The next instant cannon-fire found them again— this time from the second of the two Messerschmitts. Like a couple of cats with a mouse, he thought, as he tried to fling the heavy bomber into another abrupt turn to delay the inevitable.

To his amazement, the inevitable didn't happen. Just as suddenly as they had appeared, the Messerschmitts dived away again. For a second, Jay was utterly bewildered—until two Typhoons with RAF roundels pulled up on either side of them. The cavalry to the rescue...

As his breathing got back to normal and the sweat started to dry, Jay looked hard at Rawlings. The pilot didn't try to take control of the aircraft, and he didn't offer J.B. any explanation of what he'd done. He just cut Number Three engine again and then sat beside J.B., sipping coffee from his thermos and eating his sandwiches in sullen—almost provocative—silence. J.B. suspected he was waiting for J.B. to say something, challenge him, but J.B. wasn't ready to do that yet. He was still too shaken up to know what to say.

The Typhoons waggled their wings as they reached the coast of England and peeled off, returning to their own base. J.B. flew on to Beauchamp Rodding.

Of course they were the first aircraft back. Their premature arrival on three engines attracted a lot of attention. The fire-engines and ambulances met them. Rawlings landed, of course; the tires touched the runway hard, since they were still fully loaded. You could hear the screech. They bounced only a little and set- tled down heavy with that full load. They fishtailed a bit as Rawlings worked the brakes unevenly. Finally they slowed down and Rawlings cut Number Two engine before turning left onto the taxiway.

They parked at the hardstand and shut down the remaining two engines. A jeep with Bochanek and the S-2 was approaching at a fast pace from the Control Tower. Rawlings remarked petulantly, without even looking at Jay, "That damn engine overheated again."

"That won't wash, and you know it."

"It's the goddamned truth!" Rawlings burst out, and then, meeting Jay's eyes, he added with a curling lip, "Who's going to believe *you*, anyway? I've got eight other guys gonna back me up." He jerked his thumb in the direction of the back of the ship.

J.B. didn't answer; he just hung his oxygen mask up, climbed over his seat, and pulled his parachute over his shoulder before jumping down out of the front hatch. Two minutes later Rawlings was telling his story to Bochanek. "...and then Messerschmitts were all over us—at least six of them." The others were standing around their captain in a circle, nodding like a bunch of dumb sheep.

Bochanek's gaze shifted sharply to J.B., but he said nothing. He just ordered the men to the usual de-brief, and climbed back into the jeep and drove away. A truck groaned up, and they started to climb aboard. J.B. threw his parachute in over the tailgate and then backed off. "I think I'll stretch my legs a bit." The others were glad to be rid of him.

He walked across the field toward the maintenance hangar. He nodded to Fuentes, but he was looking for the crew chief of the *English Rose*. The man seemed to sense it. He stood up, shoving his baseball cap back on his head. "You looking for me, Lieutenant?"

"Yes, I am."

"Number Three again, huh?"

"Does it go out often?"

"Oh, yeah. Got shot up on Rawlings' third mission and it just hasn't ever been the same since." He winked at Jay, and then immediately sensed he'd made a mistake. Suddenly he was all business again. "We just can't seem to find what the problem is, sir, but you can rest assured, Lieutenant, we won't sleep until we've taken it completely apart this time. You can count on us, Lieutenant. That engine will be fixed this time! You've got my word on that, sir!" He saluted smartly, but it was a mockery, really.

J.B. returned the salute wearily and went out of the hangar. He stood in the bright, brittle sunshine of this crisp, clear autumn day and thought: "What the hell am I gonna do now?"

If he said anything to Bochanek, it would be his word against Rawlings'. And the crew chief would solemnly swear that he'd found something wrong with the damn thing. J.B. was sure of it. He wished he could call Emily. It always did him good to talk to her, but it was the middle of the afternoon. She'd still be flying.

He strolled in the direction of his Nissan hut, not really paying attention to the world around him. Some men were playing softball on that field after all. The sound of the ball hitting the bat and cheers drew his attention. Having nothing better to do, he strolled over and started watching casually. It was a couple of rookie crews—guys who hadn't been out yet. J.B. squirmed out of his monkey-suit and spread it out on the ground to sit and watch the game, his arms looped over his knees.

He didn't feel like he'd been sitting there very long, but he must have been daydreaming, because suddenly the game stopped. Everyone's head went up. The ships were coming in. J.B. dragged himself to his feet and put his hand up to shade his eyes. From a distance, the sound of those mighty engines seemed hardly more than the buzzing of a bee. But then they came nearer and nearer.

Men poured out of the hangars, out of the Messes, out of the officers' and enlisted men's quarters. Men came onto the deck of the tower and raised binoculars to the sky. Everyone was standing, squinting, pointing, counting. Three, six, seven, ten, twelve. The leading ships were still in formation. They were the undamaged ships. Behind them came the stragglers—the specks clinging to the horizon that grew larger and louder, until your own heart was throbbing with the unsynchronised howl of a ship that banked in low and cut off the planes that had gone onto the circuit politely. The red flare announced the wounded on board. As the ship banked around to line up on the runway, J.B. could see that the left-hand window of the cockpit was blown away. Suddenly Rawlings was standing beside him, and he snarled under his breath, "See what I spared you, you dumb smart-ass."

It was *Card Shark*.

J.B. found himself running. You could tell she was going to crash long before it happened. The angle of approach was too steep, the speed too great. The pilot was certainly dead. Either it was a wounded co-pilot or another member of the crew that was trying to bring her down. Either way, he was making a hash of it. It smashed onto the runway with a tearing of metal and grating of concrete, and then veered off onto the ground and spun around flinging up stone, dust and bits-and-pieces of aircraft. A propeller literally flew through the air and nearly landed amidst the group of men rushing toward the aircraft. The sirens of the ambulance and fire-engines were screaming. A moment later the gas-tanks blew.

The plane lifted up in the middle and then dropped back down, broken in two. The front of the plane had been pitched onto its nose and the tail was severed. Men started to stagger out of the waist and began running away from the flames. The last man out was on fire.

J.B. wanted to look away, but he couldn't. He was staring at a man being burned alive, and then suddenly he was knocked off his feet. There was a second explosion and debris rained down on them, but J.B. was already on the ground, grasped in the arms of a sobbing boy. It was the Kid.

"I ain't never flying with nobody but you ever again!" he declared furiously. "Never! They can lock me up and throw away the key. I ain't never flying with nobody but you."

"It's OK, Kid." J.B. held him in his arms. The Kid was shaking all over. "It's OK." Even as he said it, he looked over toward the burning ship, and saw with relief that someone had managed to get a blanket over the burning man and beat the flames out. They were lifting him up onto a stretcher. Beyond, fire engines were dousing the flames with great sprays of water, and you could hear the hissing all the way over here. The smoke started to turn white.

J.B. turned his attention back to the frightened kid in his arms. "It's OK, Kid. It's OK."

"Yeah, here. Have a fag." A man bent over them with an extended cigarette, and J.B. looked up in amazement. It was Rick.

"What the hell are you doing here? I thought you were halfway across the Atlantic by now!"

"Halfway? Hoping I'd get sunk, or what? No, I decided to stick around." As he spoke, Rick lit the Kid's cigarette for him and then offered one to Jay.

"What do you mean?"

Rick shrugged. "I signed up for a second tour."

"You did *what*?"

"I signed up for a second tour. Don't look so dumfounded, Buddy. It's all your fault."

"My fault?! What the hell have I got to do with it?"

"You introduced me to your sister, remember? What the hell do I want to be doing in some God-forsaken training base in Texas when the first decent girl I've ever dated is here in Merry Old England?"

CHAPTER 20

▼

White Waltham, England
October 1943

A Blenheim for Lichfield, a Beaufighter for Debden, then an Oxford from Winslow for Whitchurch, with a Blenheim due for on-ferrying to the northeast that she could fly back from Whitchurch to White Waltham for the night. It looked like a nice round day, if nothing went wrong. And all on her own.

Grateful as Emily was for the taxi Ansons, she actually preferred these linked flights. It hadn't always been that way. When she first started with ATA, she'd enjoyed the opportunity to talk and listen to the experienced ferry pilots. Douglas Fairweather, who often flew the taxi, especially had been wonderful about letting her sit beside him in the cockpit and teaching her gently by telling her stories of past adventures. Then, too, she had found the concentration necessary for flying exhausting, and was glad, after a delivery, to let someone else do the flying for a bit. But now, unless the weather was very bad or something terrible happened, she didn't find flying so tiring. And since she'd started the affair with Jay, she shied away from her colleagues.

It was nothing but a guilty conscience, of course. Her colleagues did not know about Jay, weren't particularly interested in her private life, and, even if they did find out, they would never say anything. Some of the younger male pilots, particularly the Irish and Poles, reputedly led quite "wild" lives in their time off anyway. Her affair with Jay might very well make her more interesting in their eyes—not that she wanted that—but it would certainly do her no *harm* in their eyes. As for the older men, they were more likely to take a fatherly approach to things, viewing her infidelity as the sad result of circumstances, something to be deplored, perhaps, but not condemned. She shied away from the American women most, however, because she felt they might be most offended that she had taken one of "their" men—but no doubt she was being unfair and imagining things. The fact was, she didn't know any of them very well, and they tended to clique together anyway.

No, it was entirely her own guilt that made her so anti-social. Or rather, her guilty conscience about being so happy and determined to keep seeing Jay. She had not seriously considered giving Jay up since that talk with Philippa after the accident. Since then she had just accepted the fact that she was in love with Jay, that being with him made her happy, and that knowing him was enriching. She even enjoyed, at some level, sharing his worries and problems. Of course, she suppressed all thought of the danger he was in—just as she had with Robin. She knew it was a possibility, one she never really *forgot*, but she refused to let it dominate her thoughts. Instead she worried about him being demoted to co-pilot, agonised with him over the misdeeds and problems of his new crew, and rejoiced with him that Rick had rejoined the squadron.

They were planning a double-date this coming weekend. Jay had been rather apologetic about it, afraid she might object, but he clearly wanted her to meet his sister. Knowing how important his family was to him, Emily felt she couldn't refuse. In fact, she was curious about his sister. After all, Jay had asked her to marry him, and even if it was a remote and rather unreal prospect, it was the goal they shared.

As Emily went through the ferrying routine, she found herself thinking about America when her thoughts were not required for the task at hand. The first delivery went without a hitch. But the Beaufighter wasn't quite ready for her, so she took time for lunch at the mess at Lichfield, and found herself remembering the food she'd had at an American base recently: pork chops and applesauce, maize and mashed potatoes with gravy—all in great quantities. Oh, yes, and ice-cream. Emily couldn't imagine how they could transport and store so much ice-cream. She hadn't had it in years, and everyone had insisted she take seconds when they'd seen her face. She'd felt very much like a child—but it had been wonderful.

At last the Beau was ready, and she took it over to Debden in the bright, almost brittle, autumn sunshine. Below her England was a particularly colourful tapestry of rust, orange, gold, yellow and greens. If it weren't for the shortening days and dropping temperatures, she might have liked the autumn best, she thought, and wondered about the seasons in America.

Jay said Michigan was bitterly cold in winter, with lots of snow. They never showed that in the movies. The movies were mostly made in California, Jay said, where there were no seasons at all—just a constant 70 degrees and sunshine. She didn't think she'd like that.

The Beau was taken off her hands with the prompt efficiency she had come to expect of front-line squadrons, and she found herself in a lorry on her way to Winslow. Bouncing along the rutted roads, she was reminded of the wide highways they always showed in the movies about America. There were always these endless ribbons of road going straight through the flat and almost empty countryside. Most of it looked rather desert-like, actually, with few trees and lots of dust.

But she reminded herself that America probably wasn't at all like it was in the movies—just as England wasn't all about grand mansions, fox-hunting or debutante balls. Her father had always raged against the cinema because it focused on the British upper class rather than "the people."

The Oxford was the basic trainer the RAF used to introduce pilots to twin-engine aircraft. It was the aircraft on which Emily had learned to fly twins as well. Because of the heavy training needs, it was one of the aircraft the ATA had to fly most frequently, and, of course, the less experienced the pilot, the more likely it was they'd be given an Oxford. Emily had flown seemingly hundreds of them in the early months of this year, and still got at least one a week. It was, therefore, one of the few aircraft in which Emily felt completely comfortable. She hardly needed to check her Pilot's Notes, but did so only out of habit and self-discipline.

Flying took little concentration as she turned southwest into the sun. Although the cloud cover was increasing as she flew to the west, it was at about 5,000 feet, and she was flying well below it with perfect visibility. She let her thoughts drift back to Jay and America again.

Jay said his family lived in a caravan-house—which was something Emily couldn't imagine, really. When she thought of living in a caravan she pictured gypsies huddled around an open fire while their shaggy ponies grazed nearby. But of course Jay's trailer wasn't like that; he said it had electricity and running water and central heating.

Jay said, too, that Michigan was flat and surrounded by lakes. Emily had looked it up in the atlas; Michigan stuck out like a big mitten outlined by large lakes. The lakes were so large you couldn't see the other side, Jay said. That seemed quite unimaginable, but intriguing, too. Emily found that she very much wanted to see more of the world. Jay had laughed when she'd asked about the Mississippi, but then he pulled her into his arms and kissed her. "You know what?" he'd teased, "You better find another one of those written-off bombers so we can fly all around America when the war is over. The Rockies and the Grand Canyon and the Redwood Forest. We could see it all together."

Emily thought she'd like that, but of course they'd never find another bomber like the Hampden they'd crashed together...

The sight of an aircraft dropping out of the sky over to her right drew her attention sharply back to her flying. Without a radio, it was impossible to get information about other aircraft in the vicinity, so there was always the danger of another aircraft popping out of the cloud unexpectedly. The ATA, however, always filed their own flight plan and, since they flew below the ceiling, the Observer Corps usually kept an eye on them as well, passing the information on to the RAF. RAF controllers were therefore usually good at alerting their own air-craft to the presence of the ATA aircraft, and Emily had never had a close encounter on clear days like this.

But no sooner did the twin-engine aircraft drop out of the cloud-bottom than it veered sharply around to its left, to pass her on her starboard side. In doing so, it lifted its starboard wing and in an instant of incredulous horror, Emily saw black crosses outlined in white. My God, she thought, it's a German! Of course she knew that the Luftwaffe still sent over lone, day-time raiders, but it was some time since anyone in the ATA had reported running into one. Most of the air encounters with the enemy had been in the early years of the war.

In a purely instinctive and irrational desire to put as much distance between herself and the enemy as possible, she shoved the throttles forward and dived away to her own left, assuming that the invader was still rushing away in the opposite direction. After all, whatever it was over here for, surely a small trainer was of no interest.

The sound was both a crack and a crunch, and it sent a shudder through the whole aircraft. Emily started in instinctive physical alarm before her brain regis-tered what had happened. Then, for an instant, she froze in sheer disbelief. She was just a ferry pilot in a trainer. If she'd been in a Spitfire or a Beaufighter, it might have been a reasonable mistake, but the Oxford was even painted bright yellow to identify it as a trainer. They couldn't have mistaken her for something dangerous!

The crunching thuds came again, and Emily shoved the stick over and kicked the rudder, to stand on her starboard wing-tip and slide down the sky in a desper-ate attempt to escape. She'd watched Hurricanes and Spitfires do this. She'd heard a thousand line-shoots about it from pilots at the bar of one mess or pub or another. She could picture it vividly in her mind's eye—and she knew she didn't have a chance. The little Oxford wasn't a high-performance aircraft like a Spit but a docile, forgiving machine designed to coddle inexperienced pilots. Even as she checked to see that the throttles were shoved as far forward as they would go, Emily was seeing that short glimpse of the aircraft in her mind again. She was almost certain she was being chased by an Me110—a lethal machine with both forward firing cannon and machine-guns.

In a Spitfire or Typhoon, even a Hurricane, she knew she could theoretically have out-manoeuvred it, turned inside its radius, got on its tail. But no one—not even the best pilot in the world—could do that in an Oxford. And she certainly couldn't out-dive it! It had a maximum speed of well over 300 mph! ***Whatever you do, don't fly straight and level!*** She heard the words hammering in her head as if Robin were in the cockpit with her. At once she went into a steep turn to the right, standing—or so it seemed to her inexperienced self—on a wing-tip. She also twisted around in her seat to try to look behind her.

The sight nearly gave her heart seizure. The Messerschmitt was so close behind her, she could see the pilot grinning in the cockpit. He was sure of his kill! She saw the flashes of light as he fired his cannon and machine-guns at her again. Emily pulled the stick back to bounce up. Anything but straight and level! Then she swung hard left and dived toward the earth. Somewhere down there was Colerne. Maybe they had a section at readiness…

The punching sound of the cannon hitting again made her want to scream. How much damage could the poor Oxford take? It was ruggedly built to deal with the rude treatment of student pilots, but not to withstand enemy fire. She hauled up again and turned hard right. Looking down for some familiar landmark. Nothing. She flipped the aircraft the other way, to look better out of the left window.

Smoke was coming from the port engine. She glanced sharply at the instruments. The oil pressure had dropped entirely. Temperature was already in the dangerous zone. It was likely to catch fire any minute. Now she started to look frantically for any field large and level enough to put down in. She banked left and right, looking out her side window and twisting to keep her assailant confused.

Colerne! Although the camouflage was very good, with "hedges" apparently cutting up the field, Emily had flown into it often enough to recognise it. She banked hard now and started to pull the Oxford around. On her left, the smoke pouring out of the engine was growing much denser and darker, but she at least had a goal and she concentrated on it.

She was greatly reassured by the frenzy of activity that appeared to greet her approach. At least the blood-wagon and fire-engine were in motion, and then right before her eyes two lovely Spitfires lifted off the far end of the field and cleared the perimeter fence several hundred yards ahead of her as she thumped the Oxford down gracelessly. It was hard to concentrate on her own flying for wanting to watch the Spitfires, as they wheeled hard to the left and strained for altitude with every fibre of their graceful frames.

A rough bounce on the uneven grass forced Emily to concentrate on her own aircraft. As soon as she had slowed down to a reasonable speed, she cut the smoking engine, and taxied the Oxford to the far side of the airfield before stopping and shutting down the still undamaged engine. Then she took a deep breath.

The sound of the sirens woke her from her daze. She unclipped her harness, and pulled off her helmet to shake her hair free. Then she climbed stiffly down out of the trainer, with her parachute over her right shoulder, into the circle of anxious rescue-workers. "Are you alright?!" they started demanding. "Have you been injured?!"

"No, I'm alright," Emily assured them, and then she saw the damage to the Oxford and felt rather weak in the knees after all.

"Here, have a sit-down," a RAF orderly suggested, and the next thing she knew she was seated on the floor of the blood-wagon, between the stretchers, watching while the fire-engine directed a stream of water at the port engine of the Oxford.

"Bloody Germans!" someone exclaimed.

"Hope the lads get him."

"He took off like a bat out of hell when he caught sight of them."

A staff car rolled up and a Squadron Leader stepped out. He was a stocky, bow-legged man with broad shoulders, whose muscular strength even the tailored uniform could not disguise. He had a dark, determined face under dark brows, and he was frowning now. At the sight of Emily he started and then looked again in evident disbelief. "Mrs. Priestman? Is that really you?"

"Smitty?" she asked uncertainly, although the face was really quite unmistakable. But the last time she had seen him, Smitty had been only a Pilot Officer.

"Good heavens, Mrs. Priestman! I never knew you could fly! I should have guessed your husband would want a pilot for a wife, I suppose, but when did you join the ATA? And are you alright? That bloody Jerry didn't get you, did he?"

Smitty spoke with a heavy West Country accent, and he had already grasped Emily's hand in his huge, square fists, nearly crushing it in his sincere concern and welcome.

"I'm just a little shaken. He dropped out of a cloud quite unexpectedly, and though I took flight at once, he seemed intent on destroying me. I suppose he thought I was a fledgling RAF pilot who deserved to be killed in the nest—so to speak."

"Bloody bastards! Let me give you a lift back to the Mess and buy you a drink. You'll need to report that that Oxford isn't going anywhere for a few days, and no doubt you'll want to call Wing Commander Priestman and let him know you're alright." He took her parachute from her and held the car door open. Emily nodded her thanks to the ambulance crew, and settled into the passenger seat. Smitty dropped her parachute in the boot and then came around and climbed in behind the wheel. As he started to drive away, he asked again: "You're sure you're alright?"

"Yes, yes. It all seemed so unreal, actually—"

"There they are!!" Smitty slammed on the brakes, flung open the door, and stepped out to be able to watch the return of his aircraft better. They were still in formation, very low and very fast. They had their undercarriages tucked up and were not making the slightest effort to line up into the wind and land. They flew right over the field, wing-tip to wing-tip, then split apart, peeling away from one another and each going into a climbing roll.

At an air-show the manoeuvre would have looked clumsy, because they didn't time it very well and their rates of climb and turn were substantially different. In fact, one of the two rather botched the roll and elicited an exasperated exclamation from his commander. But the message was clear enough: they'd got it.

"Well done!" Emily, too, had climbed out of the car to watch, and she felt like clapping in delight.

Smitty was grinning. "I think we owe you at least dinner, Mrs. Priestman. That was the lad's first victory! We're just down from Scotland and most have never seen any enemy action. They will want to celebrate, and when they discover they came to the rescue of a fair damsel in distress, I daresay they're likely to get completely carried away."

Emily just laughed. They got back into the car and drove straight over to the dispersal hut, where the two Spitfires had meanwhile landed and taxied to their sand-bag bays. The canopy of the nearest Spitfire was shoved back, and the pilot heaved himself out even before his fitter could reach him. He jumped down off the wing and came straight towards them, pulling off his helmet and grinning broadly. "He went straight in!" he called out, gesturing with his hands. "Just bang! He must have buried the nose six feet under! And then the tanks blew. We should be able to see…" He started searching the horizon and flung out his arm. "Look over there! Above the trees! See that smudge! That has to be the smoke of it!"

The other pilot jogged over from his Spitfire, parked farther away. "I got the number, too! It was M3 KL."

"Yellow K," the first pilot improved.

"No one jumped?"

"Jumped? We chased it at nought feet most of the way!"

"It nearly got away from us, too. If it could have gained a little more altitude it would have, but we didn't give it a chance." Now they went into a detailed, blow-by-blow description of the chase as the ground crews and other pilots gathered around. The two pilots were still breathless with the excitement of it all, and their colleagues looked positively green with envy, Emily thought, sparing them a glance. They were all so very young…

Eventually Smitty drew the attention of his squadron to Emily herself. "Well, you can thank your good fortune on Mrs. Priestman here. She could have lured that unfortunate Jerry over any other Fighter Station, but she took pity on you lot."

Emily laughed. "Frankly, I was desperately grateful you happened to be nearby—and not entirely certain you'd have a section on readiness."

The young men noticed her for the first time, and their astonishment was flattering. Their eyes widened, they stood straighter, and they even made the odd effort to straighten a tie here or smooth down their hair there. Smitty was making the introductions, rattling off names and nicknames, and they held out their hands one after another. Then Smitty signalled her back into the car and they started back for the mess, while the crowd of young men started for her Oxford to get a look at the damage.

"They're a good bunch," Smitty remarked proudly.

"They always are," she answered with a wry smile.

"What is Wing Commander Priestman doing these days? I haven't heard about him getting a gong for ages."

"No." Emily paused. "You must have missed the notice. He's been missing since March."

"What?!" Smitty slammed on the brakes to stare at her. Then he looked away embarrassed, and drove on stammering. "I'm so terribly sorry! I had no idea.

March—I'd just been given the squadron and was in Scotland, I suppose I wasn't—But I still can't understand—I *am* sorry."

"It's alright, Smitty, it's not your fault."

There was an awkward silence, nevertheless. They arrived in front of the Mess, and Smitty drew into the parking place reserved for him. He cut the engine, but rather than making an effort to get out of the car, turned to face Emily. "I can't begin to tell you how much I owe to him. He set the standards by which I *try* to run this squadron. And he had a much harder job than I! When I joined, half the squadron were Battle of Britain veterans who had seen it all—or thought they had, anyway—and the other half were green lads like me who'd been in training during the Battle. Those of us who'd missed the Battle had watched day after day as the losses mounted. We'd felt so frustrated not being ready or able to help— and terrified, too, that we'd fail when the time came. People are already forgetting that in April of '41 the Russians weren't in it yet, and we all expected a renewal of the Battle of Britain. We were all bracing ourselves for the next onslaught—both wishing it would start and dreading it. Making a cohesive squadron out of such diverse, over-strung material at such a time was no easy task, but your husband managed it."

Emily didn't know what to say, so she finally just murmured, "Thank you."

"And don't think we didn't know how important you were to him. He relied on you completely and trusted you absolutely. I've rarely witnessed a marriage based on such utter faith in the abilities and sense of the other."

Emily was startled. "Is that the way you saw it?" She remembered being so terribly insecure and unsure of her role.

"Oh, yes! I remember—surely you remember?—when Harry got himself in a terrible pickle taking up his Spit without authorisation? It all would have worked out if he hadn't had the misfortune to bend it trying to land after dusk. Of course, flying Spits at night really isn't easy and he shouldn't have been doing it under any circumstances, but he hadn't expected to be away that long. He'd planned to be back long before dusk. None of us had ever seen your husband so furious—he didn't say one word, just walked out on us. Harry was sure he was going to get a bowler hat—or at least posted or court-martialled. We spent all night trying to think what we could do, and then sent Mickey to see you."

Emily was smiling by now, remembering the incident, too. "I always wondered how Mickey got selected."

"He volunteered, actually. He says you were very kind."

"But not encouraging. I didn't think for a minute I could influence Robin, you know."

"So how *did* you convince him?"

"I don't know. I just told him what had happened and why, and he gave me one of his looks and walked out. About two hours later he came back and said: 'Someday I'll tell you about the Claude in Singapore.' But unfortunately, he never did."

"Did he ever tell you about getting me my commission?"

Emily shook her head.

"You remember that when I arrived at 606 I was the only Sergeant Pilot, which was a bit awkward for me, of course, but I accepted that it was the way of the world. After all, with my background and my accent I considered myself very lucky to be allowed in the cockpit of a Spitfire at all."

Smitty was thus called because he had left school at 14 to apprentice as a blacksmith in a rural community in Dorset. He'd joined the Volunteer Reserve in 1938 at the age of 23, but—only able to fly on weekends—had not progressed very far when war broke out. It had been April 1941 before he was posted to an operational squadron.

"I hadn't been with the squadron more than a week when I overheard a conversation that wasn't intended for my ears. We were on readiness as usual, and your husband was in his office in the dispersal hut, but the rest of us were out trying to catch the first bit of sun. The windows were open, and your husband had a voice that sometimes could be very clearly heard even though he didn't raise it. Alright, I was eavesdropping. I heard him say: 'I don't care how many Sergeant Pilots you send me, I'll put them *all* in for commissions.' And then after a pause, 'I have the *greatest* respect for the King's Commission, which is precisely why I refuse to let it be degraded into a social accolade. My pilots all have the same job to do and take exactly the same risks, and there is no reason for paying them different wages. *Furthermore*'—and he was getting quite pointed by this time—'if they can fight and die together, then they can damn well eat and drink together!' And within a month I was a Pilot Officer. They made quite a fuss about it, too—as if I'd earned it rather than it just being your husband's policy."

"But you *had* earned it, Smitty—just as Robin said—you were doing the same job, taking the same risks."

"Yes, of course, but I wasn't a particularly good pilot, you know. I'm still not!" He laughed at that. "Now, let me buy you that drink," he suggested, and they got out of the car.

"I need to call into my Ferry Pool and file the accident report," Emily pointed out.

"Accident Report? I'd say you need to file a Combat Report."

"In an Oxford?"

"Well, you lured the bastard into a trap, didn't you? And gave two very eager young lads the chance to prove they could do what they've been trained to do."

They went together to Operations, where by now the kill had been confirmed by both Observer Corps and the Royal Corps of Engineers, who were already digging up the remains of both aircraft and crew. The news had, in fact, already reached White Waltham, where it had been reported by several Observer Corps posts that an Oxford flown by the ATA was seen to be under attack and taking evasive action. The Observer Corps had alerted Colerne, which had scrambled a section immediately, before—in fact—Emily had led the Messerschmitt over the Station. Otherwise they would never have caught it.

In consequence, when Emily got through to White Waltham they were in an uproar, and Pauline Gower insisted on speaking with her personally. "You're quite sure you're alright?"

"Yes, but the Oxford looks a bit tatty. The port engine was smoking, too."

"Don't worry about the silly Oxford. Where did you say you landed?"

"Oh, right here at Colerne. The lads were frightfully chivalrous and sent two Spitfires to my rescue. I really feel very honoured."

"You sound like you've already been partaking of RAF hospitality," Gower remarked, undecided whether to be reproving or amused.

"Actually, no, but I was about to."

"Should we send a taxi for you?"

"Taxi?" Emily asked with a glance at Smitty, who was vigorously shaking his head. "No, the CO is going to put on transport for me." Smitty nodded. "I'll be at work first thing in the morning as usual."

"Enjoy yourself, then," Gower advised.

And she did. It seemed like ages since she'd been part of this kind of uninhibited high spirits. The squadron was fresh from Scotland and had suffered no casualties yet—a lovely change from the Bomber Stations with their omnipresent reminders of gruelling attrition. They were cock-a-loop over shooting down their first Messerschmitt, and a "task force" had been sent to collect a trophy. A large chunk out of the fin of the Messerschmitt tail with a recognisable, almost complete, swastika had been found. After a not-entirely-gentlemanly altercation with the Army, the "task force" from the squadron had returned—muddy, scratched, torn—and in triumphant possession of the coveted trophy. It was hung over the bar—but only after Emily had been induced to sign her name upon it with paint and brush brought from the squadron workshop.

Next someone brought out a camera and they had Emily sit on the bar counter, and all crowded around her for a series of photographs. In the later photographs she was wearing an RAF cap and tunic rather than her own—honorary "Section Leader" and Flying Officer.

It was getting on towards 9 pm before Emily could persuade Smitty to see about getting her home. He flew her home himself in a Hudson. They flew in silence, both enraptured by the night or lost in their separate thoughts. At White Waltham they said good-bye. "I hope I'll see more of you, Mrs. Priestman."

"Oh, certainly; I'll probably be back to collect that Oxford I so inconsiderately dumped on your erks," Emily joked.

"Yes, but, I mean, you know where to find me, if you feel like getting together."

"Thank you, Smitty," she said sincerely, adding to keep him from getting his hopes up, "but Robin is only missing. He might still turn up."

"I hope so! Your husband was one of the finest men I ever had the privilege to meet—and I've been more privileged than I deserve. Do keep in touch, at all events, won't you? Especially if he comes back. We could celebrate together." He smiled and offered her his hand.

Two nights later, Emily was sitting in a frightfully noisy night-club. The air was so laden with smoke it swirled visibly about them and made her eyes water. The music of the large band was so loud, you could not carry on a normal conversation, and so all communication had to been conducted in shouts. Emily's throat was getting sore already. The tables were crowded so closely together that the waiters could hardly get through, and it took forever for their drinks to be served.

The dance floor was crowded, too. So crowded, in fact, that even normal dancing would have been difficult enough, but some of the Americans felt that they still had to show off their fancy steps. They insisted on twirling their girl-friends, or swinging them between their legs or picking them up off the floor and all sorts of other nonsense—which usually just resulted in people getting trod upon, bumped, jostled and shoved. After only a few moments, Emily had asked Jay to return her to the table. She wasn't enjoying herself at all, although she'd been looking forward to this evening ever since Jay suggested it.

Now she looked around herself and felt completely lost and alienated. The only British uniforms she could see were a handful of RN ratings over in one corner. There were no RAF in sight—and no officers either. Emily's communist upbringing made her self-conscious for thinking that, but it was a fact.

Of course the girls were British, or predominantly so. The WACs like Jay's sister accounted for no more than a handful. But the English girls here were all doing their best to *act* like they were American—as far as Emily could see. They wore bright red lipstick and nail-polish and the ubiquitous American nylons. They danced either fast and furiously, just like their partners, or they clung to them like glue. They squealed loudly and their high-pitched voices shouting above the music were more irksome than the music itself.

Worst of all, Emily did not like Barb. She had probably been expecting too much, she told herself now. She had come expecting to find someone she would like instantly, someone who would be the sister she had never had. She had expected Barb to be like Jay. But she wasn't.

Barb was much more provincial—and content to stay that way. She wanted her American food, her American drinks, her American music. Everything British was viewed as "strange" at best or—more frequently—as simply "junk." She made jokes about the accent and the expressions of the British; she seemed to think "jolly good" was ridiculously funny for some reason, and laughed every time she made a pretence of saying it in the "right" accent. And her opinion of British food bordered on the insulting. It was as if she didn't know about rationing and that they didn't particularly *like* many of the concoctions it forced upon them, but were at least trying to make the best of things.

Barb was loud and opinionated. The conversation (such as it was in this inhospitable environment) had largely been dominated by Barb. Barb seemed to think that everyone must be interested in all her difficulties at her USAAF Base—the unfairness of the Motor Pool Staff Sergeant, the bigotry of the Exec, and all the men who made passes at her. You could tell she really loved it all, particularly the male attention.

Rick seemed content to just hang his arm over the back of her chair, press his leg against hers and light her cigarettes. Jay, however, seemed sincerely interested in all Barb was chattering about. He kept feeding her questions. They laughed a lot together, while Rick and Emily didn't even get the joke and were left looking perplexed at one another. Well, Emily supposed that was probably normal between sister and brother, but it still made her feel left out.

Now, as she watched Barb and Rick squeezing their way between the other tables back to this one, she braced herself for another flood of Barb's loud, grating words. Barb plopped herself down on the chair with a loud, "Whew! That's the hottest I've been since I got to this unheated country! Rick, Honey, do you think you could rustle up some coke?" Emily had noticed that Barb had not touched a drop of alcohol—and nor had Rick.

Rick promised to do what he could and started back in the direction of the bar. Barb turned to Emily. "Do you know where the Rest Rooms are?"

"Rest Rooms? Oh, I shouldn't think there are any here."

"WHAT? No Rest Rooms! What are we supposed to do? Go in the street?"

"She means Ladies' Room," Jay leaned forward to shout the translation into Emily's ear.

"Oh, yes, of course," Emily felt foolish needing a translator for her own language, "you need to go to the back over there and then down a flight of stairs—"

"Why don't you show me?" Barb shouted.

Emily reluctantly got to her feet and led the way. At least as they descended the flight of stairs the noise dimmed to a more tolerable level, but even here there were crowds and a line outside the ladies' room. The girls in the line were primping themselves in their compact mirrors, applying make-up or licking their hands and then pulling up their nylons. Barb leaned against the wall with a sigh and gazed at Emily. "So, let's hear it. Are you serious about my brother or just taking him for a ride?"

"For a *ride?*"

"You know what I mean: letting him buy you drinks and dinner and all that, and then it's all just 'bye-bye, sailor.'"

"Didn't you let Rick buy your dinner and drinks?"

"Yeah, well, maybe I'm serious about Rick."

"Are you?"

"Maybe—and it's not your business, anyway. He's not *your* brother."

"I see, and you think you're Jay's keeper?"

"When it comes to women, Jay needs protection. He's just a big kid, always falling for the wrong type."

"I see, you think I'm the wrong type."

"I'm not sure yet—depends on how serious you are about him. You don't act very serious."

"How does one act serious?"

Barb didn't answer right away; instead she found a pack of cigarettes in her purse, and offered one to Emily. Emily shook her head. "I don't smoke."

"Well, don't think it makes you more virtuous than me," Barb snapped back in a hostile voice. "I've seen how you put away the booze!" She concentrated on lighting up, then snapped the lighter closed and dropped it back into her purse. She inhaled deeply, exhaled slowly, and then waved the cigarette about a bit. "Like I was saying before, you don't act very serious about Jay—you're too stand-offish. You act like what Jay and I are talking about doesn't interest you at all."

"I find it very hard to hear what you are saying. The music is too loud." Emily found herself apologising.

"Don't you think the music's great?"

"No, actually I don't. I think it is very loud and very monotonous."

"Oh, I get it. You usually go to places with waltzes and that kind of thing."

"No, not really," Emily tried to explain. "But smaller bands and not so loud."

They had worked their way up to the door of the toilette, and Barb ducked inside. Emily was left before the door feeling defensive and inadequate. Shouldn't it have been the other way around? She was older and married—probably widowed, too. Why was she letting an inexperienced young woman intimidate her? Because she *was* serious about Jay…

Jay sensed that the evening had not been a great success. Emily was more withdrawn than she'd been anytime since they'd first slept together. But when he asked her what was wrong, she said 'nothing,' so they couldn't even talk about it. At last he took a stab at it. "I guess you and Barb didn't hit it off so well." He hoped she'd deny it.

"No, we didn't. She says I don't act 'serious' about you."

"Yeah, well, she doesn't know about this," Jay pulled Emily onto the bed beside him. He had already stripped down to his shorts, but Emily was still undressing and in her slip. She hadn't been expecting his move. Rather than responding playfully, she frowned and pulled away from him, remarking petulantly, "Well, what do you think she's doing with Rick right now?"

"Not this!" Jay declared definitively. "My sister's a good kid."

"And I'm not?" Emily demanded sharply, her eyebrows raised.

"You're not a kid, that's for sure," Jay retorted.

"Nor is Barb," Emily pointed out bluntly.

"Maybe not, but she's still a virgin and she'll go that way to her marriage bed. You can bet on it!" Jay's tone was increasingly aggressive.

"So did I," Emily told him pointedly, her eyes narrowed.

"OK. So what the hell are we arguing about?"

"Maybe I just don't fit into your family."

"Oh, you think you're too good for us, do you? Barb warned me about that!"

"It was Barb who spent the whole evening insulting me, my country, and my countrymen!" Emily was really angry now.

"Oh come off it! She wasn't insulting anyone. She was just having fun!"

"Well, if that's what you call it, I'm glad you enjoyed it, but it is not my idea of fun!" Emily grabbed for her dress and started to get dressed again.

"What are you doing?"

"Leaving!"

"What?! It's the middle of the night! Where do you think you're going to go?" Jay sat up on the bed in alarm.

"There are air-raid shelters all over the city—and other hotels, you know." She had her dress over her head and was zipping it up.

Jay stood up. "What the hell's got into you?"

"I don't see any point in continuing a relationship where I'm considered an object of ridicule!"

"What the *hell* are you talking about?!" Jay honestly didn't understand why Emily was so upset. He took hold of her shoulders and turned her around to face him. She turned her face away. "Nobody's ridiculing you! OK, so Barb made fun of British accents. Do you know how many Brits look down on us for *our* accents? And you aren't going to tell me you think tripe is great food?"

"No, but we have been fighting this damn war for *four* long years—and most of that time without any help! We've been *reduced* to these circumstances, and if you'd helped us sooner maybe things wouldn't have become so bad in the first place!"

"Well, don't look at me! I'm doing all I goddamned can!"

There was dead silence, and neither of them moved for an instant. Then without another word, they fell into each other's arms.

▼

CHAPTER 21

White Waltham, England
October 1943

The tannoy in the mess clicked on and a crisp voice called out: "Mrs. Priestman! Urgent telephone call! Please come immediately to the CO's office."

Everyone looked over at her. A heavy fog had rolled in during the night, and it showed no sign of lifting yet. They were all waiting to start the day. The usual card game was on in one corner, but most of the men looked up from their newspapers. The looks they cast her were curious and pitying at once. Urgent telephone calls never brought good news.

Emily let her own newspaper fall to the floor and hurried to comply with the order over the tannoy. It could only be Jay. All this week the 8th Air Force had been engaged in a furious offensive against Germany, launching raids against German cities day after day—and taking terrible losses. Philippa claimed that squadrons had been decimated and more than a thousand men lost. But they couldn't fly in this weather, either. Emily had thought he was safe today...

She knocked at the door and Miss Gower invited her in at once. She pointed to the telephone receiver lying on her desk. "Sir Howard Edward Downs, the Parliamentary Undersecretary," she announced.

More baffled than ever, Emily took up the receiver. "Priestman."

"Mrs. Priestman! Thank God I could reach you! I'm at my wit's end! I've been ringing the house all morning. Philippa is there. I know she is. I brought her back—but no one answers the phone. You must go over and see if something has happened to her!"

"Why should something have happened to her? Maybe she's just gone out shopping," Emily protested, at once annoyed that Teddy would expect her to drop everything and rush off home—as if she didn't have a responsible job. She knew too that Philippa had the day off, and the door to Philippa's bedroom had been closed when she left the house this morning. In fact, Emily had been extra quiet, thinking Philippa wanted to sleep in.

"You don't understand!" the important man said in obvious exasperation. "She was in a very queer mood last night. I don't know what it was, but she kept saying very odd things. I—I—fear she might try to take her own life."

"Philippa?" Emily could not imagine it.

"Yes, Philippa! Don't you see! This is an emergency. I could call the police, of course, but they would have to break into your house. All you have to do is go over and check on things for yourself! Of course, I *will* call the police if you refuse."

"No, I'll go and check and ring you back."

Emily hung up, explained the situation to Miss Gower, and got permission to return home. The fog was as impenetrable as ever, and it didn't look like they'd be flying for some time, anyway. A motor transport vehicle and driver was even put at her disposal. Emily asked the driver, a middle-aged woman, to come in the house with her—just in case Philippa really had done something silly.

The house was still and dark. Nothing stirred. Even Penny, thinking it was hours until anyone would be back, had settled herself to sleep, and jumped up in astonishment at the unexpected arrival of her adopted mistress. Surely that was a good sign, Emily thought. If Philippa had done harm to herself, surely the faithful dog would have sensed something was wrong?

Still she went up the steps with trepidation, while the ATA driver waited at the foot of the stairs uncomfortably. Emily knocked on Philippa's bedroom door. "Philippa?" No answer. She knocked and called louder. "Philippa!?" Still no answer. Now she was getting concerned. She tried the door. It was locked.

"I'll call the police!" the nervous driver decided.

Emily pounded in mounting alarm on the door. "Philippa! Let me in!"

The driver found the phone, and Emily could hear her giving the address to the police. Why? Emily asked herself, staring at the blank door in front of her. Why would Philippa, of all people, do something like this? Teddy was as attentive as ever. She had just been commended at work. She would soon be up for promotion. Was she pregnant, perhaps? But even that, nowadays, was hardly the scandal it once would have been—and there were ways of taking care of it, if you wanted to. It was no reason to kill yourself!

The sound of the siren drew Emily downstairs. She met the Constables at the door and led them up to the locked bedroom, explaining she'd assumed Philippa was just sleeping in late until another friend called and reported she'd been acting "strange" and wouldn't answer the phone. The ATA driver had already called in to White Waltham with a status report, but the fog was still clinging to the tree-tops, making flying impossible.

While one constable spoke with Emily and took down details of herself and Philippa, two others were working to open the bedroom door. It didn't take them very long. Emily had her ear cocked for what they would say, but they were professionals and all was silence. Then after a couple of minutes the two men came back down the stairs. Their expressions were strange—not shocked or even sober. They seemed almost to be smiling—but trying not to. At her speechless inquiry the senior constable declared, "Everything's alright, Madam. Your friend appears to be suffering from nothing more than an excess of gin."

Emily gaped. The constables grinned. Someone said she had done the right thing anyway. The constables departed. The ATA driver suggested they make some coffee, and Emily directed her into the kitchen. Then she made her way up the stairs and into Philippa's bedroom.

Philippa was lying on her stomach on her bed in her nightgown. Her arms hung off the side of the bed. Two empty bottles of gin stood on the bedside table. She was snoring slightly. Emily had just decided to let her sleep it off, when Philippa stirred, groaned, and then with a little cry, reared up and ran past Emily with her hand over her mouth. Emily could hear her being sick in the bathroom. She went back downstairs and started making toast.

She took the toast up to Philippa, who was sitting on the floor of the bathroom, her head against the wall, moaning slightly. Philippa opened one eye when she heard someone at the door, and then closed it again. "I feel like I'm going to die."

"Teddy thought you might try to kill yourself. He called and made me come check on you."

"How very chivalrous of Teddy," Philippa remarked, and Emily thought she detected a tinge of bitterness in her voice. Ah ha, she thought, she probably is pregnant, and of course he won't think of divorcing his wife…

Emily settled herself beside Philippa and offered her the toast. Philippa eyed it with one eye for a moment, then shook her head, groaned again, and leaned her head back against the wall.

"What is this all about?" Emily asked cautiously.

Philippa waved one hand through the air vaguely. "I have the day off. Surely I can drink myself into a coma on my day off without the world standing on its head."

"Yes, I suppose you can. But Teddy thought you'd said some 'odd' things last night."

"Oh, he did, did he?" Philippa's voice was very definitely poisonous.

"Did you have a fight?"

"No, no, why should we fight?" Philippa asked sarcastically. "Teddy is such a *charming* man. Not like that *beast* Steeplechase." She cut herself off. Her tone was so acid, the air was smoking.

"Did Steeplechase do something?" Emily was trying to picture some public confrontation similar to what had transpired at her own private party when the two men had encountered each other.

"Do something?" Philippa opened one eye again and fixed it on Emily. It was cold and hard. "He tried to land a damaged Lancaster in nought visibility because he had a wounded gunner on board and killed them both, that's what he did! Another stupid, worthless death! Eighty-nine operational flights, and he buys it in an English fog because he's so god-damned sure of himself. The *invincible* Steeplechase! The *immortal* Steeplechase! Well, he's dead now!" She spat it out furiously, and Emily was too embarrassed and stunned to say anything. She just sat on the floor feeling very, very sad.

Philippa rolled her head against the wall and spoke in a low moan with her eyes closed. "I thought—I thought if I didn't have anything to do with him—if I had someone else—it wouldn't hurt as much."

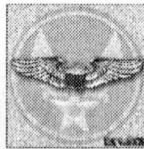

Beauchamp Rodding

The checklist had never seemed so important before, but Jay was nervous—more nervous than he'd been since that very first mission. He was back in the left-hand seat. The man beside him was a virtual stranger, a kid who'd arrived a week ago. Most of the rest of the crew were newcomers, too, but Rick had pulled rank to get on J.B.'s crew, and Webber and the Kid had both volunteered, too. That was the nicest compliment anyone had ever paid him, and J.B. hoped—and prayed—they wouldn't live to regret it.

At least today was relatively short. Bremen. It was well defended, of course, but just knowing they had several less hours in the air and more of that time with escort than without made it seem less intimidating. At least that's what Jay had told his new crew.

The new guys all looked so young to him. Which was crazy, because they weren't really younger than he was. OK, the gunners were still in their teens for the most part, but the new navigator was a "grand-dad" of 25, who'd quit his job as an insurance salesman to join up after Pearl Harbor, and even the co-pilot, Dean Jacobs, was 23 and a college grad. Dean was tall and lean and plagued by acne still. He'd played basketball and was 6 foot 6 but so skinny J.B. wondered if he was really strong enough to manhandle a B-17 around in an emergency. Well, he supposed they'd find out soon enough.

They started up the engines. It was a relatively new ship and everything still seemed tops to Jay. Poor old *Hooker* had been taken apart for scrap, and this ship, flown over in the last month, hadn't even been christened properly. She was just "T"—Thomas—at the moment. Maybe once they'd flown a couple of missions together, they'd feel more like a team and give her a proper name. Maybe they'd even choose something other than a silly pin-up girl for nose art, too.

The ceiling was still pretty low and visibility not more than a mile on the ground, but the Met officer insisted they'd have excellent visibility over the target and that this fog would have burned off or blown away by the time they got back. Jay sure as hell hoped so. There had been two crashes at High Wych the other night when returning RAF bombers had not been able to find their airfields, and had run out of fuel and crashed into the surrounding countryside. Rumours about survivors varied, but after looking at one of the burnt-out wrecks, Jay figured the rumours that said "with all hands" were right.

The tower flashed green, and Jay throttled forward so that all 55,000 lbs of aircraft started to roll forward. Jay didn't make any stupid remark about them being off on mission so-and-so, because they all had different numbers of missions to go. He noted only mentally that this was his 24th. If he survived it, he would have just one more to go.

As soon as the ungainly gaggle of hundreds of aircraft had formed up above the blanket of fog and started on its dogged way toward the enemy coast, Jay turned over the controls to Dean, and went back into the ship to check on each of his crew. It wasn't necessary, of course—he could have called in on the intercom—but he figured it wouldn't hurt to stretch his legs, and it gave him a rest while giving Dean a chance to practise formation flying. After sitting through four missions in the co-pilot's seat, J.B. had more sympathy for a co-pilot's need to keep his hand in. In fact, J.B. had insisted Dean practice take-offs and landings during their engine checks yesterday.

The two waist gunners seemed rather discomfited by his sudden appearance among them; they had been writing notes to each other, it seemed, and found his presence an invasion of their privacy. J.B. went on to the tail, however, and crouched down behind the Kid. "You OK, Kid?"

He was bundled up, as ever, in all his scarves and mittens, cap and mask and 'monkey suit,' but somehow he still seemed to be grinning. "I'm dandy, sir! I know you'll get me home safe!"

J.B. did not understand the Kid's faith in him, but he clapped him once on the shoulder and made his way back forward to the navigator. He conscientiously showed Jay where they were on his charts. J.B. turned to Rick and would have liked to chat with him, but just then Dean announced, "Passing through 10,000 feet. Everyone on oxygen." So J.B. just waved to him and returned to the flight deck. He pulled on his oxygen mask and scanned the horizon. It was indeed a clear, beautiful day up here.

It was also an enchanted day. J.B. would not have believed it possible if he hadn't experienced it himself. They seemed to float on the air, and although they heard someone over the radio reporting damage from fighters and planes dropping out of the formation, in fact they didn't see any fighters themselves. Dean pointed out some contrails, apparently from fighter-fighter engagements, but that was all. They flew on steadily like a big, peaceful convoy.

There was flak. The run into the target was, as usual, rather hot, but nothing really came close. They were shaken once or twice. The wing-tip of a Fort flying a little in front of them was shot away, but after a moment or two the pilot got it under control and continued—straight and level. Again they heard one or two distress calls over the radio, but no one in their immediate formation was hit.

They returned to Beauchamp Rodding still in perfect formation, all nine aircraft of the squadron undamaged and in position. J.B. couldn't grasp it. His 24th mission had been a milk-run! He couldn't wait to tell Emily. Just one more to go. Maybe the new aircraft and crew brought luck. Certainly being captain again was worth celebrating. This time alone—without Rick and Barb to spoil things.

Windsor

Emily looked at her watch, astonished as the door-bell rang a second time. It was only 7 pm and Jay had said he'd *try* to pick her up at 8. He must be getting really good at driving on English roads—or maybe he'd got some sort of airlift? What did it matter. She checked herself in the mirror to be sure she wasn't totally unpresentable, and then hurried to answer the door as the bell went a third time. "Really, Jay, don't be so impatient!" Emily said under her breath as she opened the door with a smile—and then froze.

It wasn't Jay. It was a postman. "Mrs. Priestman?"

"Yes."

"I have a special delivery letter for you." He held out a clipboard on which was a rough, green envelope and a form. He asked her to sign the form at the "X" and then touched his cap and climbed back on his bicycle and was gone. Emily stood staring at the curious green envelope in her hands and registered with horror that it was in German—at least the letters were all Gothic.

Her pulse, heartbeat and breathing all seemed to turn instantly erratic. Her mouth went dry. She stared at the envelope until she realised that it was from the International Red Cross. It was in both French and German, actually, and it had been posted in Zürich.

Emily backed into the house and closed the door behind her. She didn't know where to go. She looked around herself helplessly. If only Philippa had been here. She would have made Philippa open it and read it for her. She glanced toward the kitchen, then the parlour, but then walked under the stairs into the study. She switched on the light and stared at the photo on the secretary opposite. Robin stared back at her.

She went to the secretary looking for a letter opener. She could feel Robin watching her every move. He was here. She could sense it. He was here. In her hands.

She sank into the reading chair and switched on the lamp. She took the letter opener and slit the green envelope open. Inside was a thin piece of paper, rather shabby and dirty, with pre-printed headings (in Gothic type) and lines for filling in the blanks, divided into numbered boxes. She couldn't bring herself to focus on the words. Her whole body was quivering with tension. It was Robin's handwriting.

She put the letter aside and started walking around the study, unable to sit still a second longer. He was alive. He was alive. He was *really* alive. *Robin was alive!* She wanted to scream for joy. She wanted to call everyone she knew—Aunt Hattie, the Admiral, Colin, and David and Bridges and Smitty and the whole world! Robin was alive! God knew how and where, but he was alive after all. Oh, God, you will make a believer of me yet! She risked looking at the photo on the secretary.

Oh, Robin, how could I ever doubt it?

But what if he were hurt? Crippled, injured, even paralysed? It had been a terrible crash. And why had it taken so long to contact her? There had to be some reason. She stared at the green envelope on the floor and the letter on the arm of the chair. With trepidation she took up the letter, still standing, and forced herself to read:

> Apologies for not writing sooner. Prevented by concussion. Much better now. No other serious injuries. Food packages welcome. Please fly carefully. Thinking of you always. Robin

There were numbers over the boxes; he'd been allowed exactly 25 words.

Now her thoughts were in a different kind of turmoil as she tried to understand everything he hadn't been allowed to say. How could a concussion prevent him from communicating for nearly 9 months? Had he been in a coma that long? Suffering from loss of memory? Locked away in some German mental hospital? The plea for food was commentary enough on the treatment he was getting. And yet he was thinking of her.

Oh, God! And any minute now her lover would arrive! She wasn't a widow, but a married woman—and she was committing adultery, she was cheating on a man who was injured and imprisoned and thinking of her always.

Robin had done nothing to deserve what she had done to him. Not once had he ever given her the slightest reason to doubt that he was faithful to her—although he could have had his pick of any number of prettier, richer girls any time he liked. She had always told herself she must be prepared for it. That at some point he would be tempted once too often. She had told herself she was lucky to have had him at all, and must not expect to have him exclusively for ever.

And instead she had betrayed him at the first little opportunity. She felt very ill.

And then the doorbell rang.

Jay stood there in his smart dress uniform, his cap low over his eyes, holding a bottle of champagne in one hand and a dozen red roses in the other. He was radiantly happy. It hurt so much, Emily wanted to scream.

Instead she just backed up into the entrance hall, stunned and dazed and frightened.

"I'm back in the captain's seat!" Jay was explaining joyously. "It's a great crew and a great ship—Rick and Webber and even the Kid and—what's the matter?"

Emily couldn't speak. She held up her hand and fled into the study.

"Emily? What is it? What's the matter?" He followed her to the doorway to the study. He saw her pick something off the reading chair and come toward him. Her face was frozen. She handed him the letter. Jay looked down at it. "What is this?" He was about to say "I can't read German" when he understood. He looked only for the signature. "Robin."

"But it doesn't change anything!" Jay burst out. "I love you, and you can't deny you love me! You can't just go back to him!"

Emily could see how badly hurt Jay was, and that only made it worse. She didn't want to make it worse. But when he repeated, "You can't go back to him," she forced herself to point out: "But I never left him, Jay. I'm still his wife."

"That's just a technicality. You love me. If you stay with him, you'll be living a lie."

There was something in that. She couldn't deny it. It was a horrible, dreadful thought to imagine pretending to Robin that she had never betrayed him, never fallen in love with someone else, never slept with someone else. And because she didn't know what to say and said nothing, Jay was encouraged and continued. "Emily, don't you see? You can't turn the clock back. You're mine now. We belong together. We have a future together!"

"Do we?" Emily found she couldn't picture it. She couldn't picture America—not trailer homes in the snow and lakes so large you couldn't see across and endless nightclubs with loud bands and jitter-bugging youth…

"Of course we do!" Jay insisted frantically. "Oh, Emily, I can build a future for you in the greatest country on Earth! I'm sure I can get a good job at one of the automobile companies. I'll be making good money. We'll be able to have our own place and a car—everything."

"That's a long way away—when the war is over."

"Your husband won't come home until the war is over, either. But I'll be here for you, Emily." He took a step closer, setting the roses and champagne aside to take her into his arms.

Emily backed away from him, terrified she wouldn't be able to resist him if he held her in his arms. "What do you mean, you'll be here? You only have one more mission. You'll be leaving for the States in a matter of weeks."

"I can do what Rick did. I can volunteer for a second tour, and a third—whatever it takes—'till the war is over."

Emily took another step backwards, filled with an ever more acute terror now. "Don't be ridiculous!" she told him harshly.

"Emily, *nothing* is more important to me than you are!"

"That's too bad, because Robin is more important to me."

Jay had been about to take another step towards her, determined and certain that if he could just hold her in his arms, everything would be alright. He couldn't believe what she had just said. "What?"

"I said: Robin is more important to me than you are."

"And what I am then—just the next best thing?"

"Yes. That's exactly it: The next best thing."

It took several seconds before Jay had absorbed that blow enough to speak or move. Then he said very softly but acidly, "So Barb was right about you, after all. Just taking me for a ride. You bitch!" He turned on his heel and stormed out, leaving the roses and champagne behind.

E P I L O G U E

▼

Washington, DC
July 1960

"*Detroit, Michigan?!* Who the hell wants to go to Detroit, Michigan?!" Keith asked in naked outrage. The smell of coffee and fresh toast and the sound of voices from the kitchen had woken him and lured him downstairs, in eager readiness to tell about all his adventures during the last term at school. Instead he had been confronted by an incredible announcement: they were going to spend the better part of his school holidays on a trip across America to Detroit.

Keith's parents exchanged a dismayed look at his outburst, and then his father turned a cold eye on him as he said, "You will not use bad language in my house or in the presence of your mother and sister." His father didn't have to raise his voice when he said things like this. A lifetime of authority lent his words sufficient force. He looked particularly stern at the moment because he was on his way to work, dressed in the uniform of an RAF Group Captain. Keith hated it when his Dad looked like this, because it made him so unassailable and distant. When he wasn't looking so "official," he had longish dark hair that was just starting to grey at the sideburns, very dark eyes which seemed to see everything even under the surface, and the most wonderful smile.

Keith loved his Dad, but at the moment that didn't help things. "Alright," he agreed, pressing his lips together in a teenage display of resentful obedience, "but I'd still like to know why we have to go to Detroit, of all God-forsaken places? You promised me a sailing vacation!"

"Michigan is surrounded by lakes. I'm sure we'll find some opportunity to sail," his father offered weakly, looking uncomfortable.

"And we'll travel by way of upstate New York and Niagara Falls." Keith's mother entered the argument. She was dressed only casually at the moment in a skirt and blouse, but she was still slender, attractive and elegant. She wore her dark brown hair swept up into a French twist, and Keith secretly thought she was much prettier than most mothers. But at the moment none of that mattered to Keith, because she was trying to convince him that this awful trip would be fun. "We thought you'd enjoy seeing more of the country."

"But why *Detroit*?" Keith insisted. "It's nothing but an industrial city where they make cars! Why go there rather than someplace fun—like California?"

Keith's parents exchanged a look, and Keith thought his mother looked uncomfortable. His father answered, "We've been invited to stay with friends of your mother."

Keith looked at his mother in amazement. "How did you get to know some-one in Detroit?"

"It's someone I met during the war. You should be interested in meeting him, actually. He flew B-17s for the 8th Air Force."

Although at 14 Keith had by no means committed himself to one career or another, he had always taken a keen interest in flying, and had from time to time expressed a desire to follow his father into the RAF.

"Does he *still* fly?"

"I don't know. I don't think so. I think he works as an executive with one of the automotive companies. I hadn't heard from him for years, and then suddenly we got this letter inviting us to go out and stay with him and his family."

"I've got to go," Keith's father announced abruptly, getting to his feet and reaching for his cap. "Want to walk me to the Embassy, Keith?" The Embassy was a good half-hour's walk away, but Keith's father always walked in good weather. The invitation to Keith to join him was clearly an offer of a private chat, and he jumped at it.

Although still early in the morning, the air was heavy with a humid haze. Keith followed his father down the brick path to the concrete sidewalk and then fell in beside him. They walked in silence for a moment, and then his father took a deep breath and announced, "I'm sorry this trip is such a disappointment to you. I thought you'd be interested in seeing more of America. Sailing we can do at home, after all."

"When are we ever at home?" Keith countered, more resentfully than he intended. It wasn't really that he minded his father's international career, but Keith did sometimes miss having a home that belonged to them. He also thought it would have been nice to be able to relax during the holidays—not drive half-way across a continent to see some people he'd never even heard of before!

"I can insist on a posting to the UK next time, if that's important to you," his father answered softly.

Keith was a little taken aback by his father's tone. He sounded weary—or defeated. Keith looked over sharply and caught his father looking into the distance, his eyes squinting slightly—as if he were looking for Messerschmitts in the grey haze over the Potomac. He looked worried, Keith registered with a shock. He looked worried or tired. That didn't make any sense. The job here was 'a piece of cake'—no pressure, no command responsibilities, good relations all around with the rest of the Embassy staff and with the Americans. "What's the matter, Dad?"

Keith's father started slightly as he realised he'd been caught, and tried to smile. He met Keith's eyes only for an instant before—his eyes on the distance again—he asked, "Keith, please try to make the best of this trip, even if it's not what you wanted. I know how important a school holiday is, and I know what it's like to feel like it's been ruined, but this trip is very important to your mother."

"Why?" Keith wanted to know, all his resentment building up again as his father reminded him just how little time he actually had before he had to be back at school. His father didn't even glance at him. He just kept walking, his eyes on the sidewalk now. "I mean, if she hasn't heard from this bloke for years, what can be so bloody important about seeing him now?"

When his father didn't answer despite Keith's provocative use of invective, Keith opened his mouth to voice his question again, but his father finally said softly, "Because, it seems, he was very important to her then."

"How? The Americans were all there for such a short time. They just flew their 25 missions or whatever and then went back home, the war over for them. None of them stayed longer than 6 months, did they? Didn't you know him, too?"

"No." There was a pregnant pause, and Keith looked over at his father, strangely alarmed without knowing why. "I was already a POW when they met," his father explained in a soft, emotionless voice that sent a chill through Keith.

"Dad!" Keith stopped and tried to make his father look at him. His father glanced over questioningly. "What are you saying? That Mum was seeing this bloke behind your back?"

"Keith, I was in prison for over two years. Your mother had to go on living. Of course she saw people while I was away. You know how grateful I am to David Goldman and Colin Duport for looking after her for me."

"But that was different! They were *your* friends. They would never have taken advantage of the situation, but this American…" Keith just couldn't grasp it. How could his mother have done such a rotten thing? His Dad had nearly starved to death in Germany. He'd seen pictures taken just after he returned; his father was almost as thin as the people coming out of the Concentration Camps. And while he was going through that hell, his mother had been going out with other blokes? With *Americans*? Having a good time?

"Fell in love with her." His father finished the hanging sentence, and Keith could feel how hot he was becoming as he started to realise what his Dad was saying.

"Dad!" Keith insisted on his father's attention. "Are you saying they had an *affair?*"

His father looked away, his eyes focused on the distance again, and for a moment Keith thought he wasn't even going to answer. Then he realised his father was saying something without sound—just mouthing the words: I don't know.

Keith felt completely winded. His mother had had an affair! It was bad enough imagining his parents having sex, but his mother with a complete stranger? And not *before* his parents were married but *afterwards*. That made her all sorts of horrible things, adulterous to start with, but the word 'whore' also came to mind. There were so many stories about the way English girls had carried on with Yanks just for the extra food and stockings and what-not. "Why didn't you do something!" Keith blurted out furiously.

"Keith, I just told you, I was stuck in Stalag Luft III at the time." His father's tone was sharper now, starting to get angry.

"I meant, when you came back! Why didn't you confront her! How could you just go back to her?!"

"What do you think I should have done? Divorce her?" His father cocked an eyebrow at him, and Keith sensed that his father was a long ways ahead of him. He sensed that he was making a fool of himself in some way, but he just couldn't fathom how his father could forgive her! Taking advantage of his imprisonment seemed the most despicable thing imaginable.

"Yes, of course!"

"Brilliant, then she could have married him and gone off to live in America, and what would I have had? Nothing. Not your mother or you or your sister."

Keith felt dizzy as he realised that his father was reminding him he would never even have been born! He'd been conceived after the war, after his father came home.

Seeing his distress, his father continued in a gentler tone. "Besides, Keith, I don't know if she really had an affair. I know that he loved her enough to ask her to leave me. I know that after the end of the war, he wrote and begged her to come join him. I know because she showed me that letter, and one that came later, after you were born, promising that she could always turn to him if she needed someone. But that doesn't prove that *she* did anything wrong, Keith."

"She must have encouraged him!" Keith insisted with all the conviction of a teenager. But even as he said it, Keith was horrified by what he was saying. How could his mother have behaved like all the sluts they showed in the movies? The images of girls with bright-red lipstick and nail-polish clinging to "Yanks" for a pair of nylons flitted through his brain. His elegant, serious *mother* had been like *that*?

His father sighed and fixed a gaze at him that was a mixture of concern and annoyance. The annoyance apparently won. "I see I made a mistake confiding in you," his father remarked with an edge to his voice. "I thought you were old enough to understand, but if you're too immature to deal with the situation, let me set things straight." The worry Keith had seen on his father's face only moments before had apparently been banished, replaced with stern forcefulness again. The man confronting him now was back in "command," and he spoke in a soft but clipped tone that tolerated no contradiction. "Neither you nor I have any right to judge your mother. Much less have we any right to judge Mr. Baronowsky, whom we have never met."

Keith pressed his lips together sullenly. He knew better than to be openly insubordinate to his father, but that did not mean he was going to accept what his father was saying, either. His father was continuing, "This trip to Detroit is important to me, too. It's my first chance to see just what the competition was. It is more important to your mother, however, because it gives her a chance to confront the choice she made—and convince herself, I hope, that she made the *right* one. You and your sister are my greatest allies in that task. Don't let me down, will you?"

Keith had been so busy feeling resentful that he hadn't expected that appeal. He caught his breath and looked over at his father in outrage. "That's not fair!"

His father gave him a somewhat crooked smile, but there was genuine amusement in his eyes, amusement and affection. "Please, Keith, for my sake, be a sport. You wouldn't want your mother to change her mind at this stage, would you?"

"That's not fair!" Keith protested again, knowing he was completely outma-noeuvred, trapped by his father's effective tactics into a co-operation he wanted with all his heart to refuse—but couldn't.

*   *   *   *

Lathrup Village, Michigan

The silver Jaguar turned the heads of the boys playing softball at the corner; it was not only a make of car they had never seen before, it was obviously at least five years old—and in Detroit it was a disgrace to drive even last year's model. The boys called something out as the car turned the corner, but the four occu-pants of the car didn't appear to hear.

The car turned into the neatly laid-out subdivision. Sidewalks lined the street on both sides. Driveways led down to the street at regular intervals and paved walkways led from the front doors to the sidewalks. Trees had been planted every 10 yards but they were still small, protected by wooden scaffolding, and did not offer shade to the street yet. The houses, all one-and-a-half story, detached houses, were constructed on three or four different models which alternated irregularly. All were built of red or yellow brick and all had attached two-car garages. Bright, shiny American cars stood displayed in many driveways, often with the pavement wet around them from a recent wash. Water sprinklers swayed or swirled on the large, open front lawns. Flowers and shrubs were confined to the flower-beds right beside the houses, so that the entire neighbourhood was dominated by the neat cut grass of front lawns, interrupted only by the sidewalks and driveways and bright cars.

They stopped in the middle of the block. Emily checked the address from the letter in her hand: 1229. This was it. Robin cut the engine and the two kids sprang out of the back seat, anxious to escape from the stuffy car after the long, hot drive. Robin got out from behind the wheel and rolled down his sleeves before taking his double-breasted blue blazer from the back window and pulling it on. Emily was the only one not eager to get out of the car. She looked at the neat brick house with the well-tended lawn, and her throat went dry.

Robin came around the front of the car and opened the door for her. She got out and tensely led the family up the narrow walk to the front porch. She rang the bell, and heard the slow ding-dong ring inside the house. Almost at once the door sprang open and she found herself facing a tall, slender woman with dark brown hair piled up on her head as was fashionable now-a-days. She wore heavy make-up, big gold earrings and a gold necklace, as well as several very large rings on both hands. Otherwise she was simply dressed in a sleeveless shirt tucked into slacks, and her arms were beautifully tanned.

"Mrs. Baronowsky?" Emily asked. "I'm Emily Priestman, and this is my husband, Group Captain—"

"Robin Priestman." Robin leaned forward and held out his hand to her. The woman took it with a wide smile and a very bold look—or so it seemed to Emily.

"And my son, Keith," Emily continued the introductions.

Keith dutifully held out his hand and nodded his head.

"And my daughter, Charlotte."

"Please call me 'Charlie,'" Keith's younger sister said at once, holding out her hand politely but adding firmly, "I *hate* Charlotte."

The American woman laughed at the child's candour, saying directly to her, "well, I guess you're a bit of a tomboy, then—just like I was at your age. I'm Betty. Why—"

She cut herself off as her husband came up behind her. Over her shoulder he was staring out of the door straight at Emily. "Emily?" He sounded uncertain.

Emily met his gaze and answered solemnly, "Hello, Jay."

They gazed intently at each other, noting the changes.

Then Jay broke eye contact and thrust his hand out to Robin. "Hi! I'm J.B. Nice to meet you at last."

The two men measured one another.

J.B. was several inches taller than Robin, making him well over six feet, and he was broader, built like the line-backer he had been in his youth. The office work and Betty's good cooking had added pounds that were not yet unsightly but nevertheless noticeable. He was very blond and wore his hair short, as was normal in America. His open, well-proportioned face was red with sunburn at the moment, and his short nose was peeling. He had very blue eyes that were no less piercing and penetrating than Robin's.

"Well, come on in, come on in!" He gestured to everyone. "You can get the luggage later. Betty's just fixing up some lemonade to have on the back porch."

They were led through a house that was spotlessly clean, perfectly ordered and furnished with what looked like brand-new things. Everything matched, everything that ought to gleam did, and everything that was supposed to be soft and comfy was. It was like walking through the showroom of a fancy furniture store. At last they reached a screened-in porch at the back of the house, where the guests were offered lemonade on ice and fresh-baked chocolate-chip cookies. Here they also met the Baronowskys' three children: Joe, who was 13, Mary, who was 11, and Mark, who was 9. The children were sent out to play in the yard. There were various balls lying about and a volley-ball net, which soon provided a focus. A lively game developed, US vs UK.

The adults, meanwhile, discussed the trip out from Washington, the splendour of Niagara Falls, the boring industrialism of Essex County, Ontario, etc. After that Betty launched into a catalogue of options for activities during Emily and Robin's visit, and it was agreed that they would go to Lake Huron tomorrow and take a picnic lunch and swimming things. When that conversation stalled, Emily asked about Barb.

"That's right, Jay said you'd met Barb when she was in the WAC!" Betty answered. "So no doubt it won't surprise you to hear she's been married and divorced already. She just can't seem to settle down. First she thought she was too good for poor Rick Orloff. You knew him, too, Jay tells me. Instead, she married some guy with a fancy car and a house in Florida, but he turned out to be a real rat and a fake, too. Anyway, she got stuck with two kids and an ex who doesn't pay alimony. She's been trying to find work for ages, but it's tough with two kids and no college education."

"Barb's problem is she's no good at office jobs. She's applied with all the airlines to train as a mechanic, but they won't even give her a chance," Jay explained more sympathetically. "But it looks like she may have talked a small flight school into letting her train as a mechanic while working as their clerk and book-keeper."

"How is she supposed to do all that and raise two kids?" Betty wanted to know.

"What about Rick?" Emily changed the subject. "How is he doing?"

"Great! He married Cindy Caldwell, that colleague of yours from ATA, the girl from Idaho. It took them a while to get together, because Rick had his heart set on Barb, but when she got married, he finally started noticing Cindy. She's some gal, let me tell you. Got her own supply business up in Idaho and they fly a beat-up old C-47 around together. Rick moved up to Idaho with her and they're doing great."

"Well, if you call living in a run-down farmhouse with an outhouse doing 'great,'" Betty objected, adding in an aside to Emily, "I don't think they make $10,000 a year between the two of them. I don't know how they think they can raise kids on that kind of money. And neither one of them is willing to settle down and get a real job."

"They're happy," Jay insisted.

A loud shout from the yard drew attention to the children, and Emily hastened to remark how good Jay's kids looked.

This brought a big, heartfelt smile from Jay, and he said enthusiastically, "Joe's starting junior high school this fall and he's hoping to play football. But his Little League team was the best in the state two years running."

"With Jay coaching," Betty informed her guests pointedly. "Jay's so good with the boys! Before he took over the team they were the second worst. Now they are heading for the national play-offs."

"It's just a lot of fun," Jay insisted, waving her praise aside. "At that age they are still eager and docile. And Mary is doing both ballet and piano," Jay went on to say proudly. "I think she's going to be a Broadway star like that bitch Kathy never was!"

"She certainly is pretty," Emily agreed. Jay's daughter, with her bright blonde hair and sleek, tanned body, outshone her own rather mousy daughter.

"Smart, too," Jay insisted. "She's the student of the family. How about your kids?"

"They're both good at school, but Charlotte is the more ambitious. She wants to be a veterinarian—horses, of course."

"Oh, the horse phase," Betty groaned sympathetically. "I hope Mary doesn't go through that."

Emily didn't think Charlotte's interest in veterinary medicine was just a passing phase. She had insisted she wanted to pursue this field since before she could say the word. But not wanting to argue, Emily fell silent, and another awkward pause in the conversation ensued.

Jay broke it by suggesting he help Robin bring in the luggage. This, in turn, gave Betty the perfect opportunity to give Emily a tour of the house, "Just so you'll know where everything is and will feel comfortable," Betty assured her.

Betty was clearly very proud of her house, and she had every reason to be. Betty also took the opportunity of being away from Jay to remark, "Jay just got another promotion, you know? He doesn't like me to brag, but he is now running the entire department and has a staff of 14 people directly under him. He stands an excellent chance of being made vice-president next year or the year after."

"I'm so glad to hear. And you, what do you do?"

"Do?"

"Don't you have a job?"

"Oh, good heavens! Jay wouldn't *stand* for that! You know what's he's like!" She said it in a way that implied that if Emily didn't know even this, that she didn't know him at all. "He would take it as a personal *insult* if I so much as suggested it! Besides, I wouldn't dream of working as long as the kids are in school. I'm not one of those mothers who just buys cans of ready-made food. I cook everything from scratch, like the cookies we had just now, and I've made an apple pie for dinner, too. Besides, with all the things the kids are into now, I seem to spend most of my time just driving them around—baseball, band, piano lessons and ballet. And there is still so much I want to do in the house! The kitchen cupboards all need to be completely re-painted, and the curtains in the family room need to be replaced. They're so faded." Emily hadn't noticed either deficiency. Betty was continuing happily, "And Mary's room needs a make-over. It's too nursery-like for a girl her age. How could I ever find the time to make a proper home for Jay and the kids if I was holding down a job? Surely you don't work?" Betty asked, in a tone that implied it was almost an insult. "I would have thought an English air-force officer made enough money for you to get by without."

"I don't work for the money. Nor do I have a job, really, but Robin noticed that I was bored when I stopped flying, so he encouraged me to find other means to keep my mind active. In fact, he said he'd be bored to tears with a wife who could only talk about cooking, cleaning and diapers. So really, it was he who got me to start writing."

"Writing? You mean you write books?" Betty sounded quite incredulous.

"Yes, I just published a history of Frankish Cyprus." Emily waited in vain for a question about her book. Because most people didn't know there had been a Frankish kingdom on Cyprus for roughly three hundred years, they usually at least asked when it had been and how it had come about.

Betty's curiosity did not extend that far, however. "Oh, I see," she replied.

The tour over, they returned to the screened-in porch. Meanwhile, the men had finished unloading the car and joined the kids playing volleyball. From the lawn came shouting and both women looked over. Robin had removed his blazer and rolled up his sleeves again. Jay was in a polo shirt anyway. The pace picked up at once, and both men were soon smashing balls across the net with an aggression that was patent.

Emily sighed, feeling guiltier than ever for this whole fiasco. Furthermore, the conversation with Betty had stalled yet again. Betty was pushing up and then smoothing her hair, and Emily noted for a second time the huge diamond flashing beside her wedding band. It must be her engagement ring, Emily registered; the diamond was easily three times the size of the diamond set amidst five equally small sapphires that Robin had given her. "Jay and I lost touch entirely after the war," Emily ventured. "I have no idea how you two met. Would you mind telling me?"

"Not at all," Betty answered with a smile, the first genuine smile of the whole dreadful afternoon so far. "When the war ended, I was 25 and—with not a beau in sight—my parents were really putting the pressure on for me to settle down and get a job—start earning my keep, they called it. They felt I'd wasted too much time and money already and wanted me to get a job as a sales clerk or secretary—anything, just so long as I was bringing in a paycheck."

Emily nodded once. She understood all too well about parents expecting you to 'start earning your keep.'

"I thought teaching would be better than typing, so I talked them into letting me go back to college to get a teaching certificate. I'd saved enough to pay my own way, you see, and when I got accepted at Michigan they were pretty impressed. Still, I had to study hard, which meant I spent a lot of time at the UGLY—sorry, that's the Undergraduate Library.

"One day I was in the cafeteria buying a coke to keep me awake and I saw these three guys sitting at a table and gesturing with their hands, you know, like pilots do." She glanced at Emily to be sure Emily knew what she meant. Emily nodded. "I couldn't resist wandering nearer to them, as if I was looking for a place to sit, but I was really just eavesdropping. As I approached I heard them mention 'Forts' and 'Flak,' and it was obvious they were former AAF pilots. Ann Arbor was full of them, you know, all on the GI Bill and so getting their education paid by Uncle Sam, while I had to pay my own way." There was a bitterness about the way she said this that surprised Emily, and made her feel a touch guilty. She'd gone to University on a scholarship, too.

"Anyway," Betty continued, "I overheard one of these guys saying, you know, like it was the end of the world, 'and then the outboard engine quit—on the *same* side.' He was making gestures with his foot like he was standing on the right rudder and had his hands gripped around an imaginary control-column and, I don't know, but the way he was bragging and carrying on just made all my anger boil up. So I stepped up to the table and said, 'Oh, come on, a Fort's easy to fly on two engines.'" Betty clearly enjoyed telling this story.

"All three guys at the table turned and stared at me like I was a Martian or something. Then the guy who'd been telling the story rolled his eyes and groaned, 'Aw, come on! You co-eds think you know *everything*, don't you?' He would have said more, too, but I didn't let him. I interrupted to say, 'I know, because I've *flown* Forts—with two engines out on the same side, too. It's no worse than losing one engine on a C-47.' Then I turned away, because I was all worked up just talking about flying, and I heard the way they burst out laughing behind my back.

"That really hurt. I guess I should have expected it, and I should have been used to it by then. But at the time I was so miserable I just wanted to break down and cry. You see," she explained carefully, "I was a trained Army Air Forces pilot. A so-called WASP."

"You were?!" Emily was both surprised and delighted. Betty's pride in being a pilot was the first thing Emily could relate to about Betty. She added to explain her own surprise, "I didn't think you had women pilots here in the US! Jay was so amazed to see me get out of a cockpit the first time we met that he was—well— rather taken aback. He apologized to me later, but he claimed there were no women flying in the U.S."

"Well, they only hired a couple dozen women at first, and that not until the fall of 1942. I guess Jay missed all the publicity because he was in B-17 training at the time, and that's pretty intense. The larger program to actually *train* women pilots didn't produce any graduates until Jay was already in England, so it's no wonder that he never ran into any of us. But what really gets me mad when I think about it is that almost no one in America today remembers that there were actually over a thousand of us! We were trained at the only all-female training base in the world, Avenger Field in Sweetwater, Texas, and we went through *exactly* the same training as Army Air Forces cadets. Roughly half of us washed out in training, in fact. Just like the guys. We lived in barracks and we had to do drill and calisthenics and the whole spiel. Altogether, we spent more than seven months in training and by the time we graduated, we had over 200 flying hours and 30 hours on instruments as well."

"Oh, very good," Emily remarked sincerely. "I didn't get any instrument training until after the war. And you were a ferry pilot?"

"No, a lot of us were assigned to Ferrying Division, but I was thrilled to get sent to B-17 training. I flew another 130 hours on them before I was assigned to fly co-pilot at a base where air gunners were trained. Altogether I had nearly 600 hours flying, almost 400 of them on Forts, when they sent us home."

"You mean at the end of the war?"

"No, almost a year earlier!" The outrage was still there, even after 16 years. Emily had her first glimpse of a woman who could be angry and determined. Betty was explaining, "Congress refused to approve the incorporation of the WASP into the AAF, so we were told to just pack our bags and go home—at our own expense!"

"But that doesn't make sense." Emily protested. "After all that expensive training, how could they afford to just send you home before the war was over?"

"That's what I say. But you see, by then the USAAF had trained over 100,000 male pilots, too, and they were coming back after their tours in Europe and the Pacific, and everybody thought they ought have our jobs. Only it wasn't like that, really. I mean, returned combat pilots aren't the best people for flying calibration or towing targets, for example, like we WASP did. They aren't sensitive enough to fly drones like we did, either. They didn't have the patience or precision for radar tracking missions or maintenance testing—all the various things we WASP did and did well!" Betty stopped herself, noticing that she had gotten off the subject. "I'm sorry, I guess I've gotten a little carried away. I was supposed to be telling you how I met Jay."

"That's quite alright. I'm fascinated to hear there were American women pilots, too," Emily replied sincerely. Betty's pride in her accomplishments and indignation at being forgotten had been a revealing window to her that Emily found appealing. Up to now, she had been too much the perfect American housewife in her perfect house. Only now did Emily begin to see what Jay might have seen in this woman.

"I just wanted you to understand why I was so upset that day," Betty insisted. "I'd spent almost two years of my life flying 'the army way'—half that time on Forts—but I didn't get any veterans' benefits for it and no free college education. And then these three guys were sitting there just laughing at me. I really wanted to cry. I mean, I really wanted to *fly*, but no one would let me. There were so many of these guys around, you see, like the ones who were laughing at me. All the airlines and the flying clubs and the manufacturers wanted to 'give the brave boys home from the war' a job—not a girl, not even one who had trained just as hard and flown the same ships as the boys.

"So I was sitting there feeling sorry for myself, and suddenly one of those three guys—not the braggart but one of his pals—dropped into the chair opposite me. I drew back—afraid that he was going to mock me or, maybe, just afraid that he'd see I was close to tears. And he looked real hard at me and asked, 'Did you say you could fly a Fort?'

"So I told him—about the WASP and everything. Once we started talking, there seemed no way to stop. Suddenly it was dinnertime, and we'd both forgotten everything else in the world. I think that was the first time I ever skipped a class. Yeah, and so Jay took me to dinner and one thing led to another, and we got married six months later. And I've never regretted it for a minute," Betty concluded with conviction—and challengingly, too.

"What made you want to fly in the first place?" Emily asked, anxious to expand upon this common ground that she had discovered.

"I don't know. I was just fascinated by airplanes from when I was a little girl. I always wanted to fly, but we didn't have any money. But then I was in college and they opened the CPT to women. Just one in ten places, to be sure, but at least they let us train for almost nothing. From the first minute I sat in the cockpit, I was addicted to it."

Emily smiled at her. "I know the feeling."

For a moment the awkwardness between them was dissolved and they shared more than Jay.

For dinner they grilled hot dogs and hamburgers in the back yard. The kids were given the responsibility for keeping the grill going, while the adults had cocktails on the porch. Both men changed their shirts and put on their blazers. Emily had changed for dinner, too, of course, but only into a simple raw-silk dress, while Betty was in a tight-fitting cocktail dress with high heels and diamond earrings. The realisation that Betty was going to some effort to make herself look attractive gave Emily a pang of guilt. Betty shouldn't feel she was a rival. Emily made a point of complimenting her on her earrings.

"Jay gave them to me," Betty said proudly, showing off the diamonds by shaking her head a little.

"You are very lucky," Emily told her sincerely.

Betty gave a nervous laugh, and glanced toward the dining room where Jay and Robin were at the bar mixing drinks. "You didn't do so badly yourself."

"No. I didn't mean to imply that. But Jay is very special. You are very lucky to have his love."

Betty tensed; her face grew rigid for a moment. Then she asked sharply. "Do I? You know all he did was see a single, blurry photo of you in a *Life Magazine* article about the British Embassy and he couldn't sleep for nights on end. I thought something was wrong at work, but when I asked him outright, the whole story came out: how he'd met you and dated you in England. It was my idea to invite you out here. I thought Jay would discover that that girl he thought he'd loved was not like his memories at all. I guess I thought you'd turn out to be fatter, older, or uglier than the way he remembered you to be, and that the spell would be broken. But it doesn't seem be, does it? He still looks at you like you were Marilyn Monroe!" Emily hadn't noticed that. In fact, she felt as if Jay had been avoiding her. Betty was continuing. "And, you know what? I don't understand it a bit, because he says he asked you to marry him, and you turned him down. I know you hurt him terribly. He ought to hate you."

"I didn't want to hurt him, but once I learned Robin was alive, I had no choice. I couldn't very well be married to two men at once," Emily pleaded for understanding.

"I know of more than one man whose wife cheated on him while he was overseas. They got divorced afterwards." Betty looked Emily squarely in the face this time, and Emily could sense how much Betty hated and looked down on her while being afraid of her nevertheless.

She met Betty's eyes and stated softly, because the men were returning with the drinks tray, "Robin was above that."

At ten o'clock, Betty insisted that her kids go to bed, and Emily suggested that Keith and Charlotte go, too. They went cheerfully enough, but then some kind of bickering between the girls could be heard, and Betty disappeared to see what was going on. Jay started to collect the dirty things on a large metal tray, and Emily helped him. They carried everything back into the kitchen. Their hands full, they did not have a hand to flip the light switch. The kitchen was lit up only by the streetlight outside.

"You've hardly changed at all," Jay murmured, at last alone with Emily.

"Oh, Jay, I've changed in a million ways," Emily countered. "I was so provincial and insecure during the war. I'd never been anywhere but England—not even as far as Scotland. Now I've lived in Singapore and Cyprus. I've half-raised two very challenging children. I've done research and published. I'm not the same woman—girl, really—that you knew."

"Yeah," Jay remarked sourly, "but in one way you haven't changed at *all*: you still love *him*," Jay shot back bitterly.

"And I hope you love Betty," Emily countered.

"She reminded me of you."

"Jay—I don't think you should have written, and I certainly shouldn't have agreed to come. It's just opening old wounds."

"At least I now know it was a wound for you, too."

"How could you doubt that?"

"Don't you remember how it ended?"

"*Every—single—word*," Emily said slowly and deliberately. But then she asked earnestly, "But, Jay, didn't it ever occur to you that I said what I said to stop you from killing yourself?"

Jay looked at Emily hard in the darkened kitchen, and answered in a low voice. "Sometimes it did. After I got back to the States and was screwing around with a lot of other girls who didn't deserve what I did to them because I was still in love with you. That was why I wrote you after the end of the war. I thought, maybe she really loved me so *much* that she said those things to get me to go home, to make sure I'd survive the war. And I said to myself, if that's true, then she'll come to me now. But you never even answered my letters."

"How could I, Jay? Robin came home, too."

From the living room came the sound of Betty rejoining Robin and asking—with what Emily thought sounded like alarm, "Where are Jay and Emily?"

"Oh, just washing up in the kitchen," Robin answered.

"In the dark?" Betty asked.

"Let me pour you a last drink," Robin answered.

"Jay?" Betty called out, hitting the light switch to the kitchen at the same instant as she entered. If she had feared to see her husband in Emily's arms, her fears were put to rest. They were standing several feet away from one another, and Emily still had a tray in her hands. Embarrassed by her own suspicions, Betty said, "Oh, you don't have to do that. I'll take care of everything in the morning."

"I don't mind helping," Emily countered.

"No, no, don't worry about it. I've got a dishwasher." Betty was proud of that. Not everyone did.

"What are you drinking, Betty?" Robin called from the living room.

"Really, just leave that there on the counter," Betty insisted. "Come on, your husband is making us a nightcap." She led the way back into the living room determinedly.

"Then I *was* just the next best thing," Jay concluded bitterly, as if he had never been interrupted by his wife.

Emily shook her head. "No, that's not right. It's not about being better. It's about being fair. You had a life here without me, Jay. You had started to build it already and it sounded very promising—full of success and prosperity and opportunity. Your letters were laden with so much confidence and certainty of the good times to come—"

"Because I wanted to make you understand all I could offer you!" Jay explained.

"Wasn't it true, too? Weren't you on your way to success?" Emily gestured to the now-bright kitchen filled with the latest gadgets and sparkling in chrome.

"Absolutely!" Jay agreed forcefully. "I've got a great job, Emily! One that is both challenging and important. I love managing a whole team of designers, balancing engineering requirements with style and budget, and even working on the marketing strategy. And I get to see tangible results, too! I love seeing my cars in the showrooms and on the roads and being sold all across the world. Just the other day I saw a picture of one of *my* cars being driven on a German autobahn and—maybe this is going to sound corny—but it made me feel really *good*. After dumping I-don't-want-to-know-how-many tons of explosives on them, it made me feel better somehow that today—now that they've got rid of Hitler and have learned to behave like civilized people—they can buy my cars and drive them on those great roads of theirs—faster then we're allowed to do here!"

Emily smiled. "It is wonderful, really. You are very lucky to be able to have a job that enables you to contribute to making the world a better place. Robin never had those options or prospects. He didn't have a degree, remember, just Cranwell. He had no chance of a job in the civilian economy—not in England, anyway. All of Europe lay in ruins. There was still rationing. Britain was bankrupt. We were losing our colonies. You don't know how many of our friends—men who had been Squadron Leaders and Wing Commanders, men with decorations and wounds but with only wartime commissions—found themselves struggling to make ends meet as sales clerks or insurance agents.

"Robin had no choice but to stay in the RAF, and it too was ravaged by budget cuts. He was grounded, returned to his peace-time rank—which is another way of saying demoted—and then, because he'd learned to speak German in captivity, he got posted to the British Air Forces of Occupation. We found ourselves in Berlin itself, surrounded by the most appalling destruction, poverty, and—worst of all—hopelessness imaginable. It was a city populated by embittered old people, frightened women and dazed children. A city without joy, music or flowers. Half the population cowered amidst the ruins in houses without windows, electricity or running water. Listlessly the women earned a few pence each day by "cleaning up the rubble"—one brick at a time. It was there your letter found me—in a house whose Jewish owner had been killed in a concentration camp, while an SS General—our immediate predecessor—drank his wines and entertained among his lovely antiques and paintings. The SS General killed himself and his children in the garden house as the Red Army closed in in May 1945. We had a woman with a University degree as our cleaning lady, and the gardener was a former Polish slave labourer afraid to return to Soviet-occupied Poland. For a short period we even found ourselves giving refuge to a young girl who had been gang-raped by more than 20 Soviet soldiers in front of her own parents—before they were in turn shot before her eyes. Berlin was a nightmare in 1945-1949. If I'd left Robin then, it would have robbed him of the only positive aspect of his life—his tiny family. Do you really think I should have done that? To a man who'd done nothing to deserve it?"

Jay turned to look out of the kitchen toward the living room at Robin and Betty, and after a moment he shook his head. "No, I guess not." For another moment they didn't move or speak. Then Jay nodded his head again and smiled rather sadly at Emily. "You're a remarkable woman, Emily. I guess I should be grateful that we met at all—that you were there for me when I needed you. I guess I've got no right to ask for more."

"Don't make me into a romantic heroine, Jay. I'm not that special. In fact, I'm a very ordinary and rather selfish woman. More to the point: everything about me that is even a little bit remarkable I owe to Robin. It was Robin who arranged for me to learn to fly and Robin who encouraged me to research and write. I've discovered I really like writing books—almost as much as flying. I like traveling around the world with Robin and meeting all kinds of people. I don't really think—now that I've come to know America—that I would ever have fitted in here. I would have been fractious and unhappy. I certainly could never have made a beautiful house for you like this! I'm not dedicated to housekeeping or mothering the way Betty is. She loves you very much and wants nothing more in life than to make you and your children happy."

"If I'd been married to you, maybe the house and all the things in it wouldn't have been so important to me. I could have gone to South America with our international division. I wanted to, but Betty wouldn't think of it. She thought it would be bad for the children, but your kids seem to be just fine despite all the travel you've done. I know Betty wants only the best for us, but all she knows is the way she was raised. With you, things would have been different."

"Yes. But not necessarily better. More important: Have you never thought that maybe you could help Betty to get out of her rut—just as Robin helped me? She did it once before, when she learned to fly during the war. She did that on her own without any help, such as I had, and she is terribly proud of it. I suspect that under the façade of being a perfect housewife, Betty has a far more adventurous spirit that she's willing to admit even to herself. That's why you married her, isn't it?"

"What is *keeping* you two in there?" Betty called anxiously before Jay had a chance to answer.

Emily went on tip-toe and gave Jay a quick kiss. "For what it's worth, Jay, I've never stopped loving you."

Then they went back into the living room together.

Emily put the light out and climbed into the sofa bed beside her husband. Robin was so tense it was a wonder the bed didn't tremble. Emily slipped her arms around him and snuggled against him. "Thank you for letting me come. Jay and I had a misunderstanding last time we met. It was important to set it straight."

Robin had not responded to her cuddling, and asked now in a tone of voice that would not have been out of place in a parliamentary hearing, "And just where does that leave me?"

"Where you've always been, Robin—in the centre of my life and heart."

It took him a moment to accept that answer, but gradually the tension started to ease. His muscles relaxed, his breathing deepened, and he took her into his arms. He kissed the top of her head. "No regrets, then?"

"No."

"Not even in Berlin?"

"Don't be greedy, Robin. Maybe I had a moment or two of doubt now and again. Didn't you?"

"Not that I can remember."

"Selective male memory," Emily concluded, and contentedly closed her eyes.

Glossary

ATA	Air Transport Auxiliary, a civilian organisation tasked with ferrying all RAF aircraft to and from factories and maintenance units
Anson	A reliable, twin-engine aircraft ideal for transporting passengers and the mainstay of the ATA fleet of air taxis
Available	State of being on call, waiting for the order to take off, ready to be in the air in 20 minutes or less: ie not at dispersal but on the airfield
Barrage Balloon	Large helium filled balloons tethered onto steel wires which floated over major cities or important targets such as aircraft factories. The wires made it extremely dangerous to fly below the balloons and so prevented low level bombing of the areas protected by these "barrages"
Bently Priory	HQ of RAF Fighter Command
Boffins	Slang for scientists
Bomber Command	HQ for RAF bombing operations
Bowler hat	The traditional headgear of London bankers, stock-brokers and other office workers at this time; in RAF slang it meant getting "washed out" of training and sent back to civilian life
C of E	Church of England or Anglican Church
Claude	Allied designation for a Japanese fighter, the forerunner of the Zero
CFI	Chief Flying Instructor
crate	RAF slang for aircraft

DFC	Distinguished Flying Cross; a 'bar' to the DFC indicates the wearer has been awarded a second DFC etc.
Dispersal/Dispersal hut	To avoid having the aircraft concentrated in one place and thereby being an easy target, the RAF dispersed aircraft around an airfield; likewise while at "readiness" the pilots of a squadron waited for the call to action in more-or-less improvised small huts connected to the operations phone and mess by a telephone. These huts provided lockers to hang flying kit, chairs, tables, usually a gramophone, and pilots brought books, magazines, cards and board games to pass the time. They were heated by primitive stoves in winter.
DSO	Distinguished Service Order
erk	RAF slang for airman/ground crews
Fighter Command	HQ for RAF fighter operations
flap	RAF slang for panic, flutter
Flight	Sub-unit of an RAF fighter squadron consisting of six aircraft
Flying Fortress	American four-engine heavy bomber and backbone of the USAAF bomber fleet in the early years of the war
Gong	RAF slang for medal
Halifax	British four-engine heavy bomber
Hurricane	First monoplane fighter introduced into the RAF. Most Fighter Squadrons during the Battle of Britain had Hurricanes and they accounted for the most 'kills' in the Battle of Britain; continued in service in secondary theatres throughout the war.
IP	Initial Point—start of the bomb run, point at which the bombardier took command of the aircraft in the USAAF
Jerry	British slang for the Germans
kite	RAF slang for an aircraft
Krauts	American slang for the Germans
LAC	Leading Aircraftman, roughly the equivalent of a Pfc in the US Army Airforces

Lancaster	British four-engine heavy bomber, famous for taking part in the "Dambusters" raid, May 1943.
Liberator	American four-engine heavy bomber, took part in massive daylight bombing raids
loo	English slang for toilet
Main Force	RAF bombers not belonging to the Pathfinders or other special units
MAP	Ministry of Aircraft Production
Me109	Messerschmitt 109—the principal German single-engine fighter
Me110	Messerschmitt 110—a twin-engine German fighter, which proved no match for the Hurricane and Spitfire and so later converted to tactical bombing and recce functions
Mosquito	Twin-engine light, tactical bomber, used for a variety of missions including precision bombing
MP	Member of Parliament
MU	Maintenance Unit—Repair and Maintenance units where RAF aircraft requiring greater repairs or servicing than could be handled by operational groundcrews were serviced.
O T U	Operational Training Unit, a unit where pilots of the RAF were given operational and tactical training immediately prior to joining their operational Units
Oxford	Small Twin-engine training aircraft; used by the RAF to introduce pilots to flying twin-engine aircraft
P-47	American single-engine fighter, known at this time as a "pursuit" plane
Pathfinders	RAF bombers trained to lead night bombing operations by dropping flares and incendiaries over the target area, making it easier for other bombers to find the target in the dark
PM	Prime Minister
Pompii	Colloquial name for Portsmouth, England, home of the Royal Navy
Popsies	Slang for girls

prang	RAF slang for crash
RAF	Royal Air Force
RDF	British designation for radar at this time
Readiness	State of being on call, waiting for the order to take off, ready to be in the air in 5 minutes or less, i.e. waiting at dispersal
Ring	Another term for the stripes sewn on a pilot's sleeve indicating his rank: one thin ring = Pilot Officer, one thicker ring = Flying Officer, Two rings = Flight Lieutenant, Two thick rings flanking a thin ring = Squadron Leader, three rings = Wing Commander
RP	Rondezvous point, where different units of a bombing mission met up in the air before setting off.
Sally Ann	Slang for Salvation Army
Section	Sub-unit of an RAF fighter squadron consisting of three or four aircraft
ship	USAAF slang for aircraft
Shoot a line	RAF slang for telling a tall tale, bragging
Spitfire	Single-engine, high-performance fighter, made legendary in the Battle of Britain
Squarebashing	RAF/WAAF slang for marching and drill
Squareheads	American slang for the Germans
Stand-by	State of being on call, waiting for the order to take off by sitting in the cockpit with the engine ticking over, ready to be in the air in 2 minutes or less
Station	RAF base
Stripe	Another term for the rings sewn on a pilot's sleeve indicating his rank: one thin ring = Pilot Officer, one thicker ring = Flying Officer, Two rings = Flight Lieutenant, Two thick rings flanking a thin ring = Squadron Leader, three rings = Wing Commander
Sunderland	Large, four-engine flying boat used primarily for long range reconnaissance over the water and for attacking U-boats.

Tannoy	Public Announcement system, magnifying a voice and blasting out over a large area
Their Airships	RAF slang (somewhat derogatory) for senior Air Ministry officials
U/S	Unserviceable, aircraft that are not airworthy and undergoing repairs
USAAF	US Army Air Forces
WAAC/WAC	Women's Army Auxiliary Corp, later Women's Army Corp—the US women's branch of the Army and so Army Air Forces; women were restricted to a few trades and prohibited from holding command functions over men by Act of Congress. Discrimination against women was widespread and women generally used far below their capabilities in menial functions.
WAAF	Women's Auxiliary Air Force—The British women's auxiliary: WAAF were trained with RAF and filled jobs as qualified with little or no distinction due to sex. NCOs and commissioned WAAF commanded RAF of lower rank. By the end of the war, with the notable exception of flying, WAAF were allowed into all trades and branches.
Waafery	British slang referring to the WAAF quarters on an RAF station
Walrus	Small seaplane used by the Fleet Air Arm primarily for air-sea rescue duties; it could land on sea or land. ATA women pilots were cleared to land it on land only.
Wellington	Twin-engine British bomber, workhorse of Bomber Command in the early years of the war
Whimpy	RAF slang for the Wellington bomber
WRNS	Women's Royal Navy Service, the women's branch of the Royal Navy
WVS	Women's Volunteer Service, a British organisation which provided a variety of services to support the war effort including canteens for service personnel away from their bases.

978-0-595-40151-2
0-595-40151-1

Printed in the United States
55162LVS00007B/34